D0251291

KILL CITY
BLUES

KILL CITY BLUES

A SANDMAN SLIM NOVEL

RICHARD KADREY

HARPER Voyager
An Imprint of HarperCollins *Publishers*

HarperCollins books may be purchased for educational, business, or sales promotional use. For information please write: Special Markets Department, HarperCollins Publishers, 10 East 53rd Street, New York, NY 10022.

FIRST EDITION

Harper Voyager and design is a trademark of HCP LLC.

Designed by Paula Russell Szafranski

Library of Congress Cataloging-in-Publication Data has been applied for.

ISBN 978-0-06-209459-9

13 14 15 16 17 OV/RRD 10 9 8 7 6 5 4 3 2 1

To JLK, who should have

been around a little longer

ACKNOWLEDGMENTS

Thanks to my agent, Ginger Clark, and my editor, Diana Gill. Thanks also to Pamela Spengler-Jaffee, Caroline Perny, Will Hinton, Shawn Nicholls, Dana Trombley, Emma Coode, and the rest of the team at HarperVoyager. Thanks also to Dave Barbor, Sarah LaPolla, and Holly Frederick. Big thanks to Martha and Lorenzo in L.A. And thanks to Suzanne Stefanac, Pat Murphy, Paul Goat Allen, and Lustmord for the sound track to Hell. As always, thanks to Nicola for everything else.

It is evident that we are hurrying onward to some exciting knowledge—some never to be imparted secret, whose attainment is destruction.

—Edgar Allan Poe, "Ms. Found in a Bottle"

You can go a long way with a smile. You can go a lot farther with a smile and a gun.

—Al Capone

KILL CITY
BLUES

I'M IN A window seat at Donut Universe eating heart-crippling lumps of deep-fried dough with the Devil. Ex-Devil technically, but then technically we're both ex-Devils. He was Lucifer before I was. Now he's Samael and I'm back to just plain Stark.

I take a bite of an apple fritter.

"How's your donut?"

Samael eyes his glazed old-fashioned suspiciously, like maybe it's haunted.

"Charming. Did I invent these? They taste like something designed to destroy mortals from the inside out."

Candy says, "Nope. We came up with them all on our own."

"How wonderfully suicidal you people are. Donuts must be the very essence of free will."

As for the Devil job, I stuck another poor son of a bitch with that. Mr. Muninn. Some days I feel bad about it. Some days I don't. Today the sun is out, I'm eating donuts with my girl and another ex-Devil, and it's all pretty goddamn heart-warming.

Samael says, "That blond woman buying coffee. She sold me her soul for a 1956 Les Paul Goldtop. I don't think she ever learned to play it. The man behind must be a pious bore. He's virtually free of sin sign."

The Devil can see people's sins. They're like streaks of black tar on skin. Since I quit the damnation biz, I can't see sin sign, but as an angel, Samael can still pull that rabbit out of the hat. I don't miss doing that trick.

I say, "This is why I don't take you to Bamboo House. I don't want you taking an inventory of my friends."

"Sorry. It's a hard habit to break."

Candy is sitting next to Samael, trying not to let on how thrilled she is to meet the original Devil. I haven't seen her this excited since we met a furry, six-foot-tall Pikachu at the Lollipop Dolls store in Beverly Hills.

She has her pink laptop on the table, open to Wikipedia. She's updating the Sandman Slim page. And by "updating," I mean taking out all the dumbest rumors about me.

"Does it say anything about me being Lucifer?"

She nods.

"Sort of. It says you were always Lucifer and that Sandman Slim doesn't exist. He's just one of the Devil's fronts."

"You might want to take that out," says Samael. "You don't want any demon hunters or aspiring crusaders taking potshots at you."

"Yeah. Delete it all."

Candy types something over the Devil stuff.

"Is there a picture of me?"

"A drawing. It's pretty dumb. Kind of like a police composite sketch in a movie."

"Delete it, please."

"You got it, Chief," she says, channeling Jimmy Olsen.

A police sketch. I'm not surprised. They've known who I am for a while now. So why aren't there fifty patrol cars outside? Why isn't there a SWAT team waiting for me at the Chateau Marmont? I'm not lucky enough that they'd lose my paperwork and all the surveillance photos. That means somebody doesn't want me taken in, which means I have a secret benefactor. I don't think Blackburn would do it, even if I did save his wife's soul. The head of the Sub Rosa is too political to be sentimental. That means it's someone I don't know about. I don't like that. Secret friends can turn into full frontal enemies without you even knowing about it.

"I was down in Hell yesterday. Father—Mr. Muninn—sends his regards."

I smile at the image. Mr. Muninn is God. A piece of him anyway. A while back, when God finally admitted he didn't know how to run the universe, he had a nervous breakdown. He broke into five smaller Gods. The good news is that the God brothers don't like each other very much. The bad news is that the God brothers don't like each other very much. It's not doing creation any good being run by a B team that can't stand the sight of each other.

"He looks a little funny in his Lucifer armor, doesn't he? Like a beach ball in a tin can. He doesn't have what you'd call a classic warrior's physique."

Samael pushes away his donut with his fingertips.

"Are you going to eat that?" says Candy.

"It's yours," he says.

Smiling, she wraps the donut in a napkin and drops it into

her bag. Samael looks puzzled before he realizes she's going to keep it as a souvenir.

"Did Mr. Muninn fix up the armor any?" I ask.

Samael gives me a look.

"Of course not. The damage is part of the mystique. I notice that you added more than a few burns and scrapes in a very short time."

"Then you should thank me. I mystiqued it even more."

Candy says, "He was cute playing Iron Man and it was fun pretending I was fucking Tony Stark, but the armor froze my boobs at night, so I'm kind of glad it's gone."

"No, we wouldn't want one of the few intact holy remnants of the War in Heaven inconveniencing . . . your boobs," Samael says.

Candy smiles at him.

"Would you like me to update your Wikipedia page?"

He frowns.

"I have a page? I don't like that. Please remove it."

"I can't. But don't worry about it. It's mostly old Bible stories and folktales. There isn't anything about your nice suits."

"Still."

"By the way, thanks for all the swell help when I was Downtown," I say. "It took me three months to find your stupid clues in the library and escape."

"I told you to read books. If you'd been more curious, you would have found your way out sooner. You're always complaining that I don't do enough for you."

"You do plenty, but even when you help, I end up with more scars."

"Then you should thank me," says Samael. "I mystiqued you even more."

Candy giggles.

"You have no idea how hard it is not to put everything you boys say on Stark's page."

Before Samael can explain to Candy all the reasons she shouldn't call him a boy, a guy walks up and stands next to our table. He's wearing a loose, expensive-looking black jacket. A dark red silk shirt open at the neck. An alligator belt with a gold buckle. He looks like a rep from a talent agency that could have handled Traci Lords in her jailbait prime.

"I'm sorry to interrupt your conversation, Mr. Stark, but can I speak to you in private?"

"Do my friends look like cops? If you can't talk in front of them, you can't talk to me."

The guy holds up his hands defensively.

"I didn't mean to offend anyone. My name is—"

"Declan," I say.

His eyebrows furrow.

"Yes. Declan Garrett. How did you know?"

"It's just a trick I can do."

He looks skeptical, then his inner hustler takes over and he keeps talking.

"I just thought that you and the gentleman might be doing some business and I didn't want to get in the way."

"Yes, you did," says Samael. "That's exactly what you wanted. To stop a business deal."

"I see. Because he's in a suit and I'm not, we can't just be a couple of friends eating donuts," I say.

Samael looks at me.

"Are we friends, Jimmy?"

"Pipe down, Hugo Boss."

I look back at Declan.

"You just hurt my feelings."

"He's very sensitive," says Candy. "He might cry."

"I might cry."

Declan steps closer to the table. A salesman trying to establish intimacy with the mark.

"Would a million dollars soothe your wounded soul?"

Samael *tsks*.

"Do you really think a man like this can be bought with money?"

"Hell," I say. "For a million dollars you can call me Suzy Quatro."

"You're breaking my heart, Jimmy."

"Eat a jelly roll." Then to Declan, "So what do I have to do for all the tea in China?"

He opens his hands like a preacher invoking the Holy Spirit or asking for a handout.

"Give me something more precious than gold—"

"I think he means me," says Candy.

"—but that you have no use for."

Candy does a mock frown.

"Now he's hurt *my* feelings."

"Does this thing have a name?" I ask.

Declan speaks quietly. Suddenly serious.

"Come now, Mr. Stark. We both know what I'm talking about."

"No. We don't."

Samael sighs.

"He means the Qomrama Om Ya."

"Is that right?"

Declan's lips curl in a sly smile.

"He's a smart man."

"Yeah, he is. Ask nice and he'll guess your weight. What makes you think I have it?"

"Because you were seen using it. On the child ghost."

Oh, right.

The Qomrama is a weapon designed by old gods, the Angra Om Ya, to kill other gods. Namely ours. Turns out that the universe really belongs to the Angra and our God foxed them out of it. Now they're pissed and they want it back. The child ghost, Lamia, was a piece of one of the Angra that leaked through to this universe, and in a pretty blue dress and with a great big knife, she came close to destroying the world.

"You got me there. I guess I did have it."

"Did?" says Declan.

Candy nods.

"As in past tense. As in it went bye-bye, Charlie."

Declan cocks his head. A coy move I'd call him on if I wasn't sure it would cost me money.

"Come now. Who could take it from you, Mr. Stark?"

"A crazy rogue angel named Aelita."

Declan doesn't say anything for a minute, like he's thinking things over.

"If it's a question of payment, I can offer you more than money. A man like you must have a use for power objects. I can offer you the Spear of Destiny. The actual spear that pierced Christ's side on the Cross."

Samael rolls his eyes. He's heard the line before. Candy smiles. She thinks she's getting a new toy.

"No thanks. I already have one of those. Right between my Nunchucks of Fate and my Zip Gun of Doom."

"I'm disappointed to hear that," says Declan.

"How do you think I feel? I just lost a million dollars."

"Not if you find it. If, for instance, you manage to reacquire it, I wouldn't ask how."

"How open-minded of you."

Declan's eyes flicker to Samael and back to me.

"Can I ask what kind of business you are discussing?"

"I was updating their Wikipedia pages," says Candy. "Do you have one? I can do yours too."

Declan gives her an indulgent smile.

"I'm afraid I'm not nearly as colorful as these gentlemen. But thank you for the kind offer."

He reaches into an interior pocket in his jacket and pulls out a business card. He sets it on the table.

"I suppose there isn't a lot more for us to talk about here in public. If you're interested in getting serious, you can reach me here."

"If I find anything interesting under the sofa cushions."

"Exactly," says Declan. He holds out his hand. I don't shake it. After a minute he drops it to his side.

"Good-bye," he says and walks away.

"Bye," Candy calls. "It was strange meeting you."

No one talks until Declan gets outside.

Samael says, "You realize that he didn't believe a word you said. He thinks you still have the Qomrama and that you're selling it to me."

"How do you know that?"

Samael pushes Candy's hands away from the laptop and closes the lid.

"Because the man I said was a pious bore? He's about to shoot you."

He pushes Candy down and ducks himself.

The guy fires just as I turn. The shot is close enough that I feel it breeze by my ear. It hits Candy's laptop dead center. Her head pops up from under the table.

"You killed *La Blue Girl,* you asshole!"

Samael pulls her back down.

The guy pulls the trigger again, but I'm looking at him this time. I think he's more used to shooting people in the back because the moment we make eye contact his hand shakes and his next shot goes through the window, cracking the safety glass. He pulls open the door and takes off across the parking lot. I'm not wasting time going for the door. I go out the window, broken glass flying across the windshields of parked cars.

Samael was right that it looks like things haven't worked out for the shooter. He's in a tan raincoat wrinkled enough that it looks like he sleeps in it. He's an older guy. Midfifties. A bit of a gut hanging over the top of his jeans. But he runs like a fucking demon.

I chase him across Hollywood Boulevard and down La Brea. The shooter lane-splits between the gridlocked traffic, gracefully sliding across hoods and car roofs when they're too close to squeeze between. I chase him as hard as I can, but I'm not gaining much ground and I can run damned fast. This tubby sad sack isn't normal. He's potioned up or there's hoodoo on him. I could fry the shooter's fat ass with a hex, but I learned my lesson after blowing up Rodeo Drive. Zipping through traffic at Mach 5 isn't exactly low profile, but it's better than launching hoodoo RPGs at the guy. I don't need a beef with the Sub Rosa right now. So I suck it up and run faster.

He cuts to his right, running behind a gas station. I follow him but he clears a fence in one jump. I have to climb the damned thing. He's gone when I hit the ground. I take off after him again.

At the corner of Sunset the shooter turns and sees me. His chest is heaving like his lungs are going to blow up like Macy's Thanksgiving balloons. His eyes are twitching in their sockets like he's maxed out on PCP. He's definitely on a potion or two. I don't think anyone has ever caught up with him before. He looks scared.

Then all of a sudden he's calm. He smiles like a kid whose mom just tucked him in and kissed him good night.

I don't know what he's doing until he's already doing it.

The bus's engine growls. Without looking, he steps back off the curb, right in its path. It takes the bus another twenty feet to stop, but the shooter has flown forty feet. All around me people are screaming. Traffic in the intersection that was moving a second ago screeches to a halt.

I muscle my way through the crowd forming around him. He's lying facedown. I kick him onto his back, get out my phone, and photograph him. People yell at me, taking me for a gore freak looking for something hot to put on his blog. There's a tattoo on the side of his neck. I don't recognize it. I shoot that too. One of his shoes came off and his wallet is lying a few feet away. I shove my way over and pick it up. More people are yelling. I guess I've blown my low profile. For all I know there's a traffic camera shooting everything I'm doing.

I take out the dead man's driver's license and photograph that too. Then toss it and the wallet back on the ground just as a cop car pulls up. They must have been right around the corner.

Voices get shrill behind me. I don't have to look. Villagers with pitchforks are pointing out the monster to the guys with the badges. I wonder what the penalty is for pickpocketing a corpse. I can't be the first person who's done it. This is L.A.

I walk to a guy sitting on a Harley. He's a big boy. His feet are planted on either side of the bike, but his hands aren't on the handlebars. I don't have time for subtle.

With one hand, I grab the front of his shirt and lift him off the seat far enough to toss him off the bike without hurting him too much. With the other hand, I grab the handlebars so the bike doesn't fall. The keys are still in the ignition. I gun the engine and take off before either of the cops closing in on me can get within grabbing range.

The moment I take off they hoof it back to the patrol car. Which isn't going to do them any good at all. The accident has turned the street into a solid mass of cars, gawkers, and now, twenty or more amateur paparazzi, phones and cameras blasting. I steer the Harley onto the sidewalk and open the throttle, laying on the horn to clear the way. I turn the corner and head back up to Hollywood Boulevard.

I ditch the bike on the sidewalk behind a pickup truck with a camper shell big enough to hide it from patrol cars rolling by.

There are six more cop cars outside Donut Universe. Patrons are out in the parking lot yammering to the uniformed cops all at once. One takes statements but the others don't want to hear about it. They just want the cattle to wait for the detectives while putting up yellow tape around the crime scene.

I spot Candy waving to me on the opposite corner, near a Christian Science church. Samael has his hand to his ear, talking on his phone.

Candy squeezes my hand when I reach them. She worries. It's sweet. A second later Samael closes his phone.

"Did you get him?"

"He got himself. Strolled off the curb and kissed a bus."

"Why? You're not that scary."

"Yes, I am."

"If you say so."

"How much do you have to pay a guy to go out like that?"

"You don't. He chose to do it himself. It's the mark of a true believer. In what, I don't know and I don't care. But you should."

I thumb on my phone and go to the picture of the shooter's driver's license. I read it out loud.

"Trevor Moseley. Either of you ever hear of him?"

I show them his picture.

Candy shakes her head.

"I took a lot of souls back in the day, but I don't recognize his name or face," says Samael.

Candy beams at Samael.

"Sam just called some people. He's getting me a new laptop."

"Sam?" says Samael.

"Thanks," I say.

He looks at me.

"Just thanks? Nothing pithy or sarcastic?"

"I'm capable of appreciating when someone does something nice for someone I care about."

Samael looks at Candy.

"Good lord. What have you done to him?"

"Shocking, isn't it?" she says. "Pinocchio is almost a real boy."

I take a bite of my donut.

"Fuck both of you."

Samael nods.

"Ah. There's the Jimmy I know."

He looks at his watch.

"Look at the time. I should be getting back home before I'm missed."

"How are things Upstairs?" I ask.

"Just don't die anytime soon. You've seen Hell and right now I wouldn't wish Heaven on anyone. Ruach is more paranoid every day. Imagine Josef Stalin with unlimited resources."

Ruach is one of the five God brothers and the current God sitting on the throne in Heaven. Unfortunately for both humans and angels, he's the "troubled child." A stone son of a bitch. Supposedly he's cut a deal with Aelita to let her kill the other four brothers if she leaves him alone. She's already killed at least one, maybe more. Aside from Mr. Muninn and Ruach, no one knows where the other brothers are.

"At least he can't send you to Tartarus," I say.

"There are worse things than Tartarus, I'm afraid."

"Like what?"

Samael just shakes his head.

"If you want to get in touch with me, go through Muninn. Don't do it directly. Sandman Slim isn't a name I want on my contacts list right now."

And he's gone. Just blips out of existence. Interesting. With all the shit that's happened—Mason Faim's attempted war with Heaven, and God fragmenting into warring siblings—I've never seen Samael nervous before.

A couple of people in the Donut Universe parking lot are pointing our way. I wonder if the cops have put together that the hero who chased a shooter from the donut shop is the same asshole that desecrated his corpse and jacked a biker a few blocks away. This isn't the time to find out. I see a tasty shadow by the side of the church and pull Candy inside with me.

We go through the Room of Thirteen Doors and come out around the back of the Chateau Marmont. Our digs these days. Really it's Lucifer's penthouse, but until they figure out that I'm not Lucifer anymore, it's a room-service, clean-towels, and free-cable party.

BACK WHEN I was still the Lord of Flies, I'd walk through the Chateau Marmont lobby like Errol Flynn back in the day. Now that I'm not, I creep through with my head down like a flea-bitten hillbilly trying to sneak out on a bar tab. Sooner or later word is going to get out up here. The local Satanists might be nouveau riche headbangers and trust-fund creeps with a grudge against the world, but they have some good psychics on their payroll. One of them is going to pick up Mr. Muninn's vibes and start wondering how Lucifer is doing paperwork in his palace in Hell and ordering kung pao shrimp in his Chateau penthouse at the same time.

Lady Snowblood is playing on the giant plasma screen in the living room. Kasabian is at the long table he uses for a desk, surrounded by dirty plates and beer cans. He's naked, but it isn't like ordinary naked. Kasabian is a disembodied head. I'm the one who disembodied him. He shot me, so it seemed like the thing to do. He used to scuttle around on a little wood-and-brass skateboard I conjured for him. Now he gets around on a mechanical hellhound body I brought back from Downtown. Only the body has never quite worked right. Manimal Mike is trying to fix that.

Kasabian is bouncing on the balls of his two rear hound feet. His balance looks good. Mike looks up as Candy and I come inside. He points to Kasabian, looking pale and hopeful.

"Can I have my soul back now?" he says.

I watch Kasabian.

"I don't know. Can Gimpy make it down the catwalk on his own?"

Kasabian takes a step, teeters, and plants his ass on the side of the table to keep from falling.

Mike slumps into a desk chair. Wipes his face with a dirty rag. It leaves a trail of grease on his forehead and cheek. He wheels himself over and uses a delicate tool that looks like a screwdriver crossed with a spider to make adjustments to Kasabian's legs.

Mike is a Tick-Tock Man. He builds mechanical spirit familiars for the Sub Rosa chic set. He might be a drunk and nutty and a little suicidal, but he knows his way around machines. He also owes the Devil a favor. The idiot sold his soul a few years back. Now he wants it back. He still thinks I'm Lucifer, so I'm making him work off the debt by fixing up Kasabian.

While Mike works on him, I show Kasabian the dead man's bloody photo on my phone.

"Friend of yours?" Kasabian says.

"He missed, if that's what you mean."

"And now you feel guilty for offing him."

"That's the problem. I didn't. He did it to himself. And I want to know why."

I flip to the guy's driver's license. Kasabian squints at it.

"Trevor Moseley. When did he die?"

"Just now," I say. "Like twenty minutes ago."

He shakes his head.

"I won't see him for a day or so. They're not exactly state-of-the-art when it comes to sorting out the new meat Downtown."

Kasabian has a few useful skills. He's a passable computer hacker, he has good taste in movies—he once ran a choice indie video-rental place in Hollywood. Also, he can see into Hell. It's a gruesome little trick, but gruesome describes 99 percent of his life, so what's one more percent between friends?

The trick works like this: when I came back from Hell, I brought a jar of peepers with me. Peepers are eyeballs a lot like ours (no, I don't know where they come from and I don't want to know), only they work like surveillance cameras. I scattered dozens of them around Hell. Between the peepers and his ability to peek into Downtown through the Daimonion Codex, Kasabian can spyglass a good chunk of Hell. Entrepreneur that he is, he's even turning his deadeye trick into a business. Setting himself up as an online psychic. When it's up and running, he'll track down any of your dead relatives and report back on them—as long as they're in Hell. Seeing as how that's where most suckers are headed, he should be in business until the sun turns this rock into one big overcooked s'more.

"Let me know when you spot him. I might just go down and ask Mr. Moseley a few questions."

Candy says, "Can I go too?"

I should have been ready for that.

"I don't know," I say.

Candy tosses down the magazine she was thumbing through.

"We talked about this. If you leave me here and disappear down there again, you better stay down there because I swear I'll salt your skull and drink you like a daiquiri."

Candy isn't exactly human. She's a Jade. That's sort of like being a vampire, only Jades dissolve your insides and drink you, kind of like a spider. I know it sounds bad, but she's off the people juice these days. And it's kind of sexy when she lets the monster out. I just have to be around to make sure it goes back in.

"What's the difference between true love and a murder spree?" says Kasabian.

"I don't know. What?"

17

He shrugs.

"I don't know. I was hoping you lovebirds would have a clue."

He smiles, pleased with his half-assed joke.

I say, "Go bite a mailman, Old Yeller."

Mike lets go of Kasabian's leg. He flexes it and it looks like it's working all right. Mike goes to work on the other one.

"Well?" says Candy. She's right beside me, her hands balled into fists. She's not backing down on this.

"You're right. I promised. But this is only if I actually go. I'm not making any special trips down so you can take snap-shots with Stiv Bators."

"Deal."

She stands on her toes and kisses me on the cheek.

"I got it," says Kasabian. "When it's true love you know why you're getting stabbed."

"Kasabian, you romantic fool," says Candy. "You just got ten percent cuter."

He smiles at her.

"Kitten, I've got romance coming out my ass."

"And now the cute is gone."

Mike chuckles to himself. Kasabian shifts his leg, clipping him on the nose.

"Learn to stop while you're ahead," I say.

"I haven't had much practice with women since you turned me into a carnival attraction."

"I'll have you tripping the light fantastic in no time," says Mike.

As casually as he can, Kasabian says, "Stark, you still have Brigitte's number?"

"No."

"You're lying."

"Yes."

"I'm not asking for a hookup, just an introduction."

"I've put Brigitte through enough. I'm not letting you loose on her."

"You won't do me one favor, but you want me to look up your dead pal in Hell."

"Look, Mike gets your legs working, you can come down to Bamboo House of Dolls and ask her yourself. Maybe she'll say yes just for the novelty of doing a robot."

"I think she might be seeing someone," says Candy.

"Who?" says Kasabian.

"The King of Candy Land. Or was it Josie and the Pussy-cats?"

"Great. Now she gets discreet. Forget it. Chicks only want one monster in their life and Stark got to Brigitte first."

Mike stops working and Kasabian tries to stand. This time he makes it. His legs support him and he takes a few steps like, well, a circus dog doing a trick for biscuits.

I say, "You know, no matter how well you make his arms and legs work, he still looks like a mutt."

Mike sighs and nods.

"To rework his whole body so it's more human shaped, I'd have to cut it up with a plasma torch, lengthen and straighten his back legs, redo the spine, and rebalance and recalibrate the whole thing," he says. "The only way to do that is for Kasabian to get off it."

I look at Kasabian, walking steady for the first time since I've been back.

"Maybe he's right. Maybe you should go back to your skateboard for a while and let Mike do his thing."

Kasabian looks panicked. He stumbles back against his desk, his hound legs giving way.

"No way anyone is chopping up this body. I looked like a fucking bug on that skateboard. Now at least I'm mammal shaped."

"I've got all your limbs working right for the moment," says Mike. "Maybe there's some way I can do your legs without taking them off."

Kasabian sits down and slaps his computer keyboard. The screen lights up.

"Yeah. You work on that. Right now let me get back to work building my site."

As Mike packs up his tools he looks at me.

"I'm not getting my soul back, am I?"

"Not today, Mike. But keep up the good work. You're closing in on daylight."

I head into the big bedroom Candy and I share. Samael's old clothes still hang in the closet. Custom shirts and suits so sharp they could cut you like a knife. I toss my jeans and T-shirt on the bed and change into a bloodred button-down shirt and black silk trousers.

Candy follows me in and sits on the bed.

I say, "Why don't you stay here and see if Kasabian can pull up any information on Moseley when he was alive."

Candy doesn't move.

"I know you're not dressing up for me, so who's the lucky girl?" she says.

I comb my hair in the bedroom mirror. It doesn't help much. The neater I get my hair, the worse it makes the scars on my face look. There are donut crumbs on the glove that covers my prosthetic left hand, so I toss the glove onto a pile of dirty clothes and put on a clean one.

"Brigitte was there when the Qomrama disappeared, but even if she wasn't, I bet she's not the one sending hit men after me."

"Then who is?"

"I don't know. But there were only two other people there when Aelita took the 8 Ball. Saragossa Blackburn and his wife. So, I'm off to see the wonderful Wizard of Oz."

THE SUB ROSA is the underground magic community that keeps the old practices alive and secretly runs a few pieces of the world. Saragossa Blackburn is our Augur, the president and holy high chieftain of the entire Sub Rosa freak squad in California. There's no one bigger. With his heavy money Illuminati of politicians, corporate honchos, bankers, entertainment-industry lackeys, and law enforcement creeps, he's the power behind the power, and when we don't have a Sub Rosa governor running the state, Blackburn makes sure that Mr. or Ms. Civilian knows who's really calling the shots.

He's a scryer, a seer who gets glimpses of the future. All Augurs are scryers and Blackburn is supposed to be a good one. On the other hand, he didn't see me coming the last time I paid him a visit, but I was still Lucifer back then. Now that I'm just another asshole, chances are he has me right on his radar.

And here comes the proof. Men in shades and dark Brooks Brothers suits pile out of a line of blacked-out vans. The last time I dropped by, Blackburn was so sure of his untouchability that he didn't bother with security guards. He had enough wards and hoodoo mantraps around the place to hold off King Kong but not the Devil.

I don't like this. It feels too much like the bullshit I had to put up with when I worked for Larson Wells and his holy brown shirt army, the Golden Vigil.

A marine type with a blond crew cut and steroid shoulders the size of baby bulls puts his hand up.

"Excuse me, sir. Do you have an appointment?"

It's not the "excuse me" part that gets under my skin. It's the "sir." Procedures. Protocol. They're all civilized masks for contempt. I can deal with that, but I like my hate straight and up front. And these boys radiate hate like Tijuana blacktop in August. They know who I am and that I put a massive hurt on the last bunch of Sub Rosa security goons that braced me like this.

But I learned a bit of the protocol dance myself when I was playing Lucifer. Sometimes civilized is the best play. The feint they're not expecting. Besides, I'm decked out in silk and shiny shoes like Louis the Sun King's jester. Unless I crack someone's head and eat their brains, I couldn't scare a Brownie.

"I'm here to see the Augur. My name is James Stark."

"Yes, sir. Do you have an appointment?"

"No, but if you tell Blackburn I'm here, I'm sure he'll see me."

Mr. Shoulders smiles.

"The Augur is a busy man. If you call his secretary and make an appointment, we'll be happy to make sure you get inside. I can give you his secretary's phone number."

"Yeah. You see, I kind of saved his wife's soul, so he owes me a favor. Plus, someone tried to shoot me today, so I'd like to see the Augur right fucking now, pretty please with ice cream on top."

This is what Shoulders and his friends have been waiting for. An excuse. His heartbeat is going up. Microtremors in his face and hands are sure signs he's waiting for me to make a move. And if I don't do something soon, he's going to work himself up to where he'll make a move for me.

A few months ago I would already have had half of these merc fuckwits on their backs, bleeding and crying for their mommies. But I'm trying to cool some of that these days. Go with the advice Wild Bill Hickok gave men in Hell and pick and choose my fights.

"I'd really appreciate it if one of you gentlemen could call the house for me," I say. I follow it with a big, sunny smile.

Shoulders is one second from Tasing me when his phone rings. A funny, chirping ring tone. He relaxes. It's not conscious. It's reflex. He's been trained to stand down when he hears that particular tone. Besides, he has six other roid-rage behemoths behind him ready to stomp me to apple butter if I scratch my nose. But that's not going to happen. I can already see it in his body language. His shoulders are slumped. His voice is calm and low. His heart rate is dropping back to normal. When I see flat-out disappointment on his face, I know whose funny ring tone just saved my nice creased slacks.

Shoulders slaps his phone closed and sticks it back in his jacket pocket. It takes him a second to get the words out.

"Mr. Stark, I've been told that you're authorized for a visit with the Augur." Then comes the really hard part. "I hope you'll forgive any inconvenience the new security measures might have caused you."

"I forgive you," I say, "but I'm not bringing a piñata to your birthday party. You'll have to get your own goddamn candy."

In grand Sub Rosa tradition, from the outside Blackburn's mansion looks like something a wino coughed up after a night of Sterno and generic, nonfilter cigarettes. In this case, it looks like an abandoned residency hotel on South Main Street. The first floor is boarded up, covered with cryptic gang graffiti and stapled flyers for bands and strip clubs. The second and third floors are empty, burned-out shells. It's all just hoodoo, of course. Inside, Blackburn's place is a Victorian wet dream. Hell, it's so real he probably has opium addicts and lungers planted in the guest rooms to add a little more color to the place.

Inside, a guy in his early twenties in a gray suit he can't possibly afford greets me. A staff monkey. A young Sub Rosa emperor-in-training waiting to enter the big leagues. I wonder how connected you have to be to get a gig like this at his age.

"Please follow me, sir," he says in a voice smooth as buttermilk. I follow him into Blackburn's study. I killed a few people in here last month, but you'd never know it by the look of the place. No blood or a single bone fragment in sight. My compliments to your mystical janitors.

"James. Good to see you," says Blackburn, coming from

around his desk to shake my hand. He's on a first-name basis with me since I saved his wife. I'm not on a first-name basis with him because he's as close to God as we have in California.

"Thanks. And thanks for calling off your dogs. Did you hire all of them on my account? I'm flattered all to hell."

Blackburn points to a seat by the desk. I sit. He goes back around and settles down.

"Not you specifically. It's more because of . . . well, everything. Your coming in so easily was unnerving, of course, but Aelita's behavior was worse. I'm good at seeing what people really are, but I suppose that skill doesn't extend to angels. Anyway after the . . ."

"Massacre?"

"Yes, the massacre here, I decided that we finally needed to update security. The old ways of respect and even fear for the office of Augur are long gone. The twenty-first century is a fine place, but it's a little medieval too. We need our Great Companies to keep the neighbor's dog from crapping on the lawn."

"If 'Great Companies' means expensive mercs, I guess so. Still, with your money I think you could do better. At least one of your guys wanted to start trouble, not put it down."

"I know," says Blackburn. "That's why I called when I did. And he's not usually like that. He's usually a good man. It's just that you scared him."

"Me? Look at me. I'm dressed like a Deadwood dance-hall girl. How am I going to scare pros?"

"Because you're still James Stark and everyone knows the things you've done. And gotten away with."

"Now you're making me blush."

Blackburn gives me a smile. I can read people too. He's indulging me because he wants something.

"If you're really so interested in my security, why don't you come and work for me? I hear you're having some trouble with your revenue stream," Blackburn says.

"Is it that obvious these aren't my clothes?"

"I'm offering you Aelita's old position as head of my security team. Wouldn't you like to step into her shoes and show how much better you'd be at the job?"

"Don't you already have a new security chief?"

"Yes. Audsley Ishii. A very competent man. But I'd rather have Sandman Slim on my side."

"On the payroll, you mean."

"Exactly. What do you say?"

I shake my head.

"I tried the salaryman thing back with the Golden Vigil. I work a lot better on my own, thanks. And right now I'm kind of busy trying to save, you know, the world."

"I thought your chasing Aelita was a more personal thing."

"It's pretty damn personal, but she's not what I'm chasing right now."

Blackburn leans back in his chair. Steeples his hands.

"You mean the bauble."

"It's a god-killing weapon."

"I've heard the stories. All unsubstantiated."

"Do you think when the Angra Om Ya come stomping back, you'll bribe pissed-off elder gods with brunch and VIP night at Disneyland?"

Blackburn's hands go from a steeple to a dismissive little wave.

"Come on, Stark. You've seen the celestial realms. You don't really believe all this nonsense about old gods and ultimate weapons, do you?"

"I believe it because I met one of the Angra. Remember the ghost that offed the mayor a while back? Her name is Lamia."

"The little girl with the knife, you mean?"

"She killed off enough Dreamers to destabilize reality. If I hadn't stopped her, she might have destroyed the world all on her own. And she's just one little piece of what these fuckers can do."

Blackburn goes quiet for a minute. It's on his face. Am I here hustling him with ghost stories or am I telling the truth and maybe he and the other masters of the universe ought to start getting scared?

"I've looked into L.A.'s future and haven't seen anything like what you're describing."

I shrug.

"You couldn't see what an angel was angling to do. What makes you think you can see what gods want?"

He leans forward, his elbows on the desk.

"Work for me. I can give you access to more resources than you can possibly have on your own."

"Thanks, but seriously, I'm terrible. You'd want me dead in a week," I say. "But let me ask you something. Are you the one keeping the cops off me? Maybe clearing the decks just enough so I have to work for you?"

He shakes his head.

"No. Someone else is your guardian angel."

"Who?"

"I have no idea. But you're right. If you work for me, you'll never have to worry about the police again."

"I told you I already have something to do."

"You're awfully altruistic all of a sudden. What happened to Stark the monster? I seem to remember a bit of a madman storming into my house."

"I don't know what altruistic is, but I'm pretty sure I'm not it. I just want to keep a few people I like from burning in a hellfire shitstorm."

He looks away for a second and then back to me.

"You know there's a rumor that you already have the Qomrama Om Ya. That you found Aelita and took it back."

"I know. I heard about it today. Recognize this guy?"

I hold out my phone so Blackburn can see Moseley's photo. He makes a sour face and looks away.

"Warn me if you're ever going to show me anything like that again," he says. "Not everyone is as used to mangled bodies as you."

I forget that blood and dead eyes can be kind of gruesome to regular people. Something to add to the etiquette list I swear I'll start tomorrow.

"Sorry."

"Who was that?"

"The all-meat hood ornament on a city bus. He took a shot at me today after I told a buyer I didn't have the 8 Ball."

"Why do you think I might know the man?"

"I was hoping he might have been one of Aelita's crew when she ran your security."

Blackburn shakes his head.

"Aelita took care of the men herself and kept them at a distance from the household. I never got to know any of them personally."

It was a long shot but I had to try.

"If you want my opinion," says Blackburn, "you're looking at this all wrong. You see the Qomrama and immediately think of Aelita. But what about a rival? If she doesn't have it anymore—if she's lost it or is hiding it—surely there are other people in L.A. who would like to get their hands on an object with that much power."

"You included."

Blackburn shakes his head.

"It's tempting, but I don't want anything to do with Aelita or anything she's involved with."

"I'm glad to hear that."

"You might also be interested to know that someone in L.A. has put a magic object on the market recently. An object he claims is unrivaled in its importance. Sound familiar?"

"You think this asshole has the Qomrama?"

"It's possible," says Blackburn. "If I had something that powerful, I would only approach a few of the best-placed families. You don't want something like that going to the wrong sort of people. However, this person might not realize what he or she has."

"Then why would someone try to buy it from me and take a shot at me when I wouldn't sell?"

"Because the buyer is hedging his bets. He's probably made offers to both of you. The two people currently connected to the Qomrama."

"That's a lot of maybes."

"True. But if you can find out who's selling the object and who's bid on it, maybe it would point you in the direction of what you're really looking for."

I want to poke holes in Blackburn's idea, but I can't, mainly because I have no ideas of my own. I've spent the last month chasing rumors and banging my head into stone walls and come up with nothing. At least Blackburn's idea gives me something to do.

"So who's selling Aladdin's lamp?"

"I don't know. The seller is shy and only goes through intermediaries."

"What's the intermediary's name?"

"Brendan Garrett. A professional dealer in mystical exotica. I'll write down his address."

Now there's one less maybe in the world.

"Garrett? The guy who tried to buy from me today was named Garrett."

Blackburn finishes writing and hands me the piece of paper.

"That's probably your answer right there. You've been pulled into the middle of a family squabble."

"Right. One brother wants it and the other has a line to it but won't cut the other brother in on the deal. I can see some Lifetime Channel drama in that."

I look at the address. It's a glitzy hotel and a room number.

"I'm glad I could be of help. Especially if it's going to save the world. Even I have people I'd rather not see hurt in a celestial war."

Blackburn stands, letting me know my time is up.

I get up, and when he extends his hand I shake it. I wonder if he's looking into my future. I want to ask him what he sees, but I don't. I'm not sure if I altogether believe in scrying, and what does it matter what he tells me? If I live or die it doesn't change what I'm going to do: find the 8 Ball. And when I finally do die, I know I'm going back to Hell. That was easy. Now I'm a scryer too. All I need is a crystal ball and a pointy wizard hat. I can get a booth at the Renn Faire and make a mint.

On the way out a couple of Blackburn's security goons get me by each arm and shove me up against the front door. I'm one deep breath shy of putting the idiots out of their misery, then marching back in and twisting Blackburn's head off for lying to me. But another man in a suit strolls up. He's almost a head shorter than me, with a fine-boned face and hands. His skin is so pale it's almost white. Calm, blue, almond eyes set in a face so handsome it's almost pretty.

"Oh, my ears and whiskers, is that little Audsley Ishii?" I say.

He gives me a lopsided grin. Not a nice grin. The kind a headsman gives you when he doesn't like you and knows his ax is good and dull today.

"I'm not going to engage with you Stark, so don't even try."

"What's the matter? Did you hear Blackburn and me talking inside? A little nervous about your job?"

Ishii gets close enough for me to smell his fresh and minty mouthwash.

He says, "I don't want you showing up here again without an invitation."

"What you want matters as much to me as the price of pinto beans on Mars."

"I won't warn you again."

"Perfect. The next time your boys jump me, it'll give me the perfect excuse to lop off your head."

"Get out of here and don't come back."

The guys on my arms pull me away from the door and try to shove me outside. I plant my feet on the carpet and push back. I look at Audsley.

"I'm just curious. Did you know you were going to write a suicide note when you woke up this morning or did the urge just sneak up on you?"

Ishii walks way. Before I can say anything else stupid, I'm pushed out on the shitty street in front of the shitty hotel. A few of the other security hoods are standing around. They laugh when they see me get the bum's rush. I stare at them, memorizing their faces. If everything goes wrong and fire comes down from the sky, I'm making an igloo out of their bodies and taking Candy inside with me. We'll still die but I'll get to listen to these idiots roast first.

I make like I'm walking over to them. They get serious. Hands move toward gun bulges under their jackets. Just before one of them faints or pops a shot off, I disappear into a shadow on the side of Blackburn's building.

Teach your boys that trick, Ishii, you Napoleon-complex Snow White prick.

THE BEVERLY WILSHIRE Hotel is so posh it gives the Taj Mahal a hard-on. Almost four hundred rooms and a million more secrets. It's strange seeing it in daylight instead of Hell's perpetual twilight. Downtown, there's another version of the Beverly Wilshire. The penthouse was my—Lucifer's—private space in the infernal palace. Of course, there are other differences. Basement kennels full of the hellhounds. Gibbets out front for extra-naughty prisoners. Hell's legions on guard. And as far as the eye can see, the wreckage of Pandemonium, Hell's capital. The heady reek of blood tides and open sewers.

Up here, the Beverly Wilshire is where Blackburn's crowd buy and sell small countries and bang their mistresses before hunkering down in gated communities with more guns than the Third Reich.

This is the address Blackburn gave me for Brendan Garrett. The room number is for a corner suite. I have a hoodoo key buried in my chest. It lets me enter the Room of Thirteen Doors, the still center of the universe. Nothing can touch me in the Room. Not God or the Devil. It's my vacation resort and my ace in the hole. From the Room I can come out through a shadow anywhere I want. But that doesn't mean I like doing it. I especially don't like walking into rooms when I don't know what's waiting inside. But I know the Beverly Wilshire well enough that I figure I can bail safely if I barge in on a gunfight or an ether frolic.

From Rodeo Drive, I step into a shadow next to a palm tree and come out in the hall by Garrett's suite. I put my ear to the door and listen. Nothing. Just the steady hum of the hotel's air-conditioning system. I go into the suite through a shadow around the doorframe.

The room isn't too bad. Almost human in a show-offy kind of way. Gold carpet and drapes. Reds and earth tones for the pricey furniture. But even in Richie Rich hotels the art stinks. It's all vague impressionist scribbles, like minimalist portraits of whoever the artist was hitting on that day. They're not make-you-want-to-throw-up bad, they're the kind of art designed not to offend or appeal to anyone. White noise in a classy frame. If I was staying here I'd have to cover them up like I was in mourning.

The room looks lived in, like Garrett's been here awhile. Room-service menus and magazines on the coffee table. Clothes hung up in the closet and tossed over the backs of chairs in the bedroom. A half-empty bottle of Laphroaig and two glasses, one with lipstick. So he's had company. But the most interesting things are the bird and the bedside table.

The bird is a raven and it's fake. How do I know it's fake? It hasn't shit all over the floor. It's a mechanical familiar and a nice one by the look of it. It cocks its head and stares at me with its shiny black eyes, letting me know that this is its space and it's not going to move. In the bedside table I find a calfskin wallet, keys, a phone number in a feminine hand on a cocktail napkin, a thick wad of twenties and hundreds held together with a gold money clip, and five passports, all with different names but the same picture. I'm guessing Garrett's. As I lay the goods out on the bed the bird cranes its head around and I'm reminded how stupid I can be.

I was so distracted by Garrett's goods that I didn't check out the whole suite. I don't have to turn my head to know what the raven is looking at. Instead, I duck as a bullet from a silenced pistol flies by my head.

Garrett gets off another shot and hits the bedside table. That gives me just enough time to slip the black blade out of my waistband at the back and throw it. I don't want to kill him. I just want him to stop shooting so I can ask him questions. Garrett flinches when he sees the knife, but he's not quite fast enough. The blade hits the barrel of the gun and knocks it from his hand. But it doesn't fall far enough away. He dives for it. I toss an easy chair at him and follow behind it, hoping to get to the gun first. Funny thing about hope. It seldom works out. That's why they gave it a stupid name like "hope."

Garrett gets to the pistol just as I reach him. Still on the floor, he tilts the barrel up and fires. My eyesight goes black for a second as the pain hits and almost doubles me over. I have enough momentum that I go over Garrett and hit the wall behind him. He looks me in the eye, but before he can swing the gun around, I clip him good on the temple with the heel of my chic loafer. Garrett flops onto the floor and the gun falls from his hand.

Having just had some sense shot into me, I grab the pistol and check to see that Garrett is really unconscious before I go into the bathroom to look at my wound.

I'm a nephilim. Half angel, which makes me hard to kill. And I've been hurt worse than this. Hell, just in the past year Kasabian shot me in the chest, Aelita stabbed me with an angelic flaming sword, and a Hellion cut off one of my arms. Garrett was packing a light, quiet .22. Not a shoot-out weapon. More like something a hit man would pack. A .22 shell might bounce off the thick part of your skull if it was coming from any distance, but put a slug in right behind the ear, it's pennies-on-your-eyes time. So it seems like Declan and Brendan are both comfortable with killing when things don't go their way. At least Brendan does his own dirty work.

I sit on the cool tile of the bathroom floor with a towel pressed to my side. The pain from the shot has turned to a steady ache that peaks when I breathe in. I'm lucky that he didn't hit a rib or lung or I'd really be in bad shape. By tomorrow morning the wound will be healed. The bullet will still be inside me, but I'll only feel it when I do the Twist, so I can wait to get it out.

In a few minutes the throbbing eases off. I get to my feet and go back into the suite. Check that Garrett is still unconscious and then go for his bottle of Laphroaig. Unscrew the bottle with one hand while holding the towel with the other and take a long pull. And instantly regret it. Laphroaig isn't exactly my brand. I prefer Aqua Regia, Hellion moonshine. I developed a taste for it when I fought in Hell's arenas. Sure it tastes like cayenne pepper and gasoline but it's better than this Scotch. This stuff tastes like barnyard dirt and burned lawn clippings. The rich are different. They don't just own the earth, they like to drink it.

Samael's silk shirt is ruined. I'm hard on clothes. It's like my body declared a jihad on everything I wear. At least this shirt wasn't mine. But I kind of liked it. Candy isn't going to be wild when she sees my blood soaked through.

I take the bottle and limp back to Garrett. I turn out his pockets but they're empty. I pull my knife out of the floor and put it back in my waistband. Nothing to do now but wait for the guest of honor to wake up. Under other circumstances I'd dump water or a bucket of ice on him to get his ass moving, but I'm just as happy to have a few minutes of me time.

A phone on the coffee table rings. It's not Garrett's cell. It's the hotel phone. I go over and pick it up.

"Hello?"

"Mr. Garrett?"

"Yes."

"This is the front desk. A package has arrived for you. Would you like me to send it up to your room?"

"Sure. Thanks."

"My pleasure, sir."

I hang up.

I can't answer the door like this. Garrett's closet isn't any help. He's a lot bigger than I am. I'd look like I was wearing a tepee in one of his shirts. I toss the bloody towel in the bathroom and grab the hotel robe off the back of the door. I look at myself in the mirror. I'm pale and sweating, but I look more hungover than gut-shot. I set the pistol on the coffee table and drag Garrett to the bed, toss him on top, and cover him with blankets. The raven flutters over and stands on the lump that's Garrett's soon-to-be-kicked-around-the-room carcass.

There's a gentle knock on the door. I grab the money clip and peel off a twenty.

A young, freckled woman in a hotel uniform stands in the hall.

"Mr. Garrett?"

"Yes. Thanks for bringing it up," I say through my weak hangover smile.

"Of course."

She hands me the box. There's nothing on it but a tag for a local courier company.

"Is there anything else I can do for you, sir?" she asks.

"No. This is fine," I say, and hand her the twenty. I didn't get all the blood off my hands. There's a line of red along one edge of the bill. But it looks more like ink than anything else. And let's face it. This is an L.A. hotel. It can't be the first time someone handed her bloody money.

"Thank you," she says, and I close the door. That's enough social interaction for now. I can feel my side starting to leak through the robe, so I carry the box to a larger table by the wet bar and set it down. I get a new towel from the bathroom and tie it tight around my waist. It burns like a son of a bitch, but it ought to stop all the annoying fucking blood for a while.

With the black blade I slice open the courier box. Inside is a leather brief bag, something like an oversize attaché case that lawyers carry. There's another case inside that. Plastic, but heavy and substantial. Almost like a gun case. I slide it out of the brief bag, push that onto the floor, and set down the plastic one. I take a quick peek at Garrett to make sure he's not going to sneak up on me. The raven is still standing guard over him. I pop the latches on the case and push back the lid.

Lying packed in a snug black foam liner is the Qomrama Om Ya.

Color me the luckiest son of a bitch on the planet. I grab it to make sure I'm not seeing things.

Wait. Keep the son-of-a-bitch part but forget the lucky. The 8 Ball is like the bird. A fake. The real 8 Ball radiates heavy magic that you can feel through your skin. This thing looks good, but it's as magic as loaded dice.

Whoever made it isn't a complete idiot. It gives off some

minor hoodoo vibes, enough to feel real if you've never handled the real Qomrama. It's like how Russian gangs sell kindergarten terrorists radioactive junk and tell them it's plutonium. The morons think they're going to build a nuke, but all they get is cancer-therapy scrap.

The only other thing in the case is an old book. It's full of diagrams of the 8 Ball along with what look like instructions, but it's in a language I've never seen before. I put the book in my back pocket. Father Traven might have some fun with it.

In the bedroom, the raven squawks and flutters back to the chair. Garrett sits up. His eyes go wide when he sees me with his courier box.

"That's not for you!" he yells.

"Finders keepers."

He starts feeling around the bed, knocking his passports and cash onto the floor. He's looking for the gun, but it's over on the coffee table. When he can't find it, he swings his legs onto the floor and stumbles to his feet.

Just to be a dick about it, I take the fake Qomrama from the case and toss it from hand to hand like a basketball. I don't see the blinking light right away. It's down at the bottom of the compartment that held the 8 Ball. When I do notice it I have a pretty good idea what it is and I start running. So does Garrett, but the other way. He makes it to the coffee table, snatches up the pistol, and levels it at me.

"Give me back my merchandise," he says.

I'm halfway into a shadow, bent low, when the bomb goes off. The concussion blasts me the rest of the way out of the room.

I suppose I could have been a Good Samaritan. Run back for Garrett, knocked the gun out of his hand, and pulled him into the shadow with me. But it hurt when I bent down to steal his money clip and . . . well, the bastard did shoot me.

I HATE GOING through the Room straight into the penthouse at the Chateau Marmont. Whatever hoodoo keeps the penthouse hidden from both civilians and Sub Rosa makes me dizzy and nauseous every time I walk through it. That doesn't matter this time. I'm already dizzy and nauseous.

I fall near where we keep the food trays lined up buffet style against the wall. At least I don't have to worry about Candy being concerned about my belly wound. My half-blasted-off clothes will distract her. Plus, I have the cash. And the fake Qomrama.

I grab the edge of a table and pull myself to my feet with my prosthetic left arm. The explosion must have blown off the glove. The arm is ugly as Hell. It was given to me by a Kissi, an extinct race of mutant angels that lived in the chaos at the edge of the universe. My prosthetic looks like a bug claw crossed with the Terminator, but it handles things like explosions pretty well, so I can use it sometimes when the rest of my body isn't cooperating.

Before I know what's happening, I'm being steered onto one of the leather sofas. I find half a cup of Aqua Regia on the coffee table and gulp it down. When I look up Candy is standing over me. She's pulling off my shredded shirt, looking scared. And sees the bloody towel. Now her fear is mixed with annoyance.

"I let you out of my sight for ten fucking minutes," she says.

My ears are ringing, so it takes me a second to understand what she said.

She pulls out the black blade I gave her and cuts off the rest of the shirt and towel. When she sees the bullet wound she looks at me hard.

Before she can say anything, I hold out the 8 Ball.

"Look, baby, I brought you a present."

Then I pass out.

I WAKE UP in bed naked and wrapped in a sheet. There's a stain where my blood and something else has soaked through. Candy sits beside me, playing a game on her pink laptop.

Vidocq is in a chair nearby, smoking, his feet propped on a corner of the bed. *Spirited Away* plays on the big screen. It's what Candy always watches whenever she's upset. A young girl sits on a train. Some kind of Japanese folk spirit sits beside her. White oval face. All draped in black.

"Where did that come from?" I say, nodding at the laptop.

She doesn't look up from whatever she's playing. It pings and pops. Plays a silly little tune.

"I don't think she's speaking to you at the moment," says Vidocq in his smooth French accent.

I look at her. She doesn't take her eyes off the screen.

"I guess not."

I'm blistered from the explosion. I lean down and sniff the stain on the sheet. It's a strange mild acid reek with something sweet. Maybe even a little Spiritus Dei. A complicated potion. I look at Vidocq.

"One of yours?"

He smiles and inclines his head in a little bow.

"Thanks," I say.

"De rien."

Vidocq is an alchemist and a thief. He's also a hundred and fifty years old. You'd think after living in this country for a hundred years, he would have lost the accent. I don't think he wants to. It's all he has left of France. It's not like he can ever go back. Where does a hundred-and-fifty-year-old thief and murderer—he killed a couple of guys way back when. Don't worry. They deserved it—get a birth certificate? A driver's license? A passport? Yeah, he could get fake documents like Garrett had in his room, but Vidocq is too proud for that. Unless he can go back as himself, I don't think he'll ever set foot in the old country again.

I glance back at Candy. She still won't look at me. I put a finger on the top of her laptop and start to close it.

"Don't," she says. "I just got to this level and I'll lose it."

"Your computer is dead. Whose is this?"

"Mine. Samael said he'd get me a new one and he did. It's a newer model too. Lots more memory and a faster processor. Good for games."

I lie down on my back.

"So all in all a good day for you."

"Shut up," she says.

I move closer to her. Put my hand on her leg.

"This is going to happen sometimes. It's how my life works. You can't always come with me and I can't dodge every bullet. Just remember that bastards tried to kill me for eleven years in Hell and almost a year up here and no one's done it."

She says, "That's not true. You've died a couple of times."

"Not like lying-there-getting-smelly kind of dead. Just technically dead."

She hits the keyboard harder. She still won't look at me. I really want one of Vidocq's cigarettes.

"You've got to understand that if this is going to work between us."

"I don't want to," she says.

"I don't always either. But it's how things are. 'Death smiles at us all and all a man can do is smile back.' "

"Where did you hear that crap?"

"I read it in a book Downtown. It's Marcus Aurelius."

She nods.

"Quote a dead guy. Real smooth."

I kiss her leg and get up. I stink from sweat and burned skin and need a shower.

On my way to the bathroom I say, "I'm going Downtown to see Mr. Muninn. You can come with me or you can stay here and sulk."

I stand under the hot water for a long time, washing off the grime and dead skin. The wound has already closed, though I can feel the bullet inside me.

I put on a robe and go back into the bedroom.

Candy has closed the laptop. She and Vidocq are quietly watching the movie. I sit down beside her on the bed. She balls up her fist and punches my real arm.

"Ow."

"I wasn't sulking. I was mad. And not entirely at you."

"I know. Trust me. If I could, I'd be the most boring bastard in the world."

"No, you wouldn't," says Vidocq.

"Okay. Tenth most boring bastard."

Candy says, "Sometimes you get worked up. Just promise me you'll be careful."

"I'm always careful."

"Really? How does stopping to grab money in the middle of an explosion count as careful?"

The fake Qomrama and the cash are lying nearby on the bed. I pick up the money.

"Did you count it?"

"It's just shy of four thousand dollars."

"Chicken-and-waffles money."

Along the edges, the bills are as crisp and singed as I am. I show them to Vidocq. He chuckles and leans in closer.

He says, "That's a strange design on the clip. It almost reminds me of the Golden Vigil. Though not entirely."

The Golden Vigil. God's Pinkertons on earth. They were a Homeland Security offshoot that Vidocq and I used to work for. The Vigil worked with a special group of agents using angelic tech, supposedly monitoring and policing nefarious hoodoo-related activity. Zombies. Rogue vampires. Demon attacks. Hell, they even put Lucifer on a terrorist watch list. Mostly, though, they were just another set of bullheaded cops in better suits. U.S. Marshal Larson Wells and, more importantly, Aelita ran the show. That's until she went on her god-killing crusade and the government shut the Vigil down. Not a tear was shed.

"Not quite? You're sure?"

Vidocq nods.

"I'm positive. Not the Vigil."

"But still similar."

"Yes. Similar."

I toss the money back on the bed.

"I wish I could have talked to Garrett. All this cash. Passports. A mechanical familiar. Who the hell was he waiting for?"

"And who was the bomb for? Monsieur Garrett or the party buying from him?" says Vidocq.

"He had a familiar?" says Candy.

"Yeah; a good one too. I should have grabbed the asshole's wallet."

I can see Kasabian banging away on his own computer, building his Web site.

"Did Old Yeller find out anything on Moseley?"

Candy says, "Not much. He had a record but all minor stuff. He was kind of a religious nut. A couple of arrests for protesting outside abortion clinics. A fine for trashing a Scientology office and some Orthodox graves at Hollywood Forever Cemetery. It looks like he's been through every religion on the planet. There's photos of him in a dozen getups from different religious sects and cults."

"A lost soul in a hard city. A volatile combination," says Vidocq.

"I got the 8 Ball and the cash," I say to him. "You steal anything fun lately?"

He shakes his head.

"Jewelry here and there. A vase for the apartment. Helping look for your weapon puts too many temptations in my path and the old habits are the hardest to break."

He puffs his cigarette.

"And sometimes stealing a bit helps. Not everyone who comes to the clinic can pay."

Vidocq's girlfriend, Allegra, runs a hoodoo clinic for down-and-out Sub Rosas and Lurkers. Doc Kinski used to run it with Candy taking care of the front desk. Then Aelita murdered him. That bothered a lot of people, myself included. Kinski was my father.

"How is Allegra?"

"Well. She has trained two competent assistants." He looks at Candy. "She misses you working beside her." He looks at me. "And believe it or not, she misses you."

Allegra didn't take it well when she found out that I'd become Lucifer. She accused me of all kinds of nefarious shit. Mostly Sunday school stuff, which I didn't expect from her. We haven't spoken much since.

"Maybe we ought to keep it that way," I say. "Whenever we get near each other, someone says something stupid."

"Someone?" asks Candy.

"Okay. Me."

"And yet her desire to see you both remains unchanged," Vidocq says.

I toss him Garrett's cash.

"Give her this."

He nods and puts it in the pocket of his greatcoat.

"We both thank you for this."

Candy says, "Can I have the clip?"

I say, "Why? We don't have any money."

Vidocq takes the clip off the cash and hands it to her. Her eyes light up.

"I just like it," she says. "It's shiny. I'll find something to do with it."

I take off the robe. The bullet wound stings a little, but the blisters hurt like a son of a bitch. I put on my leather bike pants and boots. Find an old Maximum Overdrive video-store T-shirt that's not covered in bullet holes or blood and put that on too.

"I don't suppose you'd consider taking me along," says Vidocq.

"To Hell? I don't want to take her. Why would I subject you to it too?"

"I'd like to see the afterlife. With my condition it's doubt-ful I'll ever see it legitimately."

A hundred and fifty years ago Vidocq made himself im-mortal. It wasn't his fault. He wasn't trying to do it. Just one of his alchemical experiments took a wrong turn and left him with a condition most people would kill for. Me, I'd rather have X-ray vision. At least it would be fun at parties.

I say, "Forget it. Allegra would truly kill me dead if I took you."

He sighs, knowing I'm right.

"And she'd be right, of course. You're a terrible influence on us all."

He nods to me and blows Candy a kiss. He holds up the cash.

"And thank you for this," he says before leaving through the grandfather clock, the real entrance to our secret hide-away.

"He's right. You are a terrible influence," says Candy.

"I thought that's why you stuck around."

"There's also the free food and movies."

"Free computers too."

"And getting blown up and shot at."

"Yeah. I've got to work on my ducking skills."

"Please do." She doesn't say anything for a minute. Then, "So, we're really going?"

"You're the one who wanted to."

"Yeah, but now I'm a little scared."

"Good. That means you're sane."

"So, we just go there? No spells? We don't have to sacrifice chickens or pray to any hoary overlords of the deep or something?"

"You can dance naked around a maypole if you want. Me? I'm just walking in."

She gets up.

"Okay. Let's do it."

"Don't wear anything you really like."

"Why?"

"You're won't be springtime fresh when you get back and I'm not sure the stink of Hell comes out in the wash."

I WENT DOWNTOWN when I was nineteen. I was thirty when I came out. I've only been back on earth for around eleven months. Sometimes it seems as long was the previous eleven years.

Another magician, Mason Faim, sent me to Hell in a deal to supersize his hoodoo power. He also wanted me out of the picture. We were a pair of Sub Rosa golden boys. Way too clever and powerful for our own good. The difference between us was that Mason had to work and study his ass off to stay on top of the hoodoo heap. Me? I could always improvise a spell or hex and have it fly. That was my angel half at work, only I didn't know that at the time. When Mason got rid of me he was top dog in L.A. He murdered my old girlfriend, Alice. He tried to take over Hell and start a new war with Heaven. You have to hand it to the boy. He knew how to dream big. So I killed him.

But in a way, Mason won. He wanted to destroy me, and the one who went to Hell sure isn't who came out. I was James Stark going down but Sandman Slim when I left. Eleven years of torture and fighting in the arena to entertain monsters will alter your perspective on life.

Most nights I still dream about Hell. I can feel it inside me. It's in the stink of my sweat. Flashing on the place even for a second makes me furious and sometimes afraid and sometimes ashamed of both those things.

On the plus side, I got up close and personal with the killer inside me. I learned I was good at taking lives. Doc Kinski called me a natural-born killer, so now it's what I do. But I don't always like it, and when I do, I don't always like myself for liking it. That's what Hell is. It's the shithole bottom of the universe, but it's a place where you'll learn more about yourself than you ever wanted to know.

I GET A pack of Maledictions from a box under a table in the living room. Maledictions are the most popular cigarettes in Hell. The only brand I really like. The taste is, well, unique. Like a tire fire in a candy factory. With luck, the angel part of me is immune to cancer. If it isn't I'm going to be a solid two-hundred-pound tumor.

Richard Kadrey

Candy gives me a faint smile as I take her hand and we step through a shadow into the Room of Thirteen Doors. I open the door to Hell but I don't take her through. I hold her there looking at the place.

"Wow. It really does smell like sulfur," she says.

"Don't worry. When you get inside, between the sewers and the Hellion stink, you'll forget all about the sulfur."

"You know how to show a girl a good time."

"Nothing but the best for you."

"Whoa."

This is what I've been waiting for.

"What do you see?"

"It looks just like L.A. A more fucked-up L.A. but still L.A."

"It's called a Convergence. A kind of magical fuckup where one place gets layered on top of another. When I first landed in Hell, it was all dark palaces and cobblestone streets. Now it's L.A. None of that changes what Hell is. It just makes it easier to get around."

"Somehow, none of that is very reassuring."

"That's Hell in a nutshell. You ready?"

"Yes. No. Yes. I think so."

"Before we go in, here are a couple of rules. And they're nonnegotiable. Stay close to me. Close enough for me to grab if things get weird. If anyone starts anything let me handle it. No Jade stuff. You see any damned souls, don't look them in the eye. They're used to me but another live human could freak them out."

"I'm not human."

"You look human. That's enough. Also, don't talk to anyone but Mr. Muninn."

"Who?"

"The current Lucifer."

"Right. Mr. Muninn. You told me about him."

I squeeze her hand. She squeezes back.

"Banzai," I say, and pull her inside.

WE COME OUT on the front gates of Hollywood Forever Cemetery. The Hellion version is a train wreck. Open graves. Smashed headstones. Statues and tombs swallowed by flames. It looks like it was looted by the Golden Horde and shit on by King Ghidorah.

I lead her out the front gate, where a block-long street market has set up. It wasn't here the last time I was Downtown, but a lot of things are probably different now that Mr. Muninn is ringmaster.

We're noticed immediately. A couple of living beings, one of whom used to be Lucifer, tend to stand out down here.

Candy digs her nails into my hand, but she doesn't show any actual fear. Hellions are fallen angels. Some of them look almost human. Others are walking, talking nightmares. Like mutant versions of fish, reptiles, or insects, or all three. The crowd in the market is a nice assortment pack of all the different Hellion types.

The chatter and the hawkers' calls trail off as the crowd turns its rheumy eyes on us. The only sound is the thin Hellion breeze, the sizzle of cooked meat, and grating Hellion music from a windup player. No one moves toward us. What are they seeing? Some version of Lucifer or Sandman Slim with a dangerous Lurker on his arm?

I'm not waiting around to find out. I've seen Hellions riot and I don't need to see it again. Not with Candy here.

I head to a stall where a merchant has mugwump meat turning on a spit. The smell is somewhere between filet mignon and coffin liquor. The fire throws up some nice fat shadows. I pull Candy into one and we go back out through the Room.

My aim is better the second time and we come out in the lobby of Lucifer's palace. Back inside the Beverly Wilshire for the second time today. This time I'm not accepting any mystery packages from the front desk.

I can see a dozen guards in the lobby. I don't wait to see if Muninn has posted more. I pull Candy over to Lucifer's private elevator. Like the crowd in the market, the guards look more confused than anything else.

Candy tugs on my arm.

"Are we going somewhere soon? 'Cause there's like a hundred guys watching us through the windows."

She's right. A mob of the legions guarding the palace is clustered around the lobby windows. This isn't any time to find out if they're happy to see their old boss or if they want to flay me alive. I pull Candy to the elevator.

One of the guards all of a sudden grows a pair and yells, "Halt!"

When I look he already has his rifle leveled at us.

I let go of Candy's hand and turn and face him. Put out my arm and manifest a Gladius, an angelic flaming sword.

It's impressive anywhere, but inside the lobby it's like the sun reflecting off the skin of a cruise missile.

"Make your move, shit heel. I took Mason Faim's head and I can take yours."

He stands there for a minute pointing his gun at me. I know he's not going to shoot. There's a window on these things. Someone points a gun at you and doesn't shoot in the first few seconds, they get thinking about the consequences. And the more they think, the less likely they are to pull the trigger. This clown's been thinking long enough to whistle the long version of "Layla."

He looks around at his Hellion buddies. None of them have their guns up. Why should they? That's Lucifer upstairs, king high prick himself. If he can't handle Sandman Slim with a chick civilian in tow, then what the hell good is he?

I touch a brass plate on the wall and the elevator doors slide open. The guards stand and stare. Touch the plate inside the elevator and the doors close and we start up.

"So far Hell is a barrel of monkeys," says Candy.

"You ought to come on Halloween. Everyone dresses up like *The Brady Bunch*. Seriously. The show is huge down here."

Her heart isn't just beating fast, it's trying to pound its way out of her chest and hop a plane to Bora Bora.

"You couldn't have walked us into Lucifer's living room or something?" she says.

"That would be rude. I stuck the guy here, I have to show him a little respect."

She takes a couple of deep breaths.

"Sorry. I thought I was more ready for this. I've seen some crazy Lurker stuff, but . . ."

"But not a whole world of it? Don't feel bad. No one's prepared for this dump."

"So this is where Sandman Slim comes from."

"Yep."

"You killed a lot of those guys down here."

"Don't be sexist. There are women Hellions too. And I killed pretty much everything down here at one time or other. And when I wasn't doing it in the arena, Azazel, my old slave master, was sending me out to kill anyone on his shit list. Until I killed him."

"The monster who kills monsters."

"That's my name. Don't wear it out." Then, "Nothing's going to happen to you. I promise."

"I believe you."

She lets go of my hand and loops her arm in mine. We must look funny and weirdly formal when the doors open, like kids dressing up in their parents' clothes.

"James, so good to see you," says Mr. Muninn.

I'm not sure he means it, but he gives me a quick hug, something he's never done before. He must really be smarting to see someone besides neurotic Hellions. Now I feel bad I didn't come down sooner.

Mr. Muninn is entirely black. Like squid-ink black. He's also as round as a beach ball. He's dressed in a long brocade robe woven with a subtle fire pattern. Under it glitters Lucifer's battle armor, the ultimate symbol of power down here. It lets everyone know who's in charge. I'm not sure if I'm supposed to call him Lucifer or what, so I just take a shot.

"Nice to see you too, Mr. Muninn."

He smiles. He's already tired of being called Lucifer and all the thousand toadying variations you get with the penthouse. I know how he feels.

"You've brought a friend," he says.

Muninn looks a little bemused, like I'm a neighbor kid who brought a stray cougar cub into the living room. Is that how Muninn sees Candy? I hadn't thought about how he might react to a Jade. Maybe I'm overthinking it. I've dragged a civilian down with me into the worst place in existence and he probably doesn't approve.

"Mr. Muninn, this is my friend Candy."

"Very nice to meet you. I see you're like our friend James here, with his penchant for a single name."

"Yeah," she says. "For the longest time all I knew was Stark. It must have taken him six months to tell me the James part."

"Well, I still don't know your last name," I say.

She shrugs.

"As far as I know, I don't have one. When I have to use one I usually just go with Jade."

"Candy Jade. It sounds like one of your cartoon characters."

"Sandman Slim sounds like grout cleaner."

Muninn puts out his hand.

"Welcome to my humble home, Candy."

She shakes, but her arm tightens around mine. She's scared, like she's afraid she'll burst into flames if she touches him. But she's brave and does it anyway. No flames. No explosions. Not even smoke.

"Was it smart to bring someone more innocent than you or I to this place?"

"I introduced her to Samael and she survived. She knows about me, so she was twisting my arm to meet the new Lucifer."

Muninn says, "I wish I could meet a new Lucifer too. I don't suppose you want the job back."

"I'm afraid not."

Muninn sighs and waves us to a sitting area.

The place isn't anything like the penthouse when I lived here. I never bothered fixing it up. I left all of the anonymously expensive hotel furniture right where it was. Now the place looks like a museum. Back in L.A., Muninn lived in an underground cavern full of art, machines, toys, food, and geegaws from every civilization since the last ice age. It looks like he's moved half of it down here.

Candy and I sit on a solid-gold love seat with tentacles for armrests and shaggy horsehide cushions. From the look of the thing it's probably nestled the rear end of at least a couple of emperors. Muninn drops into a vintage La-Z-Boy recliner, but he keeps it upright for his guests.

"That's not quite the look I was expecting for the new Devil," I say.

Muninn glances across the room.

"I have a throne around here somewhere. A piece that's even grander than the seat you're on now. I wish I could greet all my guests in this chair. The throne plays hell with my back, no pun intended."

"Sorry again about sticking you down here, but I had stuff I needed to get back to in the world."

Out of the corner of my eye I catch Candy's lips flicker into a brief smile.

"I understand. I should never have let Samael play his little trick and force you into taking his place. I created Hell, which makes me responsible for its well-being."

Candy looks puzzled, and then lets it go.

I say, "So how's it going down here?"

Muninn leans back into the chair.

"Better than it was," he says.

"Better than when I ran it."

"Oh my, yes. I'm rebuilding much faster than you were and it seems to have raised everyone's spirits."

"You know I had to drag my feet, right? I had to keep these Hellion bastards running around making plans so they were too busy to get together and kill me."

"I understand completely. But it didn't help the psyches of those who had to live here."

"That's why I wanted you to take over. I knew you could make things right and hold off the wolves too."

Muninn looks at Candy.

"And what do you think, young lady? Did James's hundred days as Lucifer improve his disposition?"

"Sure. He's a pussycat now. Of course, I kicked his ass when he got home, so maybe it was that. Why don't you ask him?"

"Why don't you not?" I say. "Have you heard anything about Aelita or the 8 Ball?"

He shifts in his chair, trying to ease his back.

"Aelita still has confederates in Hell and she tried to use them to hide the Qomrama here. General Semyazah and I persuaded her that that was a bad idea."

"I wonder if she took it to Heaven?"

"I doubt it. Aelita has as many enemies as allies there. Heaven isn't a safe place for her."

"If she can't hide the 8 Ball in Heaven or Hell . . ."

"Then it's still on earth," says Candy.

"That's a relief. I got stuck with the fake Qomrama earlier today and was starting to think I'd wasted the last month chasing my tail."

"No. You are right to keep looking there," says Muninn.

"How do you know she didn't hide it in Antarctica or the bottom of the ocean?" says Candy.

Muninn says, "It's my understanding that soon after getting the Qomrama, Aelita was pursued by a contingent of loyal angels from Heaven, so she had to hide it quickly. I suspect it's still somewhere in Los Angeles."

Candy shakes her head.

"Why doesn't God just kill the bitch?" she says.

Muninn settles back in the chair and looks at me.

"Candy, remember how Mr. Muninn said that he was responsible for Hell because he made it?"

"Yes."

"Lucifer didn't make Hell. God did."

"Yeah. I thought that sounded funny."

"It makes more sense when you know that before he was Lucifer, Mr. Muninn was God."

Candy looks at me to see if I'm joking. Then she looks at Muninn.

"I'm afraid he's telling the truth," Muninn says. "And the reason I don't, as you said, kill the bitch is I can't."

"Why not?"

I say, "He's not as strong as he used to be. See, God isn't exactly God anymore. He had sort of a nervous breakdown. Instead of one big God, there's five little ones."

"Four," says Muninn. "Aelita has already killed Neshamah."

"Word is your brother Ruach is tearing it up in Heaven."

Muninn unconsciously squeezes the easy chair's arms.

"Yes. You see, Ruach is the oldest brother. The oldest fragment. He covets the power the rest of us have. He's a little mad, I think."

"Was he always that way?"

"He was always a bit fragile. Then my brother Nefesh did what he did."

"What does he do?" says Candy.

"Our quarrels became more and more violent. Finally Ruach flew into a rage. He demanded that the rest of us relinquish our powers or he would kill us all. When we wouldn't he attacked us. Nefesh was the one who finally stopped him, in much the way I cast the first Lucifer out of Heaven."

"With a thunderbolt."

"Yes. It left Ruach blind and partially deaf. His anger and fear of us grew to the point where the rest of us knew we couldn't stay."

Candy says, "So there's a God in Heaven, only he's just a little piece. And there's other pieces of God running around. And you're a piece of God and Lucifer at the same time."

"In a nutshell," says Mr. Muninn.

Candy pats my arm in mock sympathy.

"Now I understand why you are the way you are. The universe is a lot more fucked up than I ever imagined."

"Can your brothers help?" I say. "Where are they?"

Muninn waves a hand at the window.

"Here. There. Anywhere. I haven't talked to them in a long time."

"Okay. So, anything new with Merihim and Deumos? Are they at war yet?"

Merihim is a big wheel in the old official Hellion church. Hell's Vatican. Strictly an old-boys club. No girls allowed. Deumos and her sister Hellions had a little problem with that. They started their own church, worshipping a kind of goddess that's supposed to be the new post-God deity. A fairy godmother to kiss all the scraped knees and make everything all right again. One of the last things I did when I was Lucifer was give the women their own church. After I left, Merihim and his crew burned it down. What are little boys made of? Snips and snails and rotten little assholes that don't want to share their toys.

"Not quite at war but far from peace. Deumos and many of the other sisters have gone into hiding," says Muninn. "You might be amused to know that Medea Bava went into hiding with them."

Medea Bava was the Sub Rosa's Inquisition. Their ultimate enforcer. The lone-wolf cop who handed out life sentences in a little place called Tartarus, the Hell below Hell, where souls were burned to stoke the celestial furnaces. It was a place no one ever escaped from. Only I escaped and I took all the other lunatics in the asylum out with me. After that, Medea disappeared. I hate her almost as much as Aelita.

Muninn sighs.

"She lost faith in me—the God part, at least—when you

destroyed Tartarus, so she joined Deumos and the sisters. Another voice lost in the wilderness."

"Fuck Medea. She's not a voice anyone needs in their head, especially you. She's as crazy as Aelita. Deumos is the only one of the bunch who's sane, and she's completely deluded. And Merihim is just a power-hungry prick. He's long over-due for a hard fall down a long flight of stairs, if you get my drift."

"I'm afraid I do."

"I don't know how he did it, but Merihim used to crank-call me in L.A. after I left here."

"He was upset with how you left things."

"Cry me a river, pal," I say. "Isn't there something you can do to get Merihim and the church under control and off Deumos's back?"

"That would be taking sides."

"Fine. Then stop them both and make them play nice."

He looks around, uncomfortable. Slams his fist down on the arm of the chair.

"It's not that simple," Muninn shouts.

It's the first time I've heard him raise his voice about any-thing.

"You never understood how being a ruler works, James. And you have no idea what a deity is. You want me to make myself known and manifest to humankind. Do you really think that would solve anything? Or would it make things worse? You, like Samael, want total free will for the angels."

Muninn sweeps his arms out to the broken landscape of Hell.

"Behold. That is what angelic free will looks like."

"That's not fair. You took the worst of the worst, the losers and the rat-fuck crazies, and locked them at the shit-pit bottom of the universe. There was no way they were ever going to build anything but this."

"That's also Samael's argument. You two are so much alike."

"I'm not anything like Samael."

Muninn leans forward in his chair.

"Really? Does that wound in your side hurt?"

"It's nothing."

"Of course it is."

He looks at Candy.

"Samael walked around for millennia bleeding from a wound I gave him during the first Heavenly war. All he ever had to do was ask and I would have healed him."

Candy gives me a look.

"That does sound familiar."

"Samael and I aren't anything alike."

Muninn looks at Candy.

"He'll bleed with that bullet in him until the end of time before he'll ask for help."

"What if I ask?" Candy says.

Muninn raises his eyebrows.

"Ah. Here's someone unburdened by the sin of pride."

"Don't you dare," I say to Candy.

"Too late," says Muninn. "Here."

He puts something in my hand. The bullet.

Candy leans over to look at it.

"And what do we say when someone magically heals us?"

"I didn't ask him to."

She smiles at Muninn.

"He says, 'Thank you very much, Mr. Muninn.' "

"I hope you'll forgive me for snatching away your martyrdom, James," Muninn says.

"That's okay. You I can forgive but the idiot who put it in there and whoever he works for I don't. Or his bastard brother."

"Will you be seeing Wild Bill while you're here?"

"Next visit. When I'm not on the clock."

Candy holds out her hand.

"Can I have the bullet?"

"What, are you a crow all of a sudden? You want all the shiny things."

"I wanted the money clip because it was pretty. I want the bullet because you're going to conveniently lose it somewhere and I want to keep it."

"What for?"

"Who knows? Maybe when you get shot again I'll make you cuff links."

"For all the times I wear dress shirts."

Dress shirts. Clothes. The bullet in my gut. I almost forgot the whole reason I came down here in the first place.

"Mr. Muninn, I'm looking for a new damned soul. His name is Trevor Moseley. Is there any way I can find him?"

"You say he's new down here?"

Muninn shakes his head.

"I'm afraid our intake procedures aren't what they should be. Why do you want to speak to him?"

"I want to know why he was so happy to walk in front of a bus."

"That is unusual. I can put out a notice for him and let you know when he pops up on my radar."

"Thanks. I'd appreciate it. We should go. We've taken up enough of your time."

Muninn gets up.

"I'm sorry I raised my voice."

"Don't apologize. I probably deserved it."

"You did," says Candy.

"Feel free to come or go through any of the shadows in here," says Muninn. "I don't think you'll be wanting to take the long way next time."

"Not even a little. See you around, Mr. Muninn."

"It was nice meeting you," says Candy.

"Good-bye, my dear. I hope we meet again."

"Me too."

I pull Candy through a shadow and a wave of nausea and we come out in the living room in the Chateau.

Kasabian looks up from his computer.

"Where have you two been? You smell like something a dead raccoon horked up."

I look at Candy.

"Told you so."

"WHO ARE YOU calling?" says Candy.

I'm dripping on the carpet and she's still toweling off from the shower. I'm turned away dialing the phone so she doesn't have to look at the new scar I picked up from Garrett's lucky shot.

I say, "Manimal Mike. He might know who made the fake 8 Ball."

She comes out of the bathroom, takes the phone from my hand, and tosses it on the bed.

"Stop it," she says.

"Why?"

"Because you just got shot. Because you just got blown up and we just came back from Hell."

"I had a donut this morning."

"See? I didn't know that."

"You were sitting right there."

"I wasn't paying attention."

I know what she's getting at even if she doesn't want to say it. Days like this I can maybe catch a bullet, she can maybe get her laptop murdered, and maybe we can go to Hell, but doing them all the same day isn't exactly normal, even for someone as fierce as Candy.

I nod. Get a glove to put on over my Kissi hand.

"Okay, country mouse. I guess getting to Mike's in the next ten minutes isn't going to save the world. What did you have in mind? Shuffleboard or coupon clipping?"

She pushes me down so I'm sitting on the bed.

"How about sitting still for a whole sixty seconds. I think you have this illusion that you're a shark. Like you think you'll choke if you stopped moving all the time."

"The bullet's out. I'm all healed up inside."

"I know that in my head, but it doesn't feel that way yet. And I see you trying to hide the wound, so don't bother. Can we please just be here for a minute together without weird weapons or old gods or monsters between us?"

"Come here," I say, and pull her down on the bed. She curls around me with her leg over mine.

"I know I'm not always easy to be around," I say.

"No. You're fine. It's just everything you do."

"I should have listened to my high school guidance counselor and studied air-conditioning repair."

"Then you'd have all those sexy jumpsuits I could wear around the place."

"Jumpsuits aren't sexy."

"They are when you're not wearing anything under them."

She gets up and turns off the light, then comes back to bed. A few minutes later her breathing is shallow and regular. She's asleep. I close my eyes and drift off. In my dream, I'm in the arena in Hell with the mad little ghost, Lamia. We circle each other, looking for an opening.

"Are you here to kill me?" says Lamia.

I tell her the truth.

"Only if I have to."

Part of me feels like an idiot. Lamia looks like a little girl, nine or ten years old, wearing a blue party dress. She also has a knife as big her forearm. And the only thing keeping her from sticking me with it is that I have the 8 Ball. It's the only thing that's ever seemed to scare her.

But this isn't right. This isn't how I met Lamia. It wasn't in the arena. It was in the Tenebrae, the limbo land of lost and desperate ghosts too afraid to move on to Heaven or Hell.

Lamia was there, radiating crazy like a Chernobyl straitjacket and stalking the place like a Sherman tank in kneesocks. She knifed ghosts in the Tenebrae and killed people back on earth, laughing the whole time.

When I asked who she was and what she wanted, all I got

was schizobabble about the world before it was the world. Eventually she told me her name.

"I'm Lamia. I breathe death and spit vengeance."

Try having a ten-year-old tell you that and knowing they mean it. It's a Hallmark moment.

Father Traven is our resident mystical trivia expert. He used to translate books for the Church, but then he translated the wrong one. The Angra Om Ya's bible. He got the boot for that. Excommunicated. A one-way ticket to Hell.

Father Traven thinks Lamia is a demon. A "Qliphoth," he calls them. Not a little imp with a pitchfork and anger-management issues. A real demon is a broken thing. A mindless fragment of the old gods, the Angra Om Ya. But demons are basically morons, with about as much brainpower as an underachieving maggot. Some eat. Others dig. Others curse. But none of them choose it. It's what they're programmed for.

What makes Lamia special is that she's relatively smart and chatty. You might think that's a good thing, letting us get into a demon's mind so we can see how the gears work and all that forensic horseshit. But it's not good news at all.

You don't want to get anywhere near a smart demon. A smart demon is a bigger, more powerful piece of the Angra. Lamia means that more of the old gods are leaking into our universe. How long until other smart demons break through? How long before a complete Angra?

And even though I know it's wrong, Lamia and I are back in the arena, only she's not slashing me. She's slashing Candy. But I can't protect her because even though I have the 8 Ball, I don't know how it works. I'm helpless and useless.

I really want to ask Mr. Muninn about Lamia, but I haven't figured out where to even start a question like that.

"*Hey, Mr. Muninn, back when you were one big God, did you steal the universe from another race of older gods, lock them away somewhere, then pretend that you created everything and proceed to screw it all up for the next few billion years? Was that your plan? 'Cause if it was, mission fucking accomplished.*"

CANDY IS STILL asleep when I wake up. I say her name and shake her, but she doesn't budge. She gets like this sometimes. Some combination of being exhausted and her Jade metabolism. It's more like she's hibernating than sleeping. This can go on for hours. I'll go out of my mind if I sit around that long.

I turn on the light and put on new leather pants and boots. No more button-down shirts for me. I don't dress up for anyone. The only clean T-shirt I can find has a winking Japanese schoolgirl on the front over "I ♥ TENTACLES." Guess who gave me that. I also grab my coat. It's still too hot for it, but after the party at Garrett's room I'm not going anywhere without my na'at and a gun.

Going to Manimal Mike's place is a no-sweat trip I can do without anyone holding my hand. I leave Candy a note telling her where I am. She'll be pissed if she wakes and finds me gone, but it's better than lying around in the dark or watching Kasabian walk around on all fours like a Hellion windup toy.

I take the fake 8 Ball and go out through the grandfather clock. Take the elevator down to the lobby and wait for a second before going any farther.

The lobby feels all right. No hostile vibes aimed my way. The concierge nods in my direction. I nod back. Still, polite staff doesn't mean I'm off the hook. They might be playing possum while calling security. There's only one way to find out if the hotel still thinks that I'm Mr. Macheath, the Devil himself, and the rightful occupant of his gratis suite.

I pull out a Malediction and light it. In California, this is the equivalent of pissing into the pope's minestrone. But aside from a few dirty looks and make-believe coughs from a family of red-faced tourists going up in the next elevator, nothing happens.

I'm safe. For another day. I'll think I'll order lobster and a T-bone tonight.

Time to press my luck one more time.

I go into the bar and tell them to give me a sealed bottle of Stoli. The bartender hands it over without blinking.

"Thanks. Put it on my tab." Why not? Nothing actually ever gets charged to the Devil's room.

When the Chateau throws us out one day, will they try to stick me with the charges for the suite and the miles of food and booze we've put away? Good thing I'm broke.

Even with a shower and clean clothes, I still feel a little rough around the edges. Candy was right about one thing. Sleep was a good idea even if it brought on fucked-up dreams. The blisters on my side are mostly healed, but the skin is still sensitive. It's really putting me in the mood to punch something. Where's a skinhead when you need one?

I go into the garage and spot a cherry-red '68 Charger. Jam the black blade into the door and it pops opens. Jam it into the ignition and the car starts right up. I drive out into the early-evening L.A. sun, all thought of pain, the Angra, and eviction gone. Nothing improves my mood better than stealing a really nice car.

MANIMAL MIKE LIVES and works in a piece-of-shit garage in Chatsworth in the San Fernando Valley. Mike does his Tick-Tock Man work in the back while his cousins, a couple of straight-off-the-boat Russian muscleheads, try to look like they know what they're doing by pretending to fix the same cars that have been sitting in the garage for years. Mike's cousins are vucaris. Russian beast men. Kind of like what civilians call "werewolves." Like beast men, they're not too bright, but with the right motivation they can be trained to fetch or just get out of the way.

Mike's cousins wanted to gnaw my hide the first time I came here. Now I'm their best friend. I toss them the Stoli on my way in and get a couple of quick *spasiba*s before they have the cap off and are arguing over who gets the first jolt. I leave them to work that out for themselves and head for Mike's workshop in the back.

The first time I met Mike he was committing slow-motion suicide, getting blind drunk and playing a game called Billy Flinch. It's basically playing William Tell only you're trying to shoot a glass off your own head by ricocheting a bullet off the opposite wall. Good thing Mike was such a lousy shot.

Nowadays Mike's office looks less like a grease monkey's alcoholic crash pad and more like a professional workshop. I take a little credit for that. I think promising Mike his soul back gave him the kick in the ass he needed to pull himself out of the bottle and do real work. Now I just have to figure out how to wrangle his soul out of damnation so I can give it back to him.

"Hey, Mike. How's tricks?"

Mike must have been lost in his work. He lurches up from his seat like he wants to jump out of his own skin and into whatever kind of animal he's building. It looks like a Nerf ball with spikes. Mike has always been high-strung. It takes him a second to catch his breath.

"Shit. Don't sneak up on me like that."

Then he remembers he's talking to the guy he thinks is the Devil.

"Shit. I'm sorry. I didn't mean to yell."

I shake my head.

"No worries. It's about the nicest thing anyone's said to me today."

Mike's right hand is still sort of attached to the strange Nerf animal by spiderweb-thin filaments that run from a tiny clamp in his hand to the animal's back. The animal is gently suspended in the air in a larger web strung up between two long, curved pipes bolted to each side of a metal table. The pipes look like they might have come off a car's exhaust system. Mike's terrifying tools are spread out on the table. They look like things Hellions would use to perform surgery on people they don't like very much.

Once Mike has a second to process that this is an unscheduled visit, thankfully, a smaller wave of panic sets in.

"Oh God, don't tell me. Something went wrong with Kasabian's hands? His legs? I swear I'll get whatever it is working again."

"Attempt to be cool, Mike. Kasabian is fine. What's the story with your spiny friend?"

"It's a puffer fish. A fugu. Some famous Sub Rosa sushi chef is in town and one of the families wants to give him a present."

"A fish. So, if the guy made barbecue, you'd be making him a mechanical brisket?"

"No, man. Fugu is special. Like an art form. It's loaded with this stuff called tetrodotoxin. A badass neurotoxin. Cut the fish wrong and *bam*. Everyone's dead. You need a license to make it and everything."

I shrug.

"And people pay brisk money for this stuff?"

" 'Brisk' ain't the word. It's more like make-you-weep money."

"I didn't realize that civilians were as stupid as Hellions when it comes to the shit they'll stick in their mouths."

"I wouldn't know about that and hope I never do."

Mike detaches the clamp from his little fish and wipes his hands on his dirty rag.

"The commission sounds like a good thing for you. You're moving up in the Tick-Tock world."

"Yeah. Things are going okay. You didn't come by just to check up on me, did you?"

Up until now I've been holding the 8 Ball under my arm like a loaf of bread. I take it and hold it up so he can get a good look at it.

"Nothing like that. I was wondering if you'd look at something for me. It's a fake mystical object I'm guessing someone paid a lot of money for. I was hoping you'd have some idea who made it."

Mike takes it gently, like he's handling a baby duck.

"I'll have a look but I mostly know animals. Those charm- and talisman-making assholes won't give us the time of day. They talk about Tick-Tock Men like all we make are big-ass Tamagotchis. But we're artists, you know?"

"I know. That's why I brought it to you. I figure an artist knows an artist."

Mike turns the 8 Ball over in his hands, looking over every inch of it. He pulls down a magnifier mounted on the edge of the table and examines every bolt and fastening.

"Beautiful work," he says. "Incredible detail. And these materials. Brass-and-platinum skin over a core of surgical steel and cinnabar. You see these tiny sapphires by the base?"

He holds it up. There are a few blue specks on the 8 Ball's belly.

"Someone's charmed them. That's what gives it a low-level magic signature. It's gorgeous work. Does it have a name?"

"Qomrama Om Ya."

"Never heard of it. I like animals."

"If it helps, the guy had a raven in his room. Good work. Very convincing."

Mike looks up from the magnifier.

"You didn't happen to check under the tail feathers, did you?"

"You mean, did I look at the bird's ass? No. It never crossed my mind. I'd go back and try, only by now the ass is probably blown halfway to Las Vegas."

Mike goes back to the 8 Ball.

"Too bad. Lots of people sign their work in places most people don't look. That way if the bird changes hands and needs repairs, they can find the original builder."

"That's truly fascinating. I'll look under your ass if it'll help you tell me something I can use."

"Wait," says Mike. "Gotcha. Right there."

He hunches over the magnifier, holding the 8 Ball closer.

"I know who made it."

"You sure?"

He crooks a finger at me and I go around to his side of the table. The 8 Ball is huge in the magnifier. He uses one of his delicate tools to point to a single sapphire stud.

"You see that little mark etched around the sapphire? That's the alchemical symbol for verdigris. Only one Tick-Tock Man signs his work with that. You'll love him. He's a total asshole. Atticus Rose."

"Do you have a number for him?"

Mike does a sarcastic little laugh.

"Are you kidding? Rose is a golden eagle riding a gumdrop thermal over Candy Land. On a good day I'm a snail crawling across that grease pit out front. Eagles don't give their business cards to snails."

"You're not a snail, Mike. You're at least a ferret."

"Thanks," he says like he actually means it. "Anyway, like I was saying, we don't move in the same circles."

"Who would know him?"

"The high-and-mighties. Someone who can pay the equivalent of a Lamborghini for a parakeet. Someone like Blackburn. Maybe his government or showbiz buddies. You ever party with them? Me neither."

I take the 8 Ball back from Mike. It's hard for him to let go. It's like he's fallen in love and doesn't want to see his girl-friend carried off by a highwayman.

"I don't party with people like that, but I know someone who might. Thanks, Mike."

I'm halfway to the door when Mike calls after me.

"Hold up. I've been thinking about Kasabian."

"Don't do that. You'll get lesions on your brain."

"I figured it out. If you can get me another hellhound body, then I can modify that and then put new parts on Kasabian's body without taking him off."

"Great idea. I'll stop by Costco on the way home and pick up a new hellhound. Oh, wait. They only have those in Hell."

Mike frowns.

"It was just an idea. You don't have to be mean about it."

"Sorry, Mike. I was just down in Hell and it wasn't fun. I'll see about getting another hound, but I have other things to do first."

"Okay. Make sure Kasabian knows it was my idea."

"Will do."

I go out through the garage, wave to Mike's cousins, and climb back into the Charger. By the time I'm in, I've already thumbed Brigitte Bardo's number into my phone.

BRIGITTE IS MY favorite zombie hunter in the world. Except we killed off all the zombies a few months ago and she's been kind of at loose ends ever since. She was a big-time, classy porn star in Europe and she's been trying to get a legit acting career going. With her looks and brains in a town like L.A., she can really work the hell out of a room. Brigitte has more phone numbers and dirt on people in her little black book than Homeland Security.

"Jimmy," she says in her sweet Prague accent. "How lovely for you to call. How are you? Have you killed anyone interesting lately?"

"Does it count if I just happened to be in the room when the bomb went off?"

"Of course not."

"Then no."

She sighs.

"You'll have to do better. I live vicariously through you these days."

She's only half joking. We're both trained killers. Brigitte was trained for zombie hunting since she was a kid. Being a killer is a hard thing to walk away from and have a normal life.

"Listen. I wouldn't normally call you with something as boring as this."

"Boring? How could a task of yours be boring?"

"I'm trying to track someone down, and the thing is, Blackburn might know the guy, but his head of security braced me the last time I was there, so I can't ask him."

"So we won't be fighting monsters or kicking in doors?"

"Right now I'm just looking for a phone number and maybe an address."

"You were right. This is boring," she says. "Who is it?"

"A Tick-Tock Man named Atticus Rose."

"Are you looking for a pet? I can see you strolling down Sunset Boulevard with a lovely poodle. Or perhaps a white cockatoo on your shoulder. A very butch cockatoo, of course."

"How do you butch up a bird? Get it a little leather cap and chaps?"

"That's your fantasy, Jimmy. Not mine."

"Do you think you can find me a number?"

"Of course. I can get anyone's number. But just remember that everything comes with a price."

"What does that mean?"

"I'll call you later with Herr Rose's information."

"What price, Brigitte?"

Too late. The line is dead. Once a killer, always a killer.

I DITCH THE Charger by the Whisky a Go Go and walk the rest of the way back to the Chateau.

When I get back to the room, Candy is just waking up. She rubs the sleep out of her eyes and stretches like a panther. She blinks when she sees me.

"Oh. I thought you were off bringing me coffee in bed. What are you dressed for?"

"I was out talking to Manimal Mike. I tried waking you."

"Try harder next time. Where did he shoot you?"

I hold up my arms so she can see me.

"No blood. See? I made it back unmolested."

She runs her foot up my leg to my thigh.

"Maybe we should do something about that."

I close the bedroom door and turn up the new Skull Valley Sheep Kill album on the stereo. Kasabian doesn't like to listen when we smash up the furniture.

AN HOUR LATER and we've only broken one side table. The gunshot and the blast took a little more out of me than I like to admit. I light up a Malediction and look for some Aqua Regia, but the bottle is still in the living room.

Candy is lying next to me in one of the absurdly plush hotel robes.

"So what did you and Mike talk about?"

"The 8 Ball. He says he knows who made it."

"Great. Let's go pay Dr. Frankenstein a visit."

"Can't. He didn't have a number for the guy, so I called Brigitte."

"She knows the guy?"

"No. But she can probably track him down."

"Clever girl."

"They're the only kind worth knowing."

"Ain't that the truth."

We wander out to the living room. I pour some Aqua Regia into a coffee mug and Candy picks at the remains of last night's food. We always order too much and leave the food carts along the wall buffet style. I wish we could squirrel away all the leftovers. We're going to miss them when they kick us out.

Kasabian calls us from across the room.

"Check it out. My first client."

"Congratulations," says Candy.

"I didn't even know you had the site finished."

Kasabian is on the landing page for Aetheric Industries Psychic Investigations.

"The wonders of the cyberspace and desperate suckers," he says. "I put the site up an hour ago and already have three inquiries and one bona fide, already-got-his-credit-card-number customer."

"Who are you supposed to find?"

"The guy's idiot older brother. Get this. Big brother was a hoarder and hid their dad's gold coin collection somewhere in the house. My client doesn't want to spend the next ten years spelunking under old pizza boxes and soggy newspapers looking for Daddy's swag."

Candy says, "I didn't think you could get that kind of information. All you can do is look at things."

"That's right. But get this. My client thinks if I can find big bro in Hell, he can get another psychic to do a kind of Vulcan mind meld and they can talk over old times."

"That's the stupidest thing I've ever heard," I say.

Kasabian nods and smiles.

"I know. Isn't it great? See, being online so much, I learned that normal desperate people are sad and boring, but stupid desperate people are a fucking riot. And some of them have money."

"That's not very nice," Candy says.

"If my life was any lamer, I would have taken a nap in a trash compactor a long time ago, so forgive me for not farting kittens and rainbows."

"I didn't know you were that unhappy."

"I'm not. I'm realistic about my situation. And I'm honest with my clients. I spell out exactly what I can and can't do in the site's disclaimer. If someone comes along and wants to pay me to do what I said I can't, I'm not turning him down.

Stupid people's money is just as green as everyone else's."

"I might have been that desperate after Doc died," says Candy. Doc Kinski was the guy who took her off the street and gave her potions to calm her Jade bloodlust. I think he was as close to a real father as she ever had. Kind of like Vidocq for me.

"Yeah, well. You might have been desperate but you're not dumb, so it wouldn't be the same thing," says Kasabian. "And goddammit, can I have just one minute of happiness here before one of you points out what a monster I am and tries to shut me down? What do I have left then? I go back to finding weirder and weirder online porn just to keep my brain cells from imploding."

"Sorry. Of course," says Candy.

She puts a hand on his hellhound shoulder. Says, "Good luck in the Hellovision business."

Kasabian's eyes open a little more.

"Damn. I wish I'd thought of that name. I wonder if I can get that domain?"

"I guarantee you someone else already has it. Someone always has the cool names," I say.

Kasabian is already typing.

"We'll see how long they can keep it."

I say, "Did you find anything else out about Moseley?"

He shakes his head, still looking at the screen.

"Nothing except that he kind of dropped off the face of the earth a few months ago. No employment records. No bills or utilities. Nada."

"Thanks. Oh yeah. Mike says he has another idea on how to fix you up."

That gets his attention.

"How?"

"Don't get your tail bunched up, Old Yeller. It means I have to go back to Hell and maybe steal something with teeth and claws, so it's not happening this afternoon."

He turns back to the screen.

"Hurry up and wait. Story of my life."

Candy looks over Kasabian's shoulder at the screen.

"What's the weirdest porn you ever found?" says Candy.

Kasabian gives her a serious look.

"Unless you want to wake up screaming, don't ever ask me that again."

"Yes, sir."

AROUND TEN, MY phone rings. It's Brigitte.

"Hi."

"Hi yourself. You have an appointment with Herr Rose at three tomorrow afternoon."

"Thanks, Brigitte. You're my hero."

"Don't be so hasty. Remember I said that everything has a price?"

"Go on."

"The price for the address is this. I'm coming with you."

"You haven't exactly been in the field lately. What if things get hot?"

"That's why I'm coming. If I go to another audition without at least the chance to kill something, I'm afraid my behavior will become quite drastic. So you see, Jimmy, you're not just doing me a favor. You'll be doing a humanitarian service too."

"Fine. Come along. I'm sure Candy will enjoy it. You can tell each other stories about your favorite childhood kills."

A pause.

"That's the rub, you see. Herr Rose is terribly claustrophobic and only ever sees a maximum of two people at a time. It's a rule he breaks for no one."

"No problem. He'll be tickled pink when he finds you and Candy at his door."

"And where will you be?"

"Coming down the chimney."

"Through a shadow."

"Yeah."

"I miss seeing that."

"You can get an eyeful tomorrow."

"He'll hear you and throw us out."

"Hear me? I'll be as quiet as a cotton-candy mouse."

"I'm not so sure about this, Jimmy."

"Sure you are. It'll be fun. Dress pretty and bring your gun."

"A man who knows how to speak to my heart."

She gives me Rose's address. I repeat it and Candy writes it down.

I say, "See you tomorrow, Brigitte," and hang up.

Candy beams at me.

"I hope we get to shoot something. I haven't had a girls' day out in a long time."

BEL AIR IS a neighborhood that lies just west of Beverly Hills and sees its neighbor the way that neighbor sees the rest of L.A.: as a wasteland of upstarts, criminals, and wayward teens with their bongos and jungle music. If the sun ever set in Bel Air, no one would notice because its homes and residents are so luminous they'd light the night sky all on their own. It's a land where the gold standard never died and the roads are so clean you could perform open-heart surgery on any street corner.

Candy and I emerge from the shadow of a lamppost so pristine it could've been put there this morning. We're on North Beverly Glen Boulevard, across the street from the address Brigitte gave me.

The place is called Clear, an old upscale faux-Gothic hotel rebranded by one snotty nouveau chic chain or the other. The residents of these hotels are always the same. Oblivious executives in town for a day to make another billion because the billions they have aren't enough. Handsome young lovers so bursting with happiness and privilege that you want to punch the DNA that created them. And old long-term residents baffled by the bright lights and excited plastic-surgeried crowds rushing in and out of the place 24/7. Clear reminds me of palaces I saw in Hell, but in worse taste.

Brigitte is in the lobby. She's a knockout in a short green sequin dress and pearls and a little silver clutch purse just big enough for her CO_2 pistol. She looks like a flapper ninja. Candy is in her usual too-big leather jacket and Chuck Taylors. I'm in a frockcoat with guns. Which two of us don't look like we belong in the Clear?

Brigitte kisses Candy and me on both cheeks. Candy says something to her that I miss and they both start laughing. They're giddy at the idea they're going to see some action. I'm hoping we don't. And if something happens, fingers crossed that we don't start it, and by "we," I mean them.

We ride the elevator to the twelfth floor, go left, and walk almost to the end of the corridor.

"Herr Rose has two rooms, 1210 and 1212. But we've been instructed to knock only on 1210," says Brigitte.

"Easy to remember," I say. "Twelve-ten. When they signed the Magna Carta."

Both women look at me.

"Don't look at me like that. There was nothing to do in Hell but hide and read books. Is that a crime?"

Candy says, "Marcus Aurelius and now the Magna Carta? I'm starting to think that bullet unleashed your inner geek."

"I had an inner geek once. But a doctor lanced it and it went away."

"Call an ambulance. It's growing back."

Brigitte smiles.

"You two are charming together."

"I was plenty charming all on my own," says Candy. "I'm just carrying the geek so he doesn't cut himself on a bullet and bleed to death."

"Are you two done? I knew I should never let you near each other."

Brigitte says, "I think he just called us . . . What's the word?"

"Brats," says Candy.

"Yes. Brats."

"That's because you are brats."

"And who's more foolish? The brats or the man who invites the brats to a gunfight?" says Brigitte.

"No gunfights. I didn't invite anyone to a gunfight. This is a normal everyday ambush, not the O.K. Corral."

"If you're going to be boring about it, at least be entertaining. Disappear into one of your shadows while we distract Rose with our wiles."

"Yeah," says Candy. "The wiles girls are in business."

She loops her arm in Brigitte's.

I walk into a shadow by a picture window down the hall, surer than ever that I should have worn body armor.

I STILL HATE walking into unknown rooms, but I've never heard of a dangerous Tick-Tock Man, so I'm more likely to walk in on a game of Dungeons & Dragons than bear-baiting.

I come out in a room that reminds me of Garrett's. A generically elegant place, but a little more old school than his was. The wood looks like wood instead of veneer and the paintings look real instead of like overpriced prints.

Rose has two adjoining apartments. One for living and one for a workspace. The guy is either loaded or his rental agreement is so old it's written on parchment and he pays for it with shells and brightly colored beads.

He must be one of those genius types, like Tesla. Guys who would rather live in a hotel than have their own home. Live somewhere they know the sheets and towels will always be clean and where they can get a grilled-cheese sandwich from room service at four A.M. Because we're in Bel Air, I want to hate his setup, but the truth is, I understand the addiction. I love squatting in the Chateau Marmont. Plus, I never told anyone, but part of me is happy that so many of my clothes end up burned, slashed, shot up, or generally too bloody to deal with. It's a great excuse never to do laundry. I can deal with fighting in the arena in Hell, but laundry and dishes put the fear of God in me.

I can hear Rose in his workroom, so I stay out of sight in his living quarters.

At three on the dot there's a knock. Rose goes to open the door and I get my first look at him.

He's an older guy but not over the hill. In his early sixties maybe. Long, salt-and-pepper hair combed back from his forehead and over his ears. I see lab coats on the wall, but he knows company is coming, so he's wearing a pressed, old-fashioned, forties-style high-waisted blue suit and tie with a diamond pattern down the center. He could have stepped right off the set of *Out of the Past*.

He opens the door and there are Candy and Brigitte, carpet-bombing him with their wiles. Old Rose can't help but smile.

"Knock knock," says Brigitte.

"You must Mr. Blackburn's friends."

"You bet," says Candy. "Can we come in? We don't bite."

"Of course. Please come in."

Rose stands aside and Candy and Brigitte walk in like they already own the place. Old Atticus looks like he's about to hand it over to them.

"Would either of you ladies care for some coffee? If you'd like something stronger, I keep whiskey in the apartment. If you'd like wine I can have some sent up."

He speaks in a deliberate flat drawl. Not southern. Maybe Okie. I had some cousins from Oklahoma. All I remember about them was that they pronounced *theater* with a long *a*.

"No thank you. You have a lovely workshop," says Brigitte.

That's an understatement. It's a little slice of Heaven compared to Manimal Mike's jerry-rigged setup. The space is clean and stocked with every tool in this world and probably a couple of others. There's enough room for several people to work at once. Rose must have assistants because there are at least a dozen animal familiars around the room, some fully built and others just steel and gear frames.

"Thank you," he says. "May I give you ladies a tour?"

Just like I thought. Atticus, a professional recluse, can't help but want to show off his toys. He brings them over to a table where a half-constructed tabby cat lies curled up near unsewn swatches of fur.

Watching them like this isn't fun. It brings bad old feelings. This is how my hits in Hell used to go. I'd come through a shadow into someone's home and wait, sometimes hours, for them to get relaxed or distracted, and then quickly, quietly, I'd cut their throats with the black blade. Things only got messy if they had a bodyguard or a hapless, soon-to-be-dead friend strolled into the slaughter scene. No one ever got away. I was a slave and a killer and I was good at it. I don't want to be any of those things today, so I stay put and take deep breaths, letting the memories fade away.

Speaking of people who need to crank things down a notch, Rose's heart is doing its own tap dance. Brigitte got good information. This boy likes wide-open spaces. Even with two not-very-large women in the room, he's uncomfortable.

"Thank you for seeing us so quickly," Brigitte says to Rose.

"Of course. Any friends of Saragossa are welcome."

"What's this?" says Candy. She's across the workroom on her own, lost in Rose's mechanical zoo. Nearby is what looks like a wild dog with broad stripes down its back.

"That's a Tasmanian tiger, young lady. They're extinct. If you want one I'm the only Tick-Tock Man in the world who can give you an exact copy of an original, capturing both its spirit and its wild soul."

"It looks expensive."

"Very expensive," says Rose.

Candy looks at Brigitte.

"Mom, can I have one if I'm good?"

Brigitte laughs.

"Maybe for your birthday, dear."

Candy strokes the tiger's ears.

Rose's breathing and heart spike like someone rigged his scrotum to a 220 line.

"Please don't touch that," he says, and crosses the room in a few strides to where Candy is standing. She backs off and goes back to Brigitte while Rose combs the tiger's fur back the way it was.

"Do you ever make anything besides animals?" says Candy.

She's setting him up for me to knock down. Rose isn't relaxed enough to attack, but he's plenty distracted. I take off my glove and put it in my pocket.

"Like what?" says Rose.

I walk into his workspace balancing the 8 Ball on my Kissi hand.

"Something like this."

I toss the ball at Rose. He catches it. Clutches it to his chest like a life preserver.

"How did you get in here? Get out before I call hotel security."

I look at the girls.

"You know, people used to have pride. They'd keep a baseball bat by the door and hit you themselves. Now everyone has hired goons. What happened to the American can-do spirit?"

Candy and Brigitte snigger. Rose doesn't move. He's looking at my funny hand. I go to the hotel phone on the wall. Pull it out of the wall and crush it like a soda can in my trash-compactor fingers.

"Sweet Jesus," whispers Rose.

I can read Rose like the Sunday funnies. He's on the edge of panic. There are way too many people in here, but he's conflicted. Who does he ask to go? The pretty ladies or the crazy man with the mechanical meat hook? He's afraid of me but he'll weep bitter tears every night if he passes up the chance to get a better look at my Kissi arm.

I use it to take back the 8 Ball. Wave it in front of him.

"Focus. Where did you see the real 8 Ball? Who did you make the fake one for?"

Candy and Brigitte stroll around the room playing with Rose's tools. Running their hands over his animals' fur and feathers.

"The sooner you answer, the sooner we'll be gone," I say.

He glances at the 8 Ball and shakes his head.

"I've never seen that thing before in my life."

"It has your mark on it."

"Then it's a damn fake."

Candy tosses Brigitte a wriggling koi. She catches it, laughing as it tries to squirm out of her hands.

"If you think we're being unreasonable, think about it from my point of view. Not only did I lose the real 8 Ball, but your goddamn fake almost got me killed. Right now we're going to play volleyball with every kitty cat and titmouse in here until you fess up and tell me who has the real ball."

"I don't know."

"Who wanted the fake one?"

"It's all lies."

I stop for a minute. Is there a chance I'm torturing the wrong guy? I'm good at reading people, but Rose's heart rate and breathing are off the chart. His pupils are the size of baked hams. But I'm still not convinced he's all that innocent.

"Please. You people have to leave."

Reset and try another approach. I pull up my sleeve and show him my whole Kissi arm. Rose's vitals slow. He's back in his own zone. He'd love nothing more than to dismantle me piece by piece.

"I'll let you look at it if you want. Examine the hell out of it and see how it works. Just tell me about the Qomrama."

"I don't know what you're talking about."

There it is. The microtremor in his lips when I said the 8 Ball's name.

"You're lying. Who was the fake one supposed to kill? Garrett? Or the buyer? Who was the buyer?"

Candy has a diamondback curling around her arm. It looks delicate and pricey.

"Declan Garrett," says Rose.

The idiot from Donut Universe. Good.

"And who showed you the real Qomrama?"

"I never saw it. Just pictures. And diagrams in books they gave me."

Shit. Rose is telling the truth. I can feel it. He never saw the real 8 Ball. Maybe whoever commissioned the fake one might never have seen it either. Just knew about it in an old book and had Atticus run him off a mobster clone. If that's true, then chasing Moseley, getting shot, and almost getting blown to refried beans was for nothing. Still, there might be something to salvage.

"Who hired you to make the copy?"

Rose can't take it anymore. There's too many of us. We're too loud. I might kill him with my creepy hand and Candy and Brigitte might fuck up his life's work. He turns away. I think for a second that he might be crying. But he's not. When he turns back he's fished a small box, like a cable remote, from his pocket. He punches in a code with his thumb. A second later Candy slams into one of the work-tables as someone blurs by her, heading for me. I step aside at the last second and let Kid Flash fly by. When he turns, color me surprised.

It's Trevor Moseley. Upright, clean, and completely un-crushed by a number 2 bus.

Moseley comes at me like a flat-footed tornado. All fury and power but not really knowing what to do with it. I slip his first couple of punches, then give him a quick pop in the kidneys. The asshole doesn't even react. He was doped when we danced our first waltz and I guess he still is.

I go down low, giving him a good target. Moseley takes

the bait, and when he throws a kick at my head, I grab his leg and plant a boot into his balls.

I don't know what Moseley is on, but I want some of it. I've still got hold of his leg when he springs off the other and slams me on the side of the head with his foot. The world spins and I flop down flat on my ass. Moseley grabs something bright and sharp from a worktable and comes at me. I pull the na'at from under my coat, swing it like a whip so it wraps around his arm. Flick the grip so the na'at goes rigid, then twist it to break his arm. It works. A little too well. His arm snaps clean off, spewing blood, hydraulic fluid, gears, and cams all over the floor.

I retract the na'at and whip it again, this time at his head. Half of his face comes off, revealing polished wood and carved bone underneath. The fucker is one of Rose's automatons.

There's a soft explosion behind me, like a giant snake coughing. I turn and there's another Moseley on the floor with a big hole in his chest. He's oozing goo and machine parts. Across the room Brigitte has her gun out and in ready position. I nod a quick thanks for covering my back.

The other Moseley grabs me from behind. I spin and plant an elbow full force on the side of his head. And the head comes off, rolling like the world's most surprised bowling ball, coming to a rest at Rose's feet. At least I know why Moseley wasn't afraid to step in front of the bus. With all the spare Moseleys around to take his place, why not?

"You're a talented prick," I say to Rose. "Why hire help when you can build your own? Is the real Moseley still around or did you kill him after you copied him?"

A smile creeps across Rose's face like a tarantula.

"Oh, he's alive, but you're so dumb I doubt you'll live long enough to meet him."

"Did you tell him to shoot me at Donut Universe?"

"I don't ask clients what they do with my creations after I deliver them."

"I forget. What was the client's name?" says Candy.

"I forget too," says Rose, thumbing another code into the remote. "Of course, I have confidentiality agreements with all my clients, but now that you know this secret part of my work, none of you can leave."

He presses a button on the remote. Closes and locks the apartment door.

Machines kick into life around us. Saws. Drills. Lathes. Growls, hisses, and birdcalls float on top of the machine rumble. Rose has activated all of the equipment and every one of his mechanical familiars.

Candy is the first of us to attack. She goes full Jade—nails curved into claws, a mouthful of white shark teeth, and eyes like red slits in black ice—and leaps on top of a jaguar. Digs her teeth into the nape of its neck. Rakes her claws down its side. It makes a grinding, ripping sound.

Brigitte blows apart a cobra as it leaps for her and an eagle as it dives, talons out and aimed at her eyes.

Something slams me down on the first Moseley's busted carcass. Then it roars in my face like a drunken 747.

A fucking grizzly bear. It rears back, but before it can drop down and crush me, I roll out of the way, pulling the Colt .45 from under my coat.

On its hind legs, the bear is ten feet tall and half a ton. I wait until it comes down for me. When it opens its big wet mouth, I aim inside and put two slugs through its upper palate. The top of its head pops off like a toaster full of clock parts and it falls.

I look around for Candy and Brigitte, but a flock of birds—crows, starlings, and buzzards—flies around the room at jet speed, screeching and pecking at everything, including us. The air is a gray blur. I'm blind and deaf in the noise and I can't see what might be creeping up on me.

I yell, "Hit the deck," as loud as I can and bark some Hellion hoodoo.

The ceiling sizzles with flames. The fire licks down the wall like liquid. I get down on my knees and spin the na'at in circles over my head. It won't stop the fire, but it gives me something to concentrate on as I try to control the flames so they burn the familiars but don't get low enough to cook us.

It gets hard to breathe. The flames are burning off all the oxygen in the room. I bark more hoodoo and the fire dwindles to glowing ghost wisps.

"It's okay," I say.

Candy and Brigitte get up from the floor. I was expecting the hotel sprinklers to go off until I see that they're melted and fused to the ceiling.

Except for us, the room is a charred pile of splinters and crispy critters. I look at Brigitte and nod at the apartment door.

"You wanted to kick a door in."

She smiles and blows the lock off with her pistol. Kicks the door open, throws herself forward, and rolls upright, her gun out. It's nice when those reflexes kick back in. Not that they're going to do us much good. The door to the hall is open. I close it and kick a rug against the crack at the bottom so the smoke from the workroom doesn't set off the hall fire alarm.

Rose is long gone. My guess is he won't be coming back. Keeping wild animals and bloody cyborgs in a room charred like a bad night in Dresden might violate the terms of his lease.

Candy is back to human again.

"You all right?" she says.

"Fine. You?"

"Coolio."

"Brigitte. How are you doing?"

"Lovely," she says. "I haven't had this much fun in months."

Her necklace is broken, dripping pearls onto the floor. Her face and arms are scratched and bleeding, covered in soot. But she smiles like it's New Year's Eve.

"Thank you for bringing me along, Jimmy."

"Thank you for saving my ass back there."

"That was fun," says Candy. "Do we get to trash this place too?"

"No. The workshop won't do us any good, so look around here for anything like customer records or names or phone numbers. Any papers that look important."

After half an hour no one comes up with a single useful thing. Brigitte steals a mechanical parakeet in the bedroom and names it Szamanka. Candy thumbs through a big leather-bound book.

"I think this is the book Atticus was talking about," she says. "It has all kinds of drawings of the 8 Ball."

She hands it to me.

I was expecting a moldy, crumbling relic. But the book doesn't look more than a few years old. I put it under my arm and say, "Let's get out of here. I'll take this to Father Traven."

"I can take it to Liam, if you like," says Brigitte. "I'll be seeing him tonight."

I look at Candy. She moves her head microscopically. A secret nod. So that's who Brigitte is seeing. Two nice Catholic kids. A killer and an excommunicated priest. Sounds like a match made in Heaven.

"You should come and see him soon," Brigitte says. "The weight of things is hard on him. I think he drinks too much these days."

"How about tomorrow?" says Candy.

"Perfect. He'll be happy to see you."

"I didn't just get eaten by a bear," I say. "I'll be happy to see anyone."

MAYBE HAPPY ISN'T the right word. Maybe relieved is better. There isn't a lot to be happy about. Yeah, it was fun busting up the Tick-Tock Man's place, but now I'm back to square one. All my leads are blown up, burned down, run off, or dead, or as dead as a windup toy can be. Declan Garrett is still around, but he was trying to buy the 8 Ball from two different sources, so it's pretty clear he doesn't have it. I haven't even heard anything useful about Aelita or Medea. I think all I've really accomplished in the last month is making Mr. Muninn really depressed. I'm nowhere. More wasted time. Why am I doing this? I'm ridiculous. No one cares. Most people don't even believe the Angra exist much less are coming back. Hell, I'm starting to wonder myself. Am I playing this game because I've run out of legitimate things to kill? No. I saw Lamia and I know she was real, so the Angra are real. Still, maybe it's time to just walk away and let things work themselves out. We die or we don't. I've been there before. Will I have time to shout one last "I told you so" when the Angra burn the world? That's a hell of a last request. Maybe I should have given Candy her Christmas present after all. I need a drink.

WE DECIDE TO meet at Bamboo House of Dolls. It's a holy place. My second home. The best bar in L.A. A punk tiki joint. Old Germs, Circle Jerks, Iggy & The Stooges posters on the wall. Plastic palm trees around the liquor bottles. Coconut bowls for peanuts. Martin Denny and Les Baxter on the jukebox. And there's Carlos, the bartender, mixing drinks in a Hawaiian shirt. I met him my first day back from Hell. Helped him out with a skinhead problem and now I drink for free. Ain't life grand?

"Sir Galahad returns," he says when he sees me. "How's the saving-the-world biz?"

"Slow. But it's a growth industry. I expect a lot of investors when Godzilla takes a shit on Disneyland."

"Hold a place for me in the lifeboat. I'll bring my cocktail mixer and we can toast *El Apocalipsis* with Manhattans."

"Sounds yummy," says Candy.

"How are you doing, ma'am?" he says.

"Great. I'll be spectacular with a beer in me."

"You got it," says Carlos. "Aqua Regia for you?"

I shake my head.

"Black coffee. I'll be setting a saintly example tonight."

"Better you than me," says Carlos. "Hey. Put that back."

There's a skinny blond guy in a red Pendleton shirt trying to palm the cash the drunk next to him left sitting on the bar.

I reach for the guy, but before I touch him he screams. His hands have shrunk to doll size.

I don't see any witches or Coyote tricksters around. Carlos is holding a crushed paper cup in his hand. Holy water, amber, and spots of what look like red mercury wormwood drip from between his fingers. Fucking Carlos just used hoodoo on someone.

"Where did you learn that?"

"Get up and get out," Carlos tells Tiny Hands.

The money is too big for the guy to hold on to. He drops it on the floor. I think he wants to scream, but his brain has vapor-locked.

"Your hands will be okay in a couple of hours. But your head won't be if you ever come back here," says Carlos, grabbing up a baseball bat from under the bar.

Still staring at his mangled hands, Tiny Hands backs out the door.

"Neat trick, huh? Cutter Blade taught it to me for a bottle of Gentleman Jack. I keep the potion back here, and when someone gets untoward, I crush a cup while giving them the hairy eyeball. I'm the new *brujo* in town, right, motherfuckers?"

People bellied up to the bar clap and hoot. Carlos bows like it's Las fucking Vegas.

"Why do you need that hoodoo?"

Carlos moves his head from side to side like he's thinking.

"I can't have you cleaning up my messes forever. And you can't be here all the time. I decided that with all you abracadabra types around, learning a trick or two was better than taking one of those pepper-spray courses."

"That's not a bad idea. But be careful with that stuff. Crazy shit can happen when you learn on your own."

"Like what?"

"Make sure you wash that stuff off your hands before you pee," says Candy.

"I'm going to etch that on my eyeballs," he says, handing her a beer.

"I'll come by and teach you a couple of civilian-safe tricks after I find the 8 Ball."

"*Muchas gracias,*" says Carlos, and sets a cup of coffee in front of me.

I'm impressed with the hoodoo. It's hard for civilians to ever do real magic and harder still for them not to kill themselves doing it. But Carlos has always had balls of steel. He's had skinheads and zombies in here and he just cleaned up the mess and started serving drinks again. When his clientele switched from regular L.A. drunks to Sub Rosas and Lurkers, he didn't even blink. I'm not surprised he can pull off some bush magic.

Father Traven and Brigitte come in with Vidocq and Allegra. Traven looks tired. His worn soldier's face is pale and there are dark rings around his eyes. That's where the drinking comes from. He doesn't sleep, so he tries to knock himself out with booze. I've been there. It works too. But it'll kill you faster than the worst insomnia.

The father is another civilian who's picked up a little hoodoo. Before he became a professional bookworm, he was a sin eater, a priest who used bread and salt to ritually consume the sins of the dead. When he started working with us, he learned to use those sins as a weapon. He calls it the Via Dolorosa. It's like a horrible kiss when he puts his mouth over yours and spits enough sins down your gullet to book you a seat in the deepest, darkest pit in Hell.

Candy gives my arm a squeeze and goes over to the happy couples. Like we agreed, she leads Vidocq, Allegra, and Brigitte away and aims Traven at me.

"Good to see you," he says. "It's been a while."

"Sorry. I got so twisted around looking for the Qomrama that I stopped talking to practically everyone. Especially when I came up with nothing."

"I'm sorry to hear that."

"Yeah, but I almost got lucky. A guy offered me a million dollars for it a couple of days ago."

"He thought you had it?"

"How's that for a kick in the head? And there are other assholes out there who think the same thing. Whoever really has it must be laughing his ass off."

Traven gestures to Carlos.

"Evening. Could I get a gin and tonic, please?"

"He'll have coffee. Just like me."

I pick up my cup and take a drink.

Traven raises his eyebrows.

"You've been talking to Brigitte."

"She's been talking to us. She's worried about you."

He looks at her across the room.

"I suppose with reason. The last few weeks have been both wonderful and very difficult. I've never known anyone like Brigitte before. I joined the Church young. I'd never even had a serious girlfriend. I suppose I was running away from the world. Then I met Brigitte and heard about her adventures. She's opened my eyes to a lot of things."

"If everything is so *Ozzie and Harriet,* why are you turning into a lush?"

Carlos sets down the coffee. Father Traven practically drowns it in cream and sugar. I should have ordered him a milk shake.

"The certainty of Hell. The coming of the Angra Om Ya. Of having nothing, then having something and knowing it will all be taken away when I disappear into the Abyss."

"Speaking as someone who's been to Hell and had everything taken away from him, I can say that, yeah, it sucks. But it's not going to happen to you. "

Traven sips his coffee. Leans back a little and looks at me.

"You're not Lucifer anymore. You can't guarantee me anything. In fact, from what you've told me, the very God I offended by writing about the Angra is now Lucifer. If anything, that might merit me special punishment."

"No wonder they kept you in the back with the books. You're even depressing me."

"That wasn't my intention. But you asked why I was drinking and that's the best I can tell you. I'm scared."

I put my hand around the cup of coffee, feeling the hot ceramic against my skin. How do you explain to someone that you understand their fear, then convince them that it's going to be all right? In my experience, the more you talk about what scares them, the worse it gets. There's not much to do but ride out the fear with them and try to keep them away from liquor and razor blades.

What I wouldn't do for a Malediction and a shot of just about anything right now.

"You need to get out more. You've been with your books too much. Brigitte was like a kid again when we busted up the Tick-Tock Man's place yesterday. The next time I'm going someplace interesting, you should come along."

Brigitte laughs at something Vidocq says. Traven smiles.

"She's been floating on air since she came home. Yes, it would be good to do something other than poring over the same books again and again."

"What are you looking for?"

"A way out. A way that I've read the signs wrong and the Angra aren't coming."

"Did you find it?"

"I've been translating older and older texts and they all say the same thing. That the universe was not created by the deity we call God. It was created by something older and far less forgiving."

"That sounds like the Angra."

"Yes. The thin membrane of reality that separates the Angra's prison domain from ours is breaking down."

"Or they're punching their way through."

"You know, it's no coincidence that Lamia was the one to break through. There are twelve Angra in all. Six male and six female, but they're the polar opposite of the Greek and Roman myths we grew up with. The females are dominant among the Angra, and Lamia is one of the strongest."

"If they have a lot more like Lamia, we might just be fucked."

"There's no reason to think that they'll all get through. Or even one complete deity. Even one would be almost impossible to defeat. We'll have to hope that when they come, it will be in the form of something like Lamia. A larger and more dangerous fragment, but something on a scale we can comprehend."

"This isn't a pep talk, right? Because if it is, you're doing it wrong."

He looks at his coffee cup. Turns it around in his hands like he wishes there was something in there besides coffee.

"Sorry. I'm still working some of this through in my head. Talking about it helps."

"All this theoretical stuff is interesting, but how do we fight them? And how will the Angra get free in the first place?"

"That's the one piece of good news I have. It looks like they can't come back all the way on their own, no matter how many cracks appear between the universes. The full Angra can only return through a summoning."

"Great. Where's the Golden Vigil when you need them? They could set up surveillance on every Angra cult in California."

"It's not that simple. We're talking about a ritual. Something anyone with the right knowledge can do without even necessarily realizing what they're doing."

"So, some kids with the wrong book and a Ouija board could destroy the universe."

"I don't know about that exact scenario, but essentially that's it."

Richard Kadrey

"Fucking great. So we're still nowhere."

"No. I believe that the Qomrama is the key. It can kill gods, but I believe it's the key to releasing them too. We need to have it and find out if there is a way to destroy it."

"Why don't you work on that last bit? I'll keep looking until someone coughs it up or I think of something better to do."

"And you'll bring me along on your next adventure?"

"Absolutely. Now, why don't you go back with the others?"

"What are you going to do?"

"I'm not sure yet. But you'll know it when you see it."

"Thank you for the talk. Maybe there's a way out of this after all."

"One more thing. Do you think the Terminator had a soul?"

"Excuse me?"

"I mean yeah, he was a robot, but he had a human body on top of all the gears. The body was even cloned from a real guy. So could someone or something like the Terminator have a soul?"

He thinks for a minute and shakes his head.

"No. I don't think so. Why do you ask?"

"I was hoping to track someone down in Hell, but now I doubt he's there. I doubt he's anywhere."

"You'll have to explain that to me sometime."

"Sure. Sometime."

He gets up and goes and joins Brigitte with the others.

So much for tracking down Trevor Moseley in Hell and giving him the third degree. I hold up the remains of my coffee to Carlos.

"Can you make this more interesting?"

He gets a dusty bottle from under the counter and pours a shot of Aqua Regia into the cup. Just what I need to kill those last few brain cells that are getting in the way of what I think I need to do.

Carlos puts the bottle back and says, "You know, someone was asking about you yesterday."

"Did you get a name?"

He shakes his head.

"He didn't say. But he was dressed to the nines and the tens."

"Did he look like someone who might produce bad TV or good porn?"

"Neither. He was right out of *GQ*."

"Then he wasn't Declan Garrett."

"Who's that?"

"I was eating a donut and he tried to shoot me."

"Some people are like that. Anyway, the guy who is looking for you said he'd be back. He has a business deal for you."

"When he gets here tell him to fuck off. I'm beginning to I think I've spent this whole month doing things backward."

"Backward how?"

Carlos pours more Aqua Regia into my cup. The more I drink, the clearer it gets. I look around to make sure Traven doesn't see me.

"I've been looking for a thing, but what I should have been looking for is who wants it. Think of the ultimate weapon. Think of a death ray that fits in your pocket like a phone. Who would want that? In the old days, it would be the Vigil. They had a massive hard-on for hoodoo tech. Who's left in L.A. like that? Not the cops. If they had the 8 Ball, they'd have blown themselves up by now. Who does that leave? Gangsters. But not civilian ones. They're dumber than cops, so they'd all be dead. It's got to be a Sub Rosa or Lurker crew. They're the only ones who might handle the 8 Ball without setting off World War Three."

"I have no idea what you're talking about, but feel free to yammer."

He sets out coasters and drinks for other customers.

I say, "How would you feel if I became extremely unreasonable?"

Carlos leans on the bar and speaks quietly.

"Like the old days? You're not going to kill anybody?"

"Absolutely not."

He stands up and takes empty glasses off the bar.

"Things have been quiet lately. Business is off. Maybe we need a little . . . what's the French thing?"

"Grand Guignol?"

"That's it. Some of that."

I nod. Push the empty cup at him. The place is crowded for a weeknight. Civilian groupies huddle at the jukebox with a vampire holding hands with a blue-skinned Ludere. Some Razzers pick at a plate of deep fried tumors. Horned Lyphs, a tour group from Seattle, take snapshots in front of the old punk posters. A table of psychics quietly shares a bottle of tequila shaped like a Día de los Muertos skull.

"Who don't you like? I mean if they all dropped down dead, who would you not miss?"

"That's easy," Carlos says. He sets a gimlet in front of a Mal de Mer in a tight wife beater. He's shaved down the coral on his scalp so it looks like a mullet swept back to the shoulders and covered in skin like a cobra's—diamond-scaled and shiny as marble. Carlos picks up an empty glass and uses it to point across the room.

"Them," he says. "Those fucking Cold Cases."

I turn and spot a table with four of them.

Cold Cases are soul merchants. There's a lot of call for fresh souls in L.A. It's an easy town to get yours smudged up. Or maybe you get dumb and desperate and sell it to Lucifer. Don't worry. Just call your friendly neighborhood Cold Case. They have plenty of replacement souls. Most they even paid for, though there are rumors that they sometimes lift a particularly spotless soul without the owner's permission. Everyone hates Cold Cases, but enough people need them that when one of them gets in trouble, evidence gets misplaced. Paperwork disappears. Not a one of them has ever spent a night in jail.

These four are laughing together at a table, passing around a bottle of expensive bourbon. Old Cold Cases keep a low profile, but these guys are young and out to show off their wealth. Sharkskin suits. Bright ankle-length coats. Italian shoes and enough blood diamonds on their fingers and ears to finance a third-world coup.

"See their belts?" says Carlos. "They carry souls around with them these days. It's a status thing. Like how crazy GIs used to carry strings of dead enemies' ears."

I didn't notice it at first but he's right. They're all wearing skinny belts from which dangle small glowing bottles.

Carlos says, "What they do is bad enough, but flaunting and disrespecting people's souls like that, it's a sin, man. A goddamn sin."

"They good customers?"

"If I lose all my Cold Case trade, good riddance. All they do is complain about whatever I serve them. They want to hang out late at night? Let them go to Denny's."

"Okay."

I down my shot and head for their table, shouldering my way through the crowd. Pushing. Stepping on toes. I want them to see me coming. I want everyone to see me coming.

All four look up when I reach the table, but none of them move.

"Hi. I'm with the IRS. This is just a spot check see if you've paid this quarter's asshole tax."

I hold out my hand to the one closest. He has a pretty-boy face but bad-news eyes. He's the one in greenish sharkskin. He has the sleeves of his jacket pushed up to his elbows, eighties' style. That alone is enough for me to punch him.

I say, "I'm going to need to see some ID, sir."

His mean little eyes narrow.

"Who the hell are you? There are four of us, faggot."

I smile.

"Aw, I'm just kidding. You boys look like fun. Is that good? You don't mind, do you?"

I grab the bottle of bourbon and get a good mouthful. Make a face and spit it all over Mr. Sharkskin's suit.

"How can you drink that shit?"

I gesture with the bottle like a low-IQ drunk, splashing whiskey all over the table and Sharkskin's friends. All three get up, kicking their chairs back. I wait for one of them to reach into his jacket for a gun, but it doesn't happen. They're so used to being protected they're not even armed.

I take out a cigarette, spark Mason Faim's lighter, and let it fall on the table. Spilled bourbon flares up and burns with a pretty blue flame. I grab Mason's lighter and kick the burning table at the three friends. Grab the sharkskin and drag him to the middle of the bar. The place clears out like we're a bride and groom about to have our first dance. "Yadokari" by Meiko Kaji plays on the jukebox, all brittle guitar and her sad voice over lush strings.

Thoroughly kicking someone's ass is a kind of statement, but it's small-time, like a "Beware of Dog" sign. Sometimes you need to make a point that people can see from space. That kind of point is the opposite of a beating. It doesn't come from what you do but what people remember, so the less you do the better.

I bark a Hellion hex and Mr. Sharkskin rises into the air, flushed with pus-yellow light so bright you can see his bones. His belt and shoes drop off. Jewelry and bottled souls tinkle to the floor. Another bit of Hellion and his clothes catch fire, flaming off him in an instant, like flash paper.

This is showy arena hoodoo. I used to do stuff like this to opponents in Hell who really pissed me off. It's supposed to embarrass more than hurt.

Next, his skin does a slow-motion version of what just happened to his clothes. Starting at his hands and feet and moving inward, his skin peels away like a spray-on tan snowstorm. He hangs in the air like a trembling anatomy chart from a Bio 101 textbook.

"Take off your clothes," I tell his friends. "Or I'll burn them off like his."

His friends aren't dumb. They can't wait to get bare-assed

in front of a bar full of total strangers. The only thing they're careful with are their own soul bottles. They set them on their clothes like eggs nestled in henhouse nests.

I go back to the floater. I hope people are listening and not just looking. This won't work if no one hears me.

"I know you have the Qomrama Om Ya. Don't bother denying it. You have forty-eight hours to bring it to me. If I don't get it, I'll peel you down to your bones. And I'll take my time. You understand me?"

His three friends say, "Yes."

"I wasn't talking to you."

I pull the floater's big toe. His shell-shocked eyes turn down to meet mine.

"Do you understand me?"

He nods.

I bark more Hellion and the shreds of his skin float back to his body. But not his clothes. Those are ashes. The rest was an illusion. You can't really peel a civilian's skin off. I've seen it tried. Their hearts explode or they stroke out. However it happens, they always die, and dying isn't the statement I want to make today. Today is about wounding. Making the floater's buddies have to carry him home and explain to their bosses what happened and what I said. The rest of the bar is going to call everyone they know and tell them what they saw and heard. Clever me. I just phoned my demands to everyone in L.A. without using up any of my monthly minutes.

When Mr. Sharkskin looks human again, I drop him. He hits the floor and curls up in a fetal position on a pile of ashes, surrounded by his glowing bottles.

"Hey, Father. Want to save some souls?"

I stomp on a glowing bottle and crush it. There's a soft sigh as cobalt-blue smoke escapes, rising, spreading, and dissipating. One soul set free.

Traven happily crushes a bottle. Candy throws one against the wall. Brigitte, Vidocq, and Allegra start breaking them, and in a second the whole lousy bar is doing a drunken *Riverdance* on the rest of the bottles. The place fills with bright blue wisps that rise to the ceiling and vanish.

I burn the rest of the other three Cold Cases' clothes with a curse. Fish around in my pockets, and between Candy and me we come up with eight dollars. I toss it to the naked idiots.

"Bus fare, assholes. Get out."

They do. Dragging comatose Mr. Sharkskin off the floor and carrying him outside.

I go to the bar and Carlos pours me an Aqua Regia. I drink it slowly. It gives the Cold Cases enough time to get out and, if they're lucky, hail a cab that's going to jack them up for a huge tip.

A good exit is an essential part of making a statement. But you can't walk out after roughing up just one guy. People might think you had a grudge. To drive the statement home you have to spread the pain. I don't mean burn anyone else's clothes off, just make it clear that the statement is for everyone within earshot.

There's a couple of Foxy Reynards by the door. Hoodoo con men. You ever wonder why tourists on Hollywood Boulevard play three-card monte with guys at bus stops, knowing they're going to lose? The Reynards' swindle isn't the game. Any idiot can learn to palm a card. The Reynards win because they make you want to play even when you know you can't win.

I collar the older of the two.

"The same goes for you as those other lowlifes. If you know who has the 8 Ball, urge them in the strongest terms to hand it over because I'm coming for you next. Let's see how many of you bad dogs the city pound can neuter."

Now it's time to go.

I wait at the corner and light a Malediction. The others catch up to me a few seconds later. It's laughs all around. For once, even Allegra doesn't look mad at me.

I DON'T HEAR a word from the Cold Cases. No one sees any of them for the next few days. Not at any of their usual bars or restaurants or even their Wilshire Boulevard business offices. An entire industry gone to ground.

I'm not entirely surprised they ducked out. If they're going to try any retaliation, they're not going to do it themselves. They'll hire someone and they'll want a good alibi when it happens. Not that I'm sitting around waiting for a piano to mysteriously fall on my head. I hit gangs every day for the next week, sometimes two a day.

First, a big Nahual smash-and-grab collective. Their clubhouse looks like the dumbest garage sale in the world. Everything from diamonds and gold-plated tire rims to broken clock radios and dusty cassette players that have been sitting around unsold since before Atlantis pissed off to the bottom of the ocean.

I hit a couple of Ludere underground casinos. Besides gambling, they launder money for L.A.'s unsavory Sub Rosa and civilian swells. That one's sure to come back and bite me in the ass, but it was too much fun flipping the roulette and black-jack tables, like rock-and-roll Jesus versus the moneychangers.

I hit a Wise Blood coven, part of a ring selling bootleg potions. Some stolen but most nothing more than colored water and a little laudanum or strychnine for a kick. Imagine going to some old *bruja* to cure Granny's cancer and getting something as useful as a Diet Coke.

I don't let civilians off the hook. I slap around some ghost agents in the Valley. Third-rate shit birds that buy and sell the wild-blue-yonder contracts of B-list celebrities. Everyone who thinks they're anyone has a blue-yonder contract these days. It sets up their ghost with a talent agency so they can keep working after they're dead. If you're Marilyn or Elvis, it's a sweet deal. If you're a presidential candidate who lost, a one-hit-wonder singer, or someone who played the wacky neighbor on a forgotten sitcom, not so much. Your contracts gets sold off to small fries who put your ghost on the carny circuit, starring you in celebrity bum fights or snuff flicks.

I give each gang a different deadline. One day. Three. A week. Confusion is its own kind of statement, whether it's in the gangs or on the street. Fear and anarchy. Tons of fun. Maybe one of the gangs can put a bullet in me, but they know I'm hard to kill, and when I'm better I can step out of any shadow and hack off a part of them that they like.

I have to admit, it's fun busting heads. It feels like I'm becoming me again. Playing around with the Mike Hammer sleuth stuff can be fun, but it's not what I'm best at. Even the angel part of me, the smart and reasonable part, gets sick of it, especially when the clues and rumors don't go anywhere.

I know letting the arena part of my personality loose in the regular world isn't a good thing, but sometimes holding it back makes my head fill up with so much poison and fury that I want to rip it off. Candy understands, but being around me makes her all too ready to go Jade and start tearing into people, and I don't want to encourage that. All the fun and games she plays with the world . . . I know that underneath it all she feels like I do. She needs to let the beast out now and then or she'll die. It's why we're good together. Neither one of us is afraid of the other because looking at ourselves, we've seen the worst about what the other can be.

To tell the truth I'm not even sure sometimes if I'm laying into these gangsters to get info on the 8 Ball or just to pay back the world for hiding it from me. I don't want to be the goddamn savior of mankind. I'm barely over wanting to snuff the world myself. I know where the Mithras is—the first fire in the universe, the fire I could let loose and burn all of existence to ashes. I don't think I'd ever use it, but it's comforting to know that if the Angra come back and start tearing the universe apart, I could. I wonder if I'd last long enough in the flames that when the universe is gone I could set off the singularity, Mr. Muninn's backup plan. It's a sort of big bang in a box that will trigger a new universe into being. I wouldn't be there and neither would Candy or Vidocq or God or the others, but it could still be a sweet revenge on everyone. Burn the world. Barbecue Heaven and Hell, the Angra, and everything else, and then start something new. Maybe better. Maybe worse. But something that fucks over every holier-than-thou son of a bitch in existence. Reset creation to zero and let it go again.

The idea that maybe I can save Candy the way I couldn't save Alice is what lets me sleep at night. My friends are what make me wake up and start punching things because there's no way I'm going to lie down and let some old gods or whoever is hiding the 8 Ball walk away without a limp. I'll die and crawl out of Hell and do it again and again until there's nothing left of one of us. Unto the fucking end of fucking time. Hallelujah.

A COUPLE OF days later, Candy and I are walking back to the Chateau after I ditch the Audi we used to crash a necromancer key party. You haven't lived until you've busted in on a bunch of naked, pasty-ass necromancers going Playboy After Dark on a roomful of reanimated corpses. I don't have to make any threats at this point. Everyone knows what I'm there for. Candy and I just steal some beers and leave them to their smelly fun.

It's early evening. The streetlights have just come on. There's a crowd in front of the Chateau. The police have the front of the place cordoned off. Techs from the bomb squad are packing up and a hazmat team is surveying the area with handheld poison detectors. It reminds me of a Vigil operation.

Someone has staked a nithing pole in front of the hotel, a little up the driveway from where it turns off Sunset.

The pole is ten feet tall, with runes carved down its sides. On top there's a hog's head, with the skin from the body draped underneath it. Your usual nithing pole uses a horse's head. I guess the hog is supposed to be some kind of insult to go along with the curse, but really the little feet dangling in the air, bathed in the blue and red disco lights from the cop cars . . . it's more funny than it is menacing.

From across the street, Candy and I watch as the hazmat team goes to work. They put up a plastic-wrapped ladder and carefully lift the head off the pole. Put it in a double-thick plastic bag and seal it like the hog is made of plutonium.

"Who uses a *nithstang* anymore?"

"Seriously. Someone's in big trouble with PETA," says Candy.

"There's symbols carved into the pole. Can you see them?"

"It's too far away."

"Damn. I wonder if I can pickpocket a camera from one of the looky-loos."

"My phone has a pretty good zoom. I'll try to get some shots."

We cross the street and blend in with the crowd. Candy snaps away. When she's done I take her through the shadow at the corner and we come out in the hotel garage.

It's a long walk through the hotel lobby. I want to slink my way through. No one says anything, but I know the staff blames Mr. Macheath and his weirdo friends for bringing a cursing pole to their front door. I almost want to apologize. Instead, I pull Candy into the first elevator that opens and we head upstairs. I know I shouldn't order room service tonight, but seeing that hog made me hungry for pork ribs.

As soon as we get in the room Candy e-mails the photos to Kasabian.

She says, "I'm going to take a shower. I need to wash off the smell of lube and dead titties."

I go over to where Kasabian is working. The big screen is turned to a news channel. There's an aerial shot of the scene out front. Ghost-suited hazmat workers skulking around Hollywood with ritually slaughtered animal parts. Little starbursts as tourists snap away with phones and cameras. They came here hoping to see some movie stars and now they're getting a full-fledged L.A. freak show.

"Candy just sent you close-ups of the pole outside. You should get them anytime—"

"I already have them."

"Can you have a look around online and see what they mean."

"Don't have to. I already know."

He opens up some photos on the screen. The first one is a group of smiling people in what look like shitty homemade Renn Faire robes.

"Recognize anyone?"

"Nope."

Kasabian zooms in on one of the faces.

"Now?"

He has a beard but I can make him out.

"It's Trevor Moseley. What's he got to do with this?"

"Look at his robes, Sherlock. The symbols match the pole."

"I could barely see the pole."

"Oh."

He calls up Candy's pole shots and puts one beside Moseley. He's right. A lot of the badly cut and stitched symbols on his cheap robes match what's on the pole.

"So, what do they mean?"

"I'm not done. Look at this. You'd have saved some time if you'd paid more attention to Traven."

He pulls up the shot I took of Moseley's half-crushed corpse. Zooms in on a tattoo half covered in blood. It matches one of the symbols on his robes and the pole.

"Is that what I think it is?"

Kasabian nods.

"Your boy Trevor's last walk down the Yellow Brick Road was with an Angra cult. It was right there in front of you the whole time."

"But I've only been going after tinhorn bad guys. I wouldn't know where to begin looking for Angra worshippers."

"Maybe you spooked them, running all over town pissing in everybody's dream home."

He puts the three photos side by side on the screen. The answer was in front of me the whole time. But it brings up another question. Why was a clockwork Trevor Moseley playing footsie with an Angra cult? Maybe the Trevor in the photo is real—I don't know if an automaton can grow a beard—but now I'm surer than ever that the one that stepped in front of the bus wasn't any more human than the ones we found with Atticus. It also explains why Samael didn't see any sin sign on him. He wasn't human, so technically nothing he did was sinful.

I light a Malediction.

"At least I'm getting through to someone. These gangsters are getting boring. By the way, don't look for Trevor anymore. He's not going to be in Hell."

"Are you saying he's in Heaven?"

"I'm saying he doesn't have a soul."

"Lucky duck."

I puff the Malediction. Something bothers me.

"When did I send you the shot of Moseley?"

"You didn't. I took it."

"You hacked my phone?"

He looks up at me. His hellhound body whirs and clicks quietly when his head moves.

"You ask me to hack things and then you're surprised when I do it? By the way, your idea of online security wouldn't stop a mollusk with a TRS-80. If you ever want to get serious about protection, ask me."

I want to be mad, but stealing the image did answer some important questions. And if I'm going to be pissing people off, maybe I ought to learn more about security.

"What's going on with your swami gig? You ever track down that guy's hoarder brother?"

"As a matter of fact I did. He's with the misers and small-time grifters."

"Good luck getting any information out of him. Brush up on your sign language."

"I was going to ask you about that. Seeing as you're pretty acquainted with Hell—"

"No. I won't be your carrier pigeon."

"This isn't a favor, like you're always asking me to do. It's a business proposition. You'd get paid for taking messages back and forth."

"I don't think Mr. Muninn would like it."

"Right. I forgot how sensitive you are to what other people think of you. Having fun breaking thumbs?"

I tap the ash of the Malediction into an empty bottle of champagne I don't remember drinking.

"As a matter of fact I am. I might have to pencil in a rampage or two a year. It's like going on vacation."

"I remember your little moods every time I look down at where the rest of me used to be."

"You're the one that blew up your body. I just separated you from it."

"Right. How uncool of me to be upset."

Kasabian finishes off a can of beer sitting on his desk. Crushes it in his metal paw.

"You still have all that money you said you hid from Saint Stark?"

Saint Stark is my angelic half. He got loose a few months ago and went around L.A. doing good deeds and generally making himself a pain. Among his many good works was giving away most of the money a vampire collective, the Dark Eternal, gave me.

"If you want it, forget it. It's still my insurance policy in case you decide to throw me out."

"Jesus. I saved your sorry robo-dog ass from a hit squad and brought you to the best place you've ever lived and you're still going on about that shit?"

"I'm sorry. Who was the one just talking about going on rampages?"

"I just want to make sure there's some cash around."

"You're not getting it."

"I don't need it right now," I say. "These gangsters keep

bribing me not to kill them. I should have started shaking these people down a long time ago."

"If you don't want money, why are you asking about it?"

"Just sort of an inventory of assets."

He turns around in his swivel chair and drops the beer can onto the top of an overflowing trash can.

"Shit. We're not getting the boot, are we?"

"The hotel isn't happy having a pig head on the porch swing, but no one has said anything. Yet."

He turns back to his laptop. Slaps the keys hard and the photos disappear.

"Why couldn't you be a nice, boring thief like Vidocq? No one ever bothers him."

"He doesn't steal that much anymore. And he's good at it. I'm good at breaking things. The difference is that people don't always notice when their diamonds go missing, but they know when their legs bend the wrong way."

"Think about my offer. Make some honest money. You can probably do with some more friends Downtown."

"You might be right about that part."

On TV, a reporter is trying to interview a cop, but everyone behind them is pushing up their noses into pig snouts and grunting.

"One more thing. If you ever spot Medea Bava Downtown, let me know. She's supposed to be hiding with Deumos, but I don't trust the vindictive hag."

"She's the Inquisition. Even the milk on her cereal comes from angry cows."

"Just let me know if you see her. And stay out of my phone."

"Don't worry. I didn't see any of those private pictures Candy sent you."

"Fuck you."

THE HOUSE PHONE rings.

"Hello, Mr. Macheath?"

"Yes."

"An envelope arrived for you. Should I send it up?"

"You mean an envelope envelope? I don't want any packages."

"No, sir. It's just an envelope."

"Okay. Send it up."

I go out the grandfather clock and wait for the bellhop. He comes up in the elevator and gives me the note. I hand him a table lamp.

"My girlfriend has all the money and she's asleep, but I think this lamp is Tiffany, so Merry Christmas."

"Thank you, sir," he says like this happens to him all the time.

I wait until he's in the elevator before going back through the clock.

In the penthouse, I tear open the envelope. It's heavy cream-colored paper and lined with thin gold foil. Very pricey. Inside, there's a note containing three words:

Stop it.

Blackburn

Add him to the list of people who might have put up the nithing pole, though it's not really his style. That means my game has gotten under the skin of at least two people. That just leaves four million to go.

I GET AN unexpected phone call and head for Bamboo House of Dolls. Go inside for a drink and wait. I drop Declan Garrett's name a few times. Let people know I'm looking for him. What the hell? It's worth a shot. Allegra shows up a few minutes later in a jean jacket over her scrubs, looking like she came straight from the clinic. I'm going to need a smoke for this. I head outside and she follows me.

We get to the end of the building by the alley. I light up and Allegra leans against the wall, arms and legs crossed. She's nervous. So am I. We haven't been alone together in months. Not since she found out I'd been playing Lucifer.

She says, "Thanks for meeting me."

"No problem. So, what are we here for? Sorry if I'm blunt, but if you're going to yell at me and call me evil, maybe you can get started? I hear there's liquor inside."

"If I just wanted to yell, I could've done that on the phone."

She gives me a weak smile to say she's joking, but I don't smile back.

"I'm just trying to understand," she says.

"Instead of telling me you have questions, why don't you ask them?"

"Okay. You were really Lucifer? Tell me about it. What is Hell like?"

"Neither is what you think. Hell is a place like any other. I was mostly in the capital, Pandemonium. It's a city just like this. Hellions live and work there. There are markets, bars, and restaurants. There are cops and armies. Even a church. The place is on its last legs. The new Lucifer is trying to put

Humpty Dumpty back together again, but I don't think he'll make it."

Allegra crosses her arms tighter against her chest.

"What about being Lucifer?"

"You think he's all about mustache-twirling evil and temptation? Here's the truth. He's mostly a pencil pusher. You think Hell runs on its own? Being Lucifer is more like the universe's shittiest middle-management job. I spent most of my time in meetings with assholes or hiding from meetings with assholes."

"Lucifer takes people's souls."

I take a drag off the Malediction.

"Most people heading for Hell don't need his help. Most of the rest are idiots who sold their souls for fame, money, whatever. Anyway, the first Lucifer gave it all up. He's back in Heaven these days. In the loving arms of your precious Lord."

"That means there's another Lucifer, right? What's he like?"

"He's nicer than me or Samael. But he's screwed up. I wasn't any good at the Devil business and he's probably only marginally better. But he'll try harder to make Hell a better place for everyone stuck down there."

"Who is he?"

I shake my head. Blow out some smoke.

"I can't tell you that. It's too complicated. But I'll tell you this: right now the Devil isn't the problem. It's God. He's not exactly growing old gracefully."

She looks down the street like she's trying to get her bearings, then back at me.

"It's so strange to talk about the universe like Hell is just another little town over the hill. And the good people aren't that good and the bad ones aren't that bad."

"I didn't say that. Hell is a bad place full of backstabbing monsters that'd kill you as soon as blink. But some monsters are honorable. More honorable than some Heavenly halo jockeys."

"What you're saying isn't anything that I was taught or ever dreamed of."

"That's how it is. In the big scheme of things we barely matter. The Devil doesn't hate us. Neither does God, but in the end we're just bugs on his windshield. The universe didn't turn out the way he wanted and now he's hanging on by his fingernails just like the rest of us."

She opens her mouth like she's going to say something, and closes it. I flick the butt of the Malediction into the alley.

"I'm sorry about getting so mad before," she says. "It's hard to take it all in."

"Forget it. This shit is hard for anyone to understand. I don't want to."

"This thing you're looking for . . ."

"The Qomrama Om Ya."

"It's supposed to save the world from whatever's coming?"

"If we're lucky."

"So you're back to being the guy who saved the world and killed all the zombies."

"I never stopped being him. But mostly I'm just trying to keep all my stuff from getting blown up. Can you imagine the universe without *The Searchers*? I can't."

She stands away from the wall. Brushes dust off her sleeve.

"You're going to need help."

"Probably."

"Okay."

"Okay what?"

"I'll help."

"Thanks."

What do you know? People can surprise you after all. I wonder if she's been talking to Candy behind my back. Whatever it took, it will be nice not to feel like we're enemies anymore. But there's something else. Something she's not saying. She's tenser than before. She rubs a knuckle against her lower lip.

"I have something else I have to ask you."

"What?"

"It's awkward. You're going to think I invited you here and I said I'd help just because I want something."

"That depends on what you want."

I tap out another cigarette and light it, waiting for her to collect her thoughts.

"Remember when we first met back at Max Overdrive? I said I wasn't always a nice person. I had this boyfriend. He was a dealer, and when he went to jail I used his money to go to school because I didn't want to be in that life anymore."

"And now he's getting out."

She nods.

"He called me."

She holds out two fingers to ask for my cigarette. I give it to her. I didn't know she still smoked. She takes a tiny puff and about coughs her lungs up.

"He wants his money?"

"No. Yes. But he wants me too. Only, I love my life. I love Eugène. I can't go back to the way things were."

"Where is he?"

"Vacaville. He's getting out at the end of the week. He knows my old apartment."

"You still have that place? I thought you'd moved in with Vidocq."

"I keep things there and we store some of his stuff."

"The boyfriend knows the address?"

I lean against the wall and she leans next to me. We're shoulder to shoulder, but not having to look at me makes it easier for her to talk.

"Yes. I don't even bother locking it. Locks never stopped him before."

"I'll take care of it."

She puts a hand on my arm.

"Please don't kill him. I want him to go away, but I don't want to feel like I bought a hit on him just so I can hide in my nice new life."

"I'll do my best, but some people, they just don't listen."

"Please."

She sounds genuinely torn up asking me. What am I supposed to say to that?

"Okay."

She turns and hugs me. Talking about Hell and now the admission. It's been hard on her. I think she's crying. She sniffles a little.

"Don't wipe your nose on my coat."

She laughs once.

"Eugène said you would say yes, but I wasn't sure."

A cream-colored Lexus has driven past us twice. Now it stops. The guy who gets out has a haircut that costs as much as an appendectomy. He's wearing rimless glasses and a sharp but conservative blue suit. He could be an investment banker.

"Mr. Stark. Would you mind taking a ride with me?"

Allegra steps away. I shake my head.

"I'm with a friend."

He gestures at her.

"She can come too, if you like."

"Nice car, but we're fine right here. I'd invite you in for a drink, but I don't think this is your kind of place."

The Banker smiles and comes around to our side of the car.

"This isn't anything sinister. It's just a meeting to talk about possible employment."

"With who?"

"Norris Quay."

"Who's that?"

"The richest man in California."

"Never heard of him."

"Exactly."

I turn to Allegra.

"Do you want to get in the nice man's car? He says he has candy and a puppy."

She shakes her head.

"I don't think so."

I shrug.

"You heard the lady. Not interested."

He takes a couple of steps toward us.

"I assure you, this is for your own benefit. Afterward, if you decide you don't want the job, you can just—"

A bullet hits the wall, then two more. I push Allegra into the alley. The Banker crouches by his car and starts duck-walking around the front.

The shots come faster. Maybe three or four guns. AKs by the sounds of them. Wild shots spray cars and the wall behind me, sending other smokers screaming back inside the bar.

I'm kneeling on the sidewalk. I try to make it into the alley, but there's too many bullets flying. Same thing when I try to make it back into Bamboo House. The Banker is back inside the Lexus. He opens the passenger door. There's nowhere else to go. I dive headfirst into the passenger seat.

I wait a beat, expecting the Banker to get us out of there. But he's paralyzed, staring at the shooters in his rearview mirror. They're aiming at the car now. Bullets tear through the trunk and rear window. I duck and grab the wheel, stomping the accelerator. I hope no one is in the street because I can't see a damned thing.

Half a block on, the shooting stops. I hit the brake and the Banker and I bounce off the inside of the car.

I raise my head just high enough to see the shooters' car, a white Miata, smoke its wheels as it does a one-eighty and drives like hell away from us.

I look at the Banker. He's resting his head on the steering wheel, breathing hard and trying to get his breath. It doesn't help any when I pull my gun and put it to his head. I glance through the front and back windows to make sure no one is coming up on us.

Pressing my gun harder into the Banker's temple, I say, "Did you just set me up? Create a little drama so I'd get in the car?"

He gasps and holds up his right hand. It's covered in blood. His ring finger is gone.

"I wish we were that clever," he says.

I put my gun away and open the passenger door.

"I'm driving. Slide over here."

I walk around the car and get into the driver's seat.

"You're taking me home?"

"No. I'm going to meet the richest man in California. What's the address?"

The Banker tells me. He takes a handkerchief from his breast jacket pocket and wraps it around his bleeding hand. There's blood all over the steering wheel. It sticks to my palms as I drive.

"Is Norris Quay Sub Rosa?"

He shakes his head and tries to work the seat belt with his left hand. He fails miserably and gives up.

"No. He's just a regular person."

"I doubt that."

How many times in my life am I going to get an invite from the richest man in California? Why does someone like that want to hire me? I might as well have a look. It's not like I'm going back to Bamboo House right now. If someone is going take another shot at me, I'd rather it be in a car with a stranger than in the bar with people I know. Plus, I want to see Quay. Lay my eyes on a real, honest-to-goodness billionaire. Is someone like that even human? Does he sleep on a pile of vestal virgins? Does he fly to the bathroom with a jet pack? Does he sprinkle his food with gold dust and platinum the way regular people use salt and pepper? And what the hell kind of a name is Norris?

QUAY MIGHT BE a civilian, but money is the magic anyone can do. He's bought himself a Sub Rosa mansion.

We're at the abandoned zoo in Griffith Park. After a short walk we go through an old concrete enclosure. It's large and heavy, like something for big cats or bears. The interior walls are covered with graffiti. Teenybopper lovers and no-talent taggers. The Banker walks to a random crack in the floor and presses several points in the concrete, like a masseur doing acupressure. The crack creaks open on hinges like a trapdoor. He looks bad. Pale and sweating, but he minds his manners. He puts out his good hand, letting the guest know that he gets to go in first. Why not? I walk into trapdoors every day.

It's a marble staircase and for a minute I think we're back in time to ancient Athens. Underneath the zoo is where I imagine an old Greek king living. Marble everywhere. Ionic pillars supporting high ceilings. Light and dark marble squares form checkerboard patterns on the floors in the halls. Towering statues of gods and goddesses are crammed in every nook and cranny. I won't be surprised if Quay shows up in flowing purple robes and a laurel wreath on his head.

The Banker keeps his cool, but he's fading fast. He leads me into an office done up in the same Greek style, but there's a phone, a computer, and a lot of prescription pill bottles on a carved mahogany desk. Three plasma-screen TVs are mounted on the walls, all tuned to different business channels. The picture window looks out over L.A. but not this L.A. The tallest building is maybe ten floors. It's L.A. from a long time ago. Maybe from the thirties, when a lot of the big zoo enclosures were built.

A minute later someone comes in. It's almost funny. I recognize him immediately. It's Trevor Moseley, but Moseley with a good fifty more years on him. Norris Quay.

He's slightly stooped and walks with a cane. He's wearing a white button-down shirt, cream-colored slacks, and soft black slippers. This wouldn't be interesting except that everything in this place screams Grecian formality and here's Grandpa ready for an afternoon of checkers and pudding at the old folks' home.

"Ronald, you look like death," Norris says to the Banker. "Go see my doctor."

"Thank you, sir," Ronald says, clutching his bleeding hand. He still has it together enough to give me a nod before leaving.

Besides Quay, the only people in the room are two bodyguards. Massive, steroid-stinking sons of bitches. They wait in opposite corners of the room, not moving or speaking. They look rooted to each spot, like statues of Titans. But I bet they can move pretty fast when provoked.

I say, "So, how many of you are there?"

Quay hobbles to a deep blue-and-gold velvet sofa and takes his time lowering his bones onto the cushions, in no rush at all to answer me.

"You mean my simulacra? Generally no more than two or three at a time on each continent. Except Antarctica, of course. I don't collect penguins."

He smiles. The lines on his face remind me of the splitting roads in Pandemonium after an earthquake.

I shake my head.

"You've got your numbers wrong. I met three of you in just the past few days. One with Declan Garrett and two more with Atticus Rose."

"Yes. Atticus always keeps a few extras around for when one has an accident."

"The ones in Rose's workshop both had accidents. I burned them."

Quay purses his lips.

"What a waste. Never mind. I'll have Atticus run off a few more."

"You know where he is?"

"I know where everyone is."

Quay crosses his long legs and picks some lint off his trousers.

"What's the story with your clone called Trevor Moseley? He runs through every religion there is and ends up hanging out with Angra Om Ya nutcases?"

"My little Trevors, Fredericks, Pauls, Williams, and the others have insinuated themselves in various groups around the world. Groups that possess or might come to possess things I want."

I knew it.

"You want the 8 Ball."

"The Qomrama. Yes. Trevor was going to buy it from them or, if need be, take it. Then he . . . that is, I found that they didn't have it. In fact, like me they were looking for it, and all signs pointed to you having it."

"But I don't."

"Much to my dismay."

Quay makes an exaggerated sad face.

"Were you doing business with Declan Garrett? You should be more careful. He tried to blow you up."

Quay waves a dismissive hand.

"I would never do business with Declan. He's a crook. Anyway, I knew he didn't have it."

"How?"

"Because he offered it to me at a good price. He would never have done that if he'd had it."

Quay leans on the cane and the arm of the sofa and slowly pushes himself to his feet. I almost want to help the old creep, but I have a feeling if I moved an inch, I'd have a bunch of cracked vertebrae courtesy of the two meat mountains in the corners.

Quay makes it over to his desk. There's a bottle of brown booze on the far end.

"Have a drink with me, Stark."

"I'm not thirsty."

"I don't care if you're thirsty. We're going to do business and business is done over drinks."

"You don't have any Aqua Regia, do you?"

"I'm afraid not."

"Then Jack Daniel's."

He laughs.

"Of course that's what you drink."

"What does that mean?"

"It's what you drank as a young man, but because of your unique circumstance, you never had the chance to grow out of it."

"I guess you could call Hell a unique circumstance. But

like everything, it gets boring. I mean you can only be terrified for so long, right?"

He pours himself a drink in a heavy crystal tumbler.

"I wouldn't know. I'm never scared. My obscene wealth insulates me from that kind of thing."

"Is that why I've never heard of you?"

He sips his drink.

"Some people use their money to get on the *Forbes* list of richest people. Others use it to stay off."

"It must be fun having options like that."

"It is," and he gives me a smile that makes him look twenty years younger. "Get Mr. Stark his Jack Daniel's."

One of the Titans steps away from the wall and leaves the room.

I say, "Do you know what the 8 Ball is?"

"I don't care what its function is. It's an ancient object of great beauty and that's all I care about. I have the largest collection of so-called death and apocalyptic religious artifacts in the world. This isn't just morbid curiosity. It's a public service since changing government alliances and rival religious sects would have destroyed many of these objects. From time to time I've even opened my collection to museums and academics. Perhaps your friend Father Traven would like to have a look around? I'm sure he'd find my collection interesting. He'd have to sign a nondisclosure agreement, of course."

"It's a weapon."

Quay swirls the liquor in the glass.

"And it's magic, and to you Sub Rosa anything magic is beyond us mere mortals to comprehend. Well, son, I've seen magic. Hell, I live in magic and I'm just not that impressed."

I get tired of standing and sit down on the sofa. I wanted to see what this much money looked like, but now I'm annoyed by the mansion and Quay's absolute certainty in his bulletproof life.

"But you can see how I might be reluctant to sell a weapon to a stranger."

He sets down his drink and thinks.

"Just because a collector buys, say, an antique Gatling gun, does that mean he intends to rob a bank? Of course not. He admires the object for itself."

"And yet."

"You said you didn't have it."

"It means if I do, it's not for sale."

"I'm sorry to hear that."

"I'm sorry not to get paid the fortune you were going to offer me, but there we are."

"I'm starting to think that perhaps you do have it."

I lean forward.

"By the way, what you said about not being afraid? It's bullshit. I can read people. You're lousy with fear. You're like Hitler in his bunker just waiting for the commies to storm Berlin and kill him dead. And all those Trevors or whatever you call them, you didn't make them just to collect death art for fun. You're looking for a way out. You don't want to die."

He leans back in his chair.

"What man isn't looking for a way out from death? However, I assure you I'm not going to die. But the art is nothing more than appreciation for the forms. A bit morbid to most people, I suppose, but we can't deny our true natures, can we, Sandman Slim?"

His heart and breathing don't change. He's a really good liar if he's telling the truth. He really thinks he has death beat and he's just a compulsive collector. I don't know if that's better or worse. Is it worse to want the 8 Ball because you think it has the magic to make you immortal or because you want to put it on a shelf with your bowling trophies?

"Let me say it one more time and for the record. I don't have the Qomrama."

Quay sighs. Picks up a pen and doodles on a pad for a few seconds.

"I'm afraid I believe you. Were you another sort of man, I'd have Sean over there in the corner hurt you or hurt one of your friends until I was entirely convinced."

"Lucky for you you have an open mind. You touch my friends and I'll kill you."

"Naturally. As I was saying, I know it's pointless to threaten you, and anyway, I don't want us to be enemies. Do you know who has the Qomrama?"

"I know who had it."

"That's better than nothing. Let's leave things like this. If and when you recover the object, promise me you won't sell it to anybody else and we can part on amiable terms."

"I don't want to sell it to anyone."

"Excellent. We can work from there."

"Stay away from my friends."

Quay stands, but faster this time. He's excited to be just a little closer to the 8 Ball.

"If you do your best to find the device, I'll do my best to remain patient. We're done now. I'll have someone drive you home."

"You know where I live?"

"At the Chateau Marmont, of course. Lovely place. I fucked many a charming starlet there back in my prime."

"Thanks for sharing. The driver can drop me off where I got picked up."

"If that's what you want."

A flunky comes in with my drink and a piece of paper. He hands it to Quay, who scans it.

"Just set the drink down, Jeffery. Mr. Stark is leaving."

Quay stares at the paper for a few more seconds. I don't like it.

Finally he says, "You're probably wondering who that was shooting at you a few minutes ago."

"You have your cars monitored?"

He raises his eyes to mine.

"Naturally. How else would I have the license plate of the car that shot at you? The car was allegedly stolen from a used-car lot near LAX."

"Allegedly?"

"Before that, it was a rental car in the City Runaway fleet. City Runaway is owned by a small company in San Francisco which itself is owned by a much larger transportation conglomerate in Zurich, mostly investing in air and sea transport companies."

"Thanks. I'll call my broker."

"A principal shareholder in their sea freight division is Nasrudin Hodja."

Oh, shit.

"The Cold Case kingpin?"

The way Quay laughs I know that it is. He folds the piece of paper and hands it back to the flunky who brought it.

"A bit of trivia that might interest you is that Zurich is also the birthplace of our own illustrious Saragossa Blackburn, though he likes to play down his international origins."

"Is he part of the company too?"

"Not that I know of."

"And you would know if he was."

"Oh yes. Good-bye, Mr. Stark."

I'm walking out with one of Quay's Titans when he says, "Of course, there are things that get by even me. Even I don't know everyone Saragossa knows."

I turn around.

"Now you're just fucking with me."

Quay smiles.

"Have a nice evening at the Chateau. If you haven't tried the duck, do. It's to die for."

The Titan drives me back to Bamboo House of Dolls in a Mercedes SUV. He turns a classical station on the radio loud so he has an excuse not to talk to me. I go inside the bar and get very drunk. A Lyph in a Hollywood Walk of Fame T-shirt asks for an autograph. I'm too tired to refuse.

So Nasrudin Hodja wants me dead. Get in line, pal. But was Quay telling the truth about the car? He strikes me as a guy who's always playing six angles at once. He could just as easily be trying to provoke me into killing Hodja. I wonder if that's what Blackburn was doing when he sent me to Brendan Garrett. I think I get the money clip now. The symbol on the clip. It's not the Golden Vigil. It was Aelita's personal spin on the design. The design she made all of Blackburn's bodyguards wear when she worked for him. That means Brendan Garrett probably worked for Blackburn at some point. He would have sent some of his people over to clean Brendan's clock, but then big dumb me walks in and practically begs him to send me. He probably figured that Brendan would pull a gun and I'd have to kill him. He read Brendan's tea leaves and saw that he was going to die and wanted to speed it along. I can understand him wanting me to do his dirty work for him, but did he know about the bomb in the case? Was he so pissed that I turned him down that he hoped to get rid of two disloyal assholes at one time? If he did I'm in trouble. If he didn't it's good news for me. It means that since I'm part angel, he can't read my future, at least not clearly. That might come in handy sometime.

AND HERE I was under the impression we had a truce.

That's what I think when I come out of Donut Universe with a bagful of greasy death. My last trip to the Universe was interrupted by gunfire. This one is topped off by vampires waiting for me in the parking lot.

I guess the lesson tonight is to never trust a bloodsucker. Still, it's disappointing. We've stayed out of one another's way for months, and now suddenly we're in *West Side Story*. I set the donuts in the bed of a pickup truck and consider my options, which doesn't take long. I'm surrounded. It's all of them against me, and nowhere to run. Fight or die. And here I was thinking that no one could shovel more bullshit into a day like this.

There's four of them. Two male and two female. They form a loose circle around me and walk in a slow spiral, tightening the circle with each step. Trying to psych me out. It might work too if two of the bloodsuckers weren't so nervous. An older woman and a boy with acne scars. It's obvious they're new to the vampire game. They probably tagged along to get some street experience.

One of them moves with predatory calm. He's the leader. He has a young face, with his hair frizzed out in a white-boy 'fro. He's wearing a red military jacket with shiny satin pants and pointy boots. The kid's got a serious Jimi Hendrix complex. One of the women is decked in expensive custom-tailored Goth gear. The older woman and the acne kid are strictly thrift store. Note to self: the Goth girl has sharp steel tips on the toes of her boots.

I'm waiting for the gang to make a move and they're waiting for me. Weird. They should be all over me by now. I'm not going to give them any satisfaction by throwing the first punch. As long as the donuts are safe, I can take my time.

The older woman comes at me first, hands up like claws, hissing like she's watched too many late-night monster movies. I sidestep and kick her in the ass as she goes by, sending her sprawling into a Prius. The alarm goes off, which is really annoying because it covers up the sound of feet coming up behind me.

Goth girl comes at me next. Like I thought, she's more experienced than the kid and the other woman. Her nails are sharpened, so she does the claw thing too, but comes at me low and fast, aiming for my gut. Trying to disembowel me like a cat. When I move to block her, she tags me in the thigh with one of her pointy boots. It hurts like a son of a bitch. I think she drew blood. Dumb of me to let her do it.

The acned kid is next. He leaps in the air and comes down like a fucking banshee, his heavy work boots aimed at my face. The circle is tight enough now that I can't easily sidestep him. I have to slip him at the last minute, let his feet sail by but catch some of his weight on my chest, throwing me onto my back. He tries to jump me again and I catch him with my boots and flip him over, right into Goth girl. I wait for Hendrix to make his move, but he just gives me a white-fang smile.

When he's just out of my peripheral vision, he tries to jump me. Like the Goth girl, he's more experienced. I throw a back kick and he spins around it with incredible vampire speed. But I'm fast too. When I see him spin, I duck and put my shoulder into him, right about in balls territory.

This is the weirdest gang fight I've ever been in. I think they're playing with me. Instead of rushing me all at once, they're coming in one at a time like we're in an old Shaw Brothers movie. Maybe this is someone's idea of a good time, but it's not mine.

The older woman rushes me again. I imitate her boss and spin out of the way. Normally, this is something I never do. Don't turn your back on the enemy. But some rules are made to be broken. The spin covers my hand going into my coat for the na'at. It shoots it out like a qiang spear, and she's moving so fast she steps right into it. The blade splits her face open. She screams as her lower jaw wobbles in the breeze, hanging on by a few strands of gray meat.

Maybe the woman is the acne kid's aunt or something. He comes at me in a blind fury. Perfect. Dumb. His gives me the chance to do something I haven't done in months. I put the butt of the na'at into his chest, just hard enough to stun him for a second. When I step behind him, I stab the na'at so the tip goes all the way through his back and comes out between his ribs. When I twist the grip, the end opens in three backward-facing hooks. I lean my weight into it and snap the na'at back as hard as I can. The kid is still pawing himself as I rip out his spine, a trick Brigitte taught me back when we were hunting zombies. The kid has just enough time to reach back and touch his bare vertebrae before his torso collapses and he falls to ashes, kicking up a spray of fine powder. I cough up a lungful of the toothy bastard.

"Whoa," yells Jimi Hendrix. He raises his hands, the bottom one straight up and the other across the top like a T.

"Time out, man. Time out. What the fuck did you do to Phil?"

"I killed his dumb dead ass."

"Why?"

"Golly, Mr. Rogers. A bunch of bloodsuckers kick and punch a guy long enough he starts to think he's being attacked."

"You are such an asshole. We were just fooling around."

The Goth girl holds a lace-gloved hand close to her mouth. She says, "We're in trouble, man."

"No shit, Sherlock," says Hendrix.

"You kids want to clue me in on what just happened?"

Hendrix puts his hands on his head and does an exasperated three-sixty turn.

"Fuck. We were supposed to deliver a message and just thought we'd have some fun first."

"And I spoiled things. Sorry. What's the message?"

"Nnnhhnn," says the older woman, trying to talk while holding her broken jaw in place.

"The message?"

Hendrix looks at me like he's bouncing back and forth between totally panicked and numb.

"Tykho wants to see you at the club tomorrow night."

Tykho is the new boss of the Dark Eternal. I heard a freelance Bela hunter staked Jaime Cortázar, the old boss. Too bad. He once gave me an attaché case full of hundred-dollar bills. I gave him free movie rentals at Max Overdrive. But Tykho's okay. Smart too. Like Cortázar, she once assured me that "Dark Eternal" sounds a lot scarier in Latin.

"If Tykho is summoning me to demand to buy the 8 Ball, she can kiss my ass and your ass, and she can dig up Gary Cooper and kiss his ass too."

"She didn't say anything about wanting to buy anything. It sounded more like she has something for you."

Interesting. Vampires aren't the giving type.

"Okay. What time?"

"Midnight."

"Seriously? A vampire queen wants to meet me at midnight?"

Hendrix shrugs.

"She likes to watch *Leno*."

"Fine. I'll be there."

" 'Fine. I'll be there,' " says the Goth girl in a high, mocking, nasal voice. She shakes her head while she talks. "I'm not telling Tykho about this. She told you to give the creep the message. I'm not even supposed to be here."

"Are we done?"

Hendrix shoots me the finger.

I nod to the ashes.

"Good night, Phil."

I get the bag of donuts from the pickup truck and head to the Chateau. A crowd is watching us through Donut Universe's recently repaired front window.

From behind me the older woman says, "Nnnhhhnnn."

"What did she say?"

"She said fuck you sideways, asshole," yells Hendrix.

LATER, KASABIAN IS back tapping on the computer, watching Hell through his peeper like it's an old rerun of *I Love Lucy*. Candy is curled up next to me on the sofa. Too many donuts and too much wine have put her in a food coma. I want to get drunk, so I don't. I drink black coffee and light up another Malediction.

What am I doing agreeing to go for cigars and brandy with a hundred vampires on their turf? What the hell kind of life is this? Is this what I came back from Hell for? Is the marginal existence I've carved out for myself going to get Candy and the others killed the way it got Alice killed?

I keep thinking that if I try to act more like a person, I'll be less of a monster, but at night most of my dreams are about the arena and being Lucifer. Instead of running around asking questions, I'd rather be cutting off heads. But I won't. Not even Nasrudin Hodja's. Pick and choose your fights, that's what Wild Bill said, and I know in my heart of hearts he's right. A war with the Cold Cases would take over my life, and what would I get from it? A pile of skulls and a bit of idiot glee. That's not enough anymore. The moment I admitted that I was connected to the people around me and this world, that life was over. Still, I feel like I could go off at any minute. I'm not sure which is the real me anymore. The reasonable guy who can sit in a bar without hitting anyone or the guy giving idiots compound fractures because no one will cough up the 8 Ball.

Maybe I'm looking at this all wrong. Maybe reasonable guy makes monster guy stronger. People used to run when they saw me coming because they knew I was there to break things. Now no one's sure what I'm going to do and that's its own kind of power.

But how does any of that get me out of this situation? I still have to find the 8 Ball and deal with Aelita or she's going to deal with me. The only good news is that with the 8 Ball out of her hands she can't run around killing off the God brothers. They might be the only things in the universe that can stand up to the Angra Om Ya. I'm not looking forward to going at Aelita one-on-one. She's beaten me more than I've beaten her. Hell, she already killed me once. It was only one of Vidocq's potions that brought me back before my soul wandered off to Hell or Fresno.

And I'd sure like to know where Medea Bava is. She wants me dead every bit as much as Aelita. I should have gone after her when I was still Lucifer. Once I burned down Tartarus, she didn't have anywhere to run. Now she's with Deumos and I don't know what that means. I don't even know if the Sub Rosa has an Inquisition anymore. If they do, maybe a new Inquisitor has it in for me. I could ask Blackburn, but what are the chances he'd tell me the truth? Medea doesn't need any official title to come after me, and if she kills me, everyone is going to say, "He deserved it," and go have lunch.

No, I don't need a war with the Cold Cases. I've got all I can handle right now.

As vile as they were, things were so much easier in the arena. It was all pain and anger and I knew exactly what I had to do and when. I'll never stop dreaming about it and wanting things to be that simple again. The arena is my heroin. I've kicked the habit, but I'll never get completely over it.

THE DARK ETERNAL is set up in Death Rides A Horse, a posh fetish bar in West Hollywood.

The Eternal made their bones by killing off or absorbing a lot of the scattered bloodsucker street gangs, then updating and expanding their business. The Eternal has even been known to do hits or provide protection for some of the big Sub Rosa families. All very much on the down low. They make most of their money off Lurkers and vampire wannabes dealing B+. Blood Plus. It's blood infused with every kind of up, down, and Ring Around the Rosie you can think of. Addicts come to the Eternal because their product is the best. Score cheap bathtub gin from one of the outlaw gangs in Compton or San Berdoo and you're likely to OD. Or end up with permanent palsy. Imagine living forever shaking so much you can't piss straight much less sink your fangs into an unwilling throat.

Outside the club there's a line stretching all the way to the corner. I walk up to the doorman, a burly black dude with a cross tattooed on his bald scalp. It's a common vampire joke. Crosses don't work on them any more than flypaper.

He puts a hand in the middle of my chest and notices the bulge of the gun under my coat.

"We're all full up tonight. Try again tomorrow," he says with a slight Jamaican accent.

"I'm on the list."

He smiles while looking over the crowd.

"I doubt that."

"I'm on Tykho's list."

He glances at me, then back to the line.

"That's not a joke you want to be telling, man."

I take out my phone and hold it up so he can see the time.

"I have a midnight appointment. If I'm not in the club in two minutes, it's your skull Tykho is going to be gnawing on tonight. Not mine."

He thinks it over. In a second he thumbs on the radio headset he's wearing. He puts his hand over the mouthpiece.

"What's your name?"

"Stark."

"Ah," he says. "They said look for a scarred man, but damn, you're a lot uglier than I expected."

He speaks into the headset. "I got your man Stark here and I'm sending him in. What? Don't worry yourself. You'll recognize him."

He gives me a big toothy smile, showing his fangs.

"Go right in, sir."

I light a Malediction.

"What's wrong with you, man? You can't smoke inside."

"Why? None of you breathe. It's not like you're going to get cancer."

He touches his lapels.

"It makes our clothes smell bad. Bothers some of the minions."

I don't have to ask who the minions are. There's a whole army of them lined up outside the club.

I drop the smoke and crush it out with my boot.

"Leave it to L.A. to turn vampires into twelve-steppers."

I go inside the club. And am instantly rendered deaf by Totalitarian Chic doing a hard techno version of "A Fistful of Dollars" at a hundred decibels.

Years ago, Death Rides A Horse was an upscale Hollywood cowboy joint, meaning it was about as country as Lawrence Welk's massage therapist. The DE kept the cowboy theme but added the leather-and-latex aesthetic. The dance floor alone must keep half the fetish shops in L.A. in business. A cowgirl vampire rides her bouncing-pony boy minion around the edge of the dance floor. I have no idea how either of them keeps their balance. It's an impressive achievement. I have to give the DE credit. The self-conscious decadence is a lot easier to take than a bunch of middle-aged businessmen chewing Skoal dressed up like Hopalong Cassidy.

A blond kid good-looking enough to be a Michelangelo model crooks his finger at me. I push through the crowd over to him.

He doesn't say a word, just loops his arm in mine and pulls me to the back of the club.

Even in the noise and chaos, it isn't hard to spot Tykho.

Her table is in the far back, under dim lights and crowded with admirers, both dead and alive. Since she doesn't have to show off, she's in a simple black corset with a brocade dragon pattern. Her skin is full-moon white. Her spiky blue hair matches the color of her lips. The real giveaway is her eyes. The pupils are long and horizontal. A birth defect from when her mother tried to chemically abort the pregnancy after she'd been bit. Mom blew it and gave birth to a bouncing baby vampire with octopus eyes.

She waves me over and dismisses her entourage with a single elegant wave. I take her hand when she offers it. It's cold enough to chill champagne.

"Stark. How nice of you to come."

"Like I was going to turn you down?"

I sit down and a waiter bustles over to take the entourage's drinks away.

"Some of my people thought you might be too afraid to come."

"I just didn't want to ugly up your joint."

"Trust me. We get uglier faces in here every night. Fear. Greed. A civilian's terrible hope that she or he can cheat us. These do worse things to a person's face than a few scars."

"I'll drink to that."

She gestures to a waiter. He comes over and sets something on the table in front of Tykho. A dried and preserved human heart.

"And for you, sir?" says the waiter.

"Whiskey."

"Any brand?"

"Whatever costs the most."

"Of course."

Tykho stares at me like I'm the unlucky one in a "choose-your-own-lobster" tank.

I say, "Your boy Jimi Hendrix last night seemed to think you had something for me. I don't suppose it's another suitcase full of money."

She starts to reach for the heart and stops.

"You spent it all?"

"Remember when there was that other me running around the city?"

"Yes. The Mouseketeer."

"He gave most of it away."

She leans back in her seat, knuckling her upper lip, trying to cover a laugh.

"How awful for you. Betrayed by your own doppelgänger. Does that make him the evil twin or you?"

"Ask me when I have to rob a gas station to buy a cup of coffee. I'm living off bribes from gangs and ne'er-do-wells. Did you know that people will pay you cash money not to kill them?"

"We usually get the opposite. 'I'll give you my fortune if only you'll make me immortal.'"

"You ever take them up on it?"

"Rarely. Most people who come around begging for it, they're not the type you want hanging around for the next thousand years."

"I don't know if I want to hang around with anyone for a thousand years. Present company excepted, of course."

She nods at my weak compliment and pours a shot of blood from the heart flask. The stopper in the aorta has a man's face. I wonder if all the stoppers have the same face or it's a likeness of the poor slob that donated the organ.

The waiter comes back with my whiskey. Before I sip it, I say, "I assume there's no blood in this."

Tykho shakes her head.

"It's as clean as a virgin's pussy."

I raise the glass in a toast and take a sip. Whatever brand it is, it's smooth and burns just right. I know instinctively it's nothing I can afford, but I bet the Chateau has some in stock. I'll have to find out the name.

"Sorry about Phil. Your little ones play hard. I didn't know we were just roughhousing until it was too late."

"Yes. They're all in a time-out. Seeing how Phil is the first Aeternus you've killed since poor little Eleanor Vance, I think we can just chalk it up to bad luck and not a break in our truce."

Eleanor Vance. I try not to think about her. She's one of the few kills, and definitely the only shroud-eater kill, I regret. She was a teenybopper turned bloodsucker, young and still dumb enough to be reckless. I killed her for the Golden Vigil. I'll never forgive Marshal Wells and Aelita for sending me after her.

"I wish I could take back Eleanor."

Tykho runs a dyed-blue fingertip around the rim of her glass.

"It's the curse of being a predator with a brain. Creatures like you and me, we're supposed to kill and move on. We're not supposed to reflect on it. I'd say it's proof there's no God, but I know you'd disagree."

"He's around. He just has a really fucked-up sense of humor."

Or it's another of his screwups. She's right about predators. Wolves don't weep when they take down a deer. And don't tell me regret is all about having a soul. Everybody has regrets, but most people use their souls about as often as they floss, which is usually two days before they go to the dentist.

"Let's get down to it, shall we?" says Tykho. "I didn't invite you here to give you money, but despite last night's unpleasantness, I do have something for you."

"All right."

"It's about the thing you're looking for. The Qom something?"

"Magic 8 Ball is okay."

"I know you were getting nowhere finding it, so you started your blitzkrieg through the city. It unsettled everyone and made our hunting harder, so we made our own inquiries using our own methods."

I don't want to think about what their methods means.

"And?"

"We think we've found something." She takes a sip of her blood cocktail and goes on. "Your mistake was thinking all the answers lie in threatening the living. We have connections with a lot of L.A.'s nonliving residents."

"It's hard to punch a ghost."

"Lucky ghosts."

"So, a dead person told you where to find the 8 Ball."

"A friend of yours, I think. Cherry Moon?"

Cherry is one of the people I came back from Hell to kill, only I didn't have to. Another old friend, Parker, got to her first. Then I killed Parker. I tried to help out Cherry after she died. Tried to convince her ghost to cross over. No way she's going to Heaven, but an eternity in limbo has got to be worse than Hell.

"That's too bad. I'd hoped Cherry would have moved on by now."

Tykho holds up a finger.

"Was that your suggestion? It seems that she was considering that very thing and talking it over with another ghost. A very old one and a bit mad, according to her, though I'm not sure Cherry is the best judge of crazy. Anyway, she had almost decided to cross over with this odd ghost when he changed his mind at the last minute. She said he claimed to be guarding a great treasure, something both Heaven and Hell would kill to get their hands on and that he couldn't desert it."

"Did she see it? Does she know where it is?"

"Calm down, cowboy. You people always want to cut to the chase. Let me drink my drink."

By "you people" she means mortals. People with a clock ticking and a death sentence hanging over their heads. Immortals love to play this game. And this is also me paying for Phil. Tykho might not send a hit squad after me, but now that she's got me hooked, she's going to take her time giving me what I want.

Above the dance floor, boys dance with boys in one go-go cage and a bunch of girls dance together in another. They're all wearing black vests and have shaved heads. It only takes a second to see why. *Invitation to a Gunfighter* is playing on flat-screens all over the bar. I have a feeling the movie is a hit less because it's a decent studio western and more because Yul Brynner looks so good in his bad-guy black hat and vest.

Tykho finishes her drink and wipes her blue lips with a napkin.

"Where was I? Yes. The crazy ghost. He started to take her to it. They got as far as his haunt when he got cold feet. He even had a little breakdown, according to Cherry. He's supposed to be guarding some Holy Grail–like thing and here he was about to give it up to a pretty face."

"Can Cherry take me there?"

Tykho shakes her head.

"No. He scared her too much. But she told me where his haunt is. And that he's guarding the thing for an angel. You're part angel, I hear. Maybe you could talk him out of it."

I'm going to shit monkeys if Tykho drags this out much longer.

"Where's the ghost?"

She smiles. She's going to drag it out.

"Kill City."

Now I wish she'd dragged it out a little longer.

"Is she sure?"

"How many Kill Cities are there?"

"One too many for me."

"Is the great Stark afraid of a dead shopping mall?"

I finish my whiskey.

"As a matter of fact I'm terrified of shopping malls. If you'd been to Hell, you would be too. All the cute little trinket stores. Fish-eyed mannequins and ladies squirting perfume in your face. Designer toilet seats and chakra-adjusting easy chairs. It's all so fucking pointless. People using money to run out the clock, trying to find something to occupy their time before they die. It's exactly like Hell."

I signal to the waiter for another drink.

"We all have our weaknesses," says Tykho. "For us, it's daylight. For you, it's Cinnabon."

"Damn. That little girl ghost about killed me last month. I hoped I was done with ghosts for a while."

This just gets worse and worse. On top of everything else, Kill City is all the way out in Santa Monica. All those tanned tourists might be fun for bloodsuckers, but the stink of SPF 90 sends me into cardiac arrest.

"There's something else."

"Good. I was hoping this could get worse."

"We're not the only ones who know about the ghost. Don't bother asking who the other party is because I don't know, but we have every reason to believe that they're going after your 8 Ball too."

"That's all I need."

"That's not all. Medea Bava might be with them."

"No way. She's hiding out in Hell."

"That's not what I heard."

This is all I need right now. Kill City, Medea Bava, and now I have to run a footrace to find the Qomrama.

"Thanks for the information."

"You're welcome. See? All your muscling people, your Sturm und Drang, got you nowhere."

The waiter brings my whiskey and I drink it in one go.

"It got people off their asses and it got me answers, which is all I ever wanted. From where I sit, my plan worked fine. By the way, why are you helping me?"

Tykho pours another thick red shot into her glass.

"For the same reason we were grateful you took care of those pesky zombies. Self-preservation. If the stories about angry old gods are true, I doubt they'll spare the Aeternus simply because we've been shunned by the madman in the attic."

"So, you do believe in God."

"Only when convenient."

"Okay, then. Let's put a team together, go in there, and get it."

She wags a finger at me.

"No. We're not going to do that."

"A second ago you said you had a stake in this fight. Why won't you step up when it really matters?"

"Who says we won't help? The problem is this: the Dark Eternal can't enter Kill City. There's a long-standing but somewhat fragile détente with one of the federacies inside. A clan of gray fighters. Time has passed them by, but they're still dangerous. To enter the mall would be a declaration of war, and a pointless war is something we don't need right now."

"I know the feeling."

I order a whiskey for the road.

"So, how are you going to help me?"

"We're sending a representative with you."

"You just said the Dark Eternal can't go inside."

"He isn't one of the Aeternus. He's mortal."

She looks past my shoulder to a flunky lurking somewhere in the dark.

She says, "Send over Paul."

He comes from another table across the dance floor. He gives me a friendly smile and puts out his hand. I shake it. I'm not surprised by him one bit. Okay. Maybe a little, but it makes perfect sense when I get a good look.

"Stark, this is Paul Delon."

It's another Trevor. An exact copy of a young Norris Quay.

"It's good to meet you, Mr. Stark. Tykho has told me a lot about you."

"Paul, is it? How do you know Tykho?"

"We know some of the same people."

I bet you do. But I don't get the feeling that Paul knows me. Probably all of Quay's automata are drones gathering information until their master calls them home. That's good luck for me. It means he's on his own until this is over.

"Have you ever been inside Kill City?" I say.

"No."

"Ever been anywhere, you know, strange? Maybe incredibly dangerous?"

He sits down across the table from me.

"Is that what you expect?"

"From what I hear, Kill City is the last stop for the lowest of the low-life Sub Rosa families and Lurker clans that can't make it out in the world. It's a whole society of losers and they're just looking to take it out on everybody else in the world."

Paul nods. A waiter comes over.

"White wine, please," he says. Then to me, "I'm up to speed on that. I've also memorized a map of the complex and their clan territories. I've never been anywhere like Kill City, but I'm not afraid."

"You should be. If the thing the ghost is guarding is the 8 Ball, that makes Kill City the most dangerous place in L.A."

Delon frowns. I can't get a read on him. If he's like the other windup clones at Rose's studio, he's a mix of meat and machine. He has a heartbeat that's steady and mechanical.

Same with his breathing. Rose's Trevors bled, so I'm betting this Paul does too. Still, to fool a mob of blood freaks is a pretty neat trick. Atticus is worth whatever Quay is paying him.

I say, "Why don't you just give me the map and you don't have to go at all? The fewer people, the faster I can move."

"No," says Tykho. "Paul is our representative. He goes with you or you can go in alone. They don't call it Kill City for nothing. You add up the acreage aboveground and what's below, without a guide it will be like wandering the Amazon jungle blind."

"She's right," says Paul. "You'll never find what you're looking for. That's assuming the families and the Lurkers don't kill you. I know what families are there. I've studied the Lurker federacies and how to pay them off for safe passage."

"It's the Wild West in there," says Tykho. "You'll love it. What do you say?"

Tykho might not breathe or have a beating heart, but her type I can read.

"I get it. The boy is our guide but he's your man on the inside. You're afraid I might run off with the 8 Ball and take over all of Never Never Land."

Tykho leans her elbows on the table.

"Like you people say. Trust but verify."

I turn to Paul.

"I'll meet you at Bamboo House of Dolls at eight P.M. tomorrow. Don't wear those stupid loafers. Go get yourself some heavy boots. Maybe some climbing gloves."

For the first time he looks a little concerned.

"Thank you."

I stand and nod to Tykho.

"Thanks. With any luck we'll send Chuck here back with good news."

"Paul," he says. I ignore him.

"How many people know about the Kill City situation?"

Tykho shakes her head.

"Only a few among the Aeternus. Why?"

"If too many people know, it might leak back to Aelita and she'll move the 8 Ball. Don't mention this to anyone else."

"Of course."

I start to leave, when she says, "When are you reopening Max Overdrive?"

"There's not much point reopening if the world is going to end. You better hope your boy knows his stuff or the Dark Eternal is going to be another bunch of suckers streaming whatever movies the corporate big boys want you to watch."

Tykho looks up at Yul breaking windows and generally busting up the tinhorn town that hired him.

She says, "Save the world and we might find another suitcase of money so you can reopen."

"Do that and it's free rentals for as long as we're around."

"Done. Try not to die."

I take one last sip of her good whiskey.

"By the way, do you know a guy named Declan Garrett?"

"He comes in sometimes. He's always trying to sell the Crown Jewels or some such nonsense."

"If he comes in tonight tell him I'm waiting for him at Bamboo House of Dolls. We have something to settle."

"Is he selling you the Brooklyn Bridge?"

"Yeah, but I'm paying in pennies. Think he'll mind?"

Someone starts this way, sees me, and heads in the other direction. I take off after him and, when I'm close enough, grab his shirt collar and pull him back.

"Mike. What are you doing here?"

Manimal Mike looks like a kid with his hand in the cookie jar. He has a fluffy tortoiseshell kitten in a pet carrier.

Mike holds up the cat.

"Trying to earn a living. Someone's kitten's on the fritz. What, you think I only work for live people? That's racist, man."

"Calm down, Mike. I was just surprised to see you."

"Me too."

His heart is going a million beats a minute. The smell of fear sweat pours off him.

"Is there something you're not telling me, Mike? Another reason you're here?"

I let go of his shirt and he shrugs his shoulder back into place.

"Okay. Sure. You still haven't come across with my soul. These guys. They're my backup plan. I buy my way in, let one of them bite me, and I don't die and I don't go to Hell. And if I'm dead like them, I can still work."

It actually makes sense, which is more than I expect from Mike.

"I understand. It's smart to have a Plan B. Just don't do anything stupid while I'm gone. Don't let any of these guys put the fangs to you."

Mike takes the kitten and walks away.

"Give me a reason."

SOMETIMES YOU GET lucky. Or maybe the angel in my head is a little psychic. Though not nearly psychic enough. If it was, I'd see the shitstorms coming down the road and have a chance to jump in a ditch or hide in a little country church. Let the hellfire-and-brimstone preacher cleanse me of my sins. With a little luck maybe it would be near a roadhouse with local swill on tap and watered-down whiskey behind the bar. The kind of place that would at least let me smoke a god-damn cigarette while I have my drink. But with my normal run of luck, I'll shelter from the storm in a dry county where the only good times are judging the pigs at a 4-H show or chicken-fried steak at a Cracker Barrel. Like I said, my angel might be a little psychic but he's not psychic enough to do me a damned bit of good. Probably there's nothing psychic about him at all. Probably it's as simple as he talked to Tykho, but an hour after I get to Bamboo House of Dolls, Declan Garrett walks in. Candy sees him first. She elbows me.

"Salesman of the year twelve o'clock high."

He comes right over and starts in. Not even a "Hi. Sorry about interrupting your donut with gunfire." I wonder if he knows his gunman was a windup toy.

"I heard you wanted to see me."

"I'm fine, Declan. How are you?"

He's agitated. This isn't his turf. It's mine and he doesn't like it. Carlos is looking at him. I raise a hand to let him know that everything is all right and he goes back to serving other customers.

"Listen, I'm sorry we got off on the wrong foot the other

day. You're right: I do have the 8 Ball, and you can have it for the million you promised plus one more thing."

"What?"

"Who's the buyer?"

His lip curls at one corner of his mouth.

"What do you care?"

"Indulge me."

"No," he says. "You indulge me."

He sidesteps behind Candy while pulling something from under his jacket. I don't have to see the pistol to know it's there.

"Be cool, Declan. Let's all just be cool."

"I *am* cool, motherfucker. I'm a snowman eating an Eskimo Pie. You think you can call me here and cheat me out of my sale?"

"That's not it at all."

"Then what is it? . . . Oh, wait. I don't care. I want the fucking Qomrama or I'm going to shoot the pretty lady. Yeah, you'll get me, but your Charles Bronson act won't keep lead out of her spine."

Candy opens her eyes wide at me. It's not fear. She's asking me to let her go Jade on this creep and eat his face. I shake my head ever so slightly. She's mad but she listens.

"Okay, man. You've got me over a barrel. I'll take you to the 8 Ball."

"Right now, cocksucker. I mean right now."

"Sure. It's close by."

"Then let's go."

We go out to a BMW coupe parked down the block. He and Candy get in the back. He makes me drive. I take us straight down Sunset to the Chateau, obeying the speed limit and stopping for every red light. I don't know who Candy hates more right now, him or me. Given the chance, she'd probably eat us both just on principle. Him for pulling the gun, and me for not taking it from him. I'm going to have a lot of making up to do, assuming we don't end up all bullet-riddled.

Declan doesn't like it when I give his keys to the valet at the Chateau, but what's he going to do about it? We go through the lobby not looking the slightest bit suspicious. Me a few feet in front while a nervous guy is pressed so close to Mr. Macheath's squeeze that he might be giving her a high colonic.

We take the elevator to the penthouse. Declan gets extra twitchy when we arrive upstairs and he doesn't see a room right away.

"Ready to go down the rabbit hole?" I ask.

"Don't try anything cute."

I open the grandfather clock and step halfway through.

"The 8 Ball is in here, safe and sound."

He leans over and squints, trying to see past me.

"Don't fuck with me."

"No tricks. I'm not going to leave something as important as the 8 Ball in the hotel safe, am I? No. I'll keep it where no one even knows about it."

I step through the clock. A second later Candy follows, Declan holding on to her like a leech. I take a quick look around. Kasabian's laptop is open but he's nowhere in sight. Good. He's the last thing I want to have to explain to the shakiest gun in the West.

"What is this place?"

"My Batcave, where I keep all my secrets."

"You people are even weirder than I heard."

Candy cracks up and Declan tightens his grip on her arm. He doesn't appreciate her extreme lack of terror. She should probably be a little more concerned. This guy is armed and unstable, and as far as I know, Jades don't deal with bullets any better than civilians.

"You can put that gun down now. We're here and I'm going to get the 8 Ball."

"Qomrama. Show a little respect, asshole. It's a holy thing and it's going to get me a holy lot of money."

"That's clever. You wait here and I'll go get it. You okay, Candy?"

She's stopped laughing.

"Hurry up. I'm hungry. I want to order a lobster."

I give her another don't-do-anything look. She narrows her eyes at me. When this is over I'm going to need a thesaurus to show me how many ways you can say "Sorry."

The fake 8 Ball isn't in any safe. It's in the one place no one is going to go pawing around. Under a pile of my dirty clothes, the bloody ones piled on top.

I bring the 8 Ball into the living room, bouncing it in one hand. Declan tenses but doesn't let go of Candy.

"Good. Now put it on the table."

"No. Who's it for?"

"I'll shoot the bitch."

"No."

Candy looks at me.

"The bitch doesn't want to get shot," she says.

I look at Declan.

"You could have shot her before and the 8 Ball is right here, so why would you shoot her now?"

Declan's eyes flicker microscopically. He knows what will happen if he pulls the trigger and he doesn't want to die. But he also knows that I don't want Candy shot.

"Heads up," I say, and toss him the 8 Ball.

He lets go of Candy and lunges for the Qomrama. Catches it with his arms, close to his chest like a football. Candy steps away from him. Declan now has the gun leveled at both of us.

I say, "Who's it for?"

Declan looks at his bouncing baby 8 Ball and smiles.

"No one. Last time I was buying for a bunch of bankers with their own Angra group, Der Zorn Gottes. The Angra they worship is a fucking flower. Can you believe that shit? 'Zhuyigdanatha.' A real mouthful, huh? But his friends call him the Flayed Heart, so it's okay."

"But you're not selling it to them now."

"Damn right," says Declan. "Your little blitzkrieg drove the price way up. Now it goes to the highest bidder."

"That sounds dangerous," says Candy.

"Nothing ventured nothing etcetera, sweetheart. I saw the light after he killed Moseley."

"I didn't kill him. He jumped in front of a bus."

"Same thing, you fuck. He was a true believer and happy to die for the Angra cause. I'm not. Whoever ponies up can have it. That includes you, you know. You find a buyer and we can do some real business."

"You suppose your Flayed Heart buddies know how the 8 Ball works?"

"What the fuck do I care? They can give it to their kids at Christmas instead of an Elmo doll."

I don't know any other actual Angra freaks. This might be my only chance to meet some real ones.

"I know someone who wants the 8 Ball. You sell it to your people, then put me in touch so I can make a bid on it."

Declan considers this.

"I don't know that I'm going to sell to Der Zorn Gottes. Why don't you tell me your buyer and I'll sell to him? I'll give you a ten percent finder's fee."

"No. I want to meet your people."

"I have the Qomrama and the gun. What you want isn't really relevant to the discussion."

This is starting to piss me off. Ten more seconds I'll be chewing his face off myself. I could throw some hoodoo at him, but he still might get a shot off and hit Candy. I've got to find another angle.

"I have to make a tiny confession."

Declan is already edging for the door.

"What?"

"That 8 Ball is a fake."

He stops and looks at it like maybe he can tell the difference.

"It better goddamn well not be," he says, and shoots a glass vase holding some long-stemmed lilies. Thank God. I was planning on knocking the ugly thing over myself. Declan shakes the 8 Ball. Uses his gun hand to try to make it do something.

A whirring, clicking noise starts behind me.

"What are you two doing out here? Fucking each other

Richard Kadrey

with cannonballs?" says Kasabian, bleary-eyed, creaking out of his room on all fours. He sees Declan with the gun and jerks upright, which, if you aren't used to it, looks even worse.

"Shit!" yells Declan. He shoots at Kasabian, hitting him in the leg. I pull the Peacemaker from the waistband behind my back and, before he can turn the gun on me, put a hole in the side of Declan's thick skull. He drops the 8 Ball, but Candy's Jade reflexes are quick-like-a-bunny fast and she catches it before it hits the ground.

"What the fuck?" yells Kasabian, grabbing his injured leg. "Your fucking hit man crippled me," he says. He hobbles over to Declan's body. "This is exactly the kind of thing I was talking about. You don't kill me, so you bring in someone to do it for you."

"Calm down. I didn't know he was going to shoot you. I wanted to see if he knew how to use the damned 8 Ball. Someone besides Aelita must."

Candy sets the Qomrama on the coffee table and looks at dead Declan like she still wants to eat him.

"Fumbling with the 8 Ball, he looked like a junior high kid trying to take a girl's bra off for the first time."

I put the pistol back in my waistband.

"Hey, the first time can be confusing. And then some girl fools you with the kind that closes in the front and you start getting worried about how many other ways bras can open."

"That's the girl IQ test," says Candy. "Can the rat run the maze and find the cheese?"

"I knew it was a conspiracy."

"That's just the tip of the iceberg."

Kasabian drops down into his desk chair. He tries to straighten his bum leg, but can only manage to get it about two thirds out.

"I'm fine over here, Nick and Nora. Thanks for asking."

Declan has a pretty big hole in his head and it's bleeding all over the Chateau's pricey carpet.

I say, "I'm going to dump the body. Why don't you two clean up the blood as best as you can and cover what you don't get with a throw rug or the sofa?"

Kasabian shakes his head.

"Forget it. I'm not cleaning up your mess."

"I kept this asshole from killing you."

"You brought him here."

Kasabian and I have ended up here before, but this is the last time.

"You're right," I say. "I put you in danger. Maybe it's time for you to take all that money you have stashed away and find your own place."

He frowns.

"What?"

I point to Declan's corpse.

"This isn't the last time this shit is going to happen. If anything, things are going to get worse as the Angra get closer and people start scrambling for whatever they can grab."

"See? Looking for any excuse to get rid of me. I told you you'd do this."

"I brought you here to save your sorry ass, but I guess you forgot that. What we're talking about right now, though, this is your choice. You don't want to be a team player? Fine. I'll help you get back in our old room at the Beat Hotel. But just remember that from now on you're going to be watching your own back, and if you want any more work from Manimal Mike, you'll be paying for it yourself."

"You're going to let him do this?" he says to Candy.

"Sorry. I'm on the crazy man's side on this one," she says.

"This is how it is from now on. Everyone works with everyone else. You want to play lone wolf, you're on your own."

Kasabian rubs his chin with a metal paw.

"So what, we're going all Super Friends now?"

"Something like that."

"He wasn't trying to get me shot?"

Candy shakes her head.

"No. The bastard was trying to get *me* shot."

Kasabian thinks for a minute.

"Okay. You have your demands. I have mine. You drop all the 'Old Yeller' stuff. You want me to be a team player, you treat me like part of the team and not the equipment."

"That's downright cruel, man."

He holds up a finger.

"And my leg. I want it no-shit fixed."

I nod.

"I'm working on that. There aren't a lot of listings for hellhounds on Craigslist. I'm going to have to go Downtown and beg or steal one."

Candy clears her throat.

"You know, it might pique someone's interest if you call the concierge for a bunch of bleach and a body bag."

"Use the blankets and towels to get up as much blood as you can. Then call down for new ones. If they ask about the old ones, tell them we're taking care of them."

"That won't make them suspicious."

"I'm Mr. Macheath. I work in mysterious ways."

Kasabian gets up and whirs and clanks into his bathroom to get towels. Candy gives me some of the cash people have been paying me not to bend them into balloon animals.

"Sorry about making you play damsel in distress tonight."

"Tell me you didn't plan it in advance."

"I was improvising. I promise."

She looks at all the blood.

"It's like Sweeney Todd's rumpus room in here."

"I'll be back soon."

I FIND AN all-night market a few blocks from the Chateau. I buy garbage bags, bleach, duct tape, and a shovel. The clerk doesn't bat an eye. I sneak back through a shadow in the parking lot and come out in the penthouse, my stomach catching a little, not just from the typical nausea of coming through the penthouse's magic defenses, but from the thick smell of blood in the room.

While Candy and Kasabian pat down the carpet with towels and sheets, turning them bright crimson, I stick Declan's head in one of the garbage bags, securing it with tape around his neck. I don't want any more of the red stuff splashing around. I know I should feel bad about wrapping a dead man like pork chops for the freezer, but I can't work up much sympathy. He was a greedy fuck who was going to shoot Candy. That's after he almost got her shot at Donut Universe. No. Declan Garrett deserves what he got and what he's going to get.

Candy carries each soaked sheet and towel into the bathroom and throws it in the tub. The wall looks like a musk ox exploded while taking a soak.

"Where are you taking the body?" says Candy.

"Teddy Osterberg's place."

"Silly question."

Kasabian moans and groans, but he does his bit getting up the blood. I bag as many of the sheets and towels as I can carry, figuring I can come back for the rest later.

I kiss Candy on her bloody cheek. She smiles but I can tell she's still a little sore. I toss Declan's body over my shoulder, grab the bags of bloody sundries in my hands, and tuck the shovel under my arm. No one in recorded history has looked more like he's going to dispose of a body than I do right now.

I step through a shadow and come out in the garage. It only takes a couple of minutes to find Declan's Beamer. I pop the trunk with the black blade, toss Declan inside and the other goodies on top of him.

The black blade opens the door, and when I jam it into the ignition, the car starts right up. I back up carefully and drive out of the garage, giving the attendant a friendly wave as I leave.

THERE ISN'T MUCH traffic on the road at four A.M., but with a dead guy in the trunk the roads still feel crowded. All it will take to spoil the rest of the night is a bored cop pulling me over or a drunk driver plowing into me. I'm more worried about the cop. Yeah, I know I can get away from them. I've done it before. It's the dash cam that bothers me. I don't like the idea of LAPD having any more footage of me, especially with a corpse in the trunk and the murder weapon behind my back. It's a long drive out to Malibu when you have to stick to the speed limit.

I turn off the headlights when I head up the hill to Teddy Osterberg's place, driving by moonlight. I haven't been out here since I burned the place down. Teddy's mansion is a pile of rubble and some scorched beams surrounded by police tape. Teddy was a ghoul. Someone with an appetite for dead flesh. In his spare time he was a cemetery buff. He collected them like other people collect model trains. At the top of the hill, I pop the trunk and haul out the body and the shovel.

There are hundreds of grave sites sprawled in every direction. Marble tombstones and rotting wooden markers. Angel-topped mausoleums and rocky burial mounds. I take Declan out to the far end of the collection where Teddy has an old-fashioned potter's field. It's invisible from the road and seems like a good enough place for Declan to spend his retirement years.

The ground has baked hard under the California sun. I should have brought a pick to break up the soil. After about an hour of digging, I have a hole just deep enough to hold Declan. I push him over the edge with my boot and fill the hole back in, packing down the earth on top of the grave and scattering the leftover dirt around the cemetery.

Back at the car, I toss the shovel in the trunk and head down the hill, not turning on the lights until I'm back on the main road. I'm trying to decide if I should burn Teddy's car or push it into the ocean when I hear a horn behind me. I put my arm out the window and signal for whoever it is to go around, but the car just keeps honking. It's a late-sixties' cherry-red Mustang. Probably the property of some movie star's kid. At least it isn't a cop.

When the road widens enough to have a decent shoulder I pull over to let the car pass. Last thing I want is to attract attention when my coat is covered in cemetery dirt and another man's blood. Imagine my glee when the car pulls off on the shoulder behind me. I pull my gun and put it in my coat pocket.

I get out and wait. The other car's headlights are in my eyes, but I can hear the driver's door open and someone start my way. It's a woman and she's walking with purpose. All I can see is her outline. She's wearing spike heels. I cock the hammer on the pistol.

"I don't always expect tribute, but can't a girl say hello around here without every nervous Nellie pulling heat on her? You boys do love your guns."

I recognize the voice.

"Mustang Sally?"

She steps between the headlights and me and I can finally see her face. She's smiling, knowing how much she spooked me. I smile back.

"Is that a guilty conscience you're wearing tonight?" she says.

"Not guilty. Just tired. I buried a guy up at Teddy Osterberg's place. What are you doing here?"

"What I always do. Driving."

Mustang Sally is the highway sylph. The queen of the road, a spirit that's been around in one form or other since the first humans left the first mud ruts in the ground with their feet and then wagons. She drives L.A.'s roads 24/7 every day of the year and only stops when bums like me lure her over with tributes of cigarettes and road food. But tonight she stopped me.

"It's nice to see you. Thanks again for the help last time."

"Getting you into Hell or keeping you from getting run down when you got back?"

"I'm grateful for the first and pathetically grateful for the second."

She doesn't say anything for a second. I'm not the one who stopped her, but she's still a spirit that needs feeding. I pull out the closest thing I have to a tribute. Half a pack of Maledictions.

"It's all I have. I didn't expect to see you."

"That's okay. I didn't expect to see you either, but kismet," she says, and sniffs the pack.

"These must pack a wallop."

She taps out a smoke and holds it to her lips. I get out Mason's lighter and spark the cigarette for her.

"So this is what they smoke in Hell these days. A tribe that used to worship me —who was it?—they liked sage sprinkled with wolf dung, so I suppose I've had worse smokes in my time. So, what can I do for you tonight?"

I open my hands. Sally makes a face and brushes some graveyard dirt from my shoulder.

"I wasn't looking for you. You stopped me."

She shakes her head.

"Use your brain. You're on this road. I'm on this road. Spirits and mortals don't just bump into each other outside a Stuckey's without it meaning something. So, we've exchanged pleasantries. You've paid me this ludicrous tribute. All the formalities are taken care of. What's on your mind?"

I'm not sure what to say at first and then it comes to me.

"I'm going into Kill City."

"You do go to the most interesting places. Why?"

"I have to find a ghost."

"That's probably a good place for them. How many people died there?"

"In the accident, a hundred give or take."

"So, what's the problem?"

"I don't know anything about the place or where we're going. We have a guide but I don't trust him. I'm not sure what to do about it."

Sally puffs the Malediction, pulling the smoke as deep into her lungs as any Hellion.

"Here's the thing: Kill City isn't really my kind of road. I'm an open-road gal. Kill City is more of a labyrinth. You know any labyrinth spirits?"

"No."

"I know a few but they won't be any help. They're all as dizzy as clowns in a clothes dryer."

"Do you have any words of wisdom before I go in?"

She nods her head from side to side, thinking.

"You could get one of those little Saint Christopher statues for your dashboard."

"You're the only traveling saint I believe in."

She smiles. A few other cars pass us as we talk. You'd think us standing here in the middle of the night would attract rubberneckers. But no one slows down or even looks at us. It's like we're invisible.

"What I can tell you is what I tell anyone in your position. When you get lost, and you will get lost, keep going and don't stop till you hit the end of the road. There will be something there, even if it's not what you were looking for. And something is always better than nothing, isn't it?"

"That depends on how pointy something's teeth are."

She blows out some smoke and drops the Malediction on the ground, grinding it out with her shoe.

"Sorry I can't be more help," she says.

"You're always fine by me, Sally."

"I mean really sorry. I'm a spirit of the earth. Something bad is coming, and if it gets here, it will eat me like a ripe peach. And I don't want that. I love my roads and the funny people I meet along the way. I saved you once. Now you're going to return the favor, right?"

"I'm going to do my best."

"That's all a lady can ask. I'll see you around, Mr. Stark."

She turns and heads back to her car.

"I'll see you, Sally. Drive safe."

That makes her laugh. She guns the Mustang's engine and peels rubber back onto the road.

Some days are harder than others in the kill-or-be-killed game. Some days are stranger. This day might have set some new records.

I WAKE UP around noon and start calling people, telling them to come to the penthouse around three. Candy and I spend an hour rearranging furniture so the sofa, which now covers the remains of Declan's sizable bloodstain, doesn't look too out of place. Kasabian's gimp leg makes him useless for this kind of work, so he hangs out at his desk kibitzing the whole time, like a half-crocked Martha Stewart.

Candy takes me into the bedroom and gets a box down from the top shelf of the closet. It's flat and square, sealed with packing tape.

"I didn't wrap it yet because it's only Thanksgiving."

"Remind me which one that is."

"You don't know what Thanksgiving is?"

"I'm aware of its existence but I don't remember the details. We had different holidays in Hell."

"It's the one with turkey and stuffing and pumpkin pie and everyone eats and drinks too much and people fall asleep watching football or making fun of people watching football."

"Right. The one where my father broke things because he bet on the games and always lost. Always. My whole childhood, I don't remember him winning once. Shouldn't a man win once, just out of sheer statistics?"

"He wasn't your father. Doc was," says Candy.

She's right, but what difference does it make? I don't want to think about it or get into an argument about it. Doc Kinski means a lot more to Candy than he does to me. He took care of her. Got her started on the potion that makes it so she doesn't have the hunger to drink people. She loves him and I only met him after the point in my life when meeting your real father isn't much more than a technicality. Something to check off a life list. Smoke your first cigarette. See your first porn flick. Meet your real father.

Candy sees I'm not happy with her bringing it up. She picks up the box and puts it in my lap.

"I was keeping this for Christmas, but saving the world is a good time for presents too."

I unwrap the box and take out a gun.

"Do you know what it is?"

"I think so. I've seen pictures of them. It's a presentation pistol."

"It's from Tiffany's, the old jewelry place. They made fancy pistols since before the Civil War. I couldn't find one of those. This one is, like, from the eighties."

It's a Colt, with a matte-black finish and gold filigree on the cylinder and golden eagle wings along the barrel. The ivory grips are carved with talons.

"Does it work?"

"I don't know. Test it."

I pull back the hammer and dry-fire it several times. The action feels good. I know these things are supposed to be for show, but it feels like a good piece of hardware.

"Do you like it?"

"It's great. Where did you get it?"

"Doc had it. A civilian gave it to him when he fixed him up on the sly."

Now I see why she brought him up. Don't get me wrong. Doc was a good guy, considering he was a deadbeat dad and, worse, a goddamn angel. He's the one who filled me in on my background. Told me I was a nephilim, an Abomination in both Heaven and Hell and the only one of my kind left alive on earth, so, you know, lucky me. Back in Doc's prime he was known as Uriel, one of the warrior archangels. He fought in the Heavenly war against Lucifer and the other rebels. Knowing all that, I still find it hard to picture him with a gun in his hand, even if he was just stashing it in a box, never to be fired.

"Is that okay?" says Candy.

"Yeah. It's great. You're great. Thanks."

I kiss her and put thoughts about where the gun came from out of my head. I'm good at that. And I'm damned sure not going to let a good gun's origins stop me from using it.

She smiles and sits up straight.

"So, where's my present?"

"What makes you think I have one? It's only Thanksgiving."

"People have been bribing you all over town, and not just with money, I bet."

I look at her. She's still smiling, but there's something in her eyes.

"You didn't give me this because I'm trying to save the world. You did it became you don't think we're going to make it to Christmas."

She lets her shoulders fall.

"So? What if I did?"

"Assuming I have anything for you, you're not getting it now."

"Why not?"

"Because I'm more optimistic than you. You can wait for Santa."

She throws a pillow at me.

"You dick."

"If I have to twist the head off every Angra freak in L.A., we're going to make it to Christmas."

She takes the Colt and levels it at objects around the room. Snaps the gun back each time she pretend-shoots it.

"Head twisting. You know how to sweet-talk a girl. At least give me a hint."

"It's red and it doesn't fit in your pocket."

"Fuck you. That's not a clue."

"It's all you're getting."

"I repeat, you're a dick," she says, setting the gun back in the box.

We call downstairs for food. Order a real spread, like we did when we first got to the penthouse. Ordering one of pretty much everything on the menu. But not the duck. The waiters line the food carts along the wall, and because this is the Devil's room, they don't ask questions. When I sign the check, I always add a nice tip after one of these blow-outs. I still don't know who pays the bills here, if anyone. Maybe Lucifer having a room on standby is just part of the cost of doing business in L.A. For all I know, there could be other hoodoo penthouses where Odin, the Easter Bunny, and Amelia Earhart are living as large as we are and not paying one red shekel.

PEOPLE START COMING through the clock around three. First Vidocq and Allegra, then Brigitte and Father Traven. I want to grab them and start talking right away, but I keep my mouth shut. There's plenty of food and wine and beer for everyone, though I notice that Father Traven is just drinking coffee. Brigitte stays close to him. Smiling. Talking to him. Making sure he remembers to eat. She's not watching him to keep him off the booze. You can see it in her eyes. She's trying to protect him from the world.

I pass the Tiffany pistol around and everyone tells Candy about what great taste she has. She loves it. Then I can't stand waiting anymore.

"I'm going on a ghost hunt in Kill City."

That gets people's attention.

"I've been looking for the 8 Ball for over a month. All it's gotten me is tall tales that I have the shitty thing. Yesterday, the Dark Eternal told me that there's a ghost hiding in Kill City that might know where the 8 Ball is, so I'm going in to check it out."

"Do you believe what they said?" asks Vidocq.

"I have to go in and find out."

"That's not what I mean. I mean do you trust them? You have not harassed the Dark Eternal the way you have other gangs, but what's to stop you from doing so?"

"If they think you're coming for them, they might be sending you into a trap," says Brigitte.

"I don't think so. The Dark Eternal and I have steered clear of each other for a while."

"Is it true that's because they paid you a large sum of money?" asks Traven.

"Yes. And because they mostly feed on crooks and the fools that come crawling to them and I don't have a problem with that."

Traven nods. I don't know if he exactly understands, but he seems to accept that I'm not a simple sellout. I'm a complicated sellout.

"If the Dark Eternal wanted me gone, they could have sent an army. What I think is really going on is that Tykho knows the 8 Ball is valuable and that it gives whoever has it power, so she wants it. She's sending me in with a Dark Eternal rep, a guy called Paul Delon. He's the one with the map."

"Tell me about this Paul," says Vidocq. "Do we really need him? Couldn't we take his map and use it ourselves?"

I shake my head.

"First off, Paul isn't human. Candy and Brigitte would recognize him. He's another Trevor. An automaton built by a Tick-Tock Man named Atticus Rose."

"What?" says Candy. "The last two tried to kill you."

"And we killed them. There's no choice here. Robby the Robot has the map in his head. Without him I could wander around the place for weeks. All I want is to find the 8 Ball and make sure Paul never even touches it. I think I can handle that, but having more people would help. Is anyone willing to come into Kill City with me?"

Everyone except Kasabian raises their hands. I look over at him.

"You like horror movies, Kas. Aren't you interested in seeing a real-life House of Usher?"

Kasabian shakes his head. He's working over the food like he's Muhammad Ali and the buffet is Sonny Liston.

"I'll leave it to you prima ballerinas. My dancing days are over," he says, tapping his bad leg with his fork.

"You're missing all the fun."

"Bring me back a snow globe so I'll know what it was like."

"I guess that just leaves us," I say. "But I don't want all of us. Allegra, I'd like you to stay behind."

"Why?"

"Because we're basically going to the moon and that means someone is going to get hurt. If that was you, none of us knows how to fix you. And if one of us gets hurt, everyone would feel better knowing that the best doctor is at the clinic and not one of the second stringers."

"He's right, my dear," says Vidocq. "I know it's not what you want, but it's the smart thing to do."

Allegra crosses her arms and leans back in her chair.

"Fine. I'll stay."

I say, "You can also keep an eye on that other thing we talked about."

She nods.

"Yeah."

"If there are any problems with that, you can crash here with Kasabian."

Kasabian gestures with a chicken wing like he's conducting a goddamn orchestra.

"Sure," he says around a mouthful of food. "It'll be like a campout. We can set their bed on fire and roast hot dogs on a stick."

"What are we taking?" says Candy.

"Guns and lunch. I don't plan on window-shopping."

"Anything else?"

"Lights," says Brigitte.

"And water. We'll be in there for at least a few hours. Anyone with boots should wear them."

"You're going to need a first-aid kit," Allegra says. "I'll put one together."

"Good. Anything else?"

"I'll bring potions," says Vidocq. "And some of my other tools."

Vidocq might just be the best thief in L.A. That could come in handy.

Father Traven says, "I've been doing more research. I believe I've found some runes that will keep the Qomrama's magic in check. I can put them on a vessel for it if I knew how big it was."

Candy gets the fake 8 Ball from the coffee table and tosses it to him.

"Thank you."

"There's a couple of rules we're going to live by. The first is that everybody sticks together no matter what. If you're pee-shy, don't come. Second rule is that no one gets more than ten feet away from anyone else. Last rule is if we run into locals or loons, let Paul do the talking."

"You're telling us to keep our mouths shut? You?" says Candy.

"We'll meet at Bamboo House of Dolls at eight tonight."

"Why can't you take everyone in through a shadow?" says Allegra.

"I've never been inside Kill City. It's not the kind of place I want to stroll into blind. We'll go in together, one step at a time, everybody looking out for everybody else."

"Still, going in at night," says Traven.

"Less chance of being seen. And the place has been dead for years. There probably isn't much light inside, so we'll be carrying our own light night or day."

From over at his desk Kasabian says, "And what's Plan B?"

"Plan B?"

"You know, for when Plan A goes wrong. No offense, but it took your fearless leader over there eleven years to find his way out of Hell. When Plan A goes tits up, what's your backup plan for getting out of Kill City?"

Everyone looks at me.

"Thanks, Kas."

"Just being a team player, boss."

I TAKE A Toyota SUV off a parking lot on North Cahuenga. It's brown, a few years old, and with a couple of dents in the fenders. A vehicle like this is practically invisible to the highway patrol. Yeah, I could take everyone through a shadow right to Kill City's front door, but there's no way I'm letting Delon in on that trick. I figure that anything he knows, Norris Quay will eventually know, and I'm not ready to share that secret with the richest prick in prick town. If things go sideways inside, I'll drag everyone else out through the Room and leave Delon's Tick-Tock ass behind.

The others, including Delon, are waiting at Bamboo House of Dolls. Candy is waiting by the curb. When she sees me she calls inside and jumps in the shotgun seat. The others pile in the back. I head for the I-10 and turn west to the land of seashell art and crab salad. Santa Monica.

Delon sits behind me, next to Vidocq.

He leans forward and says, "So what's the plan?"

"The plan is we go in and we get out ASAP. And why are you asking me? You're Mr. Insider. What's your plan for getting us to the ghost?"

"We're going to have to deal with at least a couple of groups of crazies inside Kill City. Families and federacies."

"What's the difference?" says Traven.

"There are some intact old Sub Rosa families. Ones that have fallen so low they're completely off the map. We'll be meeting one of them when we get there. The Mangarms."

I say, "Do they know we're coming?"

"How would they?" says Delon.

"So, your plan is that we walk into their house and ask for a handout?"

Delon rustles a bag at his feet.

"I have shiny stones and beads to trade. Barter is very big in Kill City."

"Are you sure the Mangarms know anything useful?"

"If they don't they'll know who we should talk to. In any case, they're a good bunch to make nice with. They're the family closest to the outside world, which keeps them vaguely civilized."

"And how many uncivilized families will we be meeting?" says Candy.

"None if we get lucky. If we're not, who knows?"

"What are the federacies you spoke of? Are they the uncivilized groups?" says Vidocq.

"Not necessarily, but they're the ones most likely to be dangerous. They're not families. More like dog packs. Random groups of down-and-out Sub Rosa, civilians, and Lurkers. The good thing is that they're big on marking their territories, so if we keep our eyes open, we'll be able to steer clear of them."

"Luck is for suckers," I say. "Keeping us out of crazy country is your number one job. If we have to take the long way around, fine. I don't want to cage-fight a bunch of head cases where I don't know the exits."

"Understood," says Delon. "I don't want any close encounters either."

"But we might have to meet them," says Traven.

"It depends on where the ghost is hiding."

"That means we might have to."

"Yes."

"Is there anyone here who doesn't have a gun?" I say.

"I don't," says Traven.

"Do you want one?"

"No, thank you. You and Brigitte know guns. I'll end up shooting myself in the foot."

"Anyone else?"

"I don't, but I have my own defenses," says Vidocq.

Vidocq wears a custom greatcoat with dozens of pockets inside. Each pocket holds a potion he can toss like a mini-grenade at anything that needs its attitude adjusted.

"Good. What about you, Paul?"

He nods.

"I'm fine."

Great. That means the fucker is armed. At least now everyone knows. The trick is going to be keeping him in front of us the whole time we're inside.

WHEN WE REACH Santa Monica I park the van in the back on the top floor of a shopping-center parking lot. Before we ditch it, I wipe down the steering wheel and the front driver-side door, something I don't usually do. In the past, I just left the vehicle and walked away. But now that LAPD has a file on me, I don't want to make it too easy for them to track me.

We head for the beach with our bags and packs over our shoulders. Slung low on someone's back is a kid-size vinyl *Kekko Kamen* pack, featuring a mostly naked female super-hero in a red mask.

"Thanks for being discreet," I say.

Candy smiles and keeps walking.

"This is discreet. I turned off the red LEDs in her nipples. And speaking of discreet, you have so many gun bulges under that coat you look like the Elephant Man."

It's just a few blocks to the beach. We stroll along past cafés and high-priced clubs with doormen in Hawaiian shirts, like just one more group of shitheel tourists.

"What's so special about this thing we're looking for?" says Delon. "Tykho says it might be a weapon, but you don't look like the kind of person who needs more weapons."

"You can never have too many weapons."

"It is a weapon, then?"

"I didn't say that." I'm not sure how much this asshole knows, but I don't want him knowing any more than he has to. "I don't know exactly what it is, if you want to know the truth. All I know is that a very bad person wants it and that's reason enough to keep it from her."

"What's so bad about her?"

"Well, she killed me once upon a time."

Delon stops walking for a second. He has to take a couple of big steps to catch up.

"You're not a vampire, are you?"

Delon has to sidestep a gaggle of drunk bachelorettes pouring out of a limo, dragging a bewildered-looking soon-to-be bride into what's probably the third club of the night.

"Tykho said you were hard to figure out. Like whether you're just making things up to keep a mysterious image. Did you really go to Hell?"

"Many times."

"What's it like?"

"It's dark, full of monsters, and it smells bad. The upside is that people don't ask too many questions."

Delon gives me a quick look and adjusts his shoulder bag.

We reach the long street that runs parallel to the beach and he says, "There it is."

Of course, there it is. It's pretty fucking hard to miss.

For about ten minutes Kill City was the biggest shopping mall in the country. It was called Blue World Village back then and was supposed to demonstrate peace and harmony for all the countries on the planet through high-end retail consumption.

The developers stole the basic layout from the Santa Monica Pier tourist trap—upscale vomit rides for the kiddies, shit restaurants, T-shirt and crap jewelry shops, a rip-off arcade—and tacked on a glitzy mall bigger than the biggest Vegas casino. It was a whole damned Smurf-size city. Hell, if the amusement park outside wasn't enough, there was another smaller one inside.

Then, in thirty head-cracking seconds, the place went from Blue World Village to Kill City when part of the roof collapsed, taking down a couple of walls and a hundred construction workers with it. Took down a lot of investors too. The only reason the great white whale is still standing is because of all the lawsuits. The builders claim force majeure, that an act of God, an earthquake, brought the place down. A lot of investors have a lot of detectives claiming that the builders were skimming money off the top by buying inferior construction materials and using unskilled labor. Even the state and the city are fighting over who should pay to knock the damn thing down. Then there's the families of the dead, suing everyone in sight. The mall was such a mess that they never even found a lot of bodies. They just sort of vaporized under all the concrete and steel.

If anywhere in L.A. is full of ghosts and feral shut-ins, it's Kill City.

The lights by the mall, even the security lights, burned out a long time ago. There's a ten-foot-tall chain-link fence around the whole site. I take out the black blade and slice through the wire and we move inside. We stay on the concrete sidewalk around the mall. The amusement park is out on a wooden pier. Half a Ferris wheel and enough of a roller coaster left to make a nice nesting site for birds. But every Pacific storm loosens the pylons a little more. One good blow and the pier will go down, maybe taking the rest of Kill City with it. I checked the weather before we started out tonight. Clear, calm skies. Warm Indian-summer air. Just the weather for a little B&E.

In a circular courtyard by the front doors is the sky-blue globe that gave the mall its name. If they reopen the place they might have to call it Bird Shit City. Most of the northern hemisphere is buried under the white stuff and South America isn't looking so good. It's like half the world is encased in a gull-crap ice age.

The glass entrance doors are nothing but bent aluminum frames. We step through and into the pool of light on the floor. This mall lobby is pretty intact. The collapsed section is a football field's length back. The stars shine down on the rubble of a dead indoor garden.

The L.A. heat and wet ocean air have turned the inside of

Kill City into a kind of hothouse. The air is warm and thick. Water drips from the ceiling. Green fungus grows on every surface where it can get a hold. The floor is slick with the stuff. Mold leopard-spots the walls and storefronts. In the center of the lobby is a fifty-foot Christmas tree. The outside lights glitter off enormous ornaments almost lost under a layer of furred fungus.

Something crashes to the floor on the other side of the lobby, hitting hard enough to shake the Christmas tree. Candy and Father Traven have their flashlights out and shine them in the direction of the sound.

A hundred feet away, an enormous helmet has crashed to the floor. The ceiling of the lobby is twelve stories high. A mannequin Santa and reindeer, dusty chrome cherubs, and a shooting star dangle precariously on the few support wires that haven't snapped yet.

"Did anyone see it fall?"

Heads shake and people mumble no or shrug.

"An auspicious beginning," says Vidocq.

"One of the crazies might have dragged it here from another part of the mall and left it leaning against something," says Delon. "They used to have a grand bazaar up here once every couple of months. It was supposed to be neutral ground during the market, but someone always violated it. With all the violence, eventually the market died. That's when things really fell apart. The last vestiges of an organized society. Now when the crazies trade, the groups do it one-on-one and try to avoid each other the rest of the time. They're about one inch from tribes of jungle headhunters."

I say, "We should get moving," to Delon.

He goes to one of the standing mall maps. It's as tall as he is, upright and square, like one of Kubrick's monoliths from *2001*. Delon wipes fungus from the front of the map with his jacket sleeve.

"I thought you knew the mall by heart," says Traven.

"I do," says Delon. "I just want to make sure we're oriented correctly."

Everyone gets out their flashlights and clusters around him, reading off the names of the expensive shops over his shoulder. Candy comes up to me and nods at the tree.

"I told you it was Christmas. You should have given me my present."

"That's not a Christmas tree. That's Swamp Thing's summer home."

She heads to where the others are standing. I pop the cylinder on the Colt to make sure it's fully loaded. It is. I follow her over.

"Got it," says Paul. He points to a "You Are Here" arrow on the map. "I know where to go from here."

"Which way?" I say.

He points off to the left.

"Up."

Through the green-tinged dimness I see stairs and, beside them, a two-story-high pile of garbage.

"That way."

"Let's get going."

I hang back and let Delon walk point. Not that he needs any encouragement. I think he's been looking forward to being in charge. I wonder how his brain works. He's not a computer. He's goddamn Stretch Armstrong. It's not like he's downloading video to a chip in his brain. All his memories and personality must be hoodoo Atticus stuck in his head when he was screwing the skull shut. What I really want to know is if Delon knows he's a cuckoo clock or does he think he's a real boy? Part of it is cheap curiosity and part of it is self-defense. I keep thinking about Trevor stepping in front of that bus. Did he do it because he knew he was replaceable or because he thought he was sacrificing himself for the Angra cause? I'd love to get hold of a Paul or Trevor or Donny Osmond or whatever other names they have and let Manimal Mike take it apart to see what makes it run.

As we climb, I can feel people's nerves kicking in. Before this, meeting the Kill City crazies was an abstract concept. Now a machine is taking us to a meet and greet with Peter Pan and the Lost Boys. I have to admit that I'm a little concerned myself. As we reach each floor, I keep an eye open for shadows that might hide an ambush or ones dark enough that I can pull people into.

I say, "How far are we going?"

"Twelve floors. All the way to the top. There's a hotel up there with views all the way from the ocean to the city."

He sounds like a fucking real estate developer.

The empty retail spaces don't look like they were ever stores. More like strange minimalist art. Hard geometric lines and soft fungal patches behind smashed security gates. The funny thing is that the scattered glass and broken fixtures are the only things that make the spaces look like humans built them and that anything with a frontal lobe might have wanted to go inside.

"What do you know about the Mangarms?" says Traven.

"Like I said, they're Sub Rosa," says Delon. "Old-world types that specialized in black magic."

"Baleful," says Candy.

"What?"

"The correct Sub Rosa term is Baleful magic. Not black. He told me," she says, pointing to me.

"Thank you," says Delon, trying not to sound too sarcastic. "May I go on?"

"Please do."

"They were and I suppose still are black potionists. They made poisons and hexes subtle enough to get around all but the most powerful charms. The problem is that their old-school magic didn't keep up with modern medicine. Antibiotics, transfusions, and stomach pumps put them out of business."

He looks at Candy.

"The Mangarm term for it is 'scientificated magic.'"

"Cool."

Glass elevator enclosures run alongside the stairs. It looks like they haven't worked since the day the place closed down. But someone is using them. Ropes have been strung inside. There are pulleys every couple of floors. My guess is that the setup runs all the way to the top. It's probably how the Mangarms move swag from the lower floors to home sweet home. It also explains the garbage heap in the lobby. Whatever they don't want anymore goes over the railing to the floor. I wonder what living over your own garbage dump smells like in high summer.

"Stop!" yells Brigitte.

Everyone freezes where they are.

Brigitte flashes forward and knocks Delon onto his face. Something creaks and blasts by us, swinging from a wire that reaches up into the dark over our heads. It smashes into the railing on the far side of the stairs, taking out a few feet of it, before swinging back and almost clipping Traven. It cracks the opposite railing and gets stuck there. Everyone turns their flashlights on the thing.

It's smashed to bits, only held together with yards of wire and duct tape. Sharpened metal spikes stick out at all angles. The center of the thing is dull beige plastic with holes in the front where keys might have been.

Father Traven examines it, pushing pieces of crushed plastic back into place.

"It's a cash register," he says. "Sharpened rebar wrapped around a cash register."

Brigitte gets up and goes to him.

"Are you all right? It almost hit you."

He touches her shoulder.

"I'm fine. Really."

Brigitte gets on her knees, shining her flashlight on the steps until she finds what she's looking for.

"You see? Here."

Her light illuminates several feet of monofilament line stretched across one of the stairs. It hangs loose where Paul stepped on it.

"It's a trip wire," says Vidocq.

"Thank you," says Paul. He looks a little shaken. No. He doesn't know he's a machine. He thinks he's going to live a long and productive life, marry and have a pack of little toasters to bounce on his knee.

I say, "From now on, we don't all shine our lights in the same spot. Move them around. Look for other traps."

"I guess we've officially lost the element of surprise," says Candy.

Paul runs his light over the next few steps and starts up again. The rest of us follow.

"Glad you came along, Father?" I say. "What's the story about Jonah getting swallowed by the whale?"

"I was thinking more about Dante," he says.

Vidocq says, "But when Dante went up he was ascending to Heaven."

"I don't think we'll find Heaven in here, up or down."

By the tenth floor we're sweating like pigs. By the eleventh we're sweating like filthy pigs. It's a relief to hit the last staircase until it stops halfway up. There's at least a fifteen-foot gap between where we are and the top of the stairs.

Lights come on overhead. Flashlights shine down into our eyes with more lights blinking on in the hotel level above.

"Stay where you are."

It's a raspy male voice. A whiskey voice or just someone who took a hit to the throat hard enough that it never healed right. There are six other guys behind him. All are armed with homemade blades, morning stars, and slings.

"Who are you?"

Paul takes half a step forward, right to the gap.

"We're friends. We'd like to speak to Hattie."

"Would you? Why would Mama Hattie want to speak to you?"

"We have offerings."

"What kind?"

"Special. But they're only for Hattie."

The guy turns and chats away with a couple of other members of the welcoming committee. They're wearing a ragged assortment of designer robes and furs. From what Delon said, I'd guess a mix of family heirlooms and things they looted from the stores below.

Candy whispers, "Who's Hattie?"

"The family matriarch," says Delon.

The group above breaks up. The rasper comes back to the front.

"Go away. We don't need your offerings. We get what we need just fine."

"Not this you don't."

"What is it?"

"Nehebkau's Tears."

"Never heard of him."

"Shut up, you ignorant boy."

It's a woman's voice, coming from behind the group. An old woman pushes her way to the front.

The whole Mangarm crew is gaunt but the woman looks like a mummy with a hangover. But she's alive. I can hear her heart and smell her sweat, which isn't all that pleasant.

She looks at Rasper and shakes her head.

"If you were good for anything besides stealing drugs from college kids' backpacks, you'd know exactly what Nehebkau's Tears are."

She turns and looks down at us.

"Please forgive Diogo. I love my boys, but this one took one too many pretty pills and it's left him with a skull full of fiddler crabs."

She scratches the back of his head like he's the not very bright family dog. She looks Delon over. The woman might look frail but her eyes are bright and hard.

"Let me see the Tears. I've handled them before, so I'll know if you're lying. If you are, I'm going to have my boys kill you."

Delon tosses the bottle across the chasm. Hattie catches it easily. I reach up, pull Delon off the top step, and go up there myself. I have one hand under my coat, ready to pull the Colt the moment anyone twitches. A second later Brigitte is standing next to me. I can't see it but I know she has her CO_2 gun handy. If she can get it out without anyone noticing, Candy will be pulling her 9mm folding pistol. Vidocq will have palmed a noxious potion or two. I hope Father Traven has the sense to stay in the back. I don't know what Delon is doing, but it suddenly bothers me to have him behind me at a moment like this.

"What are the Tears?" Traven says.

Delon says, "One of the most potent poisons known to the Sub Rosa, mortals, or Lurkers. And it's undetectable. Worth a fortune."

Hattie opens the vial and sniffs it. Touches the underside of the stopper to her tongue. I hear Delon gasp. She swishes the stuff around in her mouth for a moment. Then half spits, half coughs it out with a wad of phlegm.

She looks at Delon and laughs.

"Don't you worry about old Hattie. I've been around poisons and potions, elixirs and venoms, every kind of nostrum and bane that you can think of. It's worn out this old body, but it's left me immune to about everything made or grown on this earth."

She looks at the bottle, smacks her lips, and puts it in her pocket.

"Let them up, boys," she says, then points at me. "But keep an eye on the scarred one. He looks shiftier than a drunken sidewinder."

Diogo and his boys grab ropes suspended over the stairs and pull. A makeshift ramp made of old pieces of scaffolding wired haphazardly together swings up into place. With a thud, the ramp bangs into the bottom of the steps and Hattie's boys tie off the ropes.

"You first, Cortés," I say, and shove Delon onto the ramp. It sways and the ropes creak and Hattie's boys laugh, but the thing holds together. Delon walks up the ramp like he's barefoot and stepping on razor blades.

"One at a time," I say to the others, and start across. I let go of the Colt so I can put out my hands to keep my balance. I don't bother looking down. I have a pretty good picture in my head of the garbage heap twelve floors below. I don't want to end up another empty juice box on the pile.

I make it across and Candy stumbles up behind me a second later. Then Brigitte and the rest.

Diogo and his boys take us into the remains of the Blue Pavilion Hotel. The place is in better shape than downstairs but could still use a good hosing down. Hurricane and smaller oil lamps light the lobby and surrounding halls. The lobby furniture is patched with duct tape and random swatches of fabric. Some of the chairs have no legs and sit flat on the floor. All the glass in the panoramic windows is covered with heavy curtains, which makes sense. They don't want anyone on the beach to see the lights from up here. Duct tape covers slits in the curtain every ten feet or so. Spy holes. It's a damp, depressing place, but at least we're high enough that there isn't fungus and mold everywhere.

"Come sit by me," Hattie says to Delon.

She perches on a heavy wood-and-gilt chair against the wall. Her secondhand throne. Delon goes over and sits in a smaller chair slightly off to the side.

Up here, the Mangarms look a little less like the *Texas Chain Saw* psychobillies I thought they were on the stairs. In here, with their patched robes and mangy furs, they look like sad, faded royalty. The bluebloods of a kingdom as long gone and dead as Atlantis.

"Tell me why you're here," Hattie says. "You didn't come for potions since it's clear you have your own. You're not looking for sanctuary because . . . well, this isn't the place for it and we aren't the kind of people likely to give it."

Diogo and the boys chuckle and elbow one another. They love their mom. I wonder how long they're going to last when she finally kicks it. I give them six months.

"We're looking for a ghost," says Delon.

Hattie leans back on her throne and laces her fingers together.

"There are many ghosts in here. Are you looking for one in particular?"

"An old one. A little mad they say. He thinks he knows secrets."

Hattie nods.

"Yes. The old Roman. I know of him. Why do you want him?"

Delon smiles.

"We want to know his secrets."

Hattie glances back at us.

"There are six of you. That's a lot of people for a dead man's secrets."

"Too many people, if you ask me," says Delon. "I'd prefer to be doing this on my own."

"Then you're a fool," says Hattie. "No one goes alone here. Especially to the old ghost. He's at the very bottom of this castle keep, in the old baths in the basement."

"You mean a spa?"

Hattie makes a face.

"No. Roman baths. Saltwater baths from the sea. Some lunatic's idea of a health balm. Me, I'd rather bathe with rats than the fetid ocean that surrounds this place."

Finally, Hattie and I agree on something.

The rest of us sit on the patched furniture across the room from Her Royal Highness. Diogo and his crew stand around us. One with close-cropped white hair has noticed Candy's shiny backpack. He pokes at it with the tip of his sword. Candy pulls the pack onto her lap.

"We were hoping you might take us to the old Roman," Delon says.

Hattie shakes her head.

"Can't. It's not in our territory. It's the Shoggots' and we don't go in there. Hell, we don't even like to trade with them."

Diogo has noticed that Vidocq is still holding a vial in one hand. He points to it with a knife and Vidocq gives it to him with a smile. He shakes it and sniffs. Opens the top and gets a face full of acrid white smoke. We're all choking and coughing by the time the idiot gets the stopper back in.

Hattie looks at our gagging group and says, "I was just telling this gentleman how we don't like trading with the Shoggots, except some of the more gullible among us do, don't we, Diogo?"

He waves away some smoke and smiles at her.

"Yes, Mama."

"Those swords and knives the boys like to show off. Trust me, they don't have the wit among them to make something like that. That's Shoggot work. They're good makers. Especially sharp things."

"Maybe you could take us to meet them," says Delon.

She raises her eyebrows.

"When I called you a fool earlier, I meant it figuratively. Now you're making me think I might have a been a bit too generous."

"But you know how to contact them."

"Why would I do that?"

Delon reaches into his bag and pulls out another small bottle.

"Salt distilled from the River Gihon in Third Heaven, which cures all poisons."

Hattie takes it from him and holds it up to the light. Satisfied with what she sees, she puts it in her pocket with the Tears.

"What else have you got in that bag?" she says.

"Nothing that would interest a lady like you."

"Really? Why don't I have my boys take it and chuck you all over the balcony."

"Excuse me, ma'am," I say.

Hattie turns to me.

"Which one of these assholes do you like the least? I'll do you a favor and kill him first."

Diogo takes a step toward me, but Hattie stops him with a short wave.

"This one looked like bad news from the moment I saw him. What's wrong with his face? No one brings a man like that along who isn't looking for trouble."

"Not with you," Delon says. "Sometimes we don't get to pick and choose who we deal with, do we? Like you and the Shoggots. He's my Shoggot."

Hattie gives a short, snorting laugh that ends in ragged coughs.

"Here I was feeling sorry for us and you've got to haul around your own monster. Look at him. He'd like to put a knife into your back right now."

I shrug.

"Nothing personal. I always want to stab someone."

"This motley crew looks like more trouble than they're worth," says Hattie. "Give them to the Shoggots. May they choke on each other."

Hattie gets up and starts down a hall with her boys.

"You wait here while we prepare. Don't steal anything. I'll know if you do."

She points to a hotel surveillance camera that hasn't worked since disco was king.

Delon comes back to where the rest of us are sitting.

"Do you trust them?" I say.

He shrugs.

"What choice do we have?"

"That's not what I asked. Does the family keep its promises?"

"Tykho said yes, but you'll notice that she's not here."

I turn to the others.

"Keep your weapons handy but don't get itchy and start shooting at shadows."

Vidocq looks at the hall that the Mangarms went down.

"I'd love to know more about their potion making. When this is over, maybe I'll come back and do some trading of my own."

"You do and I'll tell Allegra," says Candy.

Vidocq narrows his eyes.

"God does not love snitches does he, Father?"

"I wouldn't know," said Traven. "We're no longer on speaking terms."

Hattie and the boys come back, but seeing them doesn't fill me with confidence. They've left the robes and furs behind and have armored up in a garbage-dump combination of shoulder pads, padded hockey pants, hard hats, and football and baseball helmets. Diogo is looking particularly proud of his mall-cop shirt and badge. They've left their swords behind and are carrying axes and baseball bats.

"I don't believe we dressed properly for the party," says Brigitte.

"Anyone with second thoughts can still go back," I say. "After this, I'm not so sure."

Candy punches my arm.

"Stop playing Nick Fury. We're all on board."

"I just want to make sure everybody knows."

Brigitte looks at Candy.

"He's so funny when he's playing Dad."

"Isn't he just," she says.

"Sorry," I say. "I'm more used to doing these things on my own. Not as part of a school field trip."

Vidocq says, "Consider that for once you'll have people to watch your back."

"You'll need them," says Hattie, and puts on a wired-front hockey helmet. "Let's go."

We walk the twelve floors back to street level. I have a feeling they have the rope-and-pulley system rigged to get up and down faster but they don't want us to see how it works. At the bottom, Hattie and her crew lead the way with lanterns and we head deeper into the mall.

There's rubble everywhere, but we're not in the worst of the wreckage. The big concrete slabs were probably dumped there during the time when the construction crew was looking for bodies. In the dim light, the random piles of stones make the place look like a haute couture Pompeii. We're moving in a single small pool of light. Our footsteps echo off the walls. Insects buzz around our heads.

We go through a food court the size of a football stadium. The place hasn't been looted. It's been ripped to pieces by people looking for every spare corn dog and chicken wing they could find. Farther on are the dried remains of an old water park. Slides, fountains, and indoor surfing with an artificial wave machine. Nails and hooks have been driven into the walls, and clothes, all rotten now, hang in the dark. Crushed cans and plastic bottles litter the floor. People used to wash and haul water to their little fiefdoms from here.

A desiccated body lies in the bone-dry fountain. The skull is crushed. Dried blood spray on the fallen concrete and in patches on the floor. I bet this was where they used to hold bazaars and where someone broke the truce big-time. I have a bad feeling I know who did it and we're strolling right to them.

Paper crunches under our feet. Images torn from books and magazines are glued to the floor in patterns. The pages have bubbled up, are slick in the humid air, but a clear path is laid out through them. A long straight line, then a tight turn to the left. The path doubles back on itself several times in smaller and smaller curves. The pattern stretches out all round us in a circle thirty or more feet across. It's a complex maze with a kind of cloverleaf at the center. A labyrinth. A meditation path, like you see in some old churches. The path of this labyrinth is paved with photos of the world outside Kill City. Hollywood. New York. Paris. Mountains. Someone doesn't want to forget where they came from. The world as a holy relic. It's funny to think of L.A.'s short con streets as some poor slob's idea of Heaven, but there it is.

Father Traven's light dips as he trips and almost goes down. Brigitte, right beside him, grabs him before he falls. I should have looked him over better when we got out of the van. He might be sleep-deprived, coming off the booze. Also, this is a pretty odd place to drag someone who's spent his life in libraries. Was it a mistake bringing him? Brigitte never gets too far from him and I don't think she would have let him come if she thought he couldn't handle it. Still, I need to keep my eye on him.

I move the beam of my small LED flashlight over the

empty storefronts as we move beyond the food court. They look ancient. Like caves for Neanderthals. This is the part of town the Flintstones don't come to after dark.

Sofa cushions lashed together are makeshift beds for whoever lived there. Pits for cook fires are gouged out of the linoleum floors. Gray piles of ash dumped outside the folding-glass doors.

Scuffling sounds and a whisper come from a derelict high-end stereo store. Something glitters inside. Eyes. I look around at the other stores. Lots more eyes in there. I pull the Colt and cock the hammer, holding it up so everyone can see.

"Sit back and watch the show, folks. Do nothing more."

We walk for over an hour, sticking to shadows when we can. We only move out into the open when there's no other way around piles of rubble. I don't know about anyone else, but I can hear footsteps keeping pace with us one or two floors up. I walk closer to Hattie.

"Friends?"

She shakes her head.

"No one to be worried about. A mongrel Lurker pack. Bunch of softies. We've put them in their place before."

Diogo and some of the other boys throw stones up into the dark. They bounce off the walls and shatter already broken windows. You can tell from the sound that they never hit whoever's following us.

One of Hattie's other sons, a tall boy she called Doolittle, drops his pants and moons the upper floors. A second later, a stone flies down from the dark and hits him in the ass. He screams and curses. Hattie cuffs him on the ear.

"That's what you get when you act a fool."

Up ahead comes the unmistakable sound of skin slamming into skin. Boots colliding with something soft. Heavy, short breaths. Three gulping air hard. One grunting and coughing as each kick threatens to collapse bruised lungs. I run toward the sound.

The three on their feet look like extra-hard-luck street people. Layers of filthy coats and patched pants give them the look of bears in wino costumes. Whoever is on the floor is trying to fight back, throwing kicks and punches, but from that angle they don't have enough power to make the grizzlies back off.

Still running, I kick the closest one in the small of the back and he goes down on his face, teeth or something else important clattering across the tile floor. The one on my right swings a wedge of scalpel-sharp glass mounted on the end of a chair leg. I punch him in the throat, take the homemade hatchet, and slam the wooden grip into his knees, knocking him off his feet. The last of the guys is smaller than the other two. He has a butcher knife, and by the way he moves, it looks like he knows how to use it. I point the Colt between his eyes.

"Put it on the ground."

He does it.

"Now scoot before I get a finger cramp and this thing goes off."

He backs away slowly until he's out of the light. I hear someone running away and put the gun back in my pocket.

Whoever was taking the beating is still on the floor, but at least his eyes are open. He's skinny. Young-looking and small. Not much bigger than a kid. He's dressed from head to toe in dirty, loose gray clothes that look like heavy pajamas.

"You okay?"

He doesn't say anything.

"I don't think they'll be back for a while. You can get up."

The kid struggles to his feet, holding his left elbow tight to his side. His face is bruised and bloody, his upper lip swollen.

"You got a name?"

He moves slightly to his right. Hesitates. That's when I see the sword lying a few feet away. The kid dives for it, rolling more gracefully than I would have expected with his injuries. The blade is beautiful. Perfect, polished steel. It glints in the harsh LED light. Maybe the kid knows that. He flashes it, making several passes, light shining from the flat of the blade and leaving trails in the air. For a second I'm blind and I put my hand in my pocket for my gun. By the time I can see again, the kid is gone. Quiet little bastard. I didn't hear a thing.

From behind me Candy says, "Friend of yours?"

"Apparently not."

"Maybe instead of your blunderbuss you should use your na'at. Shoot the gun once and everyone in the Lower Forty-eight will know we're here."

"Yeah, but no one in Kill City knows what a na'at is, so it doesn't help to flash it. A gun is like love. The universal language."

"I can't decide if that's poetry or a desperate cry for help."

"We should keep moving," says Hattie.

The dark closes in around us again, like we're marching straight up a dinosaur's ass. Or we're lost in an old haunted fortress in a Euro-horror flick. *Tombs of the Blind Dead.* A hapless bunch of schmucks trapped in a cracked palace with an army of Templar zombies.

How do Kill City's residents live like this? I remember hearing about people living in New York's abandoned subway tunnels. Mole People, they call them. Some scavenge outside during the day, but others never leave the tunnels. I guess you get more than used to the dark. You come to think of it as home. It sounds a bit like Hell. It's the most awful place you can imagine, but after a while you start relying on the filth and blood, the cozy familiarity of betrayal and casual brutality. It's more than coping. It's adaptation. You go into the dark one species and mutate to fit your surroundings. Grow better eyes and ears. Get used to the feel of the air so you can tell when something is coming at you. After a while you're so suited to the environment you're a whole new species. Except for the ones who can't make the change. They never stop struggling with the dark. They're always looking for a way out. Those are the ones who build paper meditation walks dedicated to the world or kill so cleanly for their Hellion master that it's completely unexpected when you finally cut their throats. Of course, if you make it out, what you'll find is you're now a stranger in two worlds because the dark changes you and you'll never got back to what you were before you got lost.

"Look at this," says Vidocq. He's crouched on the floor looking at a plastic water bottle. He holds it up. "This is new. So is this." He picks up a half-smoked cigarette and sniffs it. Holds it out to me. I sniff it too. I pull off the filter and examine the tobacco at that end. It's fresh.

I say, "Tykho told me that someone else knows about the

ghost. I guess we're not alone. The question is, are they ahead of us or are they lost and stopped here to get their bearings?"

"We have to assume the worst," says Delon.

"I agree," says Brigitte. "We have to assume that they know more than we do."

"Or they're lost and are doing the simple thing," says Candy.

I say, "What's that?"

"They're circling around behind and following us since we're the ones with not one but two certified guides."

I look at Delon and Hattie.

"How much longer?" I ask the old woman.

"We go down another level just ahead. It will be harder for anyone following us to keep up."

"Let's get there and shake these fuckers."

Up ahead we come to a door marked AUTHORIZED PERSONNEL ONLY. Diogo goes in first, and when we're through, he takes out a padlock and secures the door from inside. The lock is big, but I'm not convinced it will keep any motivated people out for long. Still, any lead it might give us is a help. When we start moving again I make sure that Delon stays up front with whichever son is leading the way.

We go down to a floor with mall administrative offices and lockers full of maintenance equipment. It's cooler down here. Less green with vegetation, but there are thick black patches of mold over all the air vents and the air is thick. Water drips down from overhead pipes. Vlad the Impaler could move in and start scaring peasants from this doomsday dungeon.

Hattie looks me over in the pale lantern light.

"You're Sub Rosa, aren't you?" she says.

"How did you know?"

"You stink of it."

"Sub Rosa?"

"Judgment. About my family."

"Don't take this the wrong way, but I don't give a rat's ass—half a rat's ass—about your family. Besides, I've seen worse."

"Where?"

"Right in town. You remember the Springheels?"

"Charm makers. Used to be high-and-mighty but aren't held in much regard anymore."

"If there were any left, you'd be fighting over the same stale pretzels and moldy Big Macs."

"What happened to them?"

"The last son, Jack, he had a fetish for demons. He called up an eater one day and the party didn't go the way he planned."

"The eater got him?"

"Technically, a High Plains Drifter, a zombie—"

"I know what a Drifter is. Just because I live in the boonies, don't count me as stupid. Now go on."

"Anyway, a Drifter got him in the end, but if it hadn't been one of them, an eater would have done it sooner or later. He was begging for it."

She thinks about it for a minute.

"I suppose we look quite respectable compared to that."

"Yeah. You're mother of the year and I'm king of the Mouseketeers. We're a couple of lottery winners with money to burn."

"You'd have killed my boys back there, wouldn't you?"

"Every one of them."

"Is that how you got that face? Doing things of that sort?"

"This? I was skipping through a field and fell on some dandelions. They hurt more than you'd think."

She looks at me.

"Who's the little Lurker?"

"Don't worry about her. She's with me."

"I thought so. The face of a killer and a Jade on your arm. Your mama must be proud."

"My mother wouldn't know a Jade from a lawn flamingo."

"Once we drop you off, you won't be coming back, will you?"

"Much as I enjoyed the room service, I have another hotel to get back to."

"I have your word on that? We won't see you again?"

"Hell yes."

"All right, then."

"So, you're calling it off?"

"You mean my boys killing you all and leaving you here in the tunnels? I expect I will."

"Good call."

"We're done here."

Hattie falls back to where Diogo is walking and says something to him.

"Aw, Mama."

She slaps him.

"You mind me."

"Yes, ma'am."

We go down a long side corridor to an unmarked door. Doolittle tries the handle. It doesn't open.

"Trouble, Mama," he says.

"Allow me," says Vidocq, and gently pushes the boy out of the way. He takes a leather wrap from his pocket and opens it to reveal a set of delicate tools. Brigitte and Traven hold lights over his head and he takes a couple of them and picks the lock.

Hattie coughs and says, "A good man to have around."

"You should hear him sing karaoke."

Hattie turns to the group.

"This wasn't always locked. Guess the Shoggots are even worse about folks wandering into their territory. You sure you want to do this?"

"We have no choice," says Delon.

Hattie looks at me.

"What kind of secrets can a dead man have that you need so much?"

"I'm hoping he knows where I left my car keys."

She shakes her head.

"There's no helping some people."

A *click* echoes off the walls and the door opens a few inches.

"*Et voilà*," says Vidocq.

"Voilà yourself," says Delon. "Look at this."

On the other side of the door, twisted wire cables are bolted to both sides of the wall and the base of the doorjamb. They stretch away from us into the gloom, and it takes me a second to figure out why. There's stars above but nothing below the door except a wide rocky chasm. Sometime in the last few years this section of roof collapsed, taking several levels of floor with it. I point my flashlight down, but I can't see the bottom. The cables form a V-shaped bridge. Two tightly spaced cables are the bottom of the V with a single waist-high cable on each side to form the top. *Rickety* isn't the word for the thing. I look at Hattie.

"You're fucking kidding me."

She crosses her arms.

"You want to go? This is the way."

Delon has stepped back a few feet from the door. He's looking down the hall.

"I'm guessing this isn't on your map."

"Nothing even like it."

"Perfect."

Hattie smiles.

"We can go forward or we can go back, but either way I keep Nehebkau's Tears and the Gihon salt."

"Then we keep going," I say. I turn to the others. "Agreed?"

Everyone but Delon gives me a yes.

"You have something to say, Paul?"

He looks at his feet.

"I didn't know about this. I'm not good with heights."

Beautiful. So Norris Quay is afraid of heights. What an exciting piece of trivia. You'd think fucking Atticus would fix something like that when he made his windup clones. Maybe crossing the Grand Canyon bareback never came up before.

"We're all going. That means you too."

"I'm not sure I can."

"We're going to need the map in your head when we get across. That means if I have to tie your arms and legs and kick you across like a soccer ball, you're going."

"Threats don't help."

"That's not a threat. A threat is when I say if I have to dangle you over the side and drag you across like a sack of dirty laundry, I'll do that too."

"Stop it," says Brigitte. "Can't you see you're making it worse?"

"If you can pep-talk him across, be my guest. But we can't wait around here all night."

Brigitte talks to Delon quietly. He nods but doesn't look up from the floor.

I say, "Hattie, you and your boys have done this before. You head across and show us how it's done."

"Of course," she says.

She waves to Diogo and the others and they start across, going one by one. Even for them it's not an easy crossing. The cables were probably tight once upon a time, but over the years they've stretched and the whole bridge has started to go slack. The crossing looks like it's all about a slow and steady pace, checking your balance with each step. Lean to one side or the other and the whole bridge tips with you. Diogo shows off by tipping both ways during his crossing, righting himself easily each time. It makes my stomach clench each time he does it.

Then it's my turn. I look across the chasm at the Mangarms. I can't tell if the bridge is fifty feet long or a mile. I put my right foot on the two cables that form the walkway and test my weight. They hold. I'm kind of disappointed. If the whole thing fell down, I wouldn't have to go across. Now I have to pretend to be brave. I grab the two side cables and start across.

Each step is a new adventure in bullshit. What kind of

sadist invented bridges like this? I've seen pictures of them, so I know they exist other places in the world and that people use them every day, scurrying across like squirrels on a telephone line. I'd like to see one of them try it in Kill City over a bottomless pit. There's no way the other team came this way. With any luck, that means we're ahead of them. Unless Hattie is taking us the long way around for a laugh, which I wouldn't put past her.

I don't know if it's taken two minutes or a lunar month, but finally I make it across. Hattie's boys grab and pull me the last couple of feet onto the concrete ledge. I turn back to the others and wave like it was nothing at all, hoping I don't piss myself before the rest of them come over.

Candy is next. She puts out a foot, grabs the side cables, and crouches like a tiger, getting a feel for the bridge. She stays that way for several seconds. Long enough that I think she's frozen in place. Then she sprints forward. The bridge wobbles and sways under her, but she doesn't miss a step. What took me minutes to do, she does in a few seconds. Hattie's boys reach for her on our end, but she ignores them and jumps the last few feet onto solid ground herself. Cheers start up from the other side of the chasm. Candy waves and bows.

I put my arm around her shoulders.

"Show-off."

"Scaredy cat."

Father Traven is next. Except for Delon, he's the one I'm most worried about. I'm not convinced his footing is all that good on flat ground. While a moving walkway doesn't seem like suicide, it's still extremely stupid. There's nothing we can do but see what happens.

Vidocq and Brigitte shout encouragement as Traven plods across step-by-step. He's fine until he hits the middle, where the slack in the cables is worst. His feet wobble. He gets a death grip on the two side cables, and teeters, trying to right himself. Each time his balance starts to come back, he loses it again. He's stuck there, unable to go forward or back.

I'm so focused on Traven that I don't see Brigitte start across. She's almost as fast as Candy. When she reaches Traven she stands behind him, moving her weight back and forth, trying to counteract his movements and balance the cables. Gradually it works. Her added weight and sense of balance settle the cables into place. They come across together, a step at a time. When they're close enough, I pull Traven off the wires to clear Brigitte's path while Candy grabs her.

Traven walks to the nearest wall and collapses there. Brigitte collapses next to him. He takes her hand and they sit together in the dark.

Delon is next. Vidocq practically has to shove him onto the cables. Delon stands at the end, petrified, looking down into the chasm.

"Paul," yells Candy.

He tilts his head up slightly.

"Look at me," she says. "Don't look down. Just at me."

After a couple of minutes Delon takes an actual step forward. Then another. Every time he stops moving, he looks down, so Candy yells to him.

"You're doing fine. Look up at me. Keep looking here."

He makes it all the way to the middle of the bridge before one of the cables breaks. One of the two walkway cables comes loose with a metallic snap, coiling back to the far end and slamming into the wall. Delon goes down on one knee, desperately holding on to the side cables as the whole bridge bucks and sways. The sound of strained bolts and wires echoes off the cavern walls. After several minutes the bridge stabilizes enough for Delon to stand.

Candy starts to call to him again, but I put a hand on her shoulder. At this point I don't want anything to surprise or confuse him. Step by uncertain step Delon gets a little closer to our end. Finally he's close enough for Diogo and the boys to grab. They pull him off the wires and he pukes over the side, down into the chasm like he's trying to get even with it.

Vidocq is last to cross. He's not a big man but he's not petite and he's wearing a heavy greatcoat. Not standard issue for the Flying Wallendas. He tests the cables before he steps across, shaking the two side cables and gently putting his weight on the walkway. Satisfied, he steps back into the door and opens his coat. I don't have to see him clearly to know what he's doing. He's drinking a potion. Then another. And a third. He shudders. Breathes in and out a few times and steps onto the bridge. And sprints like a goddamn madman all the way across, not touching the two side wires and, from the way it looks, barely touching the bottom one. The wires are letting out sharp metallic screams, straining under him. He jumps the last few feet. I don't know if he felt it or if he just got lucky, but just as he launches himself, one of the two side cables breaks. Vidocq ducks as it snaps back a few inches over his head. He's shaking and his face is slick with sweat when he reaches our side.

"Not bad, old man," I tell him.

"Thank you," he says, pulling another potion from inside his coat. He downs it and tosses the bottle away. A few seconds later his breathing and heartbeat head back to normal.

"So, what did you take back there?" I ask. "Some kind of bat juice that let you float across?"

He shakes his head.

"No. One potion for balance. One for bravery. And a third to not give a damn about the other two."

Hattie's boys huddle at the edge of the chasm examining the wires. Diogo hawks up phlegm and spits it over the side. He and his brothers watch it drop like they're watching the Super Bowl.

"I don't suppose anyone following us will be able to come this way," says Traven.

I take out the black blade and slice through the remaining cables so that the bridge collapses into the chasm. There's silence and then a huge metallic rattle as it hits the far wall.

"Do you people intend to completely destroy my home?" says Hattie.

"You got paid," I say.

"We're really sorry," says Candy.

"No one ever leaves Kill City, so whoever built the bridge is still around," I say. "If it's that important, they'll come back and fix it."

"And how long will that take?" says Hattie.

I say, "From the way you talked, it sounded like you didn't come down here too often, so what do you care?"

"It's the principle."

"I doubt that. You're not the chamber of commerce. You don't give a damn about anybody else but your clan. If you did you would have said something when I stopped those guys from stomping the kid back there. I think you just want to shake us down for more gifts. We might have another bauble or two but not until we actually get somewhere. And if there are any swamps up ahead or giant spiders or fire-breathing fan dancers, you better say so before we get there. No more surprises."

She laughs and claps her hands once together.

"No surprises? In Kill City? Boy, you couldn't have chosen worse if you're looking for a place with no more astonishments."

Her sons laugh along with her. Hattie goes to the wall and takes an oil lamp down from a nail. Diogo gives her a match, which she strikes against the rough concrete. It sparks and she holds the flame to the lamp wick. It catches and yellow light fills the chamber. You can feel everyone's mood lift in the warm glow of the lamp. Our LEDs and flashlights made Kill City look like a broken-down space station. Seeing the place lit by fire, I feel like we're back on planet Earth.

Hattie opens another door and holds the lamp high.

"With all the noise you fools made, half of Kill City probably knows where we are. But I want to make sure those ahead see us coming. Don't want to spook anyone."

She leads us down another level, where the feel is different. Like we've moved into a ragged zone outsiders weren't meant to see. Bare cinder-block walls. Exposed ductwork and steam pipes overhead. We slosh through a couple of inches of dirty water from leaking pipes. No one talks. Hattie is out front, leading us like Moses through the desert. Her boys are spread out around her, as nervous as she is fierce.

The passage narrows ahead. We're getting into areas with heavier wreckage. Slabs of the upstairs floor lie on either side of us. Looking up through the hole, I can see the night sky. It's a flat, gray-black slate, all the stars washed out by the lights of Santa Monica. In the dim pools of light from the lantern and our flashlights, the rusted rebar and rows of workers' coat hooks along the walls look like props from a Roger Corman torture chamber.

Ahead is a narrow tunnel under the wreckage.

"It's hands and knees here," Hattie says.

She doesn't miss a step. Gets right down on her belly, sets the lantern in front of her, and crawls, pushing the light ahead. Her sons follow.

I shine my light into the tunnel and lean my weight on the debris. Nothing moves. The pile is solid and the passage ahead looks clear. Still, I can't see what's at the far end.

"You want to take point on this one, Paul?" I say.

"Sure."

"You're not claustrophobic?"

"Not at all."

"Great. Scream if you see dragons."

"Very funny."

Everyone takes off their bags and packs. All I have is a flashlight, so I go through next. I don't want to stick around and watch Candy trying to maneuver her *Kekko Kamen* bag so it doesn't get scratched up.

The tunnel is maybe twenty tight feet from end to end. Crawling on my elbows takes a minute or so to come out the other side. We're a long way from the world now. Dug down into the earth like bugs. Even if the bridge was still intact, there's no going back. The team following us could be around the first corner. Until I know who they are, I don't want to take a chance on running into them. That means we have no choice but to follow wherever Hattie wants to take us, and she knows it. On our hands and knees it feels like we've crossed a new barrier. We're moving forward but I don't like it.

Candy comes through the tunnel next, followed by Vidocq, Brigitte, and Traven.

The new room looks a lot like the last one, probably just an extension of it. The same rough walls and unfinished feel.

"Where to next?" I say.

"We're about there," says Hattie.

There's a grunt and a whirring sound from the other end of the room, then the growl of a generator coming to life. Bright halogen work lights come on all around us. I go blind for a few seconds.

When I can see again, there they are. I have to give it to the Shoggots. They know how to make an entrance.

The passage opens onto a wide concrete room with a metal catwalk overhead. At least twenty members of the Shoggot tribe are lined around the walls and on the walk. And they are dead-dog ugly.

Hattie and the boys pull up short. We stop behind them.

All of the Shoggots, the men and the women, are in looted designer suits. High-end stuff. But the silks and expensive wools are covered in grime and dried blood. Probably the Shoggots' own. They're definitely human, but they've been holed up down here working on their bodies for so long that at first glance they look like some peculiar flavor of Lurker. Their teeth have been filed to points. Some have split their nostrils. Others have cut off their noses or lips. Their cheeks are adorned with ritual scars and metal. Most have similar body mods on their throats, arms, or chests and many of the cuts are held open with metal hooks embedded in their skin. Some of the cuts look fresh. Others are old and infected. I see maggots in more than a few of the deeper cuts. I wish I'd quizzed Hattie on how crazy these crazies were before we came down here.

A tall Shoggot in the middle of the catwalk rests his hands on the top of the rail.

"Hattie. Lovely to see you. And you've brought friends."

"Hello, Ferox. These aren't friends. They're travelers looking for the old Roman."

"And what good is that old madman to anyone?"

Delon pushes his way up beside Hattie.

"If it's a matter of payment, I have things to trade for information."

Ferox stands up straight, scowling.

"Who was talking to you, traveler? What you want couldn't matter less to us."

Delon reaches into his pack and pulls out a long, thin knife.

"This is a Liston knife, once used by Robert Liston himself. Before the days of anesthetic, he was one of the most famous and fastest amputation surgeons in Europe."

Ferox takes a step forward to get a better look at the blade. He gestures to a couple of Shoggots on the floor nearby.

"Bring it to me," he says.

While they're carrying it up to Ferox I get next to Delon.

"Are you stupid? Giving these psychos a knife?"

"I'm trying to make us a deal."

Ferox takes his time looking over the Liston, holding it from different angles to see how straight it is. Moving it through the light to test its sheen. He makes a shallow cut inside one of his wrists, testing the amount of pressure needed to break the skin. He smiles and looks down at us.

"Hello, Officer," he says. "Would you come up here, please?"

It takes a minute before anyone figures out who he's talking to. Then Diogo takes a tentative step forward in his mall-cop shirt.

"Yes. You. That's right. Please come up and join me."

Diogo takes a couple of more steps and stops.

"Don't do it, kid," I say.

He looks at me.

"Diogo," says Hattie.

He's frozen in the middle of the room. His dim brain is overloading.

Ferox looks annoyed.

"Bring the pig up here," he says.

Shoggots grab Diogo and drag him, kicking and screaming, up the catwalk.

Hattie and the boys don't do anything. They're paralyzed. I reach for the Colt but decide to wait it out. Even with hoodoo, I don't know if I can take on this many crazies at once.

A couple of Shoggots hold Diogo as Ferox raises the kid's right arm.

"If I remember correctly from my reading, the technique was like this. A single deep curved slice, severing the skin and connective tissue in one cut. Let's see if I'm right."

He draws the blade across Diogo's biceps, digging deeper into the skin until the Liston disappears inside. He draws it all the way around so that both ends of the cut meet. Diogo screams and thrashes in the Shoggots' arms. When Ferox is finished they let him go. He falls onto his face and vomits over the side of the catwalk.

Hattie holds on to Doolittle's arm, whispering over and over, "My boy. My boy."

"Not bad for a first time, don't you agree?" The other Shoggots nod and grin. The ones with lips, at least. "We neglected to bring a saw, so we'll have to go through the bone later. Tie off his arm so he doesn't bleed to death. Leave the travelers for now. Bring me the other boys."

"No!" Hattie shouts.

Ferox points at her with the Liston knife.

"I told you not to come back here, Hattie."

I pull the Colt and take two quick shots at Ferox. The first just misses and he hits the deck before the second can get him. Two Shoggots on my level rush me and I put a bullet through their foreheads. Out of the corner of my eye I see vials fly by as Vidocq throws his potions. Candy blasts away with her folding pistol while Brigitte takes careful single shots. Delon has disappeared into the back with Father Traven. It looks like his gun is jammed.

Ferox whispers an incantation and deflects Candy and Brigitte's shots into the ceiling. So the Shoggots are Sub Rosa. I was afraid of that. Ferox tosses a ball of white-hot plasma at Doolittle, burning him from the inside like he'd swallowed a pound of phosphorus. A group of Shoggots knocks Hattie down and drags away the rest of the boys as they scream, "Mama!"

I bark some Hellion and send a stream of fat, needle-sharp projectiles at Ferox. He sees them coming and suddenly his arm looks like a skinny porcupine when he raises it to block the needles.

This time he throws a plasma ball at me. I deflect it with some defensive hoodoo and knock it into a big Shoggot rushing at me with Diogo's ax.

Before I can go after Ferox again, a couple of nearby Shoggots throw their own flashy hoodoo my way. Muscles split open beneath the open cuts in their arms and shoot out at me like quivering pink tentacles. I blast one of the tentacle throwers with the same needles I used on Ferox, catching him in the face. Another tentacle latches on to my Kissi arm and pulls hard enough to knock me off balance. I grab the black blade from under my coat and slice through the muscle in one blow. The Shoggot screams and is joined by two more.

All three hammer me with hexes. I can barely throw up enough of my own defensive hoodoo to keep them off me. I can't see Candy or any of the others anymore. I think they've been pushed back behind me to the door.

I pocket the knife and grab the na'at. Swinging it out like a sawtooth bullwhip, I take out two of my attackers. But three more join the fight. Even in the arena I never went up against this many armed fighters at once.

On the catwalk I catch a glimpse of Ferox hexing rubble, tossing it at me like hundred-mile-an-hour fastballs. I bob and weave, trying to keep off the nearby assholes, when a piece of brick slams into my ribs. I slip and go down on one knee as more debris hurricanes around me. Another brick slams into the back of my head. The nearby Shoggots keep up a stream of blasts. I can't catch my breath, trying to keep up with them. Blood runs down the side of my head and into my eye. It burns and blinds me on one side. I turn just in time to see a pipe flying at me. And the world goes dark.

I'M LOST. I'M not sure if I'm in Hell, L.A., or Kill City. It feels like I'm in the arena. I'm hunting something and I'm being hunted. I've seen the water and the smokes they left behind. But this doesn't look like the arena. Concrete corridors alternate between long straight lines and sharp turns left and right that double back on themselves. Shit. I'm in a maze. I was just in one of these, wasn't I? Something like it. I was definitely lost, with something on my tail and closing fast.

Whoever is behind me doesn't feel human. Even if it was a Lurker, I'd pick up breathing or a heartbeat. Maybe it's an angel. Maybe Aelita? Maybe Medea Bava has learned some hoodoo to hide her breath and heart so I can't see her coming.

Maybe it's simpler than that. I can't detect what's behind me because what's behind me isn't alive. What is it, then? Vampires? Is Tykho here to take the 8 Ball from me? I doubt it. She's subtler than that. Maybe it's Paul. Paul and Trevor and all their mechanical brothers.

Imagine all of L.A. filled with windup men wandering empty-headed and waiting for orders and directions and purpose. That's L.A. in a nutshell. A city of driven creatures, but no one is a hundred percent sure what they're driven toward.

Wealth. Fame. Power. Love. Revenge. These are all the obvious end points for the citizens of a spectral city, but none of them quite encompass a final goal. That's more fragile. Something that slips away like smoke the moment it's in your hands. It's a moonshine cocktail of desperation and desire, the certainty that you can find perfection through sheer willpower and the cold terror that if you do reach the goal it will have twisted into something new. A new fevered need born of the search for this one. Searching for the next goal will breed another. And on and on. L.A. and Kill City full of Pinocchios with whirring gears for brains, all wanting to be real boys but sunk in the certainty that they'll never become anything because they're nothing. They came from nothing and are headed for a further and harder nothing. Condemned by their own stupidity to end up buried deep underground with the losers, the dead, and other people's trash.

WHEN I COME to, the first thing I see is my coat wadded up on the floor across the room, which is weird because I was just wearing it and don't remember taking it off.

Gradually, the rest of the room comes into focus. More important is that when I try to move I can't. I'm chained to a wall.

I'm in a high-ceilinged room with Ferox and a handful of other Shoggots. Some have rags pressed against fresh wounds. A few have to be held up by their shithead Shoggot pals. Ferox is arranging tools and delicate surgical instruments on a table. He has the Liston knife in a belt around his waist. I pull on the chains to see if I can break them or work them out of the wall. Nothing. Just my luck. These fuckers are probably dining on rats down here, but when they left the city for this shithole, they brought their hoodoo restraints with them.

Ferox sees me squirming.

"There you are, sleepyhead. I was getting worried that I'd hit you too hard. But you're with us now, yes? Say something to let us know you understand what's happening."

"Is this the right bus? I need to get off at La Cienega."

Ferox nods, still arranging his toys.

"There we are," he says. "Wit so hot it almost burns. So good to have you back among the living."

"Speak for yourself. I was happy asleep."

"You wouldn't want to miss your coming-out party, would you, Sandman Slim?" He looks over at me. "Yes, even down here we've heard of the infamous Sandman Slim. You and I have a lot in common, you know."

"You love Night Ranger, too? Unchain me and I'll buy us a cold six."

He smiles, showing his sharp, ragged teeth.

"I meant that we're both nephilim. Though we Shoggots are a slightly more exotic variety."

"That means what? You're a mix of angel and pig fucker?"

"While you're a mix of ordinary angel and a mortal woman, we come from fallen angels."

I shake my head.

"I've been to Hell, Simple Simon. The only Hellion that can come to earth is Lucifer. The others are all stuck Downtown, going severely batshit. And even Lucifer can't make a nephilim. No fallen angel can."

"But we're living proof that it is possible. And when Father

Lucifer leads his army to take the earth for Hell, we'll be there by his side and sit at his right hand in Hell for all eternity."

I can't help but laugh a little. It makes my head hurt.

"Damn, did you back the wrong pony. Lucifer isn't coming back to skull-fuck the earth. The Angra Om Ya are. And they're not going to be impressed by your story any more than I am."

Ferox furrows his brow.

"I was hoping that being brothers of a sort, we could be civilized with each other."

"Is that why I'm chained to a wall?"

"No. That's so you won't hurt yourself moving around too much once we start the experiments."

"What experiments?"

"So, you don't believe we are who we know we are?"

"I know exactly what you are."

"Please enlighten me," Ferox says. He turns to the other Shoggots. "Everybody listen. We're about to get a lesson in metaphysics from Sandman Slim himself."

I know I should keep my mouth shut, but now it's too late to back down. All I can do is press harder.

"I don't know your family's history, but I know this from looking at you. You're not nephilim. You're losers and fuck-ups. You especially, Ferox. You drove your family from up there in the city into this sewer, and looking for a way not to have to blow your brains out, you came up with a sad fucking fairy tale about what special little snowflakes you are and how you wanted to be down here all along waiting for Ragnarok. But the Devil isn't coming for you. God isn't coming for you. You've heard of Sandman Slim? You're one up on me because I've never heard of you assholes and I bet no one I know has either. You can scare these Kill City clans, but out of here you're just another sideshow act. All you need is a two-headed calf and a pickled punk."

Ferox comes over and looks at me hard.

"How many scars do you think you have?"

"No idea."

"Let's start a new count. One."

He takes out the Liston knife and draws it across my chest, making a deep, hard cut. I grit my teeth to keep from making a sound. Just because I'm hard to kill doesn't mean that bullets and knives hurt me any less than anyone else.

He turns to the other Shoggots.

"Who here has a watch? I'd like to know how long it takes for that cut to heal. Time it, please."

He goes back to his instruments, wiping my blood off the Liston. I wonder if he did all the body mods to the other Shoggots himself or did he encourage them to do it to themselves?

He says, "Before you got here, we were planning on catching the old Roman ourselves. You see, we know about the angel and that the old ghost knows her secret. After we made him tell us what it is, we were going to sell him. But I think we'll ease him onto the back burner because now we have you. And I think Sandman Slim will fetch a better price. After I've finished my research, of course."

"I've got some research for you. Why don't you cut me loose and I'll take you to meet Lucifer and he can tell you to your face what morons you are and maybe you can haul your asses out of Kill City and do something for your family."

Ferox comes over with a magnifying glass. He sticks his fat thumb into the cut on my chest. I try not to, but I flinch a little. He studies the blood on his fingertips, and when he's done he wipes it on my torn shirt. He rips it open the rest of the way and starts examining my scars.

"Look, if this is your way of getting to know me, why don't you just friend me on Facebook?"

He lowers the magnifying glass and goes to a brazier in the corner of the room. Comes back with a small branding iron and holds it to my chest until the skin sizzles. When I'm good and cooked he tosses the iron back into the brazier and goes back to looking over my scars.

"Would someone please time how long the burn takes to set? Thank you."

He looks up at me.

"What I want to do is take you apart. Down to the smallest sliver of your being. I want to see you laid out on a table like a flesh puzzle and put you back together again in my own image. I've never had the heart to test the limits of nephilim body on my own family, and even though you and I are different sorts of nephilim, I suspect that the results will be applicable. Don't you? For instance, I wonder how many organs you can lose before you die."

He goes back to the table and brings back a scalpel. I wish I could say that this is the first time I've been tortured like this, but it isn't. The Hellions cut me up pretty nicely when I first got to Hell. They'd never seen a live human before. But for them, it was mostly just having a good time, kicking around the weak new kid. Ferox, on the other hand, seems like the real thing. A science groupie with a grudge against

God, who rejected his family, and the Devil, who hasn't rescued them. And right now my sorry carcass is the complaint department.

Ferox says, "Don't worry. I have no interest in killing you. I'm going to take you to the brink, and then let you rest and heal. When you have, we'll move on to other tests. All right? Good. Now hold still. This might sting a little."

He drives the whole head of the scalpel into my gut a few inches below the navel and starts dragging the blade north. My body shakes. I can't help it. It's rejecting the blade, this situation, the whole world, trying to shake it off like a dog with mange. I breathe deep. In through my nose and out through my mouth. I won't give this fucker the satisfaction of screaming. But I might faint and that would be embarrassing too. He cuts up three, four, five inches and stops. My legs and boots are warm with blood. My head spins. I hold my head up, not wanting to black out.

"It's been bothering me," says Ferox. "Why are you only wearing one glove? Did you lose the other?"

He pulls my glove off, and dazed as I am, I can still see his eyes go wide when he sees my Kissi hand. He pushes up my sleeve. Seeing that the prosthetic goes up farther, he slices my sleeve all the way to my shoulder, where the Kissi arm and I are attached.

"Glorious. Glorious. That's not a gift from God. Who have you been spending time with, you naughty boy?"

Ferox taps the scalpel on the arm, listening to it like it's a tuning fork. He probes it with the tip and tries to slice it. When it doesn't work he presses harder until the scalpel's head snaps off. He drops it and goes back to the brazier. It gives me a moment to breathe. I'm lucky that the feeling in the Kissi arm is a little dull. But even though he can't hurt the arm, I can feel everything he's doing. I'm getting paranoid about the cut in my belly. Like if I squirm around too much, my intestines or my liver might fall out.

Ferox comes back with the piece of flaming wood and holds it under the arm. This time I can't hold back. I don't scream but he knows why I'm groaning. His cut-up face splits into a wide smile.

"You can feel it, can't you? Not only does this lovely thing move, but it feels too. It's miraculous."

He turns to the other Shoggots.

"Who here thinks I deserve an arm like this?"

My head is spinning like a carnival teacup ride. The crowd, on the other hand, is as excited as if he was busting out with an encore of "Free Bird."

"Get me the saw," he says.

I'm losing too much blood. I can't stay awake to fight him. Who am I trying to fool? I'm way beyond fighting anyone. I can barely stay awake. Any second now, my insides are going to slide onto the floor.

I feel pressure on my arm as Ferox tests the best angles to start sawing, but where my head is taking me everything is fine and nothing hurts.

SCREAMS WAKE ME up. How shocked am I as it slowly comes to me that the screaming isn't coming from my mouth but from across the room? I can't exactly see what's happening. It looks like a fight. I think.

The brazier is on the floor and the wall is crawling with

weird shadows. I can see the Shoggots all right. Then something else. Gray streaks. Flashes of knives and swords. One of the streaks stops for a second. It's a man in a gray suit that covers his whole body except for his eyes. There's something else. He's short. About four feet tall and slashing away with a blade almost as long as he is tall. He and the other blurs move like psycho-fuck pint-size ninjas.

Then there are hands on me. Someone undoes the chains and I slip to the floor. The world is a series of blurry snapshots. I think I hear a different kind of shouting. Maybe see Candy's face. Or maybe my insides really are gone and this is a new way to feel death. That's okay. It seems like I'm lying down, even if I'm not. I'd rather die comfortably than die chained to the wall in some asshole's man cave.

And that's pretty much all there is before I stop caring and pass out.

I WAKE UP on a blanket. Candy is next to me, cross-legged, holding my human hand. We're back in the big room where the fight with the Shoggots first started. Everyone else—Brigitte, Vidocq, Traven, and Delon—is there too, talking, eating, and drinking with the gray mini-ninjas. The fuckers might be small but they're covered in an impressive amount of Shoggot blood.

"How long was I out?"

"A couple of hours. Think you can move?"

I try to sit up and make it up onto my elbows. Candy has to pull me up the rest of the way. I put my hand on my stomach. Someone has stitched me up and wrapped me in a bandage. Some kind of healing ointment seeps through the material.

"Vidocq did it," says Candy. "I think he's been getting lessons from Allegra."

Delon comes over and kneels next to us.

"How are you feeling?"

"How far are we from the baths?"

"I don't know. I'm not exactly sure where we are anymore."

"Figure it out. I'd like to be home when the world ends."

Delon nods.

"If I can find some landmarks, I'm sure I can get us there."

"That's fucking reassuring."

Delon gets up without saying anything and walks away.

My head has stopped spinning and things are starting to fall together.

"Where did you find those Grays?" I say.

"Is that what they're called? Hattie knew where to find them," says Candy.

"Sub Rosa kids told stories about them. I didn't know there were any left. They're supposed to be from England or maybe Scotland or Ireland. Somewhere with bad teeth. Ancient fuckers. Old, old magic. I don't know their real name, but don't call them fairies or goblins or trolls or any of that Peter Pan shit. They're real sensitive about it, especially around Americans."

"Hattie made a deal with them. She said there was a great wizard who would owe them a favor."

"Great. Where is she?"

"She took off before we headed back. I don't think she cared who won the fight as long as someone hurt the Shoggots."

"Christ."

"All this bullshit is because of Aelita. It's made me think. Tell me something. Why don't you ever ask me anything about Doc?"

"Doc Kinski is dead. Why would I?"

"He was your father."

"That was just a technicality."

Doc Kinski's real name was Uriel. He was an archangel and the winged bastard that fucked with my mother, left her lonely and with a kid she didn't really want. And Aelita murdered him.

"Don't talk about him that way. And you're lying. You want to know but you never ask."

"Like I said. He's dead. Deader than either of us will ever be. When an angel dies there's nothing left. It's like he was never there."

Candy looks away at the others. Brigitte looks a little past the sell-by date, though not as bad as me. Vidocq has bandaged both of her arms and her left hand. Traven has his arm around her. She leans against him.

"Doc cared about you. He never said it because you're both idiots, but he worried about you."

"Can we do family therapy later? I'm busy hemorrhaging."

Candy doesn't say anything for a minute.

I say, "I should have brought some Aqua Regia with me."

"Yeah, you need booze with a cut-up belly. You could have died back there."

"But I didn't. You Robin Hooded me."

She looks down at her hands.

"What's going to happen when we die? Am I going to go to

Hell? I've killed people. Not like today. When I was feeding."

"You're not human. I don't know that the laws are the same for you."

"Did you see any Lurkers in Hell?"

"Some."

"Then maybe they do. Besides, you're not exactly human and you're always saying you're going to Hell."

"I'm human enough. Half of me is. I figure that's enough for a ticket Downtown."

She holds the torn halves of my shirt together like maybe they'll heal like skin. They don't.

"Thanks for showing me a little bit of Hell," she says. "I'm not as afraid of it anymore."

"What's this all about?"

She takes a breath.

"What's going to happen to us when we die?"

"I don't know. I never saw any Jades in Hell and no one knows what happens to nephilim."

"Hmm," she says like she's thinking.

I say, "What you really want to know is that after we die, are we ever going to see each other again."

"Hell didn't look so bad."

"Look, I'm just speculating. I don't even know if either of us has a regular soul."

"I think if one of us dies and leaves the other alone, that's fucked."

I pull her head down onto my shoulder.

"Then let's not die. Dying's for losers."

"Sorry to tell you, tough guy, but I think that includes us."

I shrug and let her go.

"I don't have any answers. We'll have to figure things out as we go along, just like every other asshole on the planet."

"Okay. But when this is over we're going to talk about Doc."

"Oh, good. Something to live for."

One of the Grays comes over. He's a little taller and looks a little older than the rest. His hair and short beard are streaked with silver.

"Would you give us a few moments alone, lass?"

Candy kisses my bruised knuckles and goes to sit with Vidocq.

The little man sits down across from me. In the crap light it looks like he's eating chunks of venison or something. Then I see that he's cutting up one of Vidocq's Power Bars with a folding knife.

"Is that good?"

"Passable," he says. "The priest gave it to me. He's a funny one. Not as much of a stick up his arse as most of the pope's curs."

"He was excommunicated."

"Ah, I like him better already," he says. "So you're the great wizard."

"I'm Stark. Just Stark."

I put out my hand. He takes it in his surprisingly large, callused mitt and shakes.

"I'm Arawn. Leader of this lost, buggered band."

"Thanks for getting me out of there. Did you leave any Shoggots standing?"

"A few. Though not enough to trouble a church mouse, much less a grand wizard such as yourself."

He can barely get it out without laughing.

"Fuck them. No one is going to miss them."

He points to my midsection with his knife.

"You're recovering well from your wounds."

"I heal fast."

"That's good. Not always, though, is it? I heard of a vampire back in the old country. They're fast healers too, you know. This parish father got ahold of one, don't know how, but he did. Kept it in the basement of the church for weeks. Tortured it horribly. Said he was trying to understand the beast so he could conquer them for God. I think he was just having fun. Just goes to show you that healing fast isn't always a good thing. Torture him all night. Let him heal all day and then start again. I think that's what your friend back there had in mind for you."

"Interesting story. A little bird told me that you Grays don't like vampires."

He cuts off and swallows another piece of the Power Bar.

"Just the ones that make bargains they don't keep."

I'll have to ask Tykho about that sometime. Assuming she didn't send whoever is following us. Then I'll probably have to kill her.

I feel around for my coat.

"So, you're satisfied with our services?" says Arawn.

"Yeah. I think I owe you a favor now."

I take out a Malediction and light it. Instantly I feel better.

"Indeed you do."

"What do you want?"

"What can you do?"

I take a long drag off the smoke. Wonder if the smoke is

going to leak out through damaged lungs and fill my gut. I guess we'll know if I start farting smoke rings.

"To tell you the truth, most of the hoodoo I've done over the last few years has been about killing or stealing things. I'm rusty at pretty much everything else, but I'm willing to give it a try."

"That's not what I was hoping to hear."

"Sorry. Let's try it this way. Tell me the first thing that comes into your head. The first thing you want."

He sets down the knife and Power Bar.

"I'd like this century and the Sub Rosa that rose up in it to disappear like dust on the wind."

"We brought you here, didn't we?"

"Aye. You did. And forgot us when things didn't go just the way you wanted."

"What happened? How did you end up in Kill City?"

He looks away, into the lens of the flashlight, like he's staring into a campfire.

"We come from ancient magic. Powerful stuff back home, but it's weak in this new godforsaken land. We could still fight and scare the other families, but we were only half the warriors our patrons counted on and they never let us forget it."

"So they ditched you."

"Ditched. Buried. Forgotten."

"I'm not going to be able to help you turn back time or nuke L.A. Anything else you want?"

"Revenge on the house that brought us here and left us, disgraced and abandoned."

"Which house is it?"

"The Blackburns. Have you heard of them?"

What a fucking surprise.

"Everyone's heard of the Blackburns. They run the California Sub Rosa here these days."

Arawn nods. Looks at my cigarette. I hand it to him. He takes a pull and nods. Starts to hand it back.

"Keep it. I have more."

He smokes contently for a minute.

He says, "The family was strong-willed and the Sub Rosa so full of themselves. I'm not surprised that the kingdom is theirs."

"It isn't exactly a kingdom. And it's in kind of a mess right now. But they have a lovely Victorian with indoor plumbing and everything."

"You know, we weren't going to come at first, but then Hattie said it was you who rescued poor Teyrnon."

"He was the kid in gray? I don't like three against one. It upsets my delicate sensibilities."

"I took from that that you were a man of honor, but you refuse my simplest requests."

"What I'm telling you is that you and me together, my friends, your mariachis, and Patton's Seventh Army couldn't take down the Blackburns. The entire hoodoo population of California would come after us."

He throws down the cigarette.

"Powerful wizard. You're all talk. Typical Sub Rosa. Damn the lot of you."

"Why don't you just go home?"

"Our kind can't cross the open water. We'd perish."

"How did you get here?"

"Magic, you dolt."

I offer him another Malediction. He hesitates and then takes it. I light it for him.

"Okay. That's something I can do. I can take you home without going over the ocean."

"How would you go about that?"

"Ever heard of the Room of Thirteen Doors?"

"A child's tale."

"I have the key. We step into a shadow and I can take you anywhere you want. Where are you from?"

"Cambria."

"Okay. I might have to look that one up on a map."

His eyes narrow.

"If you truly have the key to the Room, why are you wandering down here?"

"I have to have some idea where I'm going before I know which door to open," I say, and nod toward Delon. "And I don't want that one to know that I can do it."

Arawn turns and looks at Delon, who's coming back inside. With luck, he's been scouting for ways to the baths.

"There is something not right about him."

"He's not a man. A Tick-Tock Man made him. He's something like a familiar, only mostly machine."

Arawn looks at me.

"And you let such a thing lead you?"

"I don't have a choice. He knows the way and we don't."

He picks up his knife.

"With a blade in your hand there's always a choice."

"What do you say? Do you want to go home?"

He shakes his head slowly.

"No. We won't return as paupers and fools. We came here as magicians and warriors, and that's how we'll return."

"I don't know what else I can give you."

He looks over his shoulder.

"The lass, the one with the short hair in the hide jacket who stays so close to you . . ."

"What about her?"

"Before she turned into a beast—and an impressive one she was—she used an equally impressive knife. Black and sharp as a crow's gaze. She said you had one just like it."

I take the black blade from my coat. The weight in my hand feels so natural and perfect. Like it's an extension of my arm. I've had it since the arena. It's one of my favorite weapons and the key to every car and bike in L.A.

"You sure you want this old thing? I bet Paul has a lot of other toys in his bag."

"If that's what I asked for, that's what I want. Or can't you honor that request either?"

I hand Arawn the knife.

"It's yours. It'll cut through anything made in this world."

"Will it, now?"

"You can start cars with it too. Do you have your learner's permit?"

Arawn walks to a pile of rubble and swings the blade. Cuts a section of concrete taller than he is cleanly in half. He goes to the wall and slices a piece out of an I-beam. He holds up the blade to check it and nods at what he sees.

He comes back over and sits next to me on the blanket.

"Yes. This will do nicely."

"We're square, then?"

"This little blade for your life? What do you think?"

"I see your point. The offer still stands. Once I find what I'm after, I can take you home."

"When we're ready we'll find you."

"If you're looking to make your fortune, make it quick. The world might be ending soon."

He stands and picks up his folding knife and the remains of the Power Bar.

"The world is always ending. A fiefdom rises. A fiefdom falls. It's the way of things."

"This time is different. If it happens, all the fiefdoms that ever were or will ever be are right down the toilet."

He cocks his head.

"Well, that's different."

"A little bit."

"Thanks for the warning. We'll see about making our way in the world a wee bit faster."

He starts away and I call after him, "Have you heard of a ghost people call the old Roman?"

Arawn stops.

"Remember when you asked if we dislike vampires?"

"Yes."

"We like ghosts even less."

His men get up and stand around him.

"Do you know how to get there?"

"Not a clue. Thanks again for the knife. Ta."

He starts up the stairs and his men follow. The Grays don't make a sound as they go. They march into the dark and in a few seconds it's like they were never there.

"I think I found something," says Delon.

He's squatting, leaning against the wall and drinking water from a bottle that's three quarters empty. How long have we been in Kill City? It seems like a couple of days, but it can't be more than a few hours.

"We turn right at the end of the hall, past a collapsed ceiling, and there's a door that leads down."

Vidocq stands and hefts his pack onto his shoulder.

"One of the Gray men told me about a door nearby. That must be it," he says.

"Saddle up, everyone. The sooner we get downstairs, the sooner we're out of Tombstone," I say. Big talker. I try to stand up and it feels like my head is spinning around like Linda Blair's. Candy comes over and helps me to my feet.

Everyone gathers up their gear and heads out. Traven takes a minute to change the batteries in his flashlight, then starts up the stairs with the rest of us. Good-bye, Shoggot country. Good riddance. If Hattie doesn't poison your water supply, I'll be very surprised.

The floor at the end of the hall is buckled like someone squeezed it from both ends like an accordion. Delon is back in the lead. Vidocq follows with Brigitte and Candy right behind. I'm at the back with Traven, stumbling along like a toddler just learning to walk.

"Are you in much pain?" he says.

"Just enough, thanks. Sorry I dragged you into this mess, Father."

"I'm sorry I haven't been more use along the way. Maybe I should have learned to use a gun."

I have to lean my arm against the wall to get over the places where the folds in the floor rise above my knees.

"You might have noticed that we have a lot of shooters and it hasn't kept us out of trouble. You'll get to show your stuff when we find the Qomrama. You know anything more about it? Where it came from? Who made it?"

Staying back with me, Father Traven has fallen behind the others. I don't like being the gimp in the group.

"Who made it is an interesting question. Most texts say it was the Angra, as a way to destroy our God. But there was speculation among a group of Byzantine scholars that God himself made it. That it's not a weapon against the Angra but against himself."

"God was going to take a bullet for the team?"

"Even that's disputed. Maybe God intended to sacrifice himself in hopes that it would appease the Angra."

"That doesn't make sense. If our God made it, and Ruach let Aelita have it, she'd know how to use it, only she doesn't. She got lucky killing Neshamah, but she can't count on getting all the brothers on luck."

"There's one more theory. A minority theory, but an interesting one. It says that a high priestess is the only one that can bring the Qomrama into this universe from where the Angra are exiled."

"How?"

"No one knows, but the theory continues that the reason the Qomrama is hard to control is that it's not just an inanimate weapon. That it's a kind of Qliphoth."

"A demon? Then it's a piece of one of the old gods. That means it's alive."

Traven shrugs. I can breathe again, so we start walking.

"As I said, it's a minority opinion, but with the Qomrama,

I wouldn't put anything out of the realm of possibility."

"Neither would I. Ever notice that we live in a very strange universe?"

Traven brushes dust out of his eyes and off his deeply lined face.

"What's left to believe in? The God in Heaven isn't to be trusted, and a piece of that very same God is also Lucifer in Hell? How are we supposed to go on knowing these things?"

"Cheer up, Father. It could have been ten."

He gives me a look.

I say, "It's a Hellion joke. When God threw the rebel angels out of Heaven, they fell for nine days."

Traven nods and says, "I get it. Things could always be worse. I suppose that's true."

"I won't tell you any other Hellion jokes. Most sound like the Three Stooges riffing on farts and vivisection."

"I appreciate that."

This part of the corridor is all raw drywall with Spackle smeared along the edges where the panels join. I feel woozy. I stop to lean against a section. And I'm falling. Not onto the floor but right through the wall.

I land flat on my back, knocking the wind out of me. It takes me a minute to get my senses back. My stitches hurt from the impact. Faintly, like he's talking through water, I can hear Traven calling my name. But I'm in no shape to answer.

I came down on a pile of mall trash and building materials. Broken drywall panels, a layer of old cups and napkins, moldy clothes, and broken beanbag chairs. A million gnat-size Styrofoam pellets float to the floor, like I'm lying in a blizzard in a garbage dump. Thin, airy laughs come from the edges of the room. They sound like the wind from the other side of a hill.

"Who's there?"

The laughter tapers off but no one answers. Looking up, I can see the hole where I fell through. It's not that far. Shadows move across it. Someone is looking for me.

I shout, "Traven. Down here. Hey!"

"He can't hear you."

Another voice says, "None of them can."

"Who is that?"

More laughs. A bunch of people down here think I'm fucking hilarious.

It's warm and damp, with the same tropical feel as the mall's atrium. My eyes slowly adjust to the room. Furred fungus on the walls glows faintly. Eidolon Whiskers. We had something like it Downtown. I look back at the opening in the wall where I fell through. It's not real. It's a phantom. A ghost wall like the one hiding the room in Hell where I first found the 8 Ball.

In a few minutes I can almost see my hand in front of my face. Then shapes in the room. I'm in the middle of a maze of improvised graves and tombs built from debris that landed here during the collapse. Someone has cobbled together a cemetery for whoever was trapped here. If this is a boneyard, I have a bad feeling about who's been laughing at me this whole time.

"Hey, dead guys. Come out, come out, wherever you are."

Gray wisps circle me. Faces resolve themselves for a second or two, then break apart into smoke.

"There you are. Why did you grab me? What did I ever do to you?"

"It was fun."

"We were bored."

"You were clumsy."

"You're alive. That's offense enough."

I shake my head.

"Is this one of those 'we're-dead-and-that-makes-the-living-our-enemy' situations, 'cause seriously . . . ? That's the best you could come up with?"

"It's not smart to mock us."

"I'm not mocking you. Hell, I'm on your side. I've been dead too. A couple of times. I know how much it sucks. Come on. We're on the same team here."

"We will be soon."

More chuckles from the peanut gallery.

"You will never leave here."

"You know you're not the first dead assholes to threaten me, right?"

"No. We're the last."

"I see why you were bored before. You're boring. You're boring ghosts and that's just sad. You have all day to figure out spooky stuff and all you've come up with is 'boohoo we're dead and everyone with TiVo has to die.' "

"You're going to die."

"Yeah, excuse me while I ignore you." I see shadows over-head. I shout, "Hey. I'm down here goddammit."

"They can't hear you."

"Stop shouting. It's annoying."

"Sorry. I didn't mean to be a bad guest. By the way, you know I'm going pee in one of the corners in a few hours, right? I mean, it's just biology. I can't help it."

Ghosts swirl around me again. When the faces resolve themselves this time, they don't look happy.

I touch the wall to see if I can find any hand- or footholds. My hand comes back wet and slimy, covered in Eidolon Whiskers. The wall is way too slippery. No way I'm climbing out. I can't see doors or openings of any kind. I take out Mason's lighter. If I can make enough of a shadow, maybe I can come out to somewhere above and find the others.

"Adios, crybabies."

I flick it on and get closer to the wall. The room is dark, but even so, the light is feeble. I hold the lighter up higher, looking for the best angle. The next second, the ghosts are all over me, whirling around my head and flying through the lighter flame. It goes out. I spark it again. They come back, blowing through the flame like a fucking annoying breeze, snuffing it out. I try cupping my hand around it, but they squeeze between my fingers and douse it again. I put the lighter back in my pocket. It was never going to work anyway. It just wasn't bright enough.

The ghosts are cackling up a storm. An easy crowd. And I wasn't even using my A material.

"You invaded our home and now you'll die here."

"Yeah, you keep saying that."

"You can starve slowly over weeks or you can end things quickly. Use one of the stones or pieces of metal to cut your wrists."

"I'm going to go with door number three. The year's supply of car wax and a weekend in Hawai'i away from Spooky Town."

A rock hits the side of my head. Someone shoves me so hard I almost fall. Pieces of drywall and metal slam into the wall around me. Some of these dead pricks are tougher than others. Not just specters but full-on poltergeists. Some scratch my face, going for my eyes. I duck and get my arms up to block them, but their spectral bodies flow around them like fog with talons. Dropping an arm to my side, I manifest my Gladius, an angelic sword of fire. I swing it in front of me, turn and raise it overhead, bringing it down again right through the thickest part of the ghostly crowd.

They burst out laughing. Big, nasty belly laughs.

"Look, everyone. The mighty wizard is using magic against us."

"I hope he doesn't kill us, don't you?"

The ghosts drift away like they've lost all interest in me. They move around the room, full-body specters now, chatting and telling jokes about what an idiot I am. I drop down onto one of the beanbag chairs.

The dead creeps are right, of course. Practically all my hoodoo is about hunting and killing. Not much use against someone who's already dead. I take out a cigarette, but when I try to light it, they again blow out the flame.

"You are the worst dead people I've ever met."

They go on with their little coffee klatch, hoping I'll go nuts and off myself.

I put the cigarette away.

"Hey, do any of you spooks know about a crazy ghost? I

mean crazier than you. He's in some kind of Roman bath or something."

A couple of them nod. One says, "No one talks to him. He's mad."

"Yeah, I think I already said that. Thanks for nothing."

So far, Kill City is living up to its name. I have no intention of letting Casper and company kill me, but I'm seriously stuck here. And I don't like cemeteries. Not one little bit.

I was around fourteen when it happened. Balthazar Roszak, the spoiled little prince of a powerful Sub Rosa family, decided he didn't like me. It had nothing to do with family rivalries or magician envy. It was just one of those dog-pack bully-and-victim games that young boys play. Balthazar played harder than just about anyone. His clan was rumored to practice heavy Baleful magic on the sly. Maybe he was out to make his bones in the family or maybe he was just a stone bastard, but when he came after me one night, I knew he was going to kill me.

I had a lot of power even when I was fourteen, but it was mostly show-off stuff. Unfocused tricks to amuse friends or impress girls. It was nothing at all like Balthazar's hoodoo. He'd been training since he was a goddamn fetus. If he wanted me dead, I knew there wasn't much I could do to stop him.

I hid in the Golden Hills Cemetery not far from my house. Golden Hills had been a big deal in the fifties, but that was a long time ago and now it was barely hanging on. The grounds were kind of weedy and the place was generally starting to fall apart.

I went inside through a place in the wrought-iron fence where I knew a post was missing. Headed straight for the trees and the big tombs where the families with money had planted Grandma and Grandpa years before. I was hoping if I stayed in the shadows, Balthazar wouldn't be able to follow me through the wet December grass. But the fucker came right along where I'd run. He wasn't even moving fast. He knew some kind of tracking hoodoo that I'd never heard of. All I could do was keep moving and hoping that he'd get bored and go home.

After an hour, I was running out of steam. It wasn't that I was tired. It was that Balthazar was relentless. No matter what I did—running straight, doubling back, climbing trees—he'd always find me. And he'd let me go to run some more. He wanted me to give up and offer myself to him. I wasn't that far from doing it.

I ran into the hills that gave the cemetery its name. The oldest part of the place. All the families that could afford the view had long since moved to better neighborhoods with better places for their dead. No one ever went up to the hills anymore. The grass was long and slippery. Some of the grave-stones were beginning to tilt in the soggy ground. A lot of the mausoleums had cracked foundations and walls. The far end of the hill was a straight hundred-foot drop to the freeway. The other end faced down the slope to where Balthazar was coming. I'd cleverly run myself right into a dead end.

I crept across the top of the hill trying to spot where Balthazar was coming up, but he was nowhere in sight. There weren't any trees up there, so I climbed on top of one of the tombs.

From somewhere below me, someone said, "Boo."

It was Balthazar. I was so startled that I started to slide

off the slanted roof and only stopped myself by jamming my heels into the raised edge. There was a crack and a crash and the whole tomb seemed to drop a few feet. I thought the roof was going to collapse and take me with it. But it held together. I couldn't hear Balthazar anymore. It was a perfect moment to finish me off, but nothing happened.

I climbed down and there he was, lying under a marble pillar from the tomb. It had come down across his chest. His head and arms flailed and pushed at the pillar, but his legs were at a funny angle and didn't move. When he saw me he tried to yell, but it came out rough and wet.

"You. You did this. You're dead."

Even hurt, Balthazar was strong. He threw a couple of fireballs at my head. They missed, but only by inches. I was stuck. Terrified of helping him. Terrified of leaving. He tried a spell to raise the pillar. He managed to get it up a couple of feet before it fell back down on his chest with a soft frightening sound.

"Help me," he said. "Or I'll kill your whole family."

I knew he meant it. I couldn't move. I was so scared of him that I wanted to help him. But I was too afraid to move. Then he started to cry. Big, wet-eyed wails. That was when I understood. I walked away and left him up there on the hill.

There was a Laundromat not too far away that still had a working pay phone. I dialed 911, didn't give them a name, but I told them that a boy was hurt inside Golden Hills. I didn't tell them exactly where. I didn't want them to find him right away. Then I went home.

The next day it was all over the local TV news. The boy who'd died in a tragic accident in a poorly maintained graveyard. When the medics had found Balthazar, they'd taken him to an emergency room at a good hospital. But it was full of civilian doctors. If they'd known to take him to a Sub Rosa clinic like Allegra's, they might have been able to save him. But I didn't want that.

I knew the moment Balthazar started crying that I was dead. No matter what he said after that, no matter what he promised or how much he pleaded, he'd never forgive me for seeing him so weak. He'd kill me the first chance he got. So I did the only thing I could do. I left him lying in the wet grass.

Balthazar was the first person I ever killed. I don't like to think about it, so I work hard at not doing it. Sometimes I see his face on an opponent when I dream about the arena. I looked him up in Hell when I was Lucifer. Found him in Butcher Valley with the other killers. Turns out I wasn't the first kid he'd come after. Still, remembering him on the ground bothers me, though not so much that I would have changed what I did.

I wonder sometimes if leaving Balthazar in a graveyard is why I'm tied so closely to the Hollywood Forever Cemetery. A cemetery was Balthazar's exit and my entrance into this world. Two fucked-up kids connected forever by a land of bones.

That's why I hate cemeteries.

The Kill City Cemetery is in even worse shape than Golden Hills. Tombs are slapped together from collapsed concrete and drywall. A few graves were hacked into the floor, but most are just covered with debris. Mini burial mounds. Someone made crosses from old water pipes. Angels are tacked on some of the graves, torn from Valentine candy displays. A

Star of David is crudely hacked out of an acoustic ceiling tile.

I pick up a Big Blue World snow globe from the floor and toss it at the nearest cross. It bounces off with a satisfying *ping*. I get up and tear the cross out of the grave, find another, and tear it out too.

"Stop that," says a ghost.

"Fuck you, Jacob Marley."

I bang the metal crosses together, shouting, "Hello. Hello. Hello."

When I don't hear anything I toss one of the crosses up and out of the ghost wall into the corridor above.

"Stop that," screams one of the ghosts.

They swarm around me, pushing and shoving, trying to knock the second cross from my hand.

"Aw. You don't like that? How about this?"

I push through them and pick up a piece of concrete with some rebar sticking from it. Using it like a sledgehammer, I bash one of the makeshift tombs to pieces.

"Stop him, someone."

"Please."

"He's insane."

A mummified body lies among the ruins of the tomb. I pick it up by the neck.

"Any of you ever see *The Muppets*? I loved that show. Let me see if I can do Kermit's voice and work the mouth at the same time."

"Stop. Please."

"Why should I stop? You can only kill me so dead."

I kick a plywood support from the side of another tomb. It leans to one side and slowly slides to the ground.

"Please. No more."

"I'm going to pull every single body out of these graves. I figure I can make half of you into lawn gnomes and the other half into ventriloquist dummies. The tourists will love 'em, don't you think?"

A spook screams in my face, "Do not desecrate our resting place."

Before any of them can stop me, I pull Mason's lighter and touch it to the corpse. It goes up like a torch in a Frankenstein movie.

"According to you assholes, this is my resting place too. If it is, I'm going to redecorate it any way I like."

"Stop. You can go."

I drop the burning body.

"What was that?"

"Please put out my corpse and we'll let you go."

I get one of the beanbag chairs and drop it on the body, smothering the flames.

"Okay. I put it out. How do I get out of here?"

"There's one more thing you must do. Take our bodies with you so they can be buried in the earth."

"Are you crazy? What are there, twenty or thirty of you? I can't carry that many bodies."

A poltergeist swoops down from the wall and flicks a knucklebone from one of the unearthed corpses at me.

"A single bone will do. One from each of us. Bury them in the ground somewhere. If you promise to do that, you can go."

"I'm going to have to mess up your little garden even more to do it, you know."

"Do what you have to, but please don't be cruel when digging us up."

"How am I supposed to carry all these bones with me?"

The poltergeist tosses something in my direction.

"Look down. There are shopping bags everywhere."

It's a thick plastic bag advertising a 50 percent opening weekend sale at Victoria's Secret. Pictures of attractive women in panties and bras. I fill the bag with bones, the smallest ones I can find from each body. Yes. This is exactly how I wanted to spend tonight.

"So, what were you? Workers getting shops ready for the mall?"

"And some construction workers."

"I was an OSHA inspector."

The others laugh.

"That's not funny," says the inspector.

I shake the bag a few times to settle the bones.

"I think that's it. Did I miss anyone?"

"No one who wants to go."

"Good. Now point me to an exit."

"No." It's a new voice. "He doesn't go."

"He's alive. He's an invader."

"He has to die."

"We had a deal," I say.

"Not with us."

Skeletal arms and bodies shoot up from the trash-covered floor. Grab on to my legs and the waistband of my pants. It's jabbers. A whole pack of them. The meanest I've ever seen. Jabbers are just animated skeletons with a little connective tissue holding them together. They're not very strong or solid, but I suddenly have dozens of hands trying to pull me down. A few more crawl completely out of the floor and pile onto my back. I'm covered in the stinking mummified remains of pissed-off clock punchers looking for some payback from the living.

I'm still weak from the Shoggots. The jabbers pull and push me down onto my hands and knees. I drop the bag of bones. They get my right hand under the floor debris. They want to pull me under and drown me in garbage. I relax and let them pull. Concentrate everything I have into my hand. The jabbers keep puling me down. I'm almost on my belly when I'm able to manifest the Gladius. I drag it from the ground, hacking through jabber bodies and sending a shower of burning trash all over the room. The jabbers back off fast. I swing the sword, ripping through their bones as the other ghosts and poltergeists dive-bomb them, driving them back underground. Another minute and it's over. I let the Gladius go out and fall against the wet wall, panting and holding on to my gut. I think I'm bleeding again, but when am I not bleeding?

A poltergeist drags the bag of bones to me. I pick it up.

"Okay. Now. How the hell do I get out of here?"

"That, I'm afraid, is your problem. The ceiling collapsed over the door and there are no windows and no ladders down here."

"Great. Can I get a small fire going?"

"Why?"

"So I can make a shadow. I can get out that way."

"All right."

I wrap some of the old clothes and paper around a pipe and

pack it together tight. Using a cinder block as a stand, I stick my MacGyver torch on top and wait for it to catch. When it does, it puts out more smoke than light. But it's enough. I know the corridor above me, so this should be easy. Right. Because everything's been so easy down here. I step into the shadow and I'm out of the cemetery. Go through the Room and I'm back in the passage upstairs. I sit and pour the bones from the bag into my coat pockets. I slit the lining of my coat and drop in the handful that don't fit. I stop and fill my lungs with air that doesn't smell like an abandoned butcher shop.

Now that I'm out, I have no idea where the others might be. For all I know, the group following us is right around the next corner, but I can't sit here in the dark forever.

"Hello," I yell. I wait. Nothing comes back. I call a couple of more times. Not a peep. I'm pretty worn out. Maybe I'm not shouting as loud as I think. I take out the Colt, cock the hammer, and fire two shots into the ceiling.

A few seconds later I hear shouts and see pinpoints of lights in the distance. If it's the other team, I'm not going to be happy. If it's another pack of ghosts, I'm fucked. I slide behind a big concrete boulder that blocks half the hallway and cock the Colt again.

I hear her before I can see her clearly. I know the sound of her sneakers slapping on the floor as she runs. I stand and she hits me like a little leather freight train. Candy throws her arms around me. I'd do the same to her, but she has my arms pinned.

"This is because I like you," she says. She lets go and punches me in the arm.

"Ow."

"And that's for disappearing again."

"It's good to see you too, baby."

I kiss her and feel the others crowd in around me, hands helping me stand up straight.

Brigitte reaches into one of my coat pockets and pulls out some bones.

"Look. You've brought presents for everyone."

"Don't lose any of those. I promised some dead people I'd get them out of this dump."

"We have to find our own way out first," says Traven.

I look around for Delon.

"How's that coming, Paul?"

He nods somewhere down the corridor.

"We found the door the Grays pointed us to."

"Show me."

Delon walks on and the rest of us follow. Candy keeps looking at me like I might keel over at any second. After my soirée with the dead, I must look pretty bad.

"Where were you? We've been looking for you for over an hour."

"And dodging the other group," says Vidocq.

"You saw them?" I say.

"Their lights," says Candy.

"Sorry to slow you. I'll tell you what happened when we're out of here."

Delon is putting his shoulder to the door when we get there. Traven helps him. They both pound on it, but the door won't budge.

"Let me try," says Vidocq. He gets to work with his lock-picking tools but stops after a few seconds.

"The door is already unlocked. Perhaps there's debris on the other side."

"Let me try," I say.

The others get behind me. I bark some Hellion and concentrate on blowing the door off its hinges. A few sparks dance around the doorframe like a bunch of drunk Tinker Bells giving me the finger. My head goes funny. I fall back against the wall. Traven and Candy grab me.

"Sorry. I think I missed."

Candy runs a hand through my hair.

"Don't feel bad. All guys have performance issues now and then."

"Unless you have some Viagra for magic in your pocket, I think I'm done for tonight."

Delon probes the door's hinges with a knife.

"At least you cleared off some of the dust. I think we might be able to pop these."

"You do that. I'm going to sit here and be useless for a while."

"Of course," says Delon. He's trying to sound neutral, but I can hear the microtremors in his voice. He's as giddy as a little French girl to see me bloody and weak.

Brigitte and Delon use their knives to pry up the hinge pins. Brigitte knocks hers out first and it clinks to the floor. A minute later Delon's pin pops out. With Vidocq and Traven's help, they lift the door out of the frame. Delon shines his light into the darkness. There's no floor. Nothing in there but a spiral stone staircase. It doesn't even look like it was built but was carved like a gargoyle from a solid piece of stone. The steps are slick with dripping water. Strands of some kind of spongy green growth hang from the sides. Underneath the dirty water and lichen are images of dragons and sea monsters surrounded by strange writing.

"Can you read any of that, Father?"

Traven comes to the front and shines his flashlight over the stairs.

"No. But the symbol pattern looks like some kind of ritual magic. An incantation. Perhaps an invocation."

"Of what?"

He shakes his head, still moving his light over the symbols.

"I'm sorry. I don't know. But it's possible that the stairs function in a similar way to a prayer wheel. Each turn along the path proclaims the prayer or offering."

"You mean, by walking down these stairs, we might be calling up something and we don't know what."

"I'm afraid so."

"We don't seem to have much choice," says Vidocq. "We can't find our way back the way we came."

"I saw something like this back home, in a cemetery outside of Ostrava," says Brigitte. "I was helping friends kill a den of vampires that had been plaguing the city. There was only one way into their tomb, but everyone who tried to enter was attacked, as if the vampires knew they were coming."

"Did they?" says Candy.

"Yes. There were runes carved into the paving stones leading to the crypt. Each step completed one part of a hex. There was only one path in, and by taking it, you were creating the spell that would lead to your death."

"What did you do?"

"We approached slowly, walking in a random and confusing manner. Forward. Backward. We jumped over stones and touched others more than once. Whatever we could do to break up the pattern of the spell."

We're Gene Kelly dancing in the rain with monsters. I guess I've done stranger things in my life.

"Since you're the one with experience, would you lead us?" says Traven.

Brigitte goes to the top of the stairs. She starts down, goes over the second step, then back from the third to the second, and down to the fourth. She repeats the pattern as she descends. Stepping over one or two stairs, going forward and then backward. It's like a demented St. Vitus's dance or a very odd torment for a soul in Hell, and definitely one of the most ridiculous things I've ever seen. On the other hand, no sea monsters burble up from below and no dragons cook us from above. Her plan looks like it could work. Like Vidocq said, we don't have any choice but to keep going. Traven goes next, slowly and methodically following Brigitte's clumsy, stuttering steps. I nod for Delon, Vidocq, and Candy to go ahead of me. I have a feeling that clog dancing with stitches in my belly is going to be slow and painful.

We go down four floors. There are no more landings or doors, just wide, empty rooms stretching out from the staircase, each room a little rougher than the one before it. None of this can be part of the original plans for Kill City. Someone put this down here or built around something that was already in place. I don't like either possibility. And I sure as shit want out of here as fast as possible.

Each floor we pass is like its own mini-kingdom. More tribes and federacies that call Kill City home. On the first is a mixed bunch of Lurkers, some Nahuals, Fiddlers, and some ragged Luderes. Fiddlers are psychics that can read objects by touching them. Like dice or a whole deck of cards. They often work with Luderes to scam civilian and Sub Rosa casinos. I'd say this bunch has lost its touch. They throw rocks and garbage at us as we go by. There's nothing we can do but duck and dance faster down the stairs.

The next floor is a beautiful fever dream. It looks like another Sub Rosa family. An old one. Their clothes look nineteenth century, patched and stitched a hundred times. They're eating fast-food garbage-can scraps from the piers on an elegant dining table set with bone china and lit by white tapers in silver candelabras. Probably the last of their fortune that they were able to save and bring down here. Who knows how many times they've had to drag this stuff from hovel to hovel over the last century.

The third floor is like a level of ghosts. We can't see any forms, just their eyes in the darkness. They're like cat eyes. Bright and reflective. With a whoop, they rush snarling at us like goddamn Drifters. Everyone ahead of me freezes on the stairs, bunching up. A bad idea.

"Move," I yell.

Brigitte starts down again, keeping to the far side of the stairs.

The clan on this level is so filthy they shine with it. It's like they're covered in oil. They lean from their perch and reach for us with hands like filthy, ragged claws. We keep going but the stairs are slick and we're walking funny. It's hard to keep a safe, steady pace.

I hear something slide and someone lose their footing. Brigitte falls against the railing on the near side of the stairs. One of the clan gets hold of her hair and pulls. She beats on his arm with her fists but can't get any footing to pull herself back onto the stairs. Traven leans over the rail and grabs the one holding on to Brigitte. Plants a kiss on his lips. The filthy guy lets go of Brigitte and screams as loud as he can through his plugged mouth. Traven holds on to him, clamping the Dolorosa on tight, spitting sin and damnation down the guy's throat. Hands reach from the dark and get hold of the man, pulling him away from Traven. The guy sputters and wails. Brigitte grabs Traven and drags him back onto the stairs. They run and the rest of us follow. Fuck incantations and maybes.

When we hit the bottom of the stairs, everyone is ready. We have our guns out and Vidocq is all set with a potion. But there's nothing down here except dull walls and a poured concrete floor. Brigitte hugs Traven. Wipes the filth from his mouth.

She says, "*Děkuji.*"

"Anytime," says Traven.

We start out and only get a few yards before rubble threatens to fill the passage where some of the upper floors have fallen into this one. We play our flashlights around the room. Delon is the first one to spot the graffiti. On both sides of the passage there are big block letters, desperate messages in a bottle.

HELP US.

WE'RE ALIVE.

DON'T FORGET US.

"My God," says Traven. "One of the construction crews must have been trapped down here."

"They never recovered all the bodies," Candy says.

I say, "Why didn't they just walk up the stairs?"

"Perhaps something prevented them," says Vidocq.

"If they got caught in a collapse this far down, it would be a bad way to go. Let's not end up like that."

"This is the only passage. Let's get going," says Delon.

It's getting on my nerves, being led around by a talking slot machine. I wonder if Kasabian's head would work on one of these mechanical bodies? Maybe I'll have to gently remove Paul's head when this is over and see.

Every few yards there's more graffiti. Each collection gets less and less coherent. No more HELP US. It's all FUCK YOUs and HOME HOME HOME. Then the words are gone and the graffiti gets completely Neanderthal. All skulls, Devil heads, and tumbling dice coming up snake eyes. Like scribblings of someone on a very bad acid trip. A few yards beyond that, the graffiti is just random streaks of color and smeared handprints. Either they had a lot of paint when they got trapped or by the end they were using other stuff on the walls. I'm going with the paint theory and ignoring the stuff that looks like teeth and skull fragments scattered in the rubble. Even that feeble lie goes south when we find the hanged men.

They're suspended by ropes and electrical wires from an overhead beam. They've been dead a long time. Long enough that they're dried out and unreal-looking, like scarecrows meant to keep anyone from getting too close. But who else is going to come down this far but rescuers and why would they want to scare them off?

"Any idea when we get out of this fucking place?"

"I'm just feeling my way along," says Delon. "If there are location markers down here, they're covered up by junk. We have to get keep going until we find another way down. A staircase or even an elevator shaft."

Our shadows flash across the far wall as lights come on behind us. For a second I think I can smell the Shoggots. I reach for the Colt in my waistband when a voice echoes off the walls.

"Don't go for your gun, Stark. We have more of them than you do."

I know that voice. It's Norris Quay. I think I would have preferred the Shoggots.

"Stay there. I'm coming to you."

Candy grabs my arm and Vidocq circles in front of me.

"What are you doing?" he says.

"Listen. I'm the only one who knows this guy. I can talk to him. The most important thing is to keep an eye on Delon. Make sure he doesn't come over."

"Why?"

"That's Victor Frankenstein out there."

Candy says, "I'm coming with you."

"Fine. Don't go for your gun unless I do."

"Okay."

I hold my hands out by my sides so they can see I'm not armed.

"Get those fucking lights out of my eyes so I can see you."

"Do it," says Norris, and the lights swing away, lighting the cavern and not burning holes in my retinas.

Quay is in the middle of a group of twelve men. He's dressed in padded overalls and wearing lightweight leg braces. An attendant on either side of him keeps hold of his elbows in case the braces aren't enough to keep him upright. Down here Quay looks so frail it's like his attendants are perp-walking a mummy. Quay's two Titans are there, each armed with HK417s, rifles you don't walk toward but flee from as fast as you can. If you have a choice about which way to go. Quay's other goons are just as heavily armed. Probably a collection of ex-military and cops. They look at Candy and me like we're a couple of baked hams with biscuits and beans. There's someone behind Quay but I can't quite make out who.

"Does the old folks' home know you're missing bingo night, Norris?"

He smiles.

"I couldn't let you and Paul have all the fun, could I? Who's the young lady? You two have seemed awfully close on the journey."

"Candy, meet Norris Quay, the richest asshole in this time zone."

Candy puts her hand up to shield her eyes from the glare of lights.

"Wow. He does look like Paul."

"Paul looks like me, dear," says Quay. "Get the lineage right."

The man behind him pushes past the attendants and points at us.

"They're the ones who destroyed my workshop. Them and some Mata Hari. Now I can't make any more familiars."

Candy waves to him.

"Hi, Mr. Rose. How are you?"

Quay holds up a hand.

"Calm down, Atticus. We'll have you set up in a new space as soon as we get what we came for."

"Which brings me to the sixty-four-dollar question. What the hell are you doing here, Norris? You already have Paul planted with us. Does he even know about you? What's going to happen if he sees you?"

"I don't give a tinker's balls what happens to him. He's an instrument. A pocket watch bought and paid for. As to why I'm here, I thought that would be obvious. Redundancy."

"There's plenty of assholes in Kill City already. We don't need duplicates."

"Did you know that when NASA sent the Apollo rockets into space, they each had three computers on board? Three, on the assumption that two would fail."

"So Paul is the first two and you're lucky number three?"

"No. Paul is one. You're two. I know you'd move Heaven and earth to get what you set out for. But what if you both failed?"

"What if I succeeded and didn't want to give the 8 Ball up?"

"That too. And now that we're this close, I don't know that a redundant system is all that necessary."

"We're not there yet."

"When the Apollo Eleven lunar module, the one that first put men on the moon, was landing, all three computers failed. Neil Armstrong had to land on the moon manually. But he was an experienced pilot and they were so close that it was not only feasible but doable. And so man landed on the moon and returned safely. I believe that from here my little team can pilot ourselves down to Mare Tranquillitatis all on our own."

Shadows move in the cavern behind Quay and his people. They're so focused on Candy and me that they don't notice.

"Do you really want the thing so bad that you're prepared to fuck up the plan this close to the end?"

"Yes. And we won't fuck it up."

"And this is all because you're an art lover and not some crazy old man who thinks the Qomrama can somehow make him live forever."

"My reasons are no concern of yours."

Whatever is moving in the dark is getting closer. I take a step toward Quay. His goons level their guns at me. I'm fast but there's no way I can get to Quay without acquiring many, many new holes in my body. Am I strong enough to throw any hoodoo? Maybe. But if the door to the spiral staircase was any indication, nothing fancy. On the other hand, maybe I won't have to do a thing.

"What if you're wrong, Norris? Did you find the bridge? Did you see the spiral stairs back there? Did your master plan include any of those? What if there's more of that ahead?"

"Of course we didn't cross the bridge. Some idiot destroyed it. But another family showed us a safe way around. You're not the only one who thought to bring trinkets to trade with the natives. As for the stairs, slippery as they were, we navigated them just fine."

"You walked straight down the stairs?"

The shadows behind Quay's men have spread out across the whole cavern. There are so many I can't count them.

"Of course. Did you expect us to fly?"

From the dark comes a grunt.

"You're not a stupid guy, Norris, but you're one dumb son of a bitch."

With another grunt the shadows behind Quay swarm over him and his men. I don't wait to see who or what they are. I bark some Hellion and practically fall over. Candy grabs me as a smoke screen fills the cavern between Quay's people and us. We head back to our group, Candy pulling me the whole way. By the time we get back I can breathe again.

Behind us it sounds like a bad night in the arena. Shrieks and curses. The crunch of bones cracked by kicks and rocks. Then gunfire. Rifle flashes explode through the smoke like stars going nova. More screams. Some human and some not. The shooting gets sloppier. More desperate. A few rounds hit the floor near us. Whatever is back there is winning and won't go home quietly once they've finished off Quay's Boy Scouts.

Candy holds out her hand. It's covered in blood.

"I think I'm shot."

Her T-shirt is ripped and there's fresh blood on the side. I tear it open until I can see the wound. There are a dozen punctures. Ragged lacerations.

"It's rocks or shrapnel. You're okay." To the others I shout, "Go, go, go."

They take off. Candy still looks a little freaked by the blood. I grab her hand and we follow.

Soon the wide passage is clogged with wreckage on both sides, narrowing the way so only one person at a time can squeeze through. Ahead is a long section of scaffold closed on both sides with lumber. Paul freezes at the entrance looking back toward the noise. Brigitte goes around him, turns on her light, and goes inside to see if the way is clear.

"Shit!" she yells, and backs out into the open. The skin on both of her shoulders is ripped and bleeding. She moves her light around inside the scaffold. The wooden planks are studded with metal. Some are wedged in sideways and sharpened like razors. Others bend back on themselves like fishhooks.

"It's very narrow inside," says Vidocq, looking past her. "We'll have to walk sideways and carefully. It will be slow."

"Then get going."

They head straight for us as the smoke screen dissipates. I can't tell how many of them there are, but it sounds like a small army. As the others file into the scaffold I try one more bit of hoodoo. Something simple, blunt, and not very powerful. I recite some Hellion and try to move just a few small stones on the nearby rubble just a little shove. Every breath I take hurts. Pain builds behind my eyes like an ice pick. But it works, in its own lame way. A few keystones shift and jagged slabs of rock and concrete slip away from the wall and crash onto the floor, blocking the narrow passage. It's not exactly the Great Wall of China, but it will slow the crazies down, and right now I'll take anything.

Candy is waiting for me at the scaffold entrance.

"Come on," she shouts.

I push her inside and get out the Colt. She starts down the metal-lined corridor trying to keep her eye on me. But she can't see what's coming and keeps cutting herself.

"Turn the hell around. I'm fine back here."

She turns and starts moving faster. The pace through the scaffold is slow enough that I can actually keep up. Little curses and whispers of pain echo off the walls. Everyone is trying to keep quiet, but the corridor is long and the metal is sharp and every inch of this place fucking hurts. But we're cooler than Steve McQueen and no one panics or rushes. Even Delon is keeping a steady, reasonable pace.

Concrete crashes to the ground behind us, followed by screams and running feet. The crazies are through and coming at us. Up ahead, Brigitte, Delon, and the others are out from under the scaffold. A second later, so is Candy. As I step out, the scaffold shakes like there's an earthquake. The crazies pour in behind us and it's not pretty.

They're not going sideways and they're not slowing down. They sprint at us full speed, teeth bared and eyes blank, ripping themselves to pieces on the blades and hooks. I try some arena hoodoo, a killing hex. I shout the words and almost throw up. It's too little too late, I played myself out collapsing the rubble. I aim the Colt and pull the trigger. It clicks.

Shit.

I fired the last two rounds in the corridor upstairs. Brigitte pushes past me and shoots at the mob.

"Go for the legs," I say.

The crazies start falling, and the fallen ones at the front are trampled by the ones behind. Each fallen body narrows the way and slows them. I reach into my coat and pull out a SIG .45, and while Brigitte shoots at the crazies' legs, I shoot at their chests. Between the two of us, we're piling up bodies fast. It's harder for each new crazy to climb over the body of its fallen, fruit-bat comrade. Soon there are so many bodies that the passage is blocked all the way to the ceiling. We can still hear screaming from behind the all-beef barricade, but no one is coming through.

I shout at Delon, "Find us a way out of here," and he sprints into the dark.

On the far side of the dead crazies, the live ones are still trying to get through. They pull bodies from the pile, then pass them back and out of the bloody passage. The whole skeleton of the scaffold shakes with their movements. I have a couple of more guns, but we're going to run out of bullets soon.

I grab Candy and Brigitte and point to a joint in the scaffold's ceiling halfway between the crazies and us.

"See that? Shoot there. Everything you have."

They both open up. I put away the SIG and take out the Desert Eagle .50 the Satanists left for me at the Chateau. Normally, I hate pistols like this because they're more suited for killing tanks and dinosaurs than shooting people. But I might have finally found a use for it.

I join the women in emptying shot after shot into the scaffold joint. Candy runs out of bullets first. Brigitte has more shots, but her CO_2 pistol is designed to punch through flesh not metal. I empty almost the whole clip from the Desert Eagle before I hear the first creak. The crazies have pulled enough bodies out of the way to start down after us again. They're rocking the scaffold so hard it's bouncing off the walls of the narrow concrete passage. The damned thing is rocking but it won't fall.

When the mob hits the area with the weak joint, the whole structure moans and bellows like a gut-shot buffalo. And comes crashing down on top of them. As metal, wood, and concrete cascade down, the crazies claw the air and crawl on crushed arms and legs, still trying to get to us. The roar of the collapse bounces around the stone walls until it feels like my eardrums are about to implode. A blinding storm of concrete dust fills the air. We cough and hack like asthmatics running a marathon in a sandstorm.

Soon the air begins to clear. The echoes of the crash and the crazies' screams fade away. There's just the gentle sound of Vidocq cursing in French and Brigitte meeting him curse for curse in Czech.

"Who the fuck was that?" says Candy. "More Shoggots?"

"No. It was the construction workers. Some of them still had their hard hats and work shirts."

"What happened to them?"

"They fucking invoked something on those stairs and then Norris and his boys invoked it again. Maybe they were going to change too, but they didn't get the chance."

Traven says, "Is that madness going to happen to us?"

"We didn't walk straight down, so maybe we got around the hex."

"Who would build something like that in here?"

"Right now I don't really care. Let's get out of here."

Delon comes back and leads us to another staircase, this one with no amusing markings on it. Sore and bloody, we head down.

Right into a dead end. There's no wreckage covering a possible exit. No windows or crawl spaces. Just a solid wall ahead and a small pile of debris behind.

"Paul," I say.

He turns and looks at me. There's already a trace of panic on his face. He knows where this is heading. I get a hand around his throat and shove him against the wall.

"What have you fucking done to us?"

He looks around like maybe a magic door will descend from Heaven above.

Candy puts a hand on my shoulder.

"Can't you take us out through a shadow?"

"Take us where? Home? Disneyland? We didn't come here for that. I want the ghost, and you, Delon, were supposed to get us to him. You're Tykho's spy and I went along with that as part of the deal, but you've been about as useful as a three-legged elephant. Why should I even explain myself to you? You're not even a real boy."

I reach under my coat for the black blade. But it's not there. Candy grabs my arm.

"Stop. Just stop."

I look at her, and for a second I see Alice's face the first time she saw me kill someone. The moment she understood what I'd become. It didn't feel good then and it doesn't feel good now. I let go of Delon and he pushes past me and climbs halfway up the stairs.

"You okay?" says Candy.

"Swell. How about you?"

"Just another day in paradise."

I want to say something more, something dumb and funny and reassuring, but in my head it's all black and full of the snake-eyed dice and Devil heads. Bad juju. Evil thoughts. I'm not taking Delon apart right now, but that doesn't make me want to do it any less. The only other thing I can think to do is what Candy said. Leave. Go out through a shadow and what then? Start over? Delon isn't coming back with us, and without a guide we'll be right where we were before we started. Maybe I could trade Tykho something for the map. Promise not to burn down her club or stake out all her toadies on the roof at sunrise. Maybe maybe maybe. It's all bullshit. This city has done its best to keep the 8 Ball from me and I think it might have won. Maybe it's time to go home, order room service, and wait for the end of the world in luxury.

"We are such fuckups," I say.

"Relax. It could have been ten," says Traven. Neither of us laughs, but I want to murder someone maybe 10 percent less. I think about what Mustang Sally said. *"When you get lost keep going till you hit the end of the road. There will be something there, even if it's not what you were looking for."* But there's nothing here at all. Just a bunch of fools and a lot of ruins.

"Let's go home," I say.

"How?" says Delon. "We're trapped. We're fucked."

"Does anyone know what this is?" says Traven. He holds out a blue plastic ball about five inches in diameter.

"Where did you find it?" says Brigitte.

"Back here. There are a lot more."

We follow Traven back along the bread-crumb trail of plastic balls. It leads to the pile of debris in back. Vidocq goes down and he and Traven pull pieces of concrete and cinder blocks from the wall. Hundreds of colored plastic balls cascade out. Red. Blue. White. Green. Then the balls stop. There are so many of them that they've plugged up the hole they were pouring through.

"What are they?" says Candy.

"A way out?" says Traven.

I say, "Let me try something."

They clear away from the hole. I get down right next to it and stick my Kissi arm into the wall of plastic. Nothing is going to bite the arm off, and if anyone is hiding on the other side, my bug arm will scare them off. But I don't feel anything except more plastic balls. I pull my arm back.

"The hole is big enough to get through. I'm going in."

"Like hell you are," says Candy. "You're hurt, you can't do magic, and you're probably out of bullets by now."

"Someone has to go through and see what's on the other side of this wall. And it's not going to be Vasco de Asshole over there," I say, looking at Delon.

"I'll go," says Brigitte. "My gun has some shots left."

"Please don't," says Traven.

"It's fine. There's probably nothing there and I'll be back in two seconds."

Traven lets go of her arm. Brigitte gets out her pistol, kneels by the opening, and worms her way inside. More balls pour into the room. When she's up to her waist, she's still burrowing. Then only her feet are showing and she disappears.

A whoop comes through from the other side of the wall. Balls begin to fall again. In a few seconds Brigitte has dug back far enough to stick her head back into the room.

"Come through," she says. "It's incredible."

Before I can say anything, Candy dives in after her. I shove Delon through next. I follow him and Traven and Vidocq follow me.

It's not much of a climb. Only a few feet. I'm suspended in plastic balls for a second when I hear Candy say, "Put your feet down, dummy."

I shift around until I clear enough balls under me to move my feet down and touch a floor. When I straighten up I find myself waist-deep in the plastic balls. The others pop up behind me.

The room is dark and smells of mold and something sweet. Like old soft-drink syrup spilled and left to go bad in wet carpets. Brigitte has her flashlight on. I can make out shapes under the collapsed ceiling. Booths. Pool tables. Pinball and motorcycle-racing machines against the walls.

"What the hell is this place?" I say.

"It's one of those family joints," says Candy. "You know. The family fills up on pizza and the kids get to run around and play games, including climbing around in ball pits."

She bounces some of the plastic balls off my chest.

"We're saved by America's shitty eating habits," she says.

Brigitte leads the way out of the pit and we follow her through the restaurant. The aluminum doors have long since been knocked down. We step over them and a small sea of broken glass and then we're back in the main floor of the mall.

I say, "Hallelujah. Back where we started."

"Not quite," says Delon.

He's standing by one of the upright mall maps.

"According to this, we're one floor above the baths."

"Lead the way," I say.

He starts down a long flight of marble stairs. There's a wet breeze coming from below and the smell of salt. Seawater?

WE COME DOWN into the middle of a whole spa complex. Massages. Manicures. Hair salons. Skin salons. Probably designer blood transfusions too. But it looks more like we landed in Dracula's forgotten root cellar. Mushrooms sprout from mist-covered cracks in the marble floor. Small, stunted palm trees and bromeliads sprout along the hall. It looks like this entire level of the mall is rotting in the salt air. The walls and ceiling have buckled from the moisture. Dripping vines dangle from the metal grid that once held ceiling tiles. In our feeble lights it looks like no one has been down here in a thousand years.

Underneath the vines and mold on one wall is a sign pointing the way to the Roman baths. As we head down there I move the bones from my pocket into the lining of my coat. Stick the SIG in my pocket. If I can't throw any hoodoo, I'm sure as shit going be ready to blast every Shoggot and monster Morlock piece of shit in Kill City.

There's a cool wind blowing between the doors to the baths. Maybe a hole that's letting in a sea breeze. Thin, dawn light filters through filthy windows in the ceiling several floors above the main bath, turning it into a strange ceremonial space. Somewhere to come for a baptism or human sacrifice after getting a perm.

There's a fake Roman temple at one end of the bathing area. The main pool is octagonal, with three tiered steps down to a foot of tea-colored water full of loose tiles and broken furniture. Delon heads for the temple. The others circle the pool, staring into the scummy water like maybe the

8 Ball will float to the surface like Excalibur and fling itself into our arms. I sit down on the top step of the pool and take out a Malediction. The flare from the lighter gets everyone's attention, but when they see it's just me, they go back to looking disappointed.

"What happens now?" says Traven. "Does anyone know how to summon the ghost?"

All their beady little eyes turn in my direction. I shake my head.

"Don't look at me. I couldn't pull a bunny out of a hat right now."

"Anybody else?" says Traven. "Brigitte. You worked with the dead. Do you know anything?"

She squats at the top of the pool and flicks in a pea-size piece of concrete with her thumb.

"This is the wrong type of dead. I know nothing about ghosts."

"Vidocq? Do you have any tricks or potions?"

Vidocq raises his hands and drops them to his sides, a gesture of exasperation.

"*Rien*. Nothing."

"We can't have come all this way for nothing."

Candy comes over and hands me her water bottle. I didn't even know I was thirsty, but once I start drinking, it's hard to stop. I hand her back the bottle.

"Any ideas?" she says.

"One."

"You better act on it before you have a mutiny."

I take a puff of the Malediction.

"Hey, asshole," I yell. "Come out, come out, or I'm going

to burn Kill City down. Also, Aelita sent us for the Qomrama."

A gust of wind stirs the water. The light from the ceiling
dims for a moment.

"Liar," comes a disembodied male voice. "Aelita wouldn't
let you pick up her laundry."

"If I say your name three times, will you show us your
pretty face, Bloody Mary?"

"Why? I'm happy this way."

"Are you afraid of us?"

"Don't flatter yourself."

"You're afraid of something," I say.

"So are you, sonny. Being afraid is one of the realities of
existence."

Delon is back by the pool. He looks around the room,
trying to pinpoint the ghost voice. Brigitte and Traven are as
wide-eyed as starstruck teenyboppers. Vidocq, Candy, and I
have all run into ghosts before. The others have never been
in a real haunted house. Welcome to the Loudmouthed Dead
Club.

"You know, for someone people keep telling us is a
madman, you don't sound all that crazy. Say something batshit for me so I know it's really you."

Silence. The cold wind blows in from a door at the back
of the room.

"Samael is back in Hell. I don't know if that's exactly crazy,
but it's pretty funny. Also, one of you isn't what he seems."

No shit, Casper. It's a real effort not to look at Delon.

I say, "I know all about that. How do you know about
Samael?"

"The same way I know when and where you got that nasty Kissi arm."

Slowly, he comes into focus, like an image on a video screen. First, the general shape forms and then it finally sharpens.

He's entirely green—head, hair, and skin. And maybe a little taller than his brothers. Definitely not as round. Calling him buff would be stretching it, but by the family standards, the guy is Captain America.

"Fuck me. I should have known one of you was behind this bullshit. Does Muninn know you're here?"

The ghost's face splits into a wide grin. Not ghost. Mr. Muninn's almost-twin. One of the God brothers.

"The five of us share some thoughts and knowledge in common, but we each have our secrets. This is one of mine."

I get up and flick the Malediction into the pool a couple of feet from him.

"Hey, Father. Let me make some introductions. Father Traven, meet God. God, meet Father Traven."

Traven's eyes narrow at me. He can't tell if I'm kidding or not. But he's a smart enough guy and we've talked enough and he's read enough arcana to work out the rest for himself.

"You're God?" he says.

"A piece of the pie, yes. You look disappointed. Turn that around, multiply it by a million, and you'll know how I feel about you people."

I stand next to Traven in case he decides to freak out or faint.

"Remember how I told you that God had a nervous breakdown and broke into little pieces? The Mr. Muninn part is in

Hell. Ruach is driving everyone crazy in Heaven. Neshamah is dead. That leaves two. Which one are you?"

"Nefesh," he says, and mimes doffing a hat. "The smart one. The one no one even looks for because he's an incorporeal, crazy old spook in a town teeming with them."

He becomes solid, standing on the water like a lime Jell-O Jesus. He points at me.

"You, pretty boy. Give an old man a cigarette."

I toss him the Maledictions and the lighter. Nefesh catches one in each hand. He rolls his eyes when he sees the cigarette brand. But he still takes one and lights up. Being a God of love, he tosses me back the lighter and smokes.

"I'm speechless," says Traven. "I devoted my life to you and now I see you're nothing but a ridiculous, foulmouthed little man."

Nefesh raises a finger to Traven. An admonishment.

"You didn't devote your life to me. You lost your calling a long time ago and hid from me in your books. And then you wrote that one particular book. Naughty, naughty."

"You're angry with me for translating a book?" says Traven. "But it was your duplicity that made it necessary for me to do it. No. You don't get to reject me. I reject you."

Nefesh lazily puffs the Malediction.

"Too late, priest. I got there first. I win again."

I say, "You have to admit it's kind of funny when you think about it. A guy powerful enough to run the universe and sneaky enough to trick the Angra out of it ends up a cabana boy in a drainage ditch. That has to make you smile just a little."

Traven looks at me. His face is gray. Drained of blood.

"You've seen these kinds of horrors before. I've only seen

them in my worst nightmares. I can't find the humor in this situation."

Brigitte puts her arm around Traven's shoulder and leads him away from the pool.

"This man will give you no satisfaction. Turn your back on him," she says.

"Do we have souls, Stark and me?" shouts Candy.

Nefesh looks at her like he hadn't even noticed her before. I pull her away, pointing a finger at him.

"Don't answer that."

I pull Candy to the wall.

"Look at that clown. Do you really care what he says? Will knowing make a difference in what we do tomorrow or the day after? Forget the question. Forget him. Let's just get the 8 Ball and get out of here."

"So, you want the Qomrama Om Ya," he says. "What for?"

"I'm starting my own magic act. You know, like Doug Henning, but with more decapitations and better music."

"Don't get snippy with me, junior. I can be gone in a second and you can explain to your friends how you wasted their time and, from what it looks like, their blood."

"I want it to use against the Angra. And to fuck with Aelita. Even if I never figure out how to use the thing, not letting her have it will be a little bit of satisfaction. Do you know where it is?"

He nods.

"Of course. I saw her hide it. Can you imagine how shocked I was to see that crazy bitch walk into my hidey-hole with the one thing in the universe that can kill me?"

"Where is it?"

"I'm not sure I'm going to say. You're not the most trust-worthy character on the planet."

"And you are? If you won't tell me, then tell the priest."

"Why? He's not even a priest anymore."

"Once a priest always a priest. However you want to split hairs, it means he's the sentimental, spiritual type. He might be mad at ghost dad, but in his heart of hearts he still loves him and doesn't want to see him die. Tell the father and he'll be the one who gets the 8 Ball and will have the final say on what happens to it."

"How do I know you won't take it from him?"

"I'm not the one you have to worry about. Keep your eye on Robby the Robot over there."

We both look at Delon. He takes a step toward the bath like maybe he didn't hear us right.

"I was wondering why you were lurking around here with one of those things."

"Why don't you ask it yourself?"

"Are you talking about me?" says Delon.

Nefesh looks at me.

"It doesn't even know, does it?"

"It doesn't have a clue."

"Know what?" says Delon.

He pulls his pistol and points it at me, swings it to Nefesh, and then back to me.

"What are you up to? I've done what I'm supposed to do. I got us here."

"Brigitte got us out of that dead end you walked us into. If you were still leading, we'd be somewhere south of Borneo by now."

"Put the gun away, son," says Nefesh.

"Son? A minute ago you called me 'it.' Why?"

" 'Son' was just me being polite. And you can put the gun down or I can turn you into a pillar of fire where you stand."

Delon swings the gun back to Nefesh again. He doesn't know where to point the damned thing. After he thinks about it, he lowers it to his side. He looks at me.

"Why did he call me 'it'?"

"Forget it. Let's just finish the job and get out of here. You'll give the Qomrama to the father, right?"

I look over at Nefesh.

"How will you keep it from Aelita?" he says.

"With the father's permission, I can hide it in the Room of Thirteen Doors. She can't get in there. Even you can't get in there."

He smokes the Malediction a bit more. Takes a couple of steps across the top of the water like he's thinking.

"Come on," I say. "Haven't you spent enough time down here floating around like a rubber duck? Just give us the 8 Ball and you can blow this place. Go stay with Mr. Muninn in Hell. He'll be happy to see you. He can use the company."

Delon sprints across the baths, and when Candy isn't looking, he grabs her from behind and puts his gun to her head.

"Someone is going to talk to me. If you're really God and this isn't one of Stark's scams, then tell me why you said what you said."

I say, "Let go of her, Delon. You're not going to like how this ends."

"I called you 'it' because that's what you are," says Nefesh.

"I'm sorry no one told you earlier, but that's how things are. You're not a man. You're a mechanism."

Candy twists and slams her elbow into the side of Delon's head. He gets off one shot but misses her. She goes Jade, her skin darkening, her teeth sharpening to shark knife points, and bites down on his wrist. Delon screams, smashing his fist onto the back of her head while she digs in her fangs. With one last deafening scream, his hand comes off. Candy knees him in the balls, and as he falls, she spits his hand at him. A few seconds later, she's Candy again, panting and wiping his blood off her face with her T-shirt.

Delon cradles his mangled arm against his chest. When he gets the guts to look at it, he sees the steel armature poking out of his wrist. The pulleys and gears, all the delicate clock-works buried under his skin.

"Fuck. What did you do to me?"

"Me?" says Candy. "Go ask Atticus Rose, you prick."

I start to tell him about Norris Quay. How he's Geppetto and Delon is his Pinocchio. But even I don't feel like rubbing it in to a guy who didn't just lose a hand but his whole life.

Delon holds out the stump of his wrist to Nefesh.

"If you're God, fix this."

Nefesh drops the last inch of the Malediction in the water.

"You don't want that arm fixed. You want me to make you real. Sorry to tell you, friend, but I'm not the Blue Fairy. The way things are these days, I'm barely me."

Delon grabs his gun with the other hand and blasts a couple of rounds at Nefesh. Bullets kick up sprays of water as they pass right through him. Nefesh smiles and looks at me.

"That's funny. I was expecting you to do that."

"If you didn't remind me of Mr. Muninn a little, I probably would have."

Delon swings the gun around so it's pointing at me. He struggles to his feet and walks toward me.

"You knew this all along and you didn't say anything? Fuck you."

Glass explodes at Delon's feet. By the time he looks down, it's too late. His legs have turned to a loose, powdery stone. As the effect moves up, he starts to collapse, his body unable to support its own weight. Vidocq stands behind him, another potion bottle in his hand. When he sees Delon go down, he puts the bottle away. Delon's powdery remains slide into the bath, dissolve, and sink to the bottom as a faint red stain floats on the surface.

"You couldn't have done that when he was back against the wall?" Nefesh says to Vidocq. "You had to get blood in my water."

Brigitte says something to him in Czech. He says something back.

"What was that?" I say.

"I told him he was already swimming in blood," says Brigitte. "He said I was a child and that I had no idea what it is to be a deity."

"Mr. Muninn said that same thing to me."

Traven says, "Are you going to tell us where to find the Qomrama?"

Nefesh looks down and takes a step back from the spreading red.

"You're going to hate me if I tell you. Maybe we should play Twenty Questions. That way you'll ease into the answer. What do you say, ex-priest?"

Traven shakes his head.

"I give up. I don't care about the world or any of this anymore."

"You were right," says Nefesh. "He *is* a sentimentalist. Okay. I'll tell you. Up in the lobby. Is there still a Christmas tree?"

"Yes," I say.

"That's where the Qomrama is. The ornament at the top of the tree."

"Merde," is the first thing I hear, then more curses echo around the room.

"I told you you'd hate me," says Nefish.

I really want a drink.

"So, we could have been in and out of here in twenty minutes?"

"I'm afraid so."

"This really is a nightmare," says Traven.

"Keep it together, Father."

I go to Candy and wipe off the last smears of blood on her face.

"Okay. The fucking thing is on the tree. How does it work?"

Nefesh comes across the surface of the water to the steps and walks out of the pool.

"Oh. I don't think I'm going to tell you that."

"It's not going to do us much good against the Angra."

"We'll see if they make it this far. I'm not convinced. If they do, maybe then I'll tell you."

"All of this is very interesting," says Vidocq, "but we're lost. We've come a long way and have no idea how to get back to the lobby."

Nefesh points out to the spa area.

"Just go up the broken escalator, then up a set of stairs. You'll be right there."

"That's impossible," say Traven. "We must have come down at least eight floors to get here."

"You went through the old tunnels? Down those funny spiral stairs? Did you happen to notice that there's some strange magic lingering around this place?"

Candy says, "Maybe that's why Aelita left the Qomrama in here. It's easy to get in but hard to get out."

"That's part of it. But I think the chapel might have been calling to her," says Nefesh.

"What chapel is that?" I say.

"On the other side of that wall is an adorable little chapel that was supposed to be used for weddings."

"Wed in a shopping mall. How wonderfully American," says Vidocq.

"It's why I like the baths. They're right next to the chapel. And part of the wall is missing, so I can ease out into the ocean and drift among the seaweed and fish from time to time."

I say, "I don't get it. There's a fast-food wedding factory so Aelita decides to leave the most valuable object in the world?"

"No. I think what called her is the chapel inside the chapel. Some clever boots brought in stones from an ancient Angra temple and built a small shrine to one of their gods right into the chapel wall."

"The shrine called to Aelita and the Qomrama without her knowing it," says Vidocq. "I wonder if whoever built it also built the spiral stairs?"

I say, "Do demons come through the shrine?"

"All the time. Another reason remaining incorporeal is convenient."

"I wonder if they collapsed the mall. The Angra might not like a Burger King on their sacred soil."

Nefesh shrugs.

"Who knows with those things? Ancient gods. Mysterious ways. If I can't figure it out, how could you?"

"Are you going to rot down here or pay Mr. Muninn a visit?" I say.

"Now that you busybodies have found me, I don't suppose I have any choice."

"Do you know where your brother Chaya is? You might tell him to go to Muninn too."

"If I knew his whereabouts, do you think I'd tell you?"

Candy pulls on my arm.

"Forget it. Let's go."

I follow her for a few steps and turn back to Nefesh.

"Every time I meet one of you little Gods, it's a ray of sunshine on a rainy day. Thanks for keeping the streak going."

We head back to the lobby to find the broken escalator. We're almost to the door when I hear Nefesh clear his throat.

"Thanks for the cigarette, Sandman Slim. And by the way, when I said one of you isn't what he seems, I wasn't talking about the mechanical man."

"What does he mean?" says Traven.

"Forget it. He's fucking with us because it's all he can do.

Play around in our heads. He can go to Hell or rot down there. Either is fine by me."

NEFESH MIGHT HAVE been playing mind games when we left, but he told the truth about the way out. Up the dead escalator. A U-turn onto the stairs and we're back in the Gothic rain forest of Kill City's main lobby. The Christmas tree is straight and huge, a fungus-covered evergreen where there should be a giant banana palm or kapok.

"What do we do now? Nefesh said the Qomrama is all the way at the top," says Traven.

Candy looks at me.

"You've used it before. Can you summon it or call it down or something?" she says.

My gut aches. I'm dizzy but I don't want the others to know right now.

"Even if I knew how, I don't think I have any hoodoo left in me."

"You're still here," says someone from across the lobby. "I thought you'd all be gone by now. Or dead."

It's Hattie. Her tattered robes are in even worse shape than they were before. Her hair is wild and dirty. Her face is scratched.

She says, "Are there any Shoggots left?"

"A few, but not enough for you to worry about. Sorry about your kids."

She nods.

"So am I. You're trying to get up the tree. Why?"

"The thing we came here for is at the top."

She smiles at us like the fools we are.

"You come all this way to end up back where you started. Ain't that a kick in the backside."

"It's a kick, but I was thinking somewhere else."

She looks Vidocq and me over.

"You're too big to climb it. It's rickety. You'll bring the damned thing down on top of us."

"I won't," says Candy.

She looks up the length of the tree like she's climbed it a million times.

I say, "That's fifty feet. You sure about this?"

She zips up her jacket. Pushes back her hair.

"Can any of you grow claws?"

"Take this," says Vidocq. He hands her a white filter mask. "I thought these might come in useful. You don't want to breathe any of that foulness into your lungs."

"Thanks."

Candy flips up her jacket collar and heads for the tree. On the way, curled claws extend from her hands as she goes Jade.

"Brave girl," says Hattie.

"Yes. She is."

"Foolish."

"You live in a garbage dump, lady. You don't get to pick and choose who's a fool."

The tree creaks as Candy climbs. Shaggy branches shake, sending down a storm of pine needles, dust, and fungus. I cover my eyes and mouth but still get a mouthful of the gritty, dirt-flavored mess. The others choke and go into racking coughs around me.

I look up through the bad air. Candy is climbing along the trunk, so I can't see her, but the moving branches show me where she is. Jades are fast and strong. She's already more than halfway up. The top of the tree sways as she gets higher. Wood snaps and pops in ways that inspire anything but confidence. Branches and glass ornaments crash to the floor.

"Are you all right?" yells Brigitte.

"Don't bother," I say. "She doesn't talk when she's Jaded out."

The tree stops shaking. A branch at the top moves. There's something silver on the end. The branch bends back toward the tree trunk.

"She's found it," says Hattie.

The treetop sways as Candy goes farther out onto the limb to drag it backward. There's a loud *crack* and the whole top of the tree comes loose like it's on a hinge, slamming into the lower branches, upside down but intact. Something falls through the branches. Not falls. Shoots like a bullet and crashes into the lobby floor, kicking up shards of marble and concrete like shotgun pellets.

I run to where it came down, not breathing. Not thinking. My head swims as I go. I stumble but I don't stop.

In a crater two feet wide and three feet deep lies the 8 Ball. The others crowd around me. I look up at the tree. Branches shake, but this time they're headed down. A few seconds later, Candy emerges from under the tree and sprints across the lobby, turning back to herself. She's covered in a fine film of dust and spores and her hair is matted with pine needles. She runs her hand through her hair and shakes her head like a dog, sending dust everywhere.

"Told you I could do it," she says.

"Good job. Now go take a shower. You smell like a love-hotel welcome mat."

Hattie stands at the edge of the hole, looking down.

"Don't look like much, does it?"

Traven says, "The core of the first nuclear bomb was only sixty-four kilograms and it leveled a city."

"That so? Aren't you a font of useless information."

"I didn't drop it," says Candy. "It shot away from me when I tried to touch it."

"Maybe it didn't like you," I say. "The father said it might be alive. Maybe your Jade form freaked it out."

"Touchy little bastard, for a weapon," says Candy.

I look at Traven.

"Okay, Father. You're up. Let's see if it likes you."

"Do you think it's safe now?" he says.

"When I had it before it only hurt anyone when I was angry or threatened. As long as you're calm, it should be fine."

"Calm," he says, and looks at me. "That's a tall order right now."

Traven's eyes are a little glassy. He looks far from a hundred percent as he gets on one knee and gently reaches for the 8 Ball.

"You'll do fine," I say. "Nice and easy. Look out for any sharp edges. It can nick you."

He hesitates before reaching down again. Lays his hand on top of the ball and holds it there for a second. Nothing happens. He relaxes and gets a grip on it and pulls it out. He's smiling when he stands up.

"I think the books were right about it being alive," he says. "It feels like it's asleep."

He brings it over to us. I'd rather have it a mile away, but beggars can't be choosers.

"We're all right," he says. "It's over."

"Let's get out of here and go home," says Brigitte.

"In a minute," says Traven. His smile is vacant. There's something wrong with his eyes.

He turns and hands the 8 Ball to Hattie. She takes it from him like she knew exactly what was going to happen.

I should have seen it before, but I've been so wrapped up in my own aches and bullshit that I missed it. One of us isn't who he seems, said Nefesh. Father Traven is possessed. Someone in Hell is using the possession key. They've taken him over and Hattie knew it was going to happen.

"What are you doing?" says Vidocq.

Hattie cradles the 8 Ball against her chest.

"Just doing what he was told," she says.

I reach for Traven, but before I can get to him, his eyes flutter closed and he slumps to the floor, his head cracking on the pavement. Brigitte starts for him but I grab her and push her behind me.

I take a couple of steps toward Hattie. I want to rip her apart. Traven is bleeding where his skull hit the floor. I want to see her bleed too. She steps back, but not because she's afraid.

"Who are you?"

"Don't you recognize me?" she says, her voice coolly amused. "You destroyed my home. You humiliated me. You're an Abomination and your presence in this city has brought it and me nothing but misery."

"What the fuck are you talking about?"

Her face shifts. Her skin crawls. The old woman becomes a young one, then cycles back to a crone, like the phases of the moon.

"Medea Bava," I say. "I heard you were Deumos's sorority sister. Shouldn't you be in Hell?"

"And leave the world to your tender mercies?" she says.

"You killed Hattie and took her place. Why?"

"For just this minute. To see the look on your face when you knew."

"Why didn't you just take the 8 Ball and go?"

"I didn't know where it was in here any more than you did. Besides . . . letting you find it for me was a chance to watch you and your friends suffer, and that alone was reason enough to watch and wait."

I pull the SIG from my pocket and aim for her head.

She holds up the 8 Ball.

"You say it works when you're angry or threatened? How do you think you make me feel?"

I lower the SIG and put it back in my pocket.

"What are you going to do with it?"

"Why, return it to its rightful owner."

She pulls out a pendant from under her robes. I recognize the shape. It's Aelita's angelic sigil. Hattie kisses it three times.

"Come to me, sister. Come and receive what's yours."

"Medea."

It happens instantly. The voice comes from behind us. Aelita, in a Maggie Thatcher power suit, shoulders her way past Vidocq and Candy. Bumps my shoulder as she goes past.

"You have the Qomrama, I see."

Medea uses it to point in my direction.

"The Abomination almost had it. I took it from him and now I want to do what's right."

"Thank you, sister," says Aelita, and reaches for the 8 Ball.

Medea's lips go from a smile to a hard straight line. The 8 Ball shoots from her hand like a cannonball, slamming into Aelita over the heart, driving her across the lobby and into the wall. Spinning blades sprout from the ball, whirring like rotary saws burrowing into her chest. An angel's scream is a terrible thing to hear. It's the death wail of something that was never supposed to die but has lived long enough to see the universe turned upside down as it now stares down death's gullet. Holy angel blood splatters the floor and our feet as the Qomrama punches through Aelita's chest and out her back. She slumps to the ground, and for a few seconds she twitches, trying to breathe, trying to focus on something besides the pain, her blood, and fractured bones. Medea hasn't moved. The 8 Ball flies from Aelita's chest and back into her hand. Aelita gasps one more time and fades away. An angel's death. Leaving nothing behind but one more hole in the universe.

Medea looks at me.

"Her war with God was a child's thing," she says. "It got in the way of the true work."

"Coming after me? I'm flattered all to hell," I say.

Medea makes a face. Behind her, Traven's eyes flutter open. He looks around for a second, unsure what's happening. With his sleeve he wipes blood from his eyes.

"You'd like to think that all this is for you, wouldn't you, Abomination?"

"You sure talk like it is."

"I call you by your true name because it's the one thing Aelita was right about. You're the filth of the universe."

"So you're not going to be in our Secret Santa pool?"

Traven gets up unsteadily behind her. I keep hold of Brigitte.

"This . . ." Medea holds up the 8 Ball. "This will do the real work now. I'll return to Deumos and my true sisters in Hell and we'll finally bring the Angra Om Ya back home."

I take a step and she steps back. Right into Traven.

"No you won't," he says. He picks up a fist-size piece of concrete and slams it into the back of her head. Medea drops the 8 Ball and lunges after it. Before she can get her hand on the thing, Traven has his hands around her throat and pulls her upright.

He says, "You want to go to Hell? I can send you there forever."

He plants his mouth over hers, like a terrible kiss. The Via Dolorosa. He spits millions of the sins he's eaten over the years into her, burning her insides, turning her soul blacker than any normal human's could ever be. Guaranteeing her the lowest depths of damnation.

But something is wrong. I've never seen the Dolorosa take this long before. Bava spasms and tries to push him away. Digs her nails into his face. Then goes slack. Traven's skin is white. He lets go of Bava, tenses, and falls onto his back in some kind of seizure. I let go of Brigitte and we run over. I hold down his shoulders and Brigitte grabs his legs until it passes. When Traven opens his eyes, they're dull and the whites are red with blood. He's blind. His face and hands are covered in deep red hemorrhages. His heartbeat is an un-steady staccato. Each of his slow, shallow breaths is harder for him to take than the one before. When he can talk, it's just a whisper.

"I'm so sorry. I don't know why I gave it to her."

"It's okay. You couldn't help it. Everyone knows."

"Does she have it?"

"No. You stopped her."

"Liam," says Brigitte. She's crying, touching his bloody face. "Don't move. We'll get you to Allegra."

Traven laughs when he hears her voice. She leans down and kisses him. He goes slack in her arms. She looks at me.

"Take us through a shadow. Now."

Traven draws a deep painful breath and grabs my arm.

"Put the Qomrama in the Room. Keep it from anyone who can use it."

I look for a dark shadow, one big enough to take all of us. I spot one by a pillar. Candy grabs the 8 Ball, but when I try to pick up Traven, he stiffens in a new round of convulsions, coughing blood.

Vidocq pushes me away. Pours something down Traven's throat. He goes still. Brigitte is trying not to scream. When the shaking starts again, Vidocq pulls out another potion. Brigitte grabs my arm.

"Do something. Some magic."

I try to remember any healing spells I used to know. I was never very good with them. I put my hand on Traven's chest and say the words. I don't feel anything. There's nothing left inside me. I'm too weak and too fucked up. My hoodoo won't work.

Brigitte shoves Vidocq aside and leans over Traven, doing CPR. She counts in Czech each time she pumps the father's chest. She pinches his nose and blows into his lungs, her mouth smearing with his blood. Traven doesn't move. I can't hear his heart or his breathing anymore. Sweat drips from Brigitte's face onto Traven's chest. No one moves. No one stops her. Let her do what she has to do even if there's nothing left of Traven to bring back. Finally, she collapses on top of him, crying. Candy puts a hand on her shoulder and pulls her up. When Brigitte sees me, she slaps me as hard as she can across the face.

"Great magician. Why can't you do anything when it matters?"

"I'm sorry. I . . . I'm sorry."

Brigitte puts her hands on Traven's bloody, red cheek and leans her forehead on his, whispering good-byes to his corpse.

I'm not even mad. I'm numb. Of course, they used the possession key on Traven. He's hardly had a glimpse of this kind of apocalyptic insanity. He's the closest thing to an innocent any of us knows. And I brought him into this shit asylum and got him tangled up in my old battles. I look at Medea's dead body. She was powerful. It must have taken every ounce of strength, every sin Traven had ever swallowed, to bring her down. Which is the real joke in all this, because for any other sin eater, it would mean they were empty of sin and they'd get a first-class ticket to Heaven. But not Traven. He was already booked on a coal cart to Hell before any of this. Candy asked if either of us has souls. Right now I hope I don't because I can't imagine a bigger, more damning sin on my record than bringing a guy like Father Traven into Kill City.

The building rumbles from below. It builds until it feels and sounds like a freight train under our feet. The whole mall slides sickly to the left. The Christmas tree sways. The trunk cracks. I pull Brigitte from Traven's body and everyone runs to the wall as the tree crashes to the floor. For a minute we're blind from the dust and fungus spores. I can hear sections of the ceiling coming down around us. The floor stops shaking, but the rumble remains, a steady background hum.

The rumbling rises and Kill City starts shimmying again. The glass around the elevator shafts shatters to the ground. I see faint light across the lobby.

"Follow me. Keep your heads down."

I grab Candy's hand and feel the weight of her grabbing someone else's. Crouching, running, feeling stitches popping in my belly wound, I head us down the stairs we just came up. Then down the dead escalator.

The windows over the Roman baths have collapsed into the main pool, flooding the whole floor in pale dawn light. I look around for a hole in the wall.

"This way. Through the chapel."

The building shifts in one direction and then the other. It's worse now. Before it felt like a solid movement from side to side. Now the motion feels soft and liquid, like we're off the foundation and floating free.

Inside, there isn't much left. A chasm has opened in the floor in front of the altar, swallowing the pews and part of the wall, destroying the regular chapel and revealing the secret Angra altar. Those fuckers are everywhere. Whatever the plan is to bring them back, it was set in motion a long time ago.

Something is crawling out of the wall. Not a crack in the wall. The wall itself, like the plaster and stone is trying to pull itself free. Its long beaklike mouth comes through first. That's all I need to see. Concentric circles of cutting fangs and grinding molars. It's a demon. An eater. We can't make it to the hole that leads to the ocean before it gets loose in the room. I shout at Candy.

"Give me your knife."

She tosses me her black blade and I rush the thing. Get a foot on some rubble and launch myself over the demon so I land right on its snout. It roars when it feels my weight and forces itself out of the wall faster. Its five spiderlike eyes emerge next and then the rest of its head. I bring the blade down as hard as I can at the base of its skull, where it meets the body, slicing through nerves connecting it to the head. The eater screams and bucks like a bronco, finally throwing me off. Halfway out of the wall, its buzz-saw mouth whirs and grinds at me, but its body won't move. It's stuck where it is. I toss Candy her knife and we head for the wall.

Vidocq and Candy jump into the water first. Brigitte comes to me slowly, looking back over her shoulder every few steps.

"What about Liam's body?"

Before I can say anything, the building drops like it's heading for the center of the earth. Back in the chapel something pushes the eater out of the wall and starts climbing out. What looks like a human hand clad in gold emerges. I grab Brigitte, toss her through the hole, and jump through after her.

The Pacific water is icy. The salt burns my gut and the burn Ferox left on my chest. The rumble grows. Around us, whole sections of the beach slip into the ocean, leaving a deep chasm below, like all of Santa Monica might be pulled down on top of us.

I don't know how deep we are underwater. I kick toward the surface, trying to keep an eye on Brigitte. As Kill City sinks the suction pulls us down with it, like the damned place is magnetic. I look back and something swims up from the churning murk below. A woman, completely covered in gold. Patterns on her skin like snake scales and circuit boards. She wears an elaborate golden headdress with swept-back wings. Half of her face is missing. An empty eye socket above a non-existent cheek and a raw, ragged jaw are all that's left on her right side. She reaches for me. I kick harder but it doesn't feel like I'm putting any distance between us. She gets hold of one of my boots, but seems to lose strength. Her body drifts down a few feet. She comes to for a minute, but it's too late. The suction is too strong that far down and she's sucked into the swirling wreckage below.

When Brigitte and I hit the surface, we swim away from shore, out into the deeper ocean, as Kill City comes around behind us. I don't know how long we swim. Maybe minutes. Maybe just one. When the noise and rumbling stop, I grab Brigitte's arm and turn her around. She looks at me wild-eyed. She doesn't want to go back. She isn't swimming away from the wreck but from Traven's body. I point her back toward shore and give her a shove. Soon she starts swimming.

We walk out of the water and collapse, exhausted and hurting. Brigitte is crying. Then it hits me.

"The 8 Ball. Where's the 8 Ball?"

"I dropped it during the quake," says Candy.

She goes to Brigitte and puts her arms around her.

Vidocq, drenched and looking every one of his hundred and fifty years, comes down to the water's edge and pulls me onto dry sand.

"All that for nothing."

"Not quite," he says. And pulls the wooden vessel Traven made for the 8 Ball from his coat pocket.

"I'm a thief, remember? Once a thing is stolen, it doesn't get away from me unless I want it to."

I'm so relieved I laugh. Then I hear Brigitte crying. A crowd of early-morning swimmers and surfers gathers behind us. The remains of Kill City slip into Santa Monica Bay, pulling a million tons of prime beachfront real estate with it. Sections of it continue to settle and collapse. Hattie's rooftop kingdom comes crashing down. Walls crush inward, revealing the food court and the dead interior amusement park. I look for bodies to bob up in the waves. Where are the rest of the Shoggots and the other tribes we saw inside? Where are the Grays? They're fighters. They'll survive. Crawl out of the water and crouch among the pier pilings until the crowds go home. Then move into Santa Monica and find another abandoned space to take over and call their own.

People pull out phones and cameras and snap photos. That's my cue to move. I look around and find a beautiful shadow by one of the broken boardwalk supports. I get everyone on their feet. While the crowd is busy watching Kill City breathe its last, I pull us through the Room and into the Chateau. I want to say it's a relief being home, but it's not.

Kasabian looks up from his work. I don't know what we

look like, but even he doesn't have anything smart to say. I curl up on the floor, waiting for the salt ache to ease up on my wounds. The others fall onto couches and chairs. No one talks. Candy brings Brigitte some whiskey. Brigitte cries like she might never stop.

I FIND A bottle of Aqua Regia and drink enough that I'm more wasted than I've been in a long time. Maybe since Alice died. Drunk enough that for a while I blot out Traven, the Qomrama, the end of the world, and every other ugly thing boring into my brain.

Things swim in and out of my consciousness. Candy. Vidocq. Kasabian tries to talk to me and I push him away. It seems like maybe Allegra is there at some point, working on me. It doesn't matter. This stupid dream is a joke. God is a joke. We're a joke. Bugs on God's windshield. If the Angra want to bite down on this shit sandwich, I say let them. What's left to lose but a world that never made any sense in a universe that's so out of control it takes a bastard like me to roust a little bit of God from his beach home and get him back in the game? Or at least to Hell, which is probably where he belonged in the first place.

I reach for the bottle but my eyes won't focus, and anyway, it looks miles away. Maybe I'll take a nap and try again later. Put on my walking shoes and make the long trek from this sofa to the coffee table.

How did any of us make it back in one piece? Mysteries within mysteries.

Man, I really wish I could reach that bottle.

SOMETIME BETWEEN KILL City and now, someone moved me onto the couch. Then someone set off Mount St. Helens in my head. Even my nose hairs ache. This isn't a hangover. It's cranial genocide. Candy is somewhere nearby. She hands me a glass full of something that smells like boiled crab ass.

"Drink it all," she says. "Vidocq left it for you. He said it would clear your head. Personally, I'd like to see you suffer for diving into the bottle like that."

"Sorry. I just."

"You feel guilty. I know. We all do. Shut up and drink."

She waves the glass in front of me. I sit up and immediately regret it. I hold my breath and swallow the potion as fast as I can. Halfway through, I hope the stuff kills me. That way I won't have to finish it. When I'm done, Candy hands me a glass of water. I gulp it down, but I can still taste the crab muck in my mouth.

"Thanks."

She takes the glass and says, "Brigitte's asleep in the bedroom. I'm going to go and check on her."

When she's gone, Kasabian limps over on his twisted leg.

"So you lost the preacher."

"You noticed."

"Too bad. He seemed like an okay guy."

"He was."

"I saw them take him away."

"Who?"

"The soul-sorting crew. I've been spending a lot of time looking around Downtown. You know, business research.

Remember how I said souls go off the radar for a while when they're being processed into Hell?"

"I remember."

The ache behind my eyes feels less like monkeys trying to hammer their way out of my head and more like guppies with rubber mallets.

"Turns out it's not the same for everyone. Murderers and rapists and your run-of-the-mill baby-eating dictators are white bread and mayo Downtown. They can take a while to get inside. But sinners against God? They're filet mignon and get priority sorting."

I rub the ache from my temples.

"Your boy Traven was in and out faster than a microwave burrito."

"Where is he now?"

Kasabian leans back in his chair, giving me a funny look.

"You were Lucifer. Don't you know?"

"I wasn't very good at the job."

"Color me surprised."

"Do you have a name?"

"He's in Helheim. A frozen patch of paradise way up north of Pandemonium. It's where everyone who has a beef with God goes. It's a lot like Antarctica, but instead of penguins they have armed guards."

"Thanks," I say, and try to stand. It almost works. I get up on the second try.

"Too bad you didn't take me up on my business offer. You could find my hoarder and say hi to the father on the way back."

"I'm going to do better than that."

"FedEx him some mittens?"

"I'm going to get him out of there."

Kasabian picks some fried shrimp off a plate someone abandoned on the coffee table. The sight of food almost makes me heave up my crab cocktail.

"I think certain people might be resistant to that idea," he says.

"I'll persuade them. Can you see Helheim? How many guards are there?"

"Not many," he says through a full mouth. "Not many. Eight maybe? The prison is in the middle of nowhere. Not many places to escape to."

I touch my stomach. Ferox's incision is closed and almost healed. Allegra did some good work on me. I'll have to thank her. And check on her ex-boyfriend she told me about. But after this. Everything can wait for this.

"What are you two talking about?"

It's Candy. She took my advice and cleaned up from her tree climb. She's beautiful. But I don't want to have to say what I'm going to say.

"You're going to love this," says Kasabian.

She sits on the end of the sofa.

"I'm going to get Traven."

She lays her hands flat on the backs of her knees, a tense gesture. She nods.

"Okay. I thought you might say something like that. I'm going with you."

"Not this time. This won't be like going to see Muninn. It's a hit-and-run trip and I need to move fast. I know Hell and half the population is already scared of me. Let me do this."

"But you promised."

I nod and slide down next to her.

"Understand something. I'm not going as me. I'm going as Sandman Slim. No stopping. No deals. No games. Anyone gets in my way dies."

She looks down at her hands.

"I hate it when you get like this."

"This is the only way it's going to work. I'll be in and out in a few hours."

"Last time it was only supposed be three days," she says. She gets up and moves to the chair across from me, putting space between us.

"I know."

"I'm not waiting for you again, you know. You have one day to get in and back. After that I'm gone."

"I understand."

"Don't tell me you understand. I don't care if you understand. I care what you do. And you have a day to do it."

She looks through the bottles by the food carts and finds a bottle of whiskey. She pours herself a drink.

"Anyway, Brigitte shouldn't be alone right now."

"Don't tell her what I'm doing. In case it doesn't work out."

She takes a belt of whiskey.

"I don't even know if *you're* coming back. You think I'm going to tell her about Liam?"

"One more thing."

"What?"

"Loan me your knife."

She's not happy at all to hear that request.

"This is a loan," she says. "Bring it back to me."

"I promise."

"You better."

She finishes the whiskey and goes back into the bedroom.

"You sure have a way with women," says Kasabian.

"Shut up."

I TAKE THE elevator down to the garage. I'm wearing a hoodie under my coat. I've reloaded all my guns with bullets dipped in Spiritus Dei. No need to worry about whether it's silver bullets or garlic or white oak you need in order to kill something. Spiritus Dei on a hollow point cutting the air at twelve hundred feet per second will kill anything dead.

The Hellion hog, a damned version of a '65 Harley Electra Glide built for me when I was Lucifer, is stashed in the back under a vinyl cover. I pull it off and look it over. There's no lock to undo. Who would steal something like this? Who except someone who's hard to kill would ride it? It's built like a mechanical bull covered in plate armor. The handlebars taper to points like a longhorn's head. The exhaust belches dragon fire and I can get the hypercharged panhead engine glowing cherry red on a long straightaway. I've only ridden it a few times in L.A. because it's like wearing a neon "Arrest Me" sign on my back and LAPD doesn't need any more encouragement.

Vidocq's potion cleared my head and Allegra did a good job healing my gut. Despite Candy being pissed at me for passing out, the sleep was good and deep. I feel strong enough to try a little hoodoo.

I whisper some Hellion, wait a few seconds, and touch my face. It isn't my face anymore. I'm just another ugly Hellion. I kick the bike into gear and it roars like a hungry Tyrannosaurus at an all-you-can-eat buffet. There's a nice shadow at the far end of the garage. I pop the clutch and lay rubber. I hope there aren't any parking attendants coming down with someone's Lamborghini because it's about to get all scratched up.

I disappear into the wall.

And blast out of the other side of the Room into Hell. I'm on the Hellion version of Sunset Boulevard, near Fairfax. The streets are in better shape than when I was Lucifer. Mr. Muninn must have the repair crews working round-the-clock shifts. The pavement along Sunset isn't buckled and I don't see a sinkhole in sight. I don't even smell any of the nauseating blood tides bubbling up from under the city. Nice work, Lucifer 3.0. I hope it's getting you some goodwill from these Gloomy Guses.

I aim the bike east, out where the street markets are clustered. The last time I was there I got into a scuffle with some army deserters when the 8 Ball went nuts and killed them all. Ground them up like fresh sausage. I'm hoping to keep a lower profile this trip. Which doesn't include worrying about stoplights and pedestrian crossings. Most of the vehicles on the road are still Unimogs and troop trucks. I'm the fastest thing in the afterlife. Eat my dust.

I SHOULD HAVE guessed that most of the changes to Pandemonium were cosmetic. Fix up the main streets to boost morale. But get off Sunset or Hollywood Boulevard and the city is still a wreck. Never recovered from when Samael, the first Lucifer, deserted the place for Heaven. Most of the regular bars, restaurants, and stores are still closed, so the big street market is packed. This is Harry Lime territory. Some of the goods are legit but just as many are black-market items, mainly from the legion's supplies. There's anything a handsome young Hellion out on the town might want. Clean clothes. Guns. Health and hex potions. High-end Aqua Regia and wine. But most of the goods are the same flea-market junk you see from L.A. to Tijuana to Narnia. Knockoffs. Stolen goods. And the things no one else wants anymore. The same goes for the food. But at least the portions are large.

I hide the hog in the same abandoned garage I did the last time I came to the market. I pull up my hoodie, still not convinced my hoodoo is a hundred percent yet. I don't want to turn back to my handsome self in the middle of a crowd. I'm a little twitchy being back here. It brings back bad memories. Not just of being Lucifer. It wasn't far from here that I got my left arm hacked off. And I know that if I head due south, I'll hit the arena, where I spent eleven years learning over and over again how close you can come to dying without ever quite making it. It's where I learned to be Sandman Slim. I don't like to think about him too much when I'm back in the world, but tonight I'm prepared to let him run wild and fancy-free.

It doesn't take long to find a bar. And then spot an officer. What I need is an officer drinking by him- or herself. At the far end of a small, tented joint I see one. A captain. Leaning on the bar with a whole company of shot glasses by his elbow. Perfect. I take out a Malediction and circle around so I come up behind him.

I get close with the cigarette out so he's looking at it and not me.

"Hey, General, got a light?"

He turns and gives me a bleary look. I must look all right because he glares at me like any other Hellion.

"I've got an extra for you if you have some flame," I say.

He pats himself down and stands when he feels a lighter in his pocket. As he gets up, I clip him on the jaw. Not hard enough to knock him out. Just enough to make his knees wobble like he's even more loaded than he really is. I get my arm around his shoulder and walk him around the back of the tent, between the market stalls where no one can see us. When I'm sure we're alone, I grab him by his collar and slap him a couple of times until he comes around.

"What happened?" he says.

"I hit you."

He looks up at me, trying to put a face and a memory together.

"You did. Didn't you?"

He reaches for his gun and I let him get it. I want him to feel it in his hand. Then I slam the pommel of Candy's knife into his temple and down he goes again. Now he knows his weapon isn't going to help. I put his pistol in my pocket and slap him again. When he comes around this time, he remembers me.

"Helheim," I say.

"What?"

"Helheim. Do you know where it is?"

"I can read a damned map."

"Take me there."

He looks at me like he didn't understand what I said. I haven't spoken Hellion in a while. Maybe I've gotten rusty.

I say, "Do you know where Helheim is?" while dragging the knife across his cheek. The sight of his black blood wakes him up fast.

"Yes. Of course. Only the lowest damned souls and the worst troops go there. Which are you?" he says. I smack him with the pommel again.

"I'm prepared to beat the brains or the attitude out of you. Which do you think will go first?"

He holds up his hands in front of his face.

"Okay. Okay. I'll tell you where it is."

"No. You're going to take me there."

He looks up at me.

"It's days from here."

"Not for me. And now not for you."

I put the blade under his chin and stand him up. Move him toward a shadow against the side of the tent and pull him in.

We come out by the garage where I hid the bike.

He looks around. Touches his head, wondering if he's even drunker than he thought.

"How did you do that?"

With the knife against his throat, I pull him into the garage and push the hood off my face. Say a few hoodoo words, and the glamour winks off. I'm me again.

"I did it because I'm Sandman Slim and I'm two seconds from turning you into a bologna sandwich."

He lurches back, more surprised than afraid. I grab him.

"What's it going to be, General? Helheim or I can leave your carcass here for a vendor to cut up and put on the spits in the market."

He says, "I'm telling you. It's days from here."

"I'm guessing there's light there."

"What do you mean?"

"Light. Enough light to throw shadows in the crevices in ice and mountains."

"Sure. Lots of shadows."

"Then it won't take days. Turn around and lean your back against the front of the bike."

I hand him two short lengths of rope.

"Tie each leg to the front forks."

"What are you going to do?"

I punch him in the solar plexus. It doubles him over and motivates him to stay down and tie himself to the bike.

"What's happening is this. I'm going to try something because I'm on a tight schedule. What you're going to do is think real hard about Helheim and I'm going to click my heels together and we'll be there in no time flat."

He finishes tying his legs and stands up.

"You're as crazy as they say."

"No. Crazy is when I break your arms and legs and bury you alive just to see if you can dig your way out. Want to play that game, General? Bet I can find a shovel or two for sale."

He shakes his head, clear-eyed. There's nothing better to sober you up than the certainty of your own imminent death.

I hand him a strip of cloth.

"Tie that around your eyes. Tight. If I don't think it's tight enough, I'll just slice your eyes out so you can't see how we're getting there."

"I'm tying it," he says through gritted teeth.

When I'm sure he isn't playing possum, I push one of his arms out over the handlebars.

"Tie your arm on. Do it tight. If you fall off, you're going to get run over."

He has to use one other hand and his teeth, but he gets it done. I have to help him tie the other side while keeping the knife to his throat. It isn't easy for either of us. When we're finished, he's spread-eagled over the front of the Hellion hog.

"How you feeling up there? Snug as a bug?"

"You are crazy. People will see us. You'll crash the bike and kill us both."

"The only thing that's going to hurt us is if you don't think of Helheim. If we end up anywhere else, you're going to be road gravy. Understood?"

"Understood."

I start the bike and check that my new best friend's legs are clear of the wheels and the road. When I'm sure, I get on the bike and ease it into first and do a one-eighty turn. There's a nice fat shadow across the street on the side of a burned-out grocery.

"Thinking of Helheim?" I shout over the rumble of the engine.

"Yes."

"You better be. Here we go."

I hit the throttle and accelerate all the way across the street, almost clipping the rear end of a pedicab on the way. When did they get those? Too late to worry. The wall comes up fast. I hope we don't end up in Hellion Fresno.

And then we're skidding on ice. The rear end starts to fishtail, so I hit the accelerator to straighten out. When we do, I throttle down and creep forward in second gear.

I've been in cold places, but this is ridiculous. The wind comes down from high snowy peaks. Every time I exhale, the frost from my breath almost covers my face. I can already feel ice forming in my nose and the corners of my lips. My hands are numb. If we don't get someplace soon, I'm going to end up with frostbite.

"What's happening?" screams Captain Sunshine.

Around the next corner I see it. Like Butcher Valley, Helheim is a deep depression surrounded by hills and watchtowers. And like the other valley, most of the towers are dark and look like they haven't been used for years. The main difference between the two places is the temperature. Butcher Valley burns with open lava pits. Helheim is a glacier, a moving river of ice scouring the valley and increasing its size forever. There will always be room for racy nuns and naughty heretics down here.

I stop the bike by a Quonset hut encased in so much snow and ice it looks like the bottom of a life-size snow globe. There are a couple of snowcats outside and a hellhound. I can't tell if it's in working order or not.

I put down the kickstand and go around the front of the bike to cut down the captain. It only takes a second to see why he stopped yelling. His lips are frozen shut. I give him a little pop in the mouth. Not to hurt him. Just to break up the ice. And to hurt him a little. Remind him whose game this is. I take off his blindfold and he looks around in wonder.

"We're here," he says.

"Looks like it. Here's what's going to happen next. You're a captain. We're going inside and you're going to do the meanest, most hard-ass officer impression of your life. Order people around. Make them salute and kiss your ass. Then tell them you want to see the new arrivals."

He shivers in his thin city coat. So do I. I put up my hoodie. The captain shakes his head.

"What if it doesn't work? Are you going to kill me?"

"Why wouldn't it work?"

"They might be in a different regiment. They might not take my orders. Sometimes soldiers stationed this far out for too long can go a little wild."

"Do your best," I say, and whisper the hoodoo that resets the glamour on my face. The captain shakes his head.

"This will never work."

"Maybe not, but isn't it more fun than getting drunk all on your lonesome?"

"No."

"You're welcome. Now go up there and be an asshole, Captain Bligh."

He moves so fast for the door to the Quonset hut I have to trot to keep up. He bursts inside with all the subtlety of a mammoth on roller skates.

Six guards stare at us. One is standing by an old wood-burning oven and the others are scattered around several tables. There used to be more guards here. The ones that remain don't like one another much. All good information to have.

The moment we get inside and the captain gets warm air into his lungs, he starts looking like an officer. He stands up straight, giving the scruffy guards the hairy eyeball. The bad news is that they give it right back. No one gets up when they see him. No one salutes. The Hellion by the oven nods and pours something thick and sludgy from a pot into a coffee cup.

He says, "Well, what did you do to get this shit duty?"

The captain doesn't answer for a few seconds.

"I don't believe I heard you say 'sir' at the end of that sentence, did I, soldier?" he says.

The soldier at the oven seems genuinely shocked.

"I guess not. Sorry. Sir."

"Quiet," says the captain. "I'm not here to correct your grammar or manners. This is an inspection. I want one of you to escort me to the new arrivals."

A scrawny recruit with a crooked nose sitting at a table by himself says, "Who's your friend?"

"Again, I didn't hear 'sir' at the end of the sentence when addressing me."

Crooked Nose sits up straighter but not because he's obeying the rules. It's sheer tension. This is how barroom brawls start.

"Who the fuck is that with you, sir? He doesn't look like any officer I've seen. Sir."

"Don't worry about him. I'm the one who can assign you to even worse duty than this."

"Worse than this?" says the guy by the oven.

"Do you enjoy the smell of rotten and congealed blood, soldier? Would you like to spend a few years patrolling the Styx?"

Crooked Nose raises his hand like he's in first grade. He's having a good time with us.

"Excuse me, sir. What general do you serve under?"

"Are you interrogating me, soldier?"

"It's a simple question, sir. Under whose authority are you here? Who the fuck would send an officer out here to the middle of nowhere in dress shoes and no heavy coat? Sir."

I can see where this is going. I lean in and whisper to the captain.

"Keep them talking," I say, and go outside.

I find a good shadow behind the closer of the snowcats and slip back inside.

I come out by the stove, so I slit that Hellion's throat before he can throw the hot cup of sludge on the captain. Let his body fall. Then step back into the same shadow. Outside, I can hear shouting over the sound of the wind. I go back in through another shadow and arrive with the SIG in my hand. I put bullets into the heads of the two guards closest to the captain. Crooked Nose stands and watches me disappear.

This time when I come in, I do it under the table where he was sitting. I spring up from underneath, using the table as a battering ram and cracking his head against the wall. One of the other two guards gets off a lucky shot and knocks the SIG from my hand. I grab Candy's knife and throw it, hitting him square in the left eye. He falls into the last guard still on his feet. The stunned guard steps back, letting the dead one slide to the floor. I pick up the SIG and aim it at him. Retrieve the knife from his dead friend's eye and wipe the black muck off on the soldier's leg. When I look around for the captain, I notice the door is open and he's gone, daddy, gone. Have fun trotting home for days through a blizzard.

I put my gun to the soldier's head.

"Guess it's just you and me, sweetheart. That okay with you?"

"Yes, sir."

"I'm not an officer, so don't sir me. But you are going to obey that other officer's order, aren't you?"

His eyes scan the room, lingering on his dead and dying pals.

"Sure. Whatever you want. The new arrivals are easy to find."

He takes a set of keys from the wall and picks up a heavy coat. He points to the soldier I got in the eye.

"It's cold outside. You might want a coat."

"Don't worry about me. Just go."

Twenty yards down a road rutted with snowcat tread marks there are heavy iron double gates. Like something you might see outside of an asylum in an old B movie. Icicles hang from the fence, as thick as a man's leg and twice as long. The old lock on the gate is as big as a pumpkin. The guard has to bang it against the metal a few times to break the ice off before he can insert the key.

"The new ones always stay by the gate. High up here on the hill. The wind isn't as bad in the valley, but they always stay up here at first. Some ice over and never make it down."

I see what he means. Down in the valley, millions of dots mill around. Damned souls. Some huddle together in the waste like penguins in a snowstorm, guarding their brood. Down the nearby hillside are the frozen souls of the ones who never made it as far as the valley floor. Among those pathetic forms are men and women, some in suits, some in jeans and T-shirts, others in rags or stark naked, standing or sitting on the hill. The wind picks up. The temperature drops and it's hard to see anything. I'm sorry now that I didn't take the dead soldier's coat.

"Traven. Father Traven," I shout. But the wind is loud enough that I'm not sure how far my voice carries.

I grab the guard.

"You shout too. Go that way and shout. The soul's name is 'Traven.'"

The soldier wanders off looking as lost as the damned and yelling, "Raven. Raven."

I get out the SIG and fire a couple of shots.

"Traven. Father Traven. Up here."

The wind keeps blowing. Visibility is shit. If Traven was standing right in front of me in a prom dress, I don't know if I'd notice him.

A figure comes trudging up the hill. It's tall and haggard, with its coat wrapped tight around it. I start down toward it. His face is still pale and blotched with the same broken blood vessels from when he died.

"Who are you? What do you want?" he yells.

I push down the hoodie and kill the glamour. His eyes narrow.

"Stark? Is that you?"

He touches my shoulders, my face, still trying to figure out if I'm real.

"Ready to get out of here, Father?"

"To where?"

Oh. Right.

"I hadn't really thought that part through. Why don't we get out of the wind and we'll figure it out."

"I'd like that."

We start up the hill. Stupid me. I'm so happy to see Traven that I forgot about the guard. He comes charging out of the blizzard with a knife in his hand. Slashes my left arm, my Kissi arm, which means he only manages to ruin yet another one of my coats. I take out the SIG and shoot him in the legs. That gets the attention of all the mobile souls on the hillside. They look around at us. Some start up the hill. When I take Traven out the gates, I leave them open. The guard crawls after us. He's yelling something but I can't hear him over the sound of the wind. Besides, he's surrounded by freezing, damned souls. I don't think he'll be shouting much longer. I throw the keys into a snowdrift.

I take Traven into the Quonset hut. He stops for a minute by the door when he sees the dead guards.

"All this death just to save me? Why?"

"Because I'm Sandman Slim. A monster and damned and those are the kind of choices I make."

Traven goes to the oven and warms himself.

"I pulled you out of that hole because I like you, but I don't want your gratitude. I did it because sending you here was as much a sin as anything you ever swallowed on earth. And saving you is a message to the people who make the rules."

"And what is that message?"

"Don't be such assholes."

That makes him laugh a little. It's good to see his face in anything but a frown or lined in deep thought. This isn't a guy who's had a lot of fun in his life. I think this last month with Brigitte might have been his best days. I suppose there are worse times to die. But it was still too soon for him.

I take a coat from the soldier I stabbed and wrap it around Traven.

"There's only one place I can take you right now. The

Room of Thirteen Doors. No one can touch you there. That includes Lucifer and God. I'll figure out what to do after you're safe."

"Can I see Brigitte?"

"No." It's a hard thing to say. "You're dead and you're not coming back. Let her grieve and deal with it."

"You're right. I wasn't thinking."

"Don't sweat it, Father. It takes a while to figure out the rules of being dead."

"You died and came back to life."

"I'm not human."

"You could have fooled me."

"Thanks."

I look out the window. The wind has died down.

"Listen. When I get you in the Room, I'll bring you some of your books. Maybe pens and paper, if you want. Not regular stuff. Like necromantic school supplies. Stuff to occupy yourself until I figure out the next move. I already put the 8 Ball there. Think of it this way. You're not some poor schmuck stuck in a room. You're what's-his-name. The knight who guarded the Holy Grail."

"Arthur was supposed to have guarded it in some legends. The descendants of Joseph of Arimathea in others. There's the story of Parsifal. Also stories about the Templars."

"Damn. You do know some trivia. No. I mean the three knights who guarded it."

Traven looks at me.

"I think you might be thinking of a movie."

"Probably."

Warmer now, he puts the guard's coat on over his jacket.

"Thank you. I don't know what else to say."

"I'm sorry I dragged you into Kill City."

"I'm not. I've looked into God's face and I've tasted the worst of his wrath. After that, I suppose I'm prepared for a room, a grail, or whatever else might come."

"Stay here and keep warm. I'm going to check on that hellhound outside. And maybe something else."

I take a gun from one of the dead soldiers and give it to Traven.

"If anyone but me comes through the door, don't ask questions. Shoot. You're in Hell, Father. Don't worry that you might shoot any schoolmarms."

"I'll think about it," he says, and puts the gun in his pocket.

Silly me. He'll never use it. He's still a priest. Sentimental.

I go out and worry about him for the hour I'm gone.

WHEN I GET back, Traven, the crazy bastard, has practically opened a soup kitchen in the Quonset hut. A hundred damned souls who've wandered up from the valley huddle inside trying to work the feeling back into their dead limbs.

"Can't leave you alone for a minute, can I?"

"Old habits die hard," says Traven. "Wait. I think I just made a joke. My first joke as a dead man."

"Congratulations. I'll send you roses and a rubber chicken. It's time to go."

I pull him outside. As we go, he gives his heavy coat to a woman in rags afraid to go into the warm building. She stares at him and kisses his hand.

"Move it, Gandhi."

He gives her a smile and comes over to me.

"Can't we take some of them back with us? How big is the Room?"

"Sure, Father. Which of them gets rescued and who has to stay in Hell forever? You choose."

"I see the dilemma."

"Lucifer, the first Lucifer, always told me my problem was that I didn't think big. Well, I'm trying to now. And stashing a few souls in the pantry isn't the way to do it."

"I trust you."

"That makes one of us."

I strap the dead hellhound to the front of the bike and put Father Traven on the back.

"This won't be a long trip, but it might be a little weird. You can close your eyes if you want to."

"You just pulled me out of damnation. I think I can stand whatever it is you're going to show me."

"Strap in, preacher."

I gun the bike and aim at the shadow of one of the guard towers. Traven tries to be cool, but I feel him tense against me and hear him, I can't fucking believe it, saying a Hail Mary as we pick up speed.

I hit the brakes when we're halfway into the Room and we slide the rest of the way in, leaving a nice line of rubber across the floor.

He gets off the bike and looks around in wonder.

"We're at the center of the universe."

"Yep."

"Where nothing can go in or out without your say-so."

"Pretty much."

"How does it work?"

"Don't know. Don't care. It works and that's good enough for me."

"That's called faith, son."

"That's called not looking a gift horse up the nose. I'll be back soon with some books. Don't worry. I'll let Vidocq pick them out."

"One thing," he says as I angle the bike to take it back to L.A.

"Yes?"

"Can you tell Brigitte that I asked about her?"

"I'll think about it," I say, but I'm lying.

I COME OUT of the Room, as usual, by the Hollywood For-ever Cemetery. I always get the copper jitters when I'm on the bike in L.A., and now I have a dead hellhound strapped across the handlebars. The only way I can attract more attention is if I was towing a Spanish galleon full of half-naked cheerlead-ers with flare guns. On the other hand, this is L.A. and I can just as easily be another moneyed airhead who scored a big movie prop on eBay. Why not? Ask nice and maybe I'll trade you Gilligan's hat for the bones of the Partridge Family's dog.

I head up Gower Street and across Hollywood Boulevard to Bamboo House of Dolls. I think about parking the bike in the alley next to the bar, but I leave it in a space out front in-stead. Let the rubes get a look at a genuine hellhound. It's not like this crowd hasn't seen its share of funny beasts before. A few people call my name as I go inside, but it's not a chitchat kind of night and I don't need strangers buying me drinks in a bar where I already drink for free.

Carlos gives me a funny look when I come in.

"Is that ice in your hair?"

"Probably."

I run my fingers through it a few times.

"Better?"

"Better. You been sticking your head in hotel ice machines again? I warned you about that."

He gets a bottle from under the bar and pours me a shot of Aqua Regia.

"I can't stay long," I say. "Tonight's a work night. Are there any Cold Cases around?"

"Again? Are you still on them?"

"Don't send them any love notes yet. They're the ones that shot up the front of your bar the other day."

He slams down the bottle.

"Those dog-dick *pendejo* motherfuckers."

I swallow the Aqua Regia.

"I'm sorry that I can't help you with that one, though. I have to make nice with them tonight."

Carlos shakes his head, staring at a table by the jukebox. Martin Denny is playing, "Was It Really Love?"

"Do what you got to do. I've got some potions back here that'll have them puking frogs and shitting bottle rockets."

"Thanks for the drink. I'll be nice as long as they are."

"Just leave some of them for me. That's all I ask."

I head over in the direction of the jukebox. The Cold Case I levitated a while back sees me coming. He stands and then the rest of them follow, grabbing for their most fearsome weapon. Their phones. I hold up my hands so they know I'm not here to hurt anyone.

"Sorry to show up still alive, boys. Tell Nasrudin no hard

feelings but he's on my naughty list. But I'm not here to talk about the past. I'm here to talk business. Who here wants me off his back? The first one to raise his hand gets a free pass from here on out."

They all raise a hand.

"I forgot to mention. You have to do something for me first."

Hands waver. A few go down. In the end, only two stay up. I pick the guy closest to me. He looks at me like he thinks I might bite off his face at any minute, so I speak in short sentences and use small words. He seems to understand. In a few minutes we have a deal. We even shake on it. I'll be washing that hand before I head home.

I TAKE BACK streets as far as I can before cutting over to Sunset to reach the Chateau. Lucky me, it's late enough that there aren't a lot of tourists around to gawk at me with a hellhound across my handlebars like demon roadkill.

I get the Hellion hog back in its space in the garage and put the cover back on. I miss it already. Who knows when I'll get to ride it again. If the world is still around at New Year's, maybe then. Put Candy on the back and take her down the Pacific Coast Highway. Open the throttle up a little. Maybe I'll even get a speedometer installed and see if we can top 200 mph.

I'm in a funny mood when I get back. Kind of light-headed. Halfway between sad and still riding on the adrenaline of the last few hours. I saved Traven from damnation, but only after I killed him. I accomplished everything I set out to do on the trip Downtown, but it doesn't feel like enough. I guess nothing will be enough for a while. A dead friend stashed under floorboards. Monsters from another universe bearing down on us. A brokenhearted friend and a girlfriend who's sick of me riding off to my doom every ten minutes. Yeah, I guess you could call the last day or so a real mixed bag. And I don't know if things are going to get any better anytime soon. Right now, though, I just want to see Candy and get something to eat.

I have to admit that I'm tempted to take the hellhound upstairs in the elevator. Just stroll through the lobby with it on my shoulder. Mr. Macheath back from another night out on the town. But I check the impulse.

The hound is so heavy I have to dance it around to get it off the bike and onto my shoulders. No showing off this time. I find the nearest shadow and go through, coming out in the penthouse. Candy is sitting on the sofa with Kasabian, drinking beer and watching *Destroy All Monsters*. She looks up at me.

"Look. The ramblin' man made it back. And he brought dinner."

I drop the hellhound on the floor. It sounds like I shot-put a piano.

"I'm glad to see you too. I told you I'd make it back in time."

"Is that what you said? I thought it was 'I'm sorry I took off again like that and I'll worship you as a goddess when I get back.'"

"That doesn't sound like me. Maybe one of your other boyfriends."

"Yeah, I have their bodies stacked on the roof. It keeps the cat burglars away."

Kasabian comes around to check out the hound. It takes him a minute to crouch on his gimpy knee, but he makes it and runs his hands over the hound like it's Ali Baba's treasure. He examines his fingertips and squints.

"This is the best you could do? It looks like you pulled this thing out of a garbage dump."

"You're welcome to go back and get one of your own."

"This falls deeply into the category of 'better than nothing.'"

"So do you, so it'll be a perfect fit."

He runs his hand along the length of the hound's spine.

"At least the legs are straight."

"Call Manimal Mike anytime you want. He ought to be able to scavenge enough parts off the thing to fix you up, Hopalong."

Kasabian looks up at me.

"What did we say about nicknames?"

"Sorry. You can't really expect me to be Miss Manners overnight."

He shakes his head, staring at the hound.

"Damn. You actually did it. And here me and your missus were making bets on whether you'd come back at all and how many more limbs you were going to lose."

"Who won?"

Candy doesn't look up from the movie.

"No one's seen you undressed yet, so the bet still stands."

"I'm calling Manimal Mike right now," says Kasabian. He clamors to his feet and squeaks and grinds away to his room.

"Let me know when he's coming over. I want to talk to him."

I sit down next to Candy, take her beer off the table, have a sip, and pass it to her.

"How's Brigitte doing?"

"You had someone you loved murdered, so you know."

"Yeah."

"Allegra and Vidocq took her to stay with them. I think seeing you burned and gutted like that scared Allegra a little."

"She patched me up pretty good. I didn't pop any rivets while I was gone."

Candy turns and kisses me. I kiss her like maybe I was afraid I wasn't coming back, which is how I always feel when I go to Hell. I hand her back her knife.

"So, I guess your plan worked out?" she says.

"Yeah. I have Traven stashed in the Room."

She pushes away from me.

"That's your master plan? Take him out of Hell so you can lock him in the attic like your crazy aunt?"

"I'm still working on the next step."

"Which is what?"

"I'll let you know when I figure it out."

I get up, checking the long slit the guard left in my coat sleeve.

"I need a shower. Will you call room service and have them send up some food?" I say. "A real spread. I just took one of the Devil's souls. I might as well steal more of his food."

I throw the coat on the pile of dirty and ruined clothes in the closet. At least it's a slash and not bullet holes or blood. A slash I can get fixed.

I step in the shower and let the hot water wash the last of Kill City and Hell off me. I should turn on the news. I wonder what people are saying happened to Kill City. And about the strange people seen swimming from the sinking mall. Shit. Some of those pricks had cameras. With luck, they were just shooting the wreckage and didn't get any shots of me. It might be about time to go totally Batman. Get a pointy mask and a cape. Maybe an hourglass-shaped muscle car. Call it the Sandmanmobile. That would really fox the cops.

The food is up by the time I dry off.

Lobster. Steak. Dim sum. Salads with vegetables they must have flown in from the dark side of the moon. Enough bread and desserts to give Canada a coronary. I love taking advantage of rich people.

I load up a plate with lobster tail and take it to the sofa. While I was in the shower they've moved on from *Destroy All Monsters* to *Godzilla vs. Space Godzilla*. Just another *kaiju* night at home with the kids.

Candy leans against my shoulder, eating dumplings. All might not be forgiven but enough is for now.

"In the attic under his Avengers collection," I say.

Candy and Kasabian look at me.

"Your hoarder," I say. "I found him in Hell. Dad's gold coins are hidden under his Avengers collection in the attic."

"Like TV–Mrs. Peel *The Avengers* or comic-book the Avengers?" he says.

"I have no idea."

"You're going to have to do better than that if you want a piece of the business."

"Don't hold your breath for any more interviews with the dead. I won't be welcome in Hell for a long time."

"You had to get messy?" says Candy.

"Well, they didn't give up Traven gratefully. I know you were pissed, but I'm glad you didn't see me doing that."

"What?"

"Murder."

"Tell me about it later."

"I'd rather not."

"But you will."

"Sure."

AN HOUR LATER Manimal Mike is in the penthouse crouched by the hound, going over every inch of it, examining the details with a flashlight.

"She has a fair amount of corrosion, but nothing I can't clean up."

He nods, satisfied.

"This will work. I can fix Kasabian's leg and use the frame to build a new torso, closer to human proportions."

"How soon?" says Kasabian.

Mike frowns and shakes his head.

"I'll have to get it back to the shop to be sure. Some of the joints are locked and I'll have to clean and reseal everything."

"How soon?"

"If I pick it up in the morning, I can probably give you a rough estimate tomorrow night."

"Great," says Kasabian.

Mike gets up and wipes his eternally grimy hands on a dirty rag he pulls from his back pocket.

"See you tomorrow," he says, and heads for the door behind the grandfather clock.

I follow him over and cut him off.

"The other night at Death Rides A Horse . . ." I say.

He holds up his hands in apology.

"Sorry about that. I was in a bad mood and embarrassed that you caught me there."

"You haven't done anything stupid, have you? Pledged yourself to some bloodsucker or let one of them put their fangs in you?"

"Nothing like that."

"Good."

I reach into my pocket and take out a small bottle.

"Here's the straight-up truth. I can't give you back your soul because it's not mine to give anymore. Never mind how or why, it's just how things are."

"Then I'm screwed."

I hand him the bottle I got from the Cold Case.

"This is a clean soul. It doesn't belong to anyone. It'll substitute for yours when the time comes."

He holds up the bottle to the light and shakes it. He gives me a doubtful look when he can't see anything inside.

"Did you think you could shake up a soul and see it like salad dressing?" I say.

"What do I do with it?"

"First off, don't lose it. Then keep it with you. When you die, your old soul will go in one direction, but you can ride this new one somewhere else. That's assuming you don't go completely Jeffrey Dahmer and stink the thing up. Do that and you're on your own, man."

"Thanks," he says, still doubtful. But he puts it in his pocket.

"Forget it. Fixing up Kasabian so he quits whining about every little thing is doing me more of a favor than him."

"I'll come by with the truck tomorrow."

"Park it by the garage entrance. I don't want to carry the hound through the lobby."

"See you tomorrow."

After *Godzilla,* we move on to *Rodan.* Not one of my favorites, but there aren't that many giant, supersonic flying lizard monsters around, so you settle for what you can get. I have my share of Aqua Regia and Candy settles into some red wine. Kasabian sticks to his beer, leaving crushed cans like autumn leaves all over the floor.

Sometime after midnight I hear someone or something scratching at the grandfather-clock door. I get a gun and go over to check it out. Find a folded piece of paper in hotel stationery lying on the floor. I bring it back to the sofa and set down the gun.

"Fan mail from some flounder?" says Candy.

I read it a couple of times to make sure I have it right.

"We're being evicted."

That gets everyone's immediate and sober attention. Kasabian turns down the sound on the movie. He doesn't turn it off, of course. That would be sacrilegious.

I read out loud, " 'The standing account for Mr. Macheath has been closed permanently. Please vacate the premises no later than noon today. There may be charges applied for each subsequent hour that the room is still occupied,' blah, blah."

Kasabian finishes his beer and throws the can at the flatscreen.

"I knew this was too good to be true. Is there anything we can do? What I really mean is, you do something."

I hand the letter to Candy. She reads it over.

"I guess Mr. Muninn knows about the jailbreak," I say.

"You do keep things interesting," Candy says. "I never got the bum's rush from a deity before."

"How do you know?"

"Good point."

"Where are we going to go?" says Kasabian.

"Where do you think?"

"Back to Max Overdrive? I can't go back to that dump after tasting paradise. Besides, the upstairs is too small for three people. Hell, it was too small for two."

"We'll fix the place up. Did you really manage to scam two hundred grand of the vampire cash?"

Kasabian looks away, then back at me.

"I might have exaggerated a little. It's more like fifty."

"That's enough to get started. Bag everything up and I'll take it to Max through the Room. That way we won't have to perp-walk through the lobby in front of everyone."

"The first thing I want to spend some money on is a bigger refrigerator. I'm not letting all of this food go to waste."

"Hell yeah."

Candy tosses the note on the table and pours herself more wine.

"Damn, boys, you sound like my first girlfriend. She called herself white trash, but I didn't really know what that meant until she moved out. Took all the canned food and toilet paper with her."

"Take the toilet paper," Kasabian says. "That's a great idea."

Everyone gets up, the good mood as dead as the lobster crumbs on my plate.

I start for the bedroom, when Kasabian says, "I was going to tell you tomorrow. I saw some other funny stuff when I was surveillance-droning in Hell."

"Yeah? What?"

"That big-time priest down there, Merihim. You said he and the wild-thing nun, Deumos, were enemies."

"And?"

"I saw them hanging around together. They didn't look like enemies to me."

That explains a lot.

"I was right when I said it. Now I'm wrong. No big deal."

"Okay. I just thought you'd want to know."

"Thanks."

"Thanks."

We both look at each other.

"That felt weird," says Kasabian.

"It did. Let's not do it again anytime soon."

"Yeah. Let's not."

Candy is in the bedroom taking clothes out of the closet and piling them on the bed.

"Hold up for a minute."

She turns and looks at me, upset but trying not to show it.

"Sit down," I say.

She drops a couple of T-shirts and sits.

I go the living room closet and come back with a cardboard box about three feet long, like a tall, thin shoe box.

"Merry Christmas."

"What happened to all that stuff about us making it to Christmas, so I had to wait?"

I put the box in her lap.

"It's been a tough couple of days. I figure that we could all use a little something."

"Yeah, I was kind of jealous when you bought Kasabian a dog and didn't get me anything."

"Open the box."

She smiles and rips the tape along the sides.

"Hell yes," she says, holding up the guitar.

"It's a midseventies Fender Duo-Sonic. The guy said it's a piece of shit, but it's just like Patti Smith's first electric guitar."

She balances it on her knees and hits a chord. It's horrible.

"I think you have to tune it first."

I sit down next to her.

"How did you get it?"

"A guy owed me a favor."

"What kind of favor?"

"I didn't break his arms."

She leans over and rests her head on my shoulder.

"What are we going to do now?"

"Pack up. Go to Max and figure things out from there."

"Saving the world is hard."

"Yeah, but at least we're not in Fresno."

She elbows me in the ribs.

"I haven't said anything to anyone, but when we were swimming away from Kill City, I think I saw one of the Angra."

Candy pushes away from me.

"It's loose in the city?"

"No. She got sucked back into the mall. But it means they're closer to getting out."

"Goddamn."

"Sorry. I needed to say something to someone. Don't tell anyone else."

"Okay."

"We should start packing."

"Okay," she says. "Thanks for the guitar. I notice you didn't get me an amp."

"No. I didn't."

"Coward."

"Damn right."

AN HOUR LATER I'm moving things over to Max Overdrive by hand through the Room. I do it all myself. It would be too strange to have Candy and Kasabian marching through and seeing Father Traven every few minutes. I apologize to him every time I come through. I bring him some pillows and a blanket. It's not like he's going to get cold in the room. The temperature never changes. But they're normal things. Things that will let him feel human in a pretty inhuman situation. I look around for a book I can give him, but all I can find is a month-old issue of *Entertainment Weekly*.

"I'll get some of your stuff from Vidocq soon. I promise."

"I know," he says. He's so fucking sincere it can just break your heart.

Downstairs in Max Overdrive, it's still a maze of drop cloths and empty paint cans from when repairs on the place stopped after the zombie riots. At least the upstairs living quarters are in decent shape. Almost like a person lived there. There's a not too small bed-sit area complete with actual windows that get sun, and an adjoining bathroom. Of course a couple of video monitors for movies. They seem small and pathetic after the drive-in-theater-size flat-screen at the Chateau. First thing we need around here is a bigger refrigerator. The second is bigger monitors.

Candy and I outvote Kasabian, so we get the upstairs room and he gets the sales floor area to himself. He can camp out on the mattress we stole from his bedroom at the Chateau. It's better for him downstairs anyway, with his hinky leg. We're just thinking of his welfare.

"We're going to have to be careful of the furniture in here, you know," I tell Candy. "It's not like we can call down to the front desk every time we break an end table or bureau anymore."

"That will just make things more challenging."

"We could cover the whole room in bubble wrap."

"And you'll finally have the padded cell you've always wanted."

Allegra knocks on Max Overdrive's front door around noon. Candy lets her in.

"I went by the hotel but they said you weren't there anymore. They asked if I knew a forwarding address. I guess some linens and furniture are missing from the penthouse."

"Come upstairs and I'll show you our almost new sofa," says Candy.

Allegra sighs.

"The penthouse was nice but I guess nothing lasts forever."

"Just scars and library fines," I say, carrying a pretty little Tiffany lamp over to Kasabian's bed. Allegra gives me a tense little wave when she sees me.

"Hey, Stark. Can I talk to you in private?"

Candy raises her eyebrows at me.

"Sure. Let's go out on the lanai."

I take her out the back door to the overflowing Dumpster. She gets a good whiff of the thing and makes a face.

"I guess you need to get some services turned back on."

"There's still water and electricity. That'll do for now."

"I wanted to talk to you about Matthew."

"He's the boyfriend."

"Ex-boyfriend."

"Right. Sorry."

She takes a deep breath.

"He's at my old apartment. He's moved in like it's his."

"Is there anything there that would tell him where you are now? I don't mean the apartment with Vidocq. That's still invisible to civilians, right?"

"Yes."

"How about the clinic? Could he track you there?"

She thinks for a minute.

"I keep some supplies there but nothing with an address. Aside from that, there's some old tables and chairs. Some of Eugène's chemistry equipment. A few books."

"How dangerous is this guy? Will he be packing when I see him?"

"Probably. He's hurt people. I know that. I don't know if he ever killed anyone."

"Okay, but that still means if it comes to it, it might be him or me. You understand?"

She touches the side of her head. Brushes some hair out of the way.

"I know it's a lousy thing to ask, but please don't kill him."

"Didn't you just hear me? If he draws down on me, I might not have a choice."

She takes a step toward me. Gropes for words.

"You know how to do these things. Trick him. Use all that strategy you learned in the arena."

"Why don't you want me to hurt him?"

"I didn't say don't hurt him. Hurt him all you want. Just don't kill him. I'd feel so guilty. He's here because I stole his money. If he dies, it will be my fault."

"I get it. I understand buyer's remorse when it comes to killing. I've had it myself. Okay. I can probably handle this without making it a terminal situation, but I need your permission to make a mess."

"As long as he doesn't die, I'll trust you with whatever you need to do."

I think the scene over. I sort of remember the layout of her apartment.

"I'm going to need you to get some things for me."

She calls up an empty note on her phone and types as I talk.

"A large painter's tarp. Waterproof. Make that two. A gallon-size jug of dishwashing soap."

"Got it. Is that all?"

"No. Glasses or empty bottles. Lots. When you think you have too many, that will be half of what I want."

She tilts her head up at me.

"Are you going to make him drink something?"

"They're not for drinking. They're for breaking."

"Don't tell me anything more. I don't want to know."

"No you don't. One more thing. I want to bring Candy along."

She gives me a pleading look.

"Do you have to? I'm already so humiliated by this."

"Candy doesn't care about bad old lovers. We've all had a few, and hell, she puts up with me. Besides, she can help. She has a mean streak, and if I do what I'm thinking, I'll have to leave Matthew alone for a while. She can babysit him."

"Fine. Just don't let Kasabian know."

"No problem," I say. "How's Brigitte doing?"

She shakes her head.

"She's stopped crying for now. I brought her to the clinic with me. She doesn't know anything about medicine, but she can file and talk to the patients. I just want her a little distracted. And I want to be able to keep an eye on her."

"She's a killer. She'll pull through."

I can tell Allegra doesn't like hearing me call Brigitte a killer.

"Is it true that Liam went to Hell when he died? Because he was excommunicated?"

"Those are the rules."

"The rules stink sometimes."

"I couldn't agree more."

"Is there anything else you need from me?"

"A key to the apartment."

"The door is unlocked."

"I know. I want to lock it. It will confuse him. Or at least piss him off. Either one's okay."

She digs in her shoulder bag for a key.

"Can you do it tonight?"

"I'll have to wait until he goes out to set up, so it depends on him."

"He goes to a bar in Westwood every night around eight."

"Perfect. I'll call you tomorrow and let you know how it went. With luck, you'll never see or hear from him again."

She hands me a key.

"And no killing."

"No killing."

She smiles for the first time since getting to the store.

"I'll pick up this stuff right now."

"I'll see you later, then. Bring Vidocq by for an early dinner. We have leftover steak and dim sum and cake from the Chateau. None of it's more than twelve hours old."

"You're living the Hollywood dream."

"It's the last good free food we're likely to see for a while."

"I'll get you your soap and tarps."

"And glass. Lots of glass. Two pairs of work gloves. And wire cutters. I'll need those too."

She starts away when I remember something.

"One more thing. Tell Vidocq to bring me some of Traven's favorite books."

"Why?"

"Do us both a favor and don't ask."

She nods and heads out. I go inside and pull Candy aside. Explain the situation to her.

"Sure," she says. "Let's do it tonight."

"Perfect. It'll give Kasabian time to change all the locks."

Kasabian limps down from upstairs, carrying sheets and pillowcases.

"What are you two whispering about?"

"We're planning your birthday party."

"Good. I like piñatas."

"And porn," says Candy.

"Piñatas full of porn. Got it."

Allegra comes back with the supplies a couple of hours later. I'll have to get a van to transport all the gear to her place. I can tell Kasabian is curious about what we're planning, but he's smart enough not to ask questions, especially after he sees the roll of barbed wire I steal off the back of a PG&E truck.

I STEAL AN Escalade from the parking lot in front of Donut Universe. It has a built-in sound-and-video system that's better than most movie theaters. Only a few hours since we left the Chateau and I'm already feeling nostalgic.

We load the Escalade in the alley next to Max Overdrive. It's a tight fit. I had to drive the Hellion hog over and it takes up a lot of room.

When we've loaded the gear, Candy and I head out to Allegra's place on Kenmore, due south of Little Armenia. Her building is a converted seventies-era motel called the Angels' Hideaway. Dying palms out front. A pool with a foot of black water out back.

Someone comes out of Allegra's apartment around eight. Heavyset white guy with his hair combed into an idiot fauxhawk. He carries himself so that everyone will notice his bulk. Typical jailhouse attitude. He doesn't look like Allegra's type, but I didn't know her back in the day, so maybe she liked big boys with cinder blocks for brains. I have a feeling he didn't spend his time in prison getting a GED or learning Latin. Probably pumped a lot of iron. Probably got dumber and meaner. By the time he walks out of sight, I don't feel at all bad about what's going to happen.

It takes two trips to carry everything into the apartment. The place has a simple layout. A short entryway that leads to a living room. A kitchen off to the side. You can't get anywhere in the apartment without going through the living room first. That's important. Candy and I shove all the boxes and furniture against the walls. Then the real work begins.

First lay down both layers of tarp. Next, cover them with plenty of dishwashing soap to turn them into slip-'n-slides, careful to leave dry areas around the edges to walk on. After that, Candy and I have a party breaking all the glasses and tossing the pieces onto the soapy tarp.

"Is this too mean?" she says. "Couldn't we just beat him with a bag of oranges?"

"Hammering people up just makes them angry. If you want to permanently modify someone's attitude, the thing to do is go full-tilt diabolical."

"This is more like a Road Runner cartoon."

"We haven't gotten to the diabolical part yet."

We put on the work gloves and roll out a few yards of the barbed wire, slicing it to length with the cutters. Then bend the wire into a wide circle and keep bending along its length until we have a spiral big enough to fit a man inside. When we're finished, it goes over by the end of the tarp farthest from the door. Lastly, we unscrew all the bulbs in the room except for one small table lamp that I keep turned off for now. The only light in the apartment is what filters in through the blinds. I close those so the place is as dark as midnight in a jug.

After that, there's nothing to do but wait for handsome, young Matthew to come home, happy and a little crocked. Candy and I sit and lean against the refrigerator.

"This is the first time we've been really alone in a month," she says.

"You're right."

"I think we should celebrate."

"Chicken and waffles?"

"I know something cheaper."

She climbs on top of me and puts my hands on her breasts. Begins to grind her crotch against mine.

"What time does your mom get home?" I say.

"Not until after her PTA meeting."

"Then we better hurry."

"You talked me into it," she says, and takes off her T-shirt. We're discreet. We don't shatter any windows or crack plaster off the wall and only break the legs off one of Allegra's kitchen chairs. I'll blame that on Matthew.

The man of the hour comes rolling back around eleven-thirty. I hear him rattle the doorknob. A little at first and then harder. He bangs on the door. Yells Allegra's name.

"I know you're in there. You think this shit is going to keep me out?"

I'm pretty sure I know the next thing that's going to happen, and it does. A bootheel to the door where the lock meets the frame. Wood splinters. There's the sound of metal on carpet as the lock slips out of the door. I stand up and get into position. Candy stays put by the kitchen door.

Matthew comes in and tries the hall light. Curses under his breath when it doesn't come on.

"Bitch, are you playing games with me? You're not funny."

Big Boy storms into the living room and straight onto the tarp. Promptly goes down on his face, into a mix of soap and razor-sharp glass.

"Fuck," he yells, and "Fuck" again, scrambling in the muck like a mule on an ice rink.

I say, "You might want to hold still."

He stops moving.

"Who the fuck is that? Where's Allegra?"

I turn on the small lamp I set aside earlier. I took off the shade so the bulb is annoyingly bright and the light harsh, better to bring out all the pretty scars on my face.

"I'm here to tell you to leave Allegra alone."

He looks at me and then around at the acre of tarp and glass. It dawns on him that he's at least moderately fucked, but he keeps up a good front.

"You're Stark, aren't you?"

"What's that to you?"

"You're the one I really wanted to see. Not that cunt."

Candy comes out of the kitchen, steps carefully onto one of the dry spots on the tarp's edge, and kicks Matthew in the ribs. He curls into a little ball of pain and surprise.

"Who's that?"

"The kick fairy. Say something stupid again and she'll leave another quarter under your pillow."

It's hard for him to catch his breath.

"Okay."

"Good. We'll deal with how you know me later. Right now I'm here to talk about you and Allegra."

"She owes me," he says, trying to sit up. He slips and goes back down again into the glass. Thin streams of red spread out into the soap. "She stole my money and left me to take the rap for everything."

"Maybe she wanted to get away from you and that life."

"Fuck the bitch."

Candy comes out and kicks him again.

"Fuck. Who is that?" he yells.

"Pay attention to me, jailbird. What I'd like to do with a guy like you is handle things simply, but I promised Allegra I wouldn't kill you."

"Suck my dick, tough guy," he says. Then looks around for Candy. Nothing happens this time. So much for chivalry.

"Instead, what I'm going to do to you is more fun."

"Why don't you come over here, pussy, and we'll settle this like men."

"First off, I'm not a man. Second, I'm comfy right here. But you're welcome to swim over my way if you can't hear me."

He stays put.

"So, I was telling you what I was going to do."

"Talk me to death?"

"You're on parole, aren't you? I'm going to dismantle you so that the only way you're ever going to see daylight again is to run as far away as fast as you can and never come back."

"How are you going to do that?"

"I thought you'd never ask. Kick him again for me, dear."

Candy comes out and gives him an especially nice shot in the lower ribs. I toss her a set of the work gloves.

"Check him for a gun. Take it and his wallet and toss them to me."

She fumbles through his clothes for a minute. I should have brought latex gloves with me, but I'm rusty at this and you can't think of everything.

Finally she comes up with a 9mm Glock and a cheap wallet with a skull and crossbones on the front. I set them on the floor by the lamp. Then grab the barbed-wire cage and hold it over him.

"Set him up straight for me?"

Candy grabs Matthew by the hair and lifts him until he's on his knees. I drop the wire spiral over his head and Candy pushes him over with her boot, so he's lying in the soap wrapped in a cage.

"If you thought the glass was bad, try getting frisky in that," I tell him.

He lets out a couple of little gasps but doesn't give any back talk.

"Now I'm going out for a few minutes. I don't want you bothering the kick fairy while I'm gone."

I hand her the wire cutters.

"Talk too much and she has my blessing to remove your tongue."

Candy smiles at me. She likes playing dress-up and femme fatale. I don't think she'll hurt him while I'm gone, but she won't be nice either. I put Matthew's gun and wallet in my pocket and pull up my hood.

"I'm going out for milk and eggs, honey. Be back in a couple of minutes."

She blows me a kiss and I head out.

There's a pharmacy a couple of blocks down Beverly from the apartment. It's a short stroll. A light rain is starting to fall. Early for this time of year. I light a cigarette and smoke until the rain picks up and the foot traffic clears off the street.

The pharmacy isn't marked around the back of the building, but there's only one door covered with surveillance cameras and alarm stickers. I pull the hood tighter so only my eyes are showing and kick the door in. The alarm goes off. I have to work fast.

I hop the pharmacy counter and head for the back. Mostly I want to make a mess and grab some Vicodin or OxyContin. I find a couple of jars of vitamin V on a top shelf in the back. I grab both. Stuff one in my pocket and tear open the other, scattering pills on the floor. On my way back over the counter, I leave Matthew's gun. I drop his wallet in the alley.

When I get back to Allegra's place, I pop the top of the Vicodin bottle, crush up a few tablets, and scatter the powder over Matthew. Put the rest of the bottle in his pocket, then take off my gloves and stick them in my pocket.

"It's raining outside," says Candy.

"Just like a good film noir, right, Matt?"

He looks up at me from the floor.

"What did you do?"

"I just broke into a pharmacy. Took some drugs and left your gun and wallet at the scene."

"Fuck," he says. "Fucking fuck you, motherfucker."

"He's kind of a poet," Candy says.

"Kind of one but not really."

Matthew shakes his head.

"This isn't going to stick, you know. The guy who told me about you, he'll fix it."

"Who's that?"

Matthew tries to roll onto his side, but it hurts too much.

"Take out my phone and call him. He wants to talk to you. Just hit the most recent call number."

I put my foot on his cage and roll him onto his back. He groans. I get a phone from his coat pocket, open it, and hit the number that comes up.

It rings a couple of times and someone with a drawl says, "Hello?"

"Who is this?"

A pause.

"That you, Stark? How's my favorite pixie?"

I know the voice. It's U.S. Marshal Larson Wells, late of the now-defunct Golden Vigil, the outfit he ran with Aelita. If the drawl didn't give him away, the way he said "pixie" would. Just the way a redneck says "faggot."

"How's tricks, kid? Been keeping busy?"

"I have a feeling you know that."

"Some. You've been making friends with the best of the best. I hear you had high tea with Norris Quay."

"I ran away from some gunmen into Quay's arms, if that's what you mean. The guy was a real piece of work."

"Isn't he just? That's the privilege of being a billionaire."

"Don't tell me you're mixed up with the guy."

"Not mixed up. He's just a concerned citizen who wants to do right by his state and his country."

"Was."

"What do you mean?"

"He's dead."

"How?"

"He followed me into Kill City and thought he could buy off all the crazies inside."

"Damn. He was going to be quite an asset."

"For what?"

"For the new project. That's why I wanted to talk to you. I want you to come work for me again."

" 'Cause it worked out so well the first time?"

"I seem to remember you bringing in your share of rogue magicians and miscreant pixies."

It's true. I did some bounty-hunter work for the Golden Vigil a while back. I was at loose ends after killing most of the people involved in Alice's murder and sending Mason Faim to Hell. I was still pretty full of unfocused rage and needed something to vent it on. Hoodoo fuckups seemed like a good idea at the time. It was while working for Wells that I killed the young vampire Eleanor Vance. Just a dumb teeny-bopper. Yeah, she tried to burn me with a flamethrower, but in the end, she was just as screwed up as I was.

I say, "Are you going to recruit Aelita for the dream team?"

"No. She's gone way off the reservation. This holy vendetta of hers, it's made her useless for any Marshals Service work."

"I'm glad to hear that. She's dead too."

Wells doesn't say anything for a minute. Once upon a time he was in love with Aelita. That was when she was just a zealot and not a batshit holy terror.

"Did you do it?"

"I wish I could take credit. But I saw it happen and I'm not sorry it did. On a personal note, you'll be happy to hear that the person who killed her is also dead."

"Who was it?"

"Medea Bava."

He laughs.

"They're both really dead? Where are the bodies?"

"At the bottom of the Pacific."

Another cold little laugh.

"It's a funny world, huh?"

"That it is. Now riddle me this, why should I work for you? I'm the one with the Qomrama. Really, you should work for me."

"But you don't know how to use the thing, do you? That's not easy information to come by, even for someone with friends like the Frenchman and Father Traven."

"Don't talk about Traven."

"Oh, so he's gone too? You're getting soft. Dead people didn't used to bother you so much."

"Well, he had my copy of *Cat Ballou* and I never got it back."

"Funny. You're still a funny guy."

Candy is giving me a what-the-fuck look. I hold up a hand, telling her to be patient.

"I used the 8 Ball a couple of times, you know. I can figure out how to use it again."

"Well enough to fight a horde of angry Devil gods?"

I don't say anything since we both already know the answer.

"Let's let bygones by bygones. We need each other now. You have the power and I have the infrastructure to fight these unholy bastards coming for our world. Work for the new Golden Vigil. We're back together and fully funded by Homeland Security."

"If I say yes, you're going to pay me."

"Of course. Same deal as before."

"Wrong. I have the 8 Ball in my back pocket. I figure that makes me kind of a defense contractor. And I ought to get paid like one, meaning grossly overpaid."

"There are rules to these things."

"I'm sick of hearing about everyone else's rules. Break the rules. You have no idea what getting back the Qomrama cost."

"You're going to let that pretty girl of yours die if you can't blackmail the U.S. government out of a few more dollars?"

"Pay me or you can fight the Angra with pitchforks and torches."

"How much do you want?"

"Someone offered me a million dollars for it. Match the offer and we're both yours."

"You know I can't do that."

"I'm the weapons guy. Tell them I invented a nuclear water balloon or something."

"You mean this, don't you? You'd kill the world for money?"

"The more people like you tell me I can't have things, the more I want them. And you're forgetting something."

"What's that?"

"I have the key to the Room of Thirteen Doors. My girl-friend that you're so worried about . . . we can hide in there. God can't get in there. Lucifer can't get in there. I bet the

Angra can't either. We can drink champagne in my own little bomb shelter while the rest of you are snacks for demon dogs."

Wells doesn't say anything. Candy winks at me. Matthew doesn't know what the fuck is going on.

"I might be able to do a hundred-thousand-dollar consulting fee."

"Not even close."

"One and a half."

"Nine."

"Two and a half."

"Eight."

"Four."

"Seven."

"Five."

"Six and a half."

"Five and a half."

"Deal," I say.

"I'll have to confirm with back east."

"Tell them if anyone tries to lowball me, the Qomrama disappears with me and mine."

Matthew yells, "Let me talk to the man."

I put the phone on speaker and hold it out to him.

"Mr. Wells? It's Matthew."

"Matthew? You're still alive? Stark really is getting soft."

Matthew frowns. He's not getting the sympathy he was hoping for.

"Listen, Mr. Wells, this psycho set me up. He robbed a drugstore and left my wallet behind."

"And a gun," I say.

"A gun? Matt, you know you're not supposed to be carrying firearms. You just violated your parole."

"I needed protection. You said you'd take care of me."

"I said to get in touch with your ex and use her to get to Stark. Not to stalk and terrorize the girl. As far at the Marshal's Service is concerned, you invalidated the terms of our agreement and we have no further obligation toward you."

"You can't hang me out to dry like this," says Matthew.

"I think he can," Candy says.

"We're done, Matthew. Stark, take me off speaker."

I push the button and put the phone back to my ear.

"It will take me a few days to work things out with Washington on the payment situation."

"Take your time. It's only the end of the world. Anyway, you have my number."

"I sure do, pal."

"Call me back before the Christmas sales start. I want a new flat-screen for the bedroom."

"Are you sure you didn't kill Aelita?"

"I wish I could say yes, but no, I didn't."

"Pity. I'd have respected you more if you'd had the wherewithal."

"That reminds me. If I work with the Vigil, you'll square me with LAPD, right?"

"If you'll stop stealing so many goddamn cars."

"Marshal Wells. I've never heard you take the Lord's name in vain before. Shame on you."

"You let me worry about me and the Lord."

"Maybe you can get me a company car. Or maybe you can get the Hellion hog declared street legal."

"The what?"

"Call me when you have an answer on the money. If things work out, maybe we'll get to spend the holidays together."

"Imagine my glee."

"I'm going to cut this idiot loose now. That okay with you?"

"Do whatever you want with the scumbag."

"Good night, Marshal."

The line goes dead.

"Matthew," I say. "I think you're about fresh out of friends. If I were you, the first thing I'd think about is getting out of California. Sorry I took your wallet and all your money."

"I'll pay you back for this," he says.

"Careful, son. I'm about to become a federal law enforcement officer. They send you to Guantánamo for threatening fine upstanding types like me."

I nod to Candy and turn off the lamp. Drop the wire cutters on the tarp next to Matthew.

"Feel free to let yourself out," I say. "And you'll want to be quick about it. The cops will be at the pharmacy by now and I kind of left a trail of pills from there to here. See you in the funny papers, Matt."

We leave and I pull the broken door shut.

Candy says, "You didn't really leave a trail of pills to the apartment, did you? Allegra could get in trouble."

"No, but Brainiac back there doesn't know that. Anyway, even if he cuts himself out of the wire, I give him forty-eight hours before he's back in county."

The rain has slacked off a bit. Just a slow drizzle. Maybe global warming will wash L.A. away before the Angra get a chance to.

Candy says, "I'm sleeping with a G-man."

"A rich G-man."

"Let's go home, J. Edgar. We have money to break furniture again."

I DUMP THE Escalade across from Donut Universe and Candy and I walk home in the rain like a stock photo on a greeting card.

When I open the front door to Max Overdrive, Kasabian gimps over to us like his tail is on fire, glancing upstairs and talking quietly. The rain has cooled down the city, but he's pale and sweating.

"What's going on?"

He looks over his shoulder.

"They're upstairs. I told them that's your room."

"Who is it?" says Candy.

Kasabian goes back behind the video racks that form the walls of his bedroom shanty.

"You deal. I don't want any part of this shit."

Candy and I look at each other. She gets out her knife and I pull the Colt. We walk into the bedroom.

Samael is sitting on the bed drinking one of Kasabian's beers. Mr. Muninn is in the swivel chair by the desk drinking coffee from a ceramic Max Overdrive mug. I hope to hell Kasabian washed the thing before giving it to him.

"Hi, Samael," I say. He raises his beer to me in greeting. "Good evening, Mr. Muninn."

He doesn't say anything for a minute. I turn to Candy.

"Why don't you go downstairs and keep Kasabian company for a while?"

"You'll be all right?"

"No, he won't," says Mr. Muninn. "Nothing is all right, young lady."

Candy stands in the doorway.

"Go on. I'll see you in a few minutes," I tell her.

Mr. Muninn says, "Don't worry. There won't be any floods or lightning bolts tonight at least. We're just going to talk like reasonable beings."

"That leaves out at least one of us," says Samael, glancing at me.

Mr. Muninn sets down his coffee cup.

"You're not helping the situation."

"Just trying to clarify which side each of us is on," says Samael.

"I presume you're here because you're on my side."

"Of course, Father. But I think I know some of Stark's argument, and for once it's not entirely dismissible."

"Fine. Then let's hear what he has to say for himself."

I say, "I'm not giving you back Father Traven."

Muninn looks at Samael.

"That's not an argument. That's a statement. Where's the argument in that?"

"Stark, would you mind elaborating a bit for Father?" says Samael.

"I don't know what else to say. I'm sorry I had to do what I did the way I did it, but I'm not letting Traven go back to Hell."

"And you think that's your decision?" says Mr. Muninn.

"As long as he's in the Room it is."

Mr. Muninn crosses his legs. Laces his fingers together.

"What I meant," say Samael, "is that perhaps you'd state your reasons why you took Father Traven in the first place."

I try to put the whole thing together in my head before saying anything.

"It's not fair," I say. "The father published a book. Big deal. Your book's gotten a lot of people in trouble over the years. Do you deserve to be damned for that?"

"You forget, Stark. I am in Hell. You sent me there."

"And you agreed to it."

"More fool me. I thought I could trust you. You're a great disappointment."

"What do you want? I'm an Abomination."

Mr. Muninn dismisses the comment with a wave.

"Please. That's no excuse."

"You don't care that I'm an Abomination, do you? You've never cared."

Samael smiles. Mr. Muninn nods.

"I see where you're going with this. You've trapped me into saying that I reject the technicality that you, a nephilim, are Abomination. And if I can do that, why can't I reject the technicality that your friend the father wrote an offensive book?"

"Well? Why can't you?"

"Because it's not that simple, is it? You made it complicated by stealing him right from under my, Lucifer's, nose. Do you know how that makes me look?"

"Of course. The three of us know all about how shitty it is to be Lucifer."

"And yet you did it anyway."

"I got a little rash maybe. Okay. Sorry. Smite me with a lightning bolt."

Samael says, "It's God that does lightning bolts. There's just us little Devils here."

"Then stick me with a pitchfork. Look, if I'd come to you and asked for Traven's soul, would you have given it to me?"

"Of course not."

"Why?"

"Why? Because there are rules that shape the universe. We might not like all of them, but without them there would be anarchy and nothing would work."

"Nothing works now."

"Now you're being melodramatic."

"Are you happy? Am I happy? Is he happy?" I say, pointing to Samael. He takes a swig of beer.

"Name me one happy creature in this universe. You can't, can you?"

" 'Call no man happy until he is dead,' " says Samael.

"That's Marcus Aurelius, right?"

He makes a *tsk* noise.

"Aeschylus. A Greek playwright. Didn't you read any of the books I left for you?"

"I remember the one where Curious George got to be a fireman."

"Getting back to the topic at hand," says Mr. Muninn. "We've had this discussion before, Stark. You want me to take sides in the religious dispute between Hell's old Church and the new. You want me to make mankind happy and cheerful and free from strife. You want me to be all things to all creatures."

"Shouldn't you?"

"Where would free will come into this scenario? The ability to make choices, good or bad."

"You never gave the angels free will. That's why this one rebelled," I say, pointing at Samael. "Maybe that's another rule you should have broken."

Samael looks away. He doesn't want to get dragged into this particular argument.

"As I said to you once before, you don't know what it is to be a ruler and you certainly have no idea what a deity is."

"Do you? Are you really a deity, or were the Gnostics right and you're just the Demiurge, a caretaker who's gotten in over his head and can't keep the plumbing working?"

"That's an offensive question."

"That's not an answer."

"I don't have to explain myself to you."

"Who are you talking to? Stark or the Abomination?"

"Both, I suspect."

"You know that both Deumos and Merihim are against you, right? They're as bad as Aelita. Just more subtle."

He looks at me hard.

"What makes you think that?"

"Things I've seen and things I've been thinking about. Hey, here's one good bit of news. Aelita is dead."

Mr. Muninn sits back in the chair. Rests his elbows on the arms.

"I'm sorry to hear that. She was a troubled child, but at one time she was one of the ones closest to me."

"You could say we rebel angels had troubled childhoods, but I blame video games," says Samael.

Mr. Muninn says, "Quiet, you. Why don't you go home and check on things at the palace." He looks at me. "It's getting crowded down there."

Samael looks disappointed.

"You said I could come along. This is Stark we're talking to. Not Mary Magdalen."

"Well, you're not helping, so please keep your contributions on topic."

"Yes, sir."

"So, Aelita is still one of your kids," I say.

"Of course. Even at his worst, so was Samael. So are you. So is all humankind."

"Let's just keep this focused. Aelita is your kid. Samael is your kid. Merihim and Deumos are your kids."

"Yes. All the rebel angels are my children."

"Then you are one child-abusing motherfucker."

"Excuse me?" says Muninn. Thunder rumbles outside.

"I'm an Abomination. A little outside everyone, right? I'm both sides and neither side of the argument. And I have your solution."

"To what?"

"Your misery. And your kids' misery."

"Please, enlighten us all with the revelation of Saint Stark."

"Close down Hell."

Samael crushes his beer can and belches.

"Excuse me."

The prick knew where I was going all along. He wanted me to say it first.

"I'm telling you as an ex-Lucifer, as someone who's seen how miserable not just the damned are but the angels guarding them. Turn off the lights. Roll up the carpets and lock the doors. Whatever point you were making by tossing the rebels there has been made. Hell hasn't redeemed the fallen angels.

It's created the biggest suicide cult in history. That's why the generals agreed to Mason Faim's idiot plan to storm Heaven. They knew it would fail and that Heaven's armies would destroy them. Suicide by cop."

Mr. Muninn picks up his coffee. Sips it and makes a face. It's gone cold. He moves his hand over it and it's hot again. He takes another sip.

"Nice trick," I say.

"Are you going to point out how weak I am now that I've split into pieces? Don't bother. I feel it every day."

"I met Nefesh yesterday."

Mr. Muninn nods.

"Yes, he told me all about it. My brother has come to stay with me."

"And me," says Samael. "Two fathers in the same house. Can you imagine my joy?"

"What about it, Mr. Muninn? Shut down Hell."

He shakes his head.

"I'll admit I've thought about it. I don't know how I'd go about doing it. What to do with the angels that still want to rebel. What to do with the lost souls. Broken as I am, I don't even know if I have the strength to do it anymore."

"Now you have Nefesh to help. Maybe the two of you could do it together."

"It's a mad idea to consider as reality. Destroying Hell is an abstract notion. A philosophical argument. Nothing more."

"Not if you don't want it to be. You can make it real."

"This is foolishness."

"You can do it and let the angels have some free will. Don't drag any of them back to Heaven. Leave Hell's gates open and let the ones that want to go back with you go and let the angels who want to stay in Hell stay. And find something better to do with all those damned souls. How many of them are like Father Traven, there on technicalities?"

"This is all very romantic and heartfelt, Stark, but I'd like to point out a flaw in your argument," says Samael. "You'll notice that I'm not in Heaven anymore. Neither are a lot of angels. Hell is becoming a very crowded place and not just with rebels and lost souls."

"Angels are fleeing Heaven in droves," says Mr. Muninn. "Ruach grows less rational by the hour."

"So you see, while your throw-the-gates-open argument might have some merit, it's impossible to implement until Ruach is made sane or removed as Heaven's guardian. And in the end, all of these arguments might be moot."

"The Angra," I say.

Samael nods.

"The Angra."

"The Angra," says Mr. Muninn.

"You broke some rules when you took the universe from them. You can break one little rule for Father Traven."

"No," says Mr. Muninn.

"I guess it's a Mexican standoff. Unless you're going to toss me into a lake of fire or something."

Mr. Muninn makes a face.

"You'd love that. It would fit right into your martyr complex."

"Then where are we?"

"I have a counteroffer. A compromise."

"Okay."

"Eleusis. The place of virtuous pagans. It's the most civilized place in Hell. Full of intellectuals and philosophers. The best of the old world. I think your Father Traven would fit right in."

"Yeah," I say. "I always hated Eleusis too. It seems to me like another bullshit technicality. Why is it their fault that they hadn't heard about your religion when it was something like nine people believed in back then?"

"The Word was there on earth. All they had to do was follow it."

"Let's not start a whole other argument," Samael says.

"Thank you."

"My answer to Eleusis is thanks but no. Traven isn't staying anywhere in Hell."

"You don't respect rules at all, do you?"

"Sure I do. When they make sense. But some don't and some are out-of-date. You keep saying you can't change the rules. Shit, man. You wrote the rules. You can break them or rewrite them any way you want."

"It's a matter of both strength and inclination, and I'm not sure I possess either at the moment. And nobody but that one," he says, looking at Samael, "has ever pressed me or spoken to me like this before."

"I'm not trying to bust your balls, Mr. Muninn. You know I like you. You're a nice guy and you took care of the dead under L.A. for all those years. But you're wrong on this and you know it. None of us here ever wanted to be Lucifer. You can make sure there are no more Lucifers ever again."

"This isn't the time for that discussion," he says.

"I might have an idea," Samael says. "A compromise for you both."

Mr. Muninn says, "I'm listening."

"Stark, as we've both pointed out, Heaven isn't the place to send anyone anymore, so your rescue of Father Traven, while brave, was ill-timed. And Father won't permit him going to paradise. So, what do you do with a soul one party won't let into Hell and the other won't permit into Heaven?"

"What?" I say.

"Blue Heaven."

"Limbo, you mean?"

"The pleasantest limbo you've ever seen," says Samael.

Blue Heaven is a place out of time, literally. Its real name translates as "the Dayward." It's a part of the universe that broke away from normal time and space in 1582 when Pope Gregory switched from the old Julian calendar to the Christian. Fifteen days were suddenly wiped out of existence. But they never really went away. They exist on their own as the Dayward. Blue Heaven.

"Have you ever been there?" says Samael.

"You know I haven't. The angel part of me has, but the rest of me can't remember what it was like. I guess I have a general sense that it was a decent enough place. I don't even know how to get there."

"Through the Room, you idiot," says Samael. "The Door of Drunken Eternity, I believe."

"How do you know that?"

"When your angel broke loose of you, he talked in his sleep."

"What, and you used to crouch over him and listen? You pervert."

"You can take the boy out of the Devil but not the Devil out of the boy," he says.

We both look at Mr. Muninn. He seems lost in thought.

He says, "If I was to agree to let Father Traven leave, would you give me the Qomrama Om Ya?"

That stumps me. I don't know what to say at first. I don't think Nefesh wanted to get near the thing.

"No," I say. "But I promise I'll use it against the Angra and fight them until the end."

"Then the answer is no."

"Let me throw you another compromise," I say.

"All right."

"Let Father Traven go and I'll come back to Hell and stay. I'll be Lucifer again."

"Ha!" says Samael. Mr. Muninn opens his eyes a bit wider. I wish I could read angels the way I can read humans. I never know what these fuckers are thinking. That goes double for God.

"You'd really do that?"

"If I can bring Candy with me, yes."

Mr. Muninn shakes his head.

"You're the definition of a troublesome child."

"What about me?" says Samael.

"You both exasperate me."

I say, "It's a gift. Well?"

"What can I say? You weren't the worst imaginable Lucifer, but you were very close. No, you won't come back as

Hell's caretaker. But I'm impressed by your offer, though I'm not rewarding you for it. I'm protecting Hell from your whims. Keep Father Traven. Put him in Blue Heaven. And this time, you'll owe me a favor."

"Cool."

I put out my hand. Mr. Muninn shakes it. It's not a happy shake. It's not even angry. It's weary. Being Lucifer will do that to you. He gives me a wicked smile worthy of Samael.

"I hope there are no hard feelings about the Chateau Marmont situation," he says.

"No. I knew it was coming. I had my hand pretty deep in the cookie jar."

"That you did, son. That you did. Well, I'm off."

"Why don't you stay? We were going to try and eat the last of the Chateau food, but I think we've lost our nerve. I figure we'll send out for something."

Muninn takes a last swig of coffee.

"And that's why you won't be Lucifer anytime soon. You don't have the most logical work ethic. I'll be heading back now to take care of business. Samael?"

"I'll be along in a bit. I have a few of my own issues to talk over with Stark."

"I'll see you at home, then."

And he's gone. Vanished. Like a God.

I look at Samael.

"We have issues?"

He shakes his head.

"Of course not. I just needed a break from home sweet home. The palace is overrun with the high and holy."

"And you're used to having your own suite."

He takes a Malediction from a gold cigarette case. Offers me one. I take it.

"You have to admit . . . it's addicting."

I nod, accepting a light.

"I'm bored to death down south. I thought you might let me raid your video collection again."

"Feel free. It's not like anyone wants to rent anything. Well, a few vampires, but that's not really a long-term business model."

He picks up a Max Overdrive bag and starts down the stairs.

"Specialization. Give the people something no one else can give them. That's the way to stay open."

"Between streaming video and BitTorrent, I'm not sure there's anything left."

Samael shrugs.

"Look harder. Consult with some younger witches. Maybe together you can conjure up a lost film or two."

"That's not a bad idea. I've always wanted to see a full version of *London After Midnight*."

"A fine place to start."

I sit down and smoke. That was all too close. Mr. Muninn might not be as strong as he once was, but he can probably still turn me into mildew on a bathroom shower mat. But I kept my promise to Traven. Maybe I'll visit Blue Heaven with him. See what the big deal is. It's not easy to get there if you don't go through the Room, so everyone there is supposed to be in the high-IQ club. Definitely the place for him. Not so much for me. Still, I haven't had a vacation in a while. Hell sure doesn't count. Maybe take Candy there for a weekend just to clear my head so I can stomach dealing with Wells again.

"Knock knock."

It's Candy.

"Can I come in?"

"Of course."

"You know the Devil is stealing all your Italian and Japanese horror movies."

"Ex-Devil, dear. Let him. He saved me and Father Traven's grapes tonight."

"Liam doesn't have to stay in the Room forever?"

I shake my head.

"Tomorrow I'm taking him to Blue Heaven."

"Where's that?"

"I'm not sure. It's supposed to be nice. You should come with us and see what it's like."

"Okay. So that's it? God stops by to argue and you get everything you want?"

"Hardly. But enough. And now I owe him a favor."

"He'll want the Qomrama."

"Yeah, but he knows he can't have that. That means it'll be something a lot harder."

She puts an arm around me.

"We'll deal with it when happens."

"Thanks."

I get up and drop the cigarette in the dregs of Mr. Muninn's coffee.

"Can I tell Brigitte about Liam getting out of Hell?"

"Don't go into details, but yeah. Why not?"

"She'll know it was you."

I say, "We should get food delivered to celebrate."

"Excellent idea. What should we get?"

"You and Kasabian work it out. He has a million delivery menus around here. I have to make a phone call."

I walk her to the stairs and call down.

"Hey, Samael. Want to stay for dinner?"

"Will there be donuts?" he says.

"No."

"Then yes."

Candy heads downstairs and I go back into a bedroom and close the door. I get out my phone and scroll back through the old incoming call numbers until I find the one I'm looking for.

"Hello? Who is this please? I don't recognize your number."

It's a man's voice. Vaguely familiar. He called me once when he was possessed.

"Talk to me, Merihim."

"Who? I think you have wrong number."

"Come on, Merihim. I know you've been in this guy's head before. Come back and talk to me."

"I'm hanging up now."

"Talk to me."

The line goes quiet but the other guy hasn't hung up.

"Stark. How nice to hear from you. We haven't talked in a while."

"I miss your crank calls. Did you lose interest in harassing me?"

"Not at all. There's just a lot of work to do down here. Busy, busy, busy. What have you been up to?"

"Killing Aelita and Medea Bava."

"That's not what I heard. I heard it was the priest who killed Bava."

"Ah. So you are keeping tabs on things."

"It's getting easier. Using the key. Possessing humans. You might have noticed."

"Yes. That was you possessing Father Traven."

"Of course."

"That's where it all came together for me. You take over Traven. He gives the 8 Ball to Medea. Medea kills Aelita to get her out of the way. That means she can come back to Hell and give the 8 Ball to Deumos. She's the key to all this. The goddess worshipper who brought the Qomrama to this universe from wherever the Angra are stuck. She wants it to do the final summoning."

"Look at you, thinking like you haven't completely pickled your brain yet."

"And this whole thing comes back to you Hellions' obsession with suicide. You think if the Angra come back, they'll destroy all of Creation and put you out of your misery once and for all."

"Why not? Father won't do it. Or can't. Who else are we to turn to?"

"I tried to save you tonight. I almost had him talked into opening Hell and letting you bastards flutter home to Heaven."

"What's the phrase? Almost only counts in hoof slippers?"

"Horseshoes. It only counts in horseshoes and hand grenades. You're right. But if you assholes hold on a little longer . . . Let Mr. Muninn—I mean Lucifer—deal with

Ruach, he can reopen Heaven and you won't have to destroy the entire fucking universe."

"Promises. Promises. We lost faith in you when you were Lucifer. Why should we listen to you now?"

"I don't know. It's something to break up the tedium."

"I tell you what, Mr. Sandman Slim. You proceed with your plan and we'll proceed with ours, and we'll see who gets there first."

"I have the Qomrama, you know. I'll use it against the Angra. And you."

"A peashooter against an army. Good luck. Is this all you called about? I'm disappointed."

"Stay in touch, asshole. I miss these fireside chats."

"We'll see. It's not as fun when you want me to call."

"Okay. Fuck you. If you wake up dead some night, don't say I didn't try to make nice first."

"Good-bye."

"Adios."

I go downstairs and find Candy sitting with Kasabian on his bed, at least a dozen take-out menus spread about between them.

"Where's Samael?"

"He kindly volunteered to go to the corner for beer. In the rain," says Candy.

"Damn. He really doesn't want to go home. Have you decided on dinner yet?"

"We're down to Indian or Thai."

"I vote Thai."

"You might get outvoted this time."

"This is why democracy is dying."

I walk around the empty movie racks and restack some of the boxes of DVDs that Samael has been pawing through. A lot of memories in this place and on these pieces of plastic. If nothing else, I hate the idea of the Angra destroying us because it would wipe out all this work. All this demented horror, action, and beauty. A universe without Terrence Malick and Lucio Fulci isn't worth living in. The Angra must be real bores. I hate them even more now. I pick up a copy of *Badlands* and go back to where Candy and Kasabian are still arguing about how hot they should order the food.

"Here's the question of the night. If we lose, what movie do you want to watch at the end of the world? I call *The Good, the Bad and the Ugly*."

"*Spirited Away*," says Candy.

"*The Snake Charmer's Daughter*, Brigitte Bardo's best porn flick."

I look around Max Overdrive. The rolled-up posters. The new-releases rack. The empty cutout bins. Fuck the world. I'll kill the Angra to save my movies.

I say, "We're going to need more TVs."